FOLLOWER

There was a light clicking sound, like long nails brushing the door by the handle. Then the handle began to turn, the brass glinting dull in the neon glow, and the door began to open.

The room suddenly went dark as the hoarding hit the beginning of its programmed cycle; first the outlines of the letters, then the fill, and then building up the background to the brilliance of day. Each stage put more light into the room, and the last reached the figure that stood in the doorway.

It was Per Lindegren. The neon reflected on his glasses. One lens was smashed, and there was dried blood on the cheek below it. His anorak was open, and it had been torn. His hands were hanging limp by his sides, the knuckles blackened and bruised, and he carried his head at a strange angle.

He spoke. There was more blood around his mouth, and his teeth were black with it. His voice was hoarse, almost a whisper.

'Whatever's following you, boy,' he said. *'Get rid of it.'*

About the author

Stephen Gallagher is the author of six other books
published by New English Library paperbacks,
including *Rain*, *Chimera* and *The Boat House*. His
latest novel is *Nightmare, with Angel*.

STEPHEN GALLAGHER

FOLLOWER

NEW ENGLISH LIBRARY
Hodder and Stoughton

First published in Great Britain in 1984 by Sphere Books Ltd

Reissued in 1991 by New English Library hardbacks

New English Library paperback edition 1993

Printed and bound in Great Britain for Hodder and Stoughton Paperbacks, a division of Hodder and Stoughton Ltd., Mill Road, Dunton Green, Sevenoaks, Kent TN13 2YA. (Editorial Office: 47 Bedford Square, London WC1B 3DP) by Clays Ltd., St Ives plc. Typeset by Rowland Phototypesetting Ltd., Bury St Edmunds, Suffolk.

British Library CIP

Gallagher, Stephen
    Follower.
    I. Title
    823 [F]

ISBN 0-450-54062-6

ONE

It had been a bad start to the winter, and the signs were that it was going to get worse. The emergency road that led from the inlet village to the light-keeper's house on the headland had been ploughed three times in the first two weeks of snowfall. On the night after the latest ploughing, the light-keeper's wife turned her face from the pulsing of the shore beacon and tried to bury herself in her pillow. Tonight she finally accepted that, after the violent fiasco of three days before, she wouldn't be seeing her afternoon lover again.

Everyone in the village had their preoccupations, like keeping the streets clear and breaking the plate ice that was already beginning to form around those boats that had been moored too close inshore. Her own interior space was crammed with despair, and its tenancy was getting to be more than she could handle. She made fists in the covers and screwed them tight, and she fought the sobs until she felt that she'd break like a wire. When she felt herself weakening from the effort of holding out, she slipped from under the covers and left the bedroom, barefoot and silent on the pine boards. Back in the second bed her husband slept on, breathing to the even rhythm of the light.

In the cool air of the upper landing she paused for a moment, and then she made her way down towards one of the other bedrooms on the blind side of the house. Her husband had built the frame house from Swedish plans with some help from the village, but he hadn't added much

1

in the way of imagination. Even though nobody ever stayed over there were beds in every bedroom, and he'd placed them just as the drawings had shown. Her own contribution had been to keep everything scrubbed and immaculate for him, too good to be touched.

The agony gave her another sharp twist, this time from an unexpected direction – a reminder of the complexity of the monster that struggled within her and defied any hope of understanding. The light-keeper had tried to give her the best home that he could, but he'd never really known how.

The second bedroom stood neat and precise in the graininess of her night-vision, dimly perceived in a handful of angles and planes. She went to the divan and crawled under the daytime dust cover, feeling the embroidered satin of the mattress cold against her face. *Paris*, she thought, and for a moment she felt a sense of hope, of release; Paris had been wonderful, the kind of place that she'd left the islands for. Her love of the city had even been enough to overcome the awkward disappointments of the honeymoon – the light-keeper had tried his best, but he'd been scared to death. Anywhere with more than four streets and one hotel scared him to death, and he couldn't sleep without the steady beat of his lamp. But then on their return the reality of her future had been waiting, and it had wrapped itself around her like an iron shawl.

She gently brushed the peachy down of her cheek against the brocade, her young life in ruins without hope of restoration. Inside her the monster turned, twisting her despair a little tighter; she could have borne the thick-skulled fishermen and their jealous wives if only they'd left her with her afternoon secret. But now even that was gone, and she'd never again be called a gem, a china doll, never again feel skin against her naked skin in the delicious guilt of daylight.

Once more it turned a heart-stopping turn, once more she held on and tried to absorb the pain of it. She felt like a ripe fruit, ready to split. Crying might have helped, but she couldn't cry; instead she tried to whisper the one name that might serve as a charm to bring her comfort.

And the monster knew.

It bellowed its rage from deep inside, a rapidly-expanding fire of raw emotion. The reaction was so fast and so strong that it seemed, for a moment, to be a punishing force that exceeded the limits of her sorrow; it had fed too fast and broken loose, and without even thinking or knowing how she pulled herself back and felt it rush by.

It was like a near-miss by an express train, but it didn't last for long. After it came . . . nothing.

She waited.

She couldn't believe it. She felt cleaned-out, restored, almost as if she was a child again and back in the islands. Life out there hadn't been any tougher or any easier than it was now, but she'd been amongst her own kind, and from the age of five until she was nine she'd had Katya. Katya was a crossed husky and German Shepherd bitch, the meanest-looking dog imaginable with the nature of a teddy bear. At nights when the house was dark she used to sneak down and open the kitchen door so that the dog could follow her back to bed. Katya would curl against her, fitting into the spaces that she'd left and tainting the air sweetly with the musk of her breath. Before morning, the dog would be back in the kitchen again on her blanket by the old stove.

Twice a year Katya would come into season and they'd have to shut her in the yard until it was over. For a week or so afterwards she'd walk around looking doleful and carrying a soft toy in her mouth. One spring, the gate hinges gave and the dog got loose. When Katya managed to drag herself home, she was so badly torn up that her father spent a couple of minutes checking her over on the yard cobbles and then went for his shotgun. She'd been down by the quay at the time, watching the mailboat come in. It was only weeks later that she remembered she'd heard the shot, and had thought nothing of it.

Even though nothing really terrible had happened to her in the next ten years, she always remembered it as the start of the bad times. Nine-years-old had been when she'd started to grow, like it or not. It was strange to be back. *I'm dreaming*, she thought sadly, *that's all*; she wasn't home in the islands, and there was no warm pressure of Katya against her side. She waited for the dog to lose its form as the dream-kaleidoscope turned and gave her self-pity other, less remote shapes.

The mattress bounced a little as the animal stood, and then stretched, and then jumped down to the floor. She could hear the faint clicking of its claws on the boards as it crossed to the landing and started down the stairs. *Morning already?* She rolled over into the warm space where the dog had been, only there was no warm space.

She sat up slowly, pushing the hair out of her eyes.

Katya? she thought. But Katya was dead, buried as deep as the thin soil would allow and covered over with stones.

She got up, and went to check the other rooms. She saw nothing, just the cold empty spaces of a house laid out by mail order. She shivered a little in the thin night-dress. The cold empty space where her pain had been was just as real. Without switching off the lights, she returned to the second bedroom.

The covers were rumpled, as she'd left them. Down on the floor the amber-coloured boards were dotted with white scars, translucent as a fingernail, running in a widely-spaced line from the bed to the door. She knelt to touch them, almost expecting that they'd fade away, but there was nothing imagined about them; she could feel rough flecks on the surface of the wax.

They seemed to spell out a message. The message was, *the worst is over*. She touched the marks again, reassured by the contact.

The bad times were over. For the first time in three days, she smiled.

TWO

John Visco's journey with Per Lindegren had begun to develop into a hard-luck story on four wheels. The rear-tyre blowout was only the start.

They stood on an empty stretch of the highway by the Hardangerfjord. Lindegren seemed dazed, shaking his head slowly at the sight of his Fiat van with one rim down on the tarmac. He was a short, round man, a bespectacled dealer in ladies' dresses. He'd been making this run for six years without any hitch, and a breakdown now seemed to violate some natural law.

'Two of us can switch it,' John suggested. He was already starting to shiver in the cold away from the shelter of the high-sided van. 'Have you got a jack?'

After a moment, Lindegren looked at him. It was impossible for John to tell whether the Norwegian was in a mild state of shock or if he simply hadn't understood. 'To lift the wheel off the road,' John went on, trying to show what he meant, but already Lindegren was shaking his head again.

'This never happened to me before,' he said, hollowly.

John fought down the urge to reach out and grab Lindegren's collar and shake him back into life. 'How about a breakdown wagon?' he said.

It took a couple of moments, but then the sun seemed to rise behind Lindegren's glasses. 'Yes,' he said, 'I can call a breakdown wagon!' And he trotted around to the far side of the van to rummage around in the glove compartment for his auto club documents. His world was back in balance.

John took a stiff walk to the edge of the road, and looked out across the water.

The fjord was the colour of chopped steel, and the valley sides were mostly under snowcover. It was also bitterly cold away from the shelter of the high-sided van – he could feel the wind cutting through the blue serge of his surplus-store jacket, and it stripped through his jeans as if they weren't there. Jesus, he thought, I'm mad – work in a place like this? And he pushed his fists deeper into his pockets and reflected that at least the cold would be working to keep them both awake.

They'd had three exhausting days and three sleepless nights, Lindegren in a ship's cabin and Visco up above on the passenger deck. There were better routes across to Norway, but they closed down at the end of the tourist season and left only the Faroese lines making the North Sea crossing. They'd had engine trouble after the call at Hanstholm, and within a couple of hours of their first landfall at Stavanger the galley stores had run out and the restaurant had closed. Up until the blowout, John had been watching Lindegren for any signs of fatigue at the wheel, but he'd either seen none or was too far gone himself to recognise them.

Lindegren emerged from the cab. He'd found the document wallet, and he was checking through it for his membership card as he crossed the road towards the water.

John hunched his shoulders, turned his back into the wind, and waited.

'Hey, Visco,' the little man said. His English was good but it was strangely put together, like a jigsaw from two different boxes. He looked over both sides of the card and then held it out.

'Do something for me, will you?' he said. 'Go telephone these people, the Automobil-Forbund. Tell them to get a wagon out here.'

John looked doubtfully at the card. 'Me?' he said hollowly. 'Come on, Per, I only just got here.'

'It's no problem,' Lindegren said. 'I'd go myself, but I can't be leaving my stock. My whole life's tied up in that van.'

John glanced around. The road was long, wide, and empty. When he weighed the demands of courtesy against his chances of getting another lift, the scales came down heavily on one side. It would take him less than an hour to walk back the mile and a half to the last buildings that they'd passed, or else he could plant himself by the gravel shoulder and stand there until his hitching arm froze at right angles to his body.

Besides, what was he scared of? A little confusion, a risk of embarrassment. Some way or another, he ought to be able to get the message through. If not, he should have stayed at home, because it was going to be nothing compared to the challenge that he was hoping to take on.

'Sure,' he said. 'What do you want me to say?'

After twenty-five hours on the road for a trip that shouldn't have taken half a day, Lindegren's mind was made up. He didn't say so in as many words, but he'd decided that there was a powerful source of misfortune sitting across from him in the cab.

John Visco started to be aware of it after the second blowout. Lindegren had not only lost a tyre, but he'd also ruined the wheel rim in a final five-hundred yard sprint to get them onto the forecourt of an isolated general store.

He'd made his own phonecall this time, and John had got out of the van to stretch. It had been early evening. The wind had been almost as keen as before, and now it carried a thin scattering of snow before it. The forecourt had been brightly lit, snowfall that had been beaten down and gritted; where artificial light spilled it was yellow like ivory, but beyond the ring was the chill and even blue of an unspoilt drift. A couple of other buildings had been showing windows higher on the valley side, and behind

7

them had been the more solid darkness of woodland. Lindegren had been looking up at the single bulb in the phonebooth with an expression of agony like a plaster saint in an alcove.

They hardly talked at all during the three-hour wait for the breakdown truck that followed. They took turns at kicking around the forecourt and sitting in the cab, and John slowly became aware that Lindegren seemed to be giving him a long, thoughtful stare whenever his back was turned. He caught him doing it a couple of times, but the Norwegian didn't explain what was on his mind.

In fact, only one scrap of conversation from that wasted part of the evening was later to stick in John's memory.

Lindegren climbed back into the cab. The engine was running, and the heater fan was on. A snowplough was going by for the second time that night, an immense spitting yellow lorry with a V shaped blade that bounced on the ground ahead of it. Lindegren watched it pass. Casually – almost *too* casually – he said, 'You ever hear of a *fylgja*?'

'A what?'

'A *fylgja*. There isn't an English word for it.'

John shrugged. 'No, I never did.'

'It's like a piece of bad luck. Only it walks.'

John looked across the cab, but Lindegren was carefully studying the pattern of the snowflakes on the windscreen in front of him. John could see what he was getting at, although he wasn't sure that he could believe what he was hearing.

'You mean a jinx,' John said carefully, watching for a reaction.

Lindegren thought it over, but the concepts didn't quite seem to match. 'Jinx is close,' he conceded, but he went no further. He didn't develop the point, and he didn't explain.

As far as John was concerned, he didn't have to.

Out on the forecourt and looking for the eighth or ninth time into the unlit window of the general store, John shivered in the cold and let his anger blow off. The fat little fuck didn't even carry a decent jack in the van, and now he was trying to shift the blame for his lack of preparation onto his passenger. What was he supposed to do, shoulder his pack and walk off into the blizzard taking his 'bad luck' with him? No chance, not at this hour and not so far out from any sizeable town or shelter. Even if the cold didn't get him, the snowplough might; they'd have to scrape him off the blade like dried-on gruel.

He went back around the van. Most of the rear offside tyre had peeled away, and the wheel rim was bent all out of shape. It was ruined, but Lindegren had managed that all by himself. The fat little fuck.

John Visco climbed back into the cab. Lindegren was asleep over the wheel, and he didn't wake up.

Help arrived around midnight, with the wrong size of tyre; Lindegren had misread the figures in the Fiat's handbook. Help went away again, and didn't return until morning.

When the day arrived, the weather started to improve. Lindegren's air of desperation didn't.

By nine o'clock, they should have been rolling into the city's outskirts on the flat stretch of land at the head of the Oslofjord. But they were still on a mountain road, and they seemed to be climbing; if there had been any signs to suggest that they should have done otherwise, they'd missed them. Lindegren reached across John to the dashboard glove compartment and pulled out a clipboard, trying to steady the van with one hand as he did. On the front of the clipboard was a stack of invoices held down under an elastic band, and tucked under the band on the reverse side was a city map.

John watched the road apprehensively as Lindegren divided his attention between the map and his driving. There was a rise in the ground ahead, and no way of seeing what might be climbing up the other side of it. No way of listening, either, because Lindegren was keeping the Fiat in low gear even though it sobbed and strained to move up. As it turned out, it wasn't another car that was the problem; they came over the brow squarely in the middle but without meeting anything, but then Lindegren lost the Fiat.

The ragged urging of the engine had become a roar as the van's nose pointed downhill, and the leap forward as he finally changed up surprised him; he hit the brakes, and lost the back end. He knew enough to attempt to steer with the skid; he probably knew enough to take his foot off the brakes, too, but he didn't do it. Instead of the complete spin that it had been attempting, the Fiat coasted broadside-on into the high bank at the side of the road. Visco was thrown against Lindegren, Lindegren was squashed against the driver's door, and about a ton of polythene and assorted fabrics shifted in the back.

John had to get out so that Lindegren could climb across his seat to go and look at the damage.

It wasn't so bad. The snow had only been falling for a few weeks, and so the roadside walls raised by the ploughs hadn't had the chance to harden and become like the sides of a bobsleigh run. The van had demolished a length of the banking, but when Lindegren brushed the clinging ice away he uncovered only a few shallow dents.

But the van was nearly new, and he'd been making this trip for six years and never had a hitch, and . . .

He fixed John with a long and mournful look, and there was no disguising it this time. He couldn't explain how or why, but he knew – somehow – where the blame lay.

He tried to back out, but his wheels spun and wouldn't bite. John knew better than to ask if he carried snow chains; this was a man who didn't even carry a jack. He watched from the road as Lindegren revved so hard he made the clutch squeal, spinning the back wheels and digging himself even deeper into a couple of ruts. Then as he came around to see if he'd managed to get himself anywhere, John said tentatively, 'Anything I can do to help?'

'Anything you can do?' Lindegren said, wheeling on him. He had a day's stubble and his hair was raised in

10

spikes. He looked like a supporting player in a Popeye cartoon. 'Anything you can do? You can stay out of my way, that's what you can do.'

John shrugged. 'Doesn't seem like much.'

'It's enough. Believe me, it's enough.' And he bent with his hands on his knees to take a closer look at the rutted ground under his wheels.

John began, 'You could put something under the wheels . . .'

'I *know*,' Lindegren said with exaggerated patience, making a little motion with his hands as if to push John away. 'I live here, remember?'

He opened the back doors of the van, groaned at the way his stock had shifted around, and then started rummaging underneath it. He came out with an expensive-looking cardboard dress box which had been folded flat. He opened it out and ripped it in two with difficulty, jamming half under each of the drive wheels to improve traction.

At first it didn't look like he was going to do it; again he spun the wheels too fast, and the cardboard began to shred whilst the van stayed in place. But then it jerked a few inches and rolled back, and Lindegren seemed to be getting the idea. He started to rock the van with short blips on the pedal, and on the fifth attempt he gave an extra burst and rolled free.

He carried on for nearly fifty yards down the road before he stopped; for a moment John didn't think he was going to stop at all, but then the brakelights glowed and John ran to catch up.

Lindegren was staring straight ahead. He seemed to be angry with himself over something. As he climbed in, breath feathering in the cold air, John said, 'There's something wrong, isn't there?'

Lindegren's expression made it clear that there was no sane reply to such a question.

It was about ten minutes later that they passed the first vehicle they'd seen in an hour or more; it was a yellow

11

Citroën with a loaded ski rack on its roof, two adults in the front and three children in the back. Lindegren was no longer trying to read the map as he drove. It was on the seat beside him, and he didn't even glance at it. Within the next few minutes they'd passed three more cars, all of them carrying skis and all of them climbing towards the hills behind. When Lindegren saw a half-buried sign for a parking area, he pulled across the road and through the gates.

The area was a cleared oval about the size of an ice rink. The plough must have gone over it within the last couple of hours, because the ground had been scraped down almost to the bone of the night's fall, and the tread of its big tyres with their teeth of chain still showed fresh. There was only one car already there, a black Mercedes with its radiator covered by a piece of old cardboard. It had a ski rack but no skis, and there was no sign of where the Mercedes people might have gone.

Lindegren put the Fiat alongside the other car. 'We break down, now we get lost,' he said almost philosophically, and started to zipper his quilted anorak in preparation for getting out. It came as a surprise to John; he'd been assuming from the evidence that they were on or near one of the city's main roads and heading in more or less the right direction.

He said, 'What now?'

'We get out and ask, that's what now.'

'You want me to do it?'

'And get directions maybe to Sverige. No thanks, Visco, I ask for myself.' And then he opened the door, squirmed around on his foam cushion, and dropped the short distance to the ground. The cushion eased back into shape with a sigh.

John climbed out, buttoned his jacket as high as it would go and turned his collar up as Lindegren did his usual double-check of the locks. It took him longer than usual, allowing for the extra time he spent shaking his head over the new dents and scratches on the driver's side. John

12

could sense that something was going through the little man's mind, but he couldn't guess what.

They set off across the rink towards the road, their boots crunching on the fresh snow. Lindegren seemed to have some definite idea of where he was going, which didn't exactly tie in with his claim that he was lost. John let him lead the way, and he watched from a few paces behind; the Norwegian seemed to be working his way slowly through a problem, as if he hadn't had much practice.

They crossed the road and climbed over the snowbank at a point where it had been tramped hard into a bridge of grey ice. John saw the marks of ski sticks on the bank alongside, and in the clearing beyond he saw ski tracks, hundreds of them covering an area the width of a motorway, slicing on downhill through a clearing in a stand of high snow-laden conifers. Lindegren had his head down and was already twenty yards ahead, and John moved to follow.

It was an easy ski slope, and obviously heavily used by somebody. The untouched snow to the side was more than knee deep, but where the tracks ran it was compressed enough for walking. John wondered if Lindegren might have seen a light or a building to head for, but that didn't seem to be so; the trees hid everything.

Lindegren was really moving. It took John more than a minute to make up the lost distance, and when he drew near he could hear that Lindegren was muttering to himself. As John came level, he said abruptly, 'Listen, Visco. I'm a nice fellow, right?'

'If you say so,' John said, but it didn't seem to be enough.

'Look, I take you off the ferry, I give you the lift. That make me pretty nice fellow, right?'

John nodded, and waited for whatever came next. Which was Lindegren hammering at the same issue, as if it was a point to be forced home before the next stage of the argument could be considered. 'I come rolling off the boat and see you shivering there at the dock gates and I think, what hell. That's what I'm like – you ask my wife, ask my friends, ask anybody.'

'I don't understand what you're trying to say.'

'I'm trying to say you bring me bad luck. I'm trying to say you're a jinx, John Visco. I'm sorry, but there it is.'

The picture ahead came a little clearer as they emerged from the woodland and began a slightly steeper descent. There was a group of fair-sized buildings about a quarter of a mile on, and a railway track that cut across before them. The road was to their right, and the path would meet it again to bring them into the settlement. John started to say, 'But I don't see how –'

But Lindegren had gone.

His legs had shot from under him in a pratfall that carried him half a dozen feet on down the path, and he was only just coming to rest when John reached him and helped him up. At first he accepted the hand with breath-less gratitude, but then he remembered that it was the hand of the jinx and pulled away in what seemed like genuine fear.

'Don't touch me, please,' he said. 'Just don't.'

He unzipped his anorak and reached gingerly inside, bringing out a silver and leather hipflask that would hold maybe a quarter pint of spirits. He probed the ribs under where it had been lying, staring around into nowhere like he was feeling for rabbits in a hole. Then he said defiantly, 'You're slipping, Visco, I break nothing. Big bloody bruise, though, thanks.' He slipped the flask into an out-side pocket, and tramped on. He had trouble getting his zip refastened. John, having no real choice, followed.

Lindegren slowed to let him catch up when they were almost at the point where they rejoined the road for the last few yards. Most of the annoyance seemed to have boiled out of him, and he said, 'I'm sorry, Visco. Call you names, give you a bad time. It's not like me, I'm a nice fellow, really. It's just . . .' and he flapped his hand, indi-cating a frustration that could never really be expressed.

'Yes,' John said. 'I know.'

14

'Come on. I buy you coffee.'

The place they were heading for was a rambling wooden lodge, a snow-covered roof with timber ends carved into dragonheads and a terrace before it, around which a dozen or so cars were parked. Some of them had been there overnight and were almost buried.

There was firewood stacked under the eaves and the basement windows were shuttered, and they bowed their heads as they came in around the side to avoid being blinded by the fine mist of snow that was being blown from the roof's edge.

'Restaurant,' Lindegren explained, 'big ski-ing place about twelve, thirteen kilometres out. Oslofjord somewhere over there.' And he pointed vaguely across the terrace before climbing the steps to the main entrance, stamping the snow off his boots as he went.

'I thought you were lost,' John said as they moved through a double porch. Oslofjord, if it had been anywhere at all, had stayed out of sight behind the mists. They came through into a large dimly lit room built mostly around a double-chambered stone fireplace. Lindegren blinked and craned his head to look around; it was early and most of the tables were empty, but his glasses had misted up.

He said, 'Damn roads all look the same in snow,' and took his glasses off. He started to reach for his handkerchief, remembered the condition it was in and changed his mind, and then waved them around vaguely as if that might clear them. Then he walked into a chair.

They finally made it to a table by the fire, and a white-jacketed waiter took their order. Lindegren polished his glasses on a corner of the tablecloth, and held them up to the light of a chandelier made of reindeer antlers. He held them for longer than he needed to, but it gave him an excuse not to look at John as he said, 'I'm an honest fellow, me. Ask anybody. There's something coming on behind you, John Visco, and you have to get rid of it.'

'Something behind me? Like what?'

'Just an expression, a way you say things. Bad luck like yours, it isn't natural.' And with the worst of it said, he put his glasses on and looked around. Two children in a family group three tables down had to look away quickly, stifling giggles.

John said, 'It kind of seems to me that the bad luck was all yours.'

'Six years I've been driving to England,' Lindegren began, but fortunately the return of the waiter cut him short. There was an enforced truce for thirty seconds or so until he moved away, during which John and Lindegren looked in opposite directions. John noticed for the first time that there was a dog under the next table, a chestnut-brown setter with grey splashes on its paws and muzzle. It had been staring at him eagerly, and when it saw that it had been noticed its tail began to switch from side to side; but its leather harness had been roped by a couple of turns of nylon line to one of the table legs, and the best it could manage was a signal. Hadn't Mark Twain written something about the difference between a dog and a man? Something like, you take both in off the street and feed them when they're starving, and the dog won't bite you.

As the waiter moved away, John got in first with, 'Six years is plenty of time for the odds to stack up. Where did you learn English?'

'Sesame Street,' Lindegren responded automatically, and then checked himself. 'No, that was joke. All over.' The coffee had arrived in a silver service, old but well polished, and Lindegren reached for the jug. He was about to say something more but he hesitated, and held the jug higher. With his free hand, he tried to smooth down the four or five distinct spikes of hair that he saw reflected there. No good.

He set the jug down, pushed his glasses up onto his forehead, and massaged at the shiny spots either side of the bridge of his nose. His shoulders were heaving gently, and John thought that the little man had cracked; but he was laughing.

16

'Jesus damn,' he said, 'sitting here like a fucking porcupine.' He wiped his eyes, put his glasses back into place, and took a deep breath to shake him back to rationality. 'What am I talking about? Couple of flats, a day late. What the hell.'

'What the hell,' John agreed, and poured the coffee. Except that he somehow missed the cup, and poured it straight into Lindegren's lap.

The dog joined in the howling, and John ran to get some paper towels. The men's room was on the upper floor across a kind of minstrels' gallery, and when he got there he found only cloth towels on rollers; so he grabbed a handful of soft toilet paper and headed back.

He couldn't see Lindegren from the gallery, and when he got back to the table he found a ten-krone note held down by the sugar bowl. He looked around, and the young woman with the family group said something he couldn't understand. What he understood was that maybe Lindegren was grabbing the chance to abandon him – and almost everything that he owned was locked in the back of the little man's Fiat van.

He ran out onto the terrace. Lindegren was either hiding or moving at one hell of a clip, because John could see for some distance along the looping road that had brought them to the lodge. There was a car just coming into sight, its tyres raising a thin smoke of snow powder which immediately dispersed in the wind, but nobody on foot. Could Lindegren have flagged down some vehicle for a ride up the hill? If he had, John had no chance of catching him. But as he crossed the terrace and descended the few steps to road level, another thought occurred to him.

Lindegren had never been lost – well, maybe at first, but only then. When he'd put the map aside and pulled into the oval parking area, he'd known exactly where he was. He'd also known the path to the lodge, and followed it with the obvious confidence of someone who'd walked that way many times before. But why leave the van so far away, when the road came over a dip and ran down by the side of the lodge itself?

The intention had been to dump John, to make sure that the so-called jinx couldn't follow Lindegren home and begin the slow process of total ruin. John began to trot up the road, unaware for the moment of the flapping of his unbuttoned jacket or the handful of toilet paper that streamed out behind him like the tail of a kite; he concentrated on the ground ahead, watching for the patches of black ice that would so easily scoop his feet from under him. There was no pavement, just a shoulder of grey mush thrown by passing cars, and the ice was baked hard underneath.

Lindegren had to move with the same kind of care. But he only had half a minute's start at the most, and he was nowhere in sight.

John stopped, and tried to think. He felt sharpened by the cold air and the long days without sleep, but it was deceptive; for all his sharpness, he couldn't grab hold of a tumbling idea for long enough to examine it.

He rolled the toilet paper into a ball, and stuffed it into his pocket. Then he buttoned his jacket. If Lindegren wasn't on his way back to the van, he must be hiding, waiting for John to go away. But John wouldn't go without his pack – could Lindegren have forgotten as much? – and all he'd have to do would be to wait by the van. And the van was so far off . . .

That was it, that was the reason. They'd come down the hill on a looping path that more or less followed the line of the road; but Lindegren must know another, a path that cut through the trees and across the loop, one that would get him to the van and away before John could even cover half the distance.

John turned back to the lodge. He was a couple of hundred yards away from it by now, and he'd climbed enough to be about level with the roofline. Back of the timbered building was more or less a solid snowbank up to the eaves, broken only by a boarded-up souvenir kiosk

18

and a telephone booth. Behind them was the spidery line of the top inch or so of a picket fence.

Beyond the fence was more woodland, with children's voices in amongst the trees. The power and telephone wires zigzagged up the hill above the spruce and pine to link with the railway's lines above. On each of the poles there was a light glowing dimly in the grey of the morning, angled down onto the ground beneath.

Where there were lights, there had to be some kind of ski run. Or a path.

John left the road and started to cut across country to join the lines. The snow pulled him down at first, but where it was held together by a depth of brushwood under the surface he was able to keep going; staying close to the flaking birch seemed to be best, and within minutes he broke through onto the path Lindegren must have taken.

It was much steeper than the one they'd come down, and instead of being conveniently packed by ski tracks this trail had been almost polished. Which was good news – Lindegren wasn't too steady on his feet, and this would help to slow him down.

He stepped aside at a bend to let a party of downhill skiers pass. They were all boys of school age, and they coasted on past without any show of effort. He'd yet to catch sight of Lindegren – the little man must be scrambling up the trail in a panic. And for nothing; there was no reason why he couldn't simply say this is it, the ride ends here, best of luck for the next one, and then set him down at some intersection to stand with his sign.

John guessed that he was about halfway when he reached the railway line. There was a station, nothing more than an open-sided hut and cleared areas on either side of the rails, and a man and a girl in bobcaps and tracksuits were standing in the shelter. He wondered whether to stop and ask them if they'd seen Lindegren, but he decided against it almost immediately; he could be wasting time in making himself understood, and confirmation wouldn't really be any help. And if he was wrong, and the trail led off across into the mountains somewhere, then it was almost certainly too late to head back and start again.

But he wasn't wrong. The little trail carried on beyond the railway and Lindegren was struggling on ahead, a small, stumbling figure about a quarter of a mile upslope, arms waving as he tried to keep his balance. John stopped for a moment to gather himself for the long-haul effort to overtake; Lindegren had quite a lead, and it wasn't going to be easy.

He started to climb, kicking up snow as he went. The muscles in his legs started to protest after only a few dozen strides, but he ignored them. The gap was already starting to close, but Lindegren was now beyond the woods and on the edge of the clearing which would lead him back to the road and the parking area, and when he reached the middle of the broad ski run John saw him turn and look back.

John wasn't going to make it.

Lindegren turned and floundered towards the road. He didn't look first, which was a mistake. Three skiers gliding silently downhill had to split to avoid him; one of them shouted a warning, but it was too late.

He collided with the second man in the party. John could hear the thump across the snow, a flat sound without echo. One ski flipped over and nailed itself into the snow at an angle whilst the two bodies rolled on for some distance. The other skiers executed braking turns and began to shuffle back to where Lindegren and their winded fellow lay half-buried.

To Lindegren, it would confirm the escalation of the jinx – a glance back to see John in his tracks, and then immediate disaster. John pressed on, making the most of the time he'd been given whilst the skiers helped the two fallen men to their feet. There was no time for any kind of argument to start, because as soon as he could balance on his own Lindegren went staggering off feebly, churning his way through unbroken snow in a last desperate attempt to get to the road before John.

He made it, but only just. His snow-spattered back was disappearing through the gates of the parking area as John slid over the embankment and down to the road.

Another four or five cars had joined the Fiat and the black Mercedes, making a neat row at the far end of the oval. John came across cautiously, thinking that Lindegren might be desperate enough to make a last effort to get away, in which case he might put the van into a skid across the rink without meaning to. But the van's engine wasn't even running, and when John came around the side he saw that Lindegren hadn't even managed to open the door yet; he'd dropped his keys, and was down on the ground trying to find them.

He looked up when he heard John. He was almost in tears. Christ, John thought, the man's an authentic mental case, and he tried to speak but found he didn't have the breath. He leaned on the side of the van and took a deep swallow of air that burned his lungs, and Lindegren wiped his eyes and found his keys and stood up.

John said, 'What about my bag?'

Lindegren was embarrassed, and was clearly stung by the implied accusation. 'I wasn't going to take your bag, what you think I am? Thief?' He sorted through the keys on his ring, and his hands shook. As he went around to the back of the van he said, 'Nothing personal in this, Visco. But I got people to see and deliveries to make, and I want to be alive to do it. With you along, I'm not so sure.' He unlocked the doors and swung them open. John's pack had shifted, probably turned on its side after the bump with the snowbank, and it was crushing a few of the more expensive-looking lines up against the inside of the van. Lindegren made a fatalistic, what-else-did-I-expect gesture, and took hold of the frame to pull it out. One of the buckles snagged on something, and Lindegren jerked it free with a tearing sound. He didn't even look to see what had been ruined as he set the pack down before John and pointed across the slope they'd just climbed.

'You see the bridge?' he said. 'You see the line? That's the T-Banen, the electric trains, five kroner will take you anywhere you want to go. Here, look,' and he put a hand in his pocket and came out with a fistful of notes and change. He held it out without even counting it, and when John didn't respond he took his hand and pressed the money into his palm. He said, 'I pay your fare, anything; ask at the lodge and they'll tell you how. Have another coffee, have what you like, all on me, eh? Please, Visco?'

John found himself holding onto the money, and Lindegren took a step away in case he tried to offer it back. There was a mute pleading in his eyes, a terror so deep that John had never seen anything like it before; he said, 'I didn't think Norwegians were superstitious.'

'You have to push us. Please, Visco.'

He shrugged, and lifted his pack by one of the straps to sling it around and onto his shoulder. Lindegren quickly secured the back of the van and scampered around the side, as if he was afraid that John might change his mind and withdraw permission. He was so eager to get away that he stalled the engine twice before he was moving, then he was out of the parking area and turning down the road without a wave.

John opened his hand and looked at Lindegren's money. There were about thirty kroner in notes and coins. An authentic mental case. He shoved it into the pocket of his jeans and reached behind him for the other shoulder strap, and then he shrugged against the weight a couple of times to get the pack settled for the descent.

He had a list of six addresses in the city, and after the half-hour ride down in the T-Banen carriage he set about checking them out. They were all inexpensive *pensjonats* in quiet back streets around the university area, but the list proved useless; the first three places he checked had all been turned over to become Vietnamese refugee centres, and so six o'clock that evening found him in line at the accommodation counter in the East railway station.

They offered him cheap or they offered him central, but he couldn't have both. By now he was almost too weary to think with much logic but he decided to take the more expensive option – it would be easier to find, and it would have a phone in the room, which could be important. Besides, when he got the job he was after then the expense wouldn't be significant. He changed his money at the kiosk next door, and then he was on his way.

They'd placed him in an older hotel which overlooked the city's main central plaza. It also had a sidestreet entrance which was squeezed between shopfronts and difficult to find. There was no lobby, just a desk and an open-fronted elevator, and even these had to share space with a small hair-dressing salon. He signed in and was given a key attached to a brass globe that could have choked an elephant.

He was in number five-fifteen, the top floor with a view of the Gate below. It had two single beds with duvets against one wall, a window with a deep ledge and a heater below it, and an old-fashioned Electrolux refrigerator with a press-button handle. Visco set his pack down against the end of one bed, opened the window and then turned down the heater. He opened the Electrolux; no light inside, but two bottles of Pils lager, one Coke and one tonic.

There was also a bathroom, with so much white tile that he'd have been blinded if age hadn't dulled the glaze. The mirror over the sink didn't flatter him; it made his skin pale and put dark rings under his eyes, and he only stayed long enough to splash his face and then dry himself on one of the hotel's cheap towels.

His own towel was in the zippered compartment at the bottom of his pack, not to be unrolled except behind locked doors. He sat on the bed and pulled it out with difficulty; for some reason he couldn't unscramble the order of doing things, because he was still in his boots and heavy jacket. From the towel he took the greased frame of a Swiss 9mm SIG automatic pistol. The slide was wrapped in polythene at the bottom of his soapcase, and the magazine was between two paperback books in a side pocket of his pack. The five rounds for the magazine were hidden in the case of his travel alarm.

He was dog-tired. This was really something that could wait until tomorrow, but he went ahead anyway. Within five minutes, he'd completed the assembly.

He sat there with the gun in his hand, grinning like a kid. There was no feeling like it. He could still remember the first time that he'd ever held a real pistol, one with actual killing-power. He'd been working at a disco-bar in South Wales, and two or three of them had gone along for an after-hours nightcap to the manager's home. It was a split-level house on a hillside, architect-designed and no more than four years old; it had a landscaped Japanese garden, a complete mirror-glass wall on one side of the lounge, and a basement den with an attached firing range. Barry had opened up the cabinets to show them his weapons collection; they couldn't use the range because it was late and Barry's children were asleep, but they handed the guns around and experienced the strange sensation of completeness and authority that seemed to come as part of the deal.

It was weird, but John knew then that he was hooked. The part of his life that he always referred to as 'the struggling phase of my autobiography' had already begun to drag on for too long, but here was a drug that could float the anxiety away for a while.

He'd told himself on that same evening – if ever the chance came for him to get a gun of his own, something compact that he could carry as he travelled, he was going to grab it however much it cost him. He wasn't interested in marksmanship or in joining a pistol club; in fact, it didn't even matter if he never got to pull the trigger on a loaded chamber or magazine. He just wanted that rare sensation, that peculiar fix of power, that feeling of being somehow *extended* and enlarged.

So, here it was. He raised the automatic, and sighted along his arm to the window. There was a blue neon Ford sign across the Gate; one well-placed shot could take out the window and the sign as well. He placed his left hand over the gun, and pulled back the slide.

A round moved up into the firing chamber.

Now, this meant business.

He couldn't understand why he was still feeling so sharp. He'd been three nights without a cabin on the sea crossing, with another night on the road to be added to that. Either he was fooling himself, and the table was about to be kicked from under the house of cards that was his consciousness, or else he'd come through some kind of barrier and he was never going to have to sleep again.

He was fooling himself. Somewhere in the distance, the City Hall clock began to chime; he'd just blinked, and lost a quarter of an hour. He was still sitting on the bed, but the gun was no longer levelled at the neon.

It was under his chin, with the end of the barrel just fitted into the soft space between his jaw and his windpipe. The weight of his finger was resting on the trigger.

Slowly, he took it away. He'd almost been pressing hard enough to bruise the skin. What had he been doing, dreaming? Whatever the cause, he'd managed to give himself a bad scare. He'd never done anything like that before, ever. He lowered the gun and put it down on the towel.

At the same time, he couldn't help wondering what it would be like. It would make a mess, but he'd never see it – maybe just a blinding red behind the eyes before the bullet took out his brain and the top of his head. Although he'd probably screw it up, break a cheekbone and pop out an eye or something, just enough to make it a painful and lasting embarrassment . . . either way, it wasn't in line with what he had in mind. A suicide was a nobody, a broken shell in a zippered bag.

That wasn't what John Visco had in mind. Not at all.

He went across to the Electrolux, and took out a beer.

What the hell. He drank from the bottle as he undressed, letting his clothes fall in a heap on the floor. Here's to the Teamverk Geological Survey, and the end of the jinx forever.

He dropped onto the bed. He could dream about blowing Per Lindegren away.

Fat little fuck, he thought as the shadows closed in.

THREE

Jerry Fraser almost had to dig his way out of the head of the shaft; the canvas cover that he'd fitted three months before was stiff and frozen so that it hung more like a board than a flap, and enough snow had drifted under the edge to give him a problem kicking it open. Getting worse every day, but it wasn't going to last.

Fraser was a junior field geologist with the Teamverk number nine survey in Tromstad, about fifteen hours' drive north of the Arctic circle when the roads were open. The title of junior didn't sit very well with a man of thirty-three years who'd picked up his late qualifications in a more exacting school than many of the others on the survey but Fraser did his best to let it pass. Perhaps it wasn't too late for him to learn patience, as well, although some of the talk around the field office and the cabins didn't make it easy.

He dumped the tin sample box outside the cover, put the duffel bag with his own gear on top of that, and then gave the shaft head a final check before he ducked out after. His bad leg twinged as always at the first touch of cold, and then settled to the regular ache that he'd learned to ignore. He tied the flap down behind him; there were still some climbing pieces and the field telephone inside, but there was no point taking out either until the main office gave its decision on the site.

He was now in half of a ruined hut, the useless half that gave no shelter, but the sky above was a blue so clear that he could almost see through it to darkness and stars. He was in the wagon shed that had been the headworks of the mine's gravity railway, cars full of ore descending and controlled by a chain winch bringing up the wagons for the next load; most of the gear was now gone, and what hadn't been removed or destroyed had become rusted, overgrown. Until the snows came, of course, filling in the spaces between the parallel sets of rails and silting down through the open roof, burying the dead apparatus until the spring melt came and the corpse pushed its way back to the surface.

He left the sample case with its load of tagged and graded tailings – no need to stagger with it when he could get help. He walked across the loading bay platform and jumped down to the tracks, and then dusted the snow from his gloves as he went out through a doorless arch in the end wall to the old wagon yard. He was hardly limping at all.

There were seven trucks still on the rails, all corroded solidly into place, and Teamverk's number two Land-Rover was nosed in at an angle near the end of the line. Fraser had been trying to bring it around to get it into the shelter of the hut's most complete wall, but as he'd changed through the gears he'd felt the clutch pedal suddenly give a couple more inches than it was supposed to, and on the return it had locked into place. As Fraser approached the Rover now, he called out, 'Well, Olav, am I mobile?'

Olav Nystrom crawled out from under the vehicle, squinting as he moved from darkness to weak sunlight. He was dark-haired and nineteen years old, Teamverk's only local recruit. He said, 'Mobile if you walk. Your clutch is locked.'

'Something big?'

'Something small. Take a look.' He handed Fraser two pieces of a sheared rod about five inches long, and bent to pick up some snow. Fraser held the pieces together. It was no factory part but a workshop botch, a piece of threaded metal that had been built up to length with several welds.

He said, 'Is that all?'

'It's enough,' Nystrom said, wiping the oil from his hands. 'I'll take the pieces down and see if I can cut a bolt for a patch-up repair.'

'That means both the Rovers are out, then.'

'Until the snows melt and you can get a tractor to pull the other one out of its hole, yes. Somebody should tell Skipper Ashton not to take the corners with his eyes closed.'

'Ashton was stoned out of his mind when he did it, and so were the others. That's why nobody stayed with it.'

'They sent a boy to knock on my door,' Nystrom said, reaching under the Rover and pulling out the plastic sheet he'd been lying on. 'As if I could do anything alone.'

'Maybe they thought you'd mobilise the village for them.'

'They thought wrong, Jerry. If things were different, there's Lidman with the machine shop behind the chandlers could turn out one of those rods in half an hour. As it is, we'll have to order the part and fly it in.'

If things were different. If Teamverk got anything more than minimal co-operation, if Tromstad moved to show the strangers any welcome at all. Nystrom rolled the plastic sheet, and Fraser stepped aside as he took it around to stow it in the back of the Rover. This wasn't the first cheap repair that the boy had found in either of the machines; like most old Land-Rovers, they had ownership histories too dense to unravel. And they let in the rain, their heaters were poor and their wipers a joke, and their brakes squealed like a bicycle's, but they climbed the icy tracks in the hills over Tromstad like a couple of monkeys.

Or at least, they had. Now both vehicles were out, and it was a two-mile walk down to the cabins that were Teamverk's operational centre and almost another mile further to the village. Fraser said, 'What about the rod from the other Rover?'

'Depends how bad you want it. The snow's up to the roof and it's hard like a stone.'

'Forget it, then. If Kreiger gets desperate, let him send Skipper Ashton out with a shovel.'

Nystrom grinned. 'I want to watch the sparks when he tells him,' he said, and slammed the door. It didn't catch the first time, and he had to do it again. All the Rover's windows shook, but the door held. Then he looked at Fraser and said, 'Give you a hand?'

'You could help me with the case, tailing samples from gallery four. And there's some of my kit, but I can manage that.'

They started to walk alongside the line of trucks, and Nystrom said, 'Moving out at last?'

'Moving out early. I wasn't going to bring anything down until tomorrow, but that animal's been around again.'

'You mean your wolf?' Nystrom said as they passed through the arch and climbed up to the level of the loading platform, and Fraser beckoned him across to where the snow lay thinnest.

There were marks that hadn't been fully covered. They weren't really distinct enough to be called animal tracks with any certainty, but the rare presence of a wolf in the valley was no longer in doubt. The latest sighting had been three days before, in the hay fields above the village; a group of children which included Ingrid and Anja, Nystrom's two small cousins, had seen it break from one stand of trees across the field to another, hurdling the fence between with ease. Fraser pointed and said, 'It got the canvas open and went sniffing around again.'

'Did it break anything?'

'No, nothing. But what scares me is the idea that it might be down there waiting for me sometime. It chews on the phone lines, as well.'

'For what?'

'Don't ask me, maybe it likes the taste. I was getting breakup on the field line, so I ran it through my hands for a couple of hundred yards and found it down to the metal in one place.'

'I'm surprised you got any signal at all.'

The sample case had a rope handle at either end, and they swung it between them. Jerry Fraser put the weight on his best side, and they carried it across to the edge of the platform and set it on the snow before they climbed down. Fraser said, 'What I thought of doing was taking the two batteries out of the Rovers and wiring them in series for a night. See if I couldn't make its eyes light up in the dark.'

'And when Kreiger picks up the phone in the morning . . .'

'Pow. More likely one of the other bastards spoofing me again. They watch me set out and they give me long enough to get down through the galleries, and then they start cranking the handle. First couple of times I climbed all the way back to answer it.'

'What did they say?'

'Nobody spoke, but I could tell they were listening. Bastards. So now I have to sit down there in the dark and listen to it ring half a mile away and wonder if it might be genuine.'

'If it might be Kreiger?' Nystrom said as they emerged into the wagon yard. Fraser made a face at the name of his team leader.

'Kreiger's as bad as the rest. You know he wouldn't have given you a job if they hadn't told him he had to hire a token viking.'

Now it was Nystrom's turn to look pained. 'Please,' he said, 'I heard enough from my father.'

'Still giving you a bad time?'

'No, but . . .' He shook his head. Sometimes when he talked to Jerry it was like talking aloud to himself; he was never afraid of his secrets being handed around later for everybody to turn over and laugh at, but when it came to the growing feeling of being a stranger within his own family – well, there just didn't seem to be the words for it.

The snow-cut track mostly followed the line of the old

railway, and it showed as a crisp edge of shadow running downhill ahead of them. The shaft and workings to which Jerry Fraser had been assigned were much older than the large open-cast copper mine which was the main subject of the survey; nobody else had shown much interest in this unpromising and hazardous-looking piece of hardrock digging, and so Ray Kreiger had tossed it to the last in line and told him to go ahead with it. Fraser mapped and classified his territory alone and some way higher than the open slopes where the rest of the team were involved in a seismic survey, and on the days when the Rovers were needed elsewhere he had to shoulder his tools and climb all the way.

The descent got steeper towards the village. From here they could see only a narrow slice of the stacked roofs and then the black fjord waters beyond, catching a little of the sun and sparkling nearly three miles down. They could reach the Teamverk centre in an hour, and the outskirts of the village about twenty minutes after that.

There was enough width in the cut for them to walk level and with the awkward case between them. The line for the field telephone ran alongside them, pinned every now and again by a short metal pole to hold it clear of the snow. Fraser was watching it as he said, 'What will you do when the team pulls out? Back to the boats?'

Nystrom shook his head firmly. He was proud of being a good, instinctive mechanic, but he didn't want to spend the rest of his life below decks in the fishing fleet. Whether he stank of diesel or of fish, it didn't matter; he said, 'I think I'll be leaving Tromstad.'

'You could hang on for the verdict on the mines. Teamverk would give you a job.'

'They called me Quisling once already. Twice I can do without.' He glanced ahead and to the right, where most of the old copper workings lay. 'You think they'll decide to reopen?'

'Right now it isn't worth it. But in three or four years, if the boom comes and the market gets hungry . . . well, maybe.'

'My uncles will be sitting in the roads with shotguns.'

'Better tell the Oslo bureau. They'll need to include that in their projections.'

They stopped to switch sides around the box, setting it down and bending some life back into their mittened hands before starting off again. Nystrom was silent, looking out over the bleak massif. Fraser knew what he was thinking. He'd kicked over the same problems himself, sixteen years before on a Florida beach; a desperate need, impossible to satisfy because it refused to take shape, and an urge to reach out even when there was nothing obvious to reach for. Stay in place, and it could burn you up; start to run, and it could as easily burn you out.

Nystrom said, 'It's a hard decision to make, Jerry. What would you do?'

'No easy answers from your Uncle Jerome.' He might have said forget it, the military draft has a way of solving these things for you, but something else had taken his attention. He said, 'Has that line gone slack?'

Nystrom glanced at the staked wire alongside the track. They were coming up to the middle point between two anchorages, and the line had drooped low enough to disappear under the snow for six feet or more. He said, 'I don't know. How should it look?'

'Give it a pull and see.'

They stopped, and Nystrom reached over with his free hand and took hold of the wire. It lifted easily, as if there was plenty under the snow to spare. Then they put the sample case down and Fraser pulled the line in; four feet along he came to the sheared end with the wire core showing bright. He said, 'How long ago did I call for you?'

'An hour and a half, maybe two. I wasn't counting.'

'Was the line in one piece when you came up?'

'I didn't follow it.'

Fraser tested the side of the cut. It was frozen, but it wasn't solid enough to take his weight. He kicked a couple of deep footholds and stamped them firm before he carefully raised himself to get a better view of the snow around the wire.

He seemed to find something that he'd been expecting. He beckoned to Nystrom to climb up beside him, and said, 'Are those wolf tracks, Olav?'

Nystrom, who'd never seen a wolf track in his life, said, 'I'm only a token viking. How many wolves do you think we get around here?'

There was a mess of trampled snow around the chewed wire, and a single line of tracks that led away. The animal, wolf or whatever, must have made its approach along the man-made cut before snapping the line and heading off cross-country. Where they hadn't been kicked over, the prints were clear and well-formed. They were also big – Nystrom could almost have fitted his spread hand into a single depression.

Fraser was beginning to scramble over the edge of the cut. He said, 'I want a look at the bastard that's harassing me.'

Nystrom took a second look at the wolf's traces – personally, this was as near as he cared to get. He said, 'It could be two, three miles away.'

'Or a couple of hundred yards and running.' Fraser tested his weight on the snow; a film crust had formed over deeper layers, and he could stand upright without breaking through. Neither of them was carrying snowshoes – Nystrom hadn't expected to need his, and Fraser didn't own any. No-one had known that the survey would run so late into the year. He slipped his duffel bag off his shoulder and lowered it into the cut, swinging it a little to land by the sample box as Nystrom stood alongside him.

Nystrom tested the snow with his heel. He'd known sub-zero conditions for two-thirds of his nineteen years, and he'd learned that snow shouldn't easily be trusted – especially on high, sloping ground. Its depth was never even but consisted of layers of plate frost and looser, refrozen crystals. In a mature bank those layers could shear under their own weight and begin to avalanche, and it took only the slightest push to begin the reaction.

Alone, he'd have stayed on the safe ground of the cut. But he was with Fraser. Besides, the snow was young and comparatively shallow; the crust would take their weight out on the exposed slopes, but they'd have to watch for wind-sheltered hollows where the sun might have acted to soften up the surface. He said, 'Okay, but no running,' and Fraser nodded his agreement without having to ask for an explanation.

They took it slowly. The wolf trail was easy enough to follow, but as Fraser tried to push ahead he broke through almost immediately into thigh-deep snow, and he floundered for several yards before he was able to regain the surface. By then he was panting heavily, and the inside of his woollen shirt was greasy with sweat. Nystrom waited as Fraser struggled – he couldn't offer a hand, as their combined weight would drag both of them down. He was expecting Fraser to say, 'forget it, let's go back,' but he didn't. He pressed on without even stopping to beat the snow off his parka, and so Nystrom followed.

The wolf obviously had no problem with the snow. Its gait had been long-reaching and even, breaking trail as it went. After a few hundred yards it had begun to angle downslope, and each stride had become longer as the going eased.

Nystrom said, 'This kind of speed, we should be bringing it down in a couple of minutes, right?'

'I only want a look at it.' There wasn't much spare meat on Fraser and when he pushed himself hard he seemed to be all leather and sinew, like a runner. He pulled down his parka zip a couple of notches to let himself cool off, and added, 'Maybe we'll scare it up.'

'And maybe it will roll over laughing.' Nystrom couldn't shake himself of the thought that maybe the wolf had been behind him as he'd climbed the fjell in response to Fraser's call. How far? Close enough to watch his back, perhaps.

He couldn't recall turning at any point and looking down the length of the trail that he'd covered.

It seemed that the wolf had a destination in mind. Its tracks arrowed on down towards the old copper mine workings.

Open-cast mining is the least hazardous way of getting ore out of the ground. It's also the least expensive form of mine to operate, and the one with the most serious and lasting effects on the landscape; simply blast and collect, blast and collect, following the ore seams where they reach the surface and leaving a wasteland where nothing can grow. The scars on the land above Tromstad were nearly forty years old, and they'd barely even begun to close when Teamverk arrived to probe around.

They'd covered about half a mile from the cut, but it seemed like more. Fraser hadn't said anything for a while but he was obviously feeling the strain as his leg started to stiffen and drag. Nystrom thought this is it, now he's got to turn back, but Fraser wasn't having any of it; there was defeat in simply giving in and turning around, and every step would be a reminder of effort wasted. If he couldn't get close enough to see the wolf – and now it seemed ridiculous that he'd ever believed he might – then he'd have to pick some simpler target and try to be satisfied with that. Like his swimming coach had said in those early painful days of therapy, it doesn't count if you don't touch the end of the pool.

There was a group of ruined buildings around what had once been the quarry's main yard. Now they stood alone out on the fjell, unvisited and untended. The trail led straight on through – and that, for Fraser, would have to be the end of the pool.

'Christ,' he said as they came into the yard, 'whose mad idea was this?'

Most of the buildings were of weatherbeaten wood, and they were too frail to risk approaching. He saw an uneven brick wall that had once perhaps been part of an explosives

36

shed, and went across. He cleared the top of snow before he turned and lowered himself onto it.

Nystrom said, 'Your leg is bad?'

'It's okay when it's rested. I think we lost.'

Nystrom nodded; in his opinion it had never even been a competition. He said, 'Two of us alone with no gun, I think it's best.' He dusted down a section of the wall for himself, and Fraser hitched along a couple of inches. Looking out across the yard, he tried to follow the line of the trail but found he couldn't; the snow wasn't smooth, but flowed in an uneven blanket over the rubble it buried.

Fraser said, 'How many wolves do you get?'

'Last one was ten, twelve years ago.' Anywhere other than Tromstad the answer would probably have been none; the wolf in Scandinavia was close to extinct, and the hunting groups tended to stay in the more remote uplands away from the main roads and villages. Two sightings in a dozen years had to be no more than a double fluke, although in the first case at least there had been an explanation. Fraser narrowed his eyes and looked out across the dazzling white of the snowfields as Nystrom told him the story.

There had been some agreement that the wolf had come into the area towards the end of an extremely bad winter, crossing a frozen inlet of the fjord alone. One opinion was that it was old and slow and had been left to look after itself when the pack moved on, another was that it was sick and had been driven out. The most popular and least informed view was that the wolf was just mean, and that it had chosen to prey on the village because it had a natural hatred of the innocent.

Whatever the explanation, the first evidence of its arrival came in the spring. Tromstad's year was sharply divided to follow the seasons; deep winter was for fishing the cod and the herring in the Lofoten waters and beyond, and in the spring the boats were laid up and then men of Tromstad became farmers. There wasn't enough of a summer for a decent crop, so they raised cattle; as soon as the mountain passes opened they would drive the herds to the upland pastures and use the lower fields around the village to grow barley, which they cut green and stored as feed for the next winter.

The wolf had hit on the second night, taking one calf and maiming another. There wasn't much doubt about the cause, even though some of the men had to be shown the mauled carcase before they'd believe it. The injured calf had to be killed, and they'd cut it open and dosed it with strychnine before hauling it to the edge of the woods and leaving it. They checked it the first couple of nights and found nothing, but on the third they found that the wolf had defecated onto the bait. That was the same night that it entered the fields again, starting a stampede that woke the man on guard and startled him so much that he'd fired both barrels of his shotgun into the air before he'd even remembered where he was.

So it was wise to poisons. And it obviously had no intention of moving on after a single kill – easy prey that couldn't fight was too good to ignore. And so Tromstad got wolf fever.

Nystrom remembered watching his father in the kitchen at home, working on the scrubbed wooden table. He was taking steel fishhooks and rolling them back on themselves, binding them with gut and then wadding the deadly spring into a ball of tallow. He followed as his father scattered twenty or thirty of these deadly treats around the springs and streams where the wolf might be expected to go; it only had to swallow one, and as the gut dissolved in its juices the hook would open out and begin slow murder. Per Brøndsted, one of Nystrom's uncles, came up with a similar ruse but using rolled whalebone in suet; as he was dropping them in the woods he stepped into a powerful trap made by Sven Lidman in his machine shop, and narrowly missed severing his Achilles tendon. A teenaged boy was knocked unconscious by a rock in a deadfall

– a stroke of luck which prevented him from dumping a bag of cyanide in the stream that also provided Tromstad's main water supply. When Lars Nilssen's bitch was in heat, he staked her out in the fields with the idea of luring the wolf down and clubbing him to death during the tie – he caught Leif Lokkeberg's mongrel three nights running.

All the ingenuity went for nothing. The wolf, meanwhile, went on doing its best to stay alive.

After three weeks of the fever, the village decided to make a community effort. It was Nystrom's grandfather who came up with the basic idea, and he offered the use of the family's *seter*, the one-storey wooden farmhouse that was their summer home in the mountains. They took a young calf and tethered it in the open some distance upwind; the animal was barely weaned, and it began to cry as soon as it was left alone. The sound carried well in the still mountain air, and the men returned to the *seter* for akvavit and stories of the open sea. Two stayed on guard, waiting out of sight with their shotguns, and two more came out to relieve them after a couple of hours.

The crying stopped around midnight. The calf had exhausted itself and fallen asleep. The watch continued, but no wolf came. The next day they made sure that the calf got no water in the hope that it would call louder and for longer, and in the evening about an hour after sundown they were rewarded.

Olav was staying up late; his mother was still down in the village, and his father's ideas about child-rearing were well intentioned but imprecise. The large main room of the *seter* took up one complete end of the building and had views on three sides into the valley across an encircling verandah. There was a fire of pine logs burning in the grate but all of the windows and the verandah doors were open to the night, and so when the first shots came they were easy enough to hear.

The men ran down the central hall and into the kitchen, collecting their guns and spilling out of the back door. The noise they made as they ran up the hill would have been enough of a signal to any wounded or startled animal that might be heading their way, but by now they were men trying to impress other men, and the wolf had become a convenient accessory.

Those on guard had reloaded and fired again by the time that the party arrived with Olav tagging along behind. The calf was still bleating, and in the darkness it was the only target they had. The men fired as they arrived, some of them barely stopping to aim, and with the thunder of the guns Olav thought that his eardrums would burst.

Nystrom paused in his telling of the story. He was remembering the sight of the calf as they'd come upon it with lanterns, stripped down to the bone in places by the storm of buckshot. The moment was special in his memory, but not in any way that he wanted to describe.

Fraser said, 'Did they get it?' It was a moment before Nystrom realised that he was talking about the wolf, not the calf.

'They hit it and it didn't come back, but there wasn't a body.' There had been a few splashes of blood on the grass leading away – 'wolf blood,' his father had confidently called it after touching the grass and smearing it between his fingers, and everyone had stepped forward and done the same. It was only in the morning that the reservations had begun. 'My uncle said they got bad luck because it wasn't a clean kill, said it would affect the winter fishing.'

'Did it?'

'They got a bad season, but it wasn't because of any wolf. There were trawlers to the North taking the cod as they came down to spawn. Every village's catch was bad, but you couldn't tell them that. They're hardheaded farmers, but when it comes to the winter fishing there's a rule and a superstition for everything. Your leg any better?'

Fraser raised his knee and tested it, and he seemed

satisfied when it didn't actually creak. He said, 'It eases after a while. I put too much of a strain on it.'

Nystrom said, 'How long before you have to leave, Jerry?'

'I'll be away as soon as Kreiger stops finding me little jobs to do around the site. He's let most of the others go.' Failed to stop them was nearer the truth, but this was only Fraser's second contract and he didn't want to take risks with his record.

Nystrom took the information without any obvious pleasure. Sometimes it seemed that Jerry Fraser was his only friend in the village, and when he left . . . Nystrom said, 'Is Sara coming back?'

'Only if it really looks like Kreiger's going to spin it out. Otherwise she'll be finding us a place in Oslo for the season. Give me a hand up, will you?'

Nystrom stood up and stretched; he was stiff after resting, but he knew that it would go after a couple of minutes' walk. He put out a hand to Fraser, and it was as he was pulling him up that the wolf broke from the shelter of the ruined building behind them.

Fraser started to express surprise as he was jerked up and around, but then he saw the animal. It wasn't bolting from cover, and it didn't even seem to be in any real hurry. It covered a few paces at a sideways lope, and then turned back to give them an even stare.

It wasn't quite as big as he'd expected, but it was full-coated and powerful. Fraser's first thought was that this was no wolf; it looked more like somebody's dog. But then, what did *he* know? He'd never hunted anything more ambitious than rabbits or birds.

As it turned its head, Fraser saw that its face was marked in a diabolic patterning of black and grey. Its ears were pointed, and they lay back slightly on its skull. Well, maybe it *was* a wolf, at that; no dog had ever fixed him with the long, cool stare of an equal as this animal now did.

Is it you? the question formed in his mind, coming out

of nowhere and fading so fast that he didn't even have the time to be surprised.

'No,' he said, without fully understanding why. Olav gave him a curious glance.

The animal turned to go.

Once it had turned away, it didn't look back. Crossing the yard it was cautious, watching the ground ahead, but as it reached the open *fjell* it began an easy, loose-limbed trot.

As the ground dropped away, it disappeared from sight. Fraser watched the *fjell* for a little longer, but there was nothing else to see. So this was it, the prowler that snapped his lines and came sniffing around his territory when he wasn't there. Thoughts of a gun and a couple of hounds were now right out of his mind. As the immediacy of the experience started to fade, he was wishing for his camera.

It was Nystrom who spoke first. As Fraser unconsciously shifted his weight to try out his leg, he said, 'Feeling better?'

For a moment it looked as if Fraser had forgotten how to answer, but then he made an effort to concentrate. He said, 'Not fit for the sprint, but I can dance again.'

They followed their own tracks back up the snowplain towards the cut. They'd been moving almost parallel with the fjord's edge and were some way down from the village, and when Nystrom looked towards the shore he could see the coast road where the sun gleamed on a ribbon of ice. It was now mid-morning but the sun was as high as it was going to get; late afternoon and it would be dusk, and soon after that the sea mists would start to roll in from the Atlantic. Fraser didn't say much, but on the return he paced himself better.

When they stumbled back down into the cut, the sample case had gone. Nystrom said with some bewilderment, 'Wasn't it here?'

Fraser kicked at a neat square depression in the snow where the box had been standing. He said, 'Probably someone collected it. Kreiger must be getting anxious.'

'Anxious for what?'

'Tonight's supposed to be the final data crunch before the big report and the hookup tomorrow. All the directors and the bureau staff in a two-way TV conference and all pretending they know what they're talking about. Just the kind of thing to get Kreiger's balls aching.'

Nystrom glanced at the chewed telephone line. 'And he couldn't call you . . .'

'So he sent some goons to find out why I'm late. Another popularity point for Jerry Fraser.'

'Think of the good things. We don't have to carry any rocks.'

'I know, but they wouldn't carry any of my gear for me. Wait a minute.'

Fraser looked around, and after a moment spotted what he was looking for; about fifteen yards up the cut, a destroyed-looking piece of the side wall showing where someone else had climbed to the level of the plain. He went over to it and climbed after. There were no tracks, but after scanning for a couple of seconds he could see the dark corner of his duffel bag sticking up against the white, about as far away as a man could expect to throw it. He went out and brought it back, brushing the powdery snow from the canvas as he rejoined the young Norwegian.

'Bastards, Jerry?' Nystrom hazarded.

'You said it,' Fraser replied.

FOUR

It had been almost a year before when John Visco had managed to fix a half-hour meeting with Teamverk's London man. Lewis Alexander was a transplanted US national like the rest of them, living and working out of two rooms in a hotel close to Regents Park, ready to fold his operation and pull out quietly at four hours' notice if he had to. John caught him at lunch, a plate of hotel sandwiches (nearly all garnish and not much of anything else) and a half-bottle of wine set out on a coffee table next to the telephone. The colour TV in the corner was switched on, but the sound was turned down.

John saw a powerful man going to seed, his best days behind him. He looked tired, and he reminded John of Errol Flynn in the last years of his life, a game adventurer in a body that was no longer game for adventures. His eyes were hard and his talk was cynical, but after less than ten minutes of listening John knew that Teamverk had to be the target for his one desperate shot.

The company which operated under the name of Teamverk A/S was actually a puppet outfit through which the parent company could direct its investment in safety. They had a Norwegian sleeping partner and a prestige address in an Oslo hotel, and it was from here that the contract survey teams scattered throughout the country were controlled. Alexander gave him a rundown of the personnel, starting with Kendall Riggs, the bureau chief; skinny as a shoelace, he was the main man to look out for. He wore the clothes of a man half his age, and because of his build he could get away with it – there was a trace of bitterness in the way that Lewis Alexander described the man who was his immediate superior, and he went on to say that without the wardrobe Riggs would probably look like something from the fright show taking an afternoon off. And he was screwing his secretary, Rachel Hellstrom, a forty-three-year-old career woman who'd worked her way up from the pool to being boss of a pool of her own. Everybody knew about it and pretended they didn't, and Rachel went on spraying Riggs' cologne onto the pillows every morning to mask the scent of her perfume.

John should have been able to guess from this that Lewis Alexander was setting up his own exit from Team-verk sometime soon, but he didn't. He kept thinking *Kendall Riggs, the main man to look out for*, over and over so that it couldn't slip away. Alexander was telling him about some of the others, but they barely registered; Glenn Dossman, an old Europe hand, looks like a bag of shit if shit could sit up and say hello, but underneath sharper than any of them; the little Dutchman who ran the computer side of things, the guy with the wet handshake who ran finance . . .

Kendall Riggs, John kept thinking, and he wished that he could write it all down. As soon as he got out of the room he did, as much as he could remember, but before that he asked Lewis Alexander for the letter.

A letter of introduction was an essential first step in the rest of John's plan, a lever to use on some crack in the international jobs market so that he could prise it open wide enough to slip in. He'd spent too long answering ads and getting nowhere, wasting his time in unskilled hotel work and watching the sunlight slowly fade out of his bright future. He'd begun to get desperate; of all the dreams he'd had of the life that lay ahead, none of them had been at all like this. He found himself watching people, mostly aimless old people in parks and on the streets, and getting a terrible sense of premonition that was like a shadow passing through his soul.

Alexander had scribbled him a few lines on some company paper. The words themselves didn't matter, and although John read them over and over in the months that followed he never really remembered what they said. They became more like a spell, or a charm; his one piece of proof that he wasn't out of the game altogether. When his belief in himself was at a low, Lewis Alexander's casual note was his lifeline to a preferred version of reality.

So here he was, one summer season and a lot of hard saving later, sleeping off his exhaustion in an Oslo hotel room. It was a room that he could barely afford, and paying for it would rob him of any margin that he might have been preserving for his ticket home. He was preparing himself to chase a vacancy that quite probably didn't exist – but then, this was the world. There were no guarantees, anywhere.

He dreamed the same dream as always – at least, it started the same, with the railed park in the city square and the woman bumping the trolley down the steps of the town house as John watched from the trees. Her route could vary but it always ended with John following her down to the pond, where she'd stop by the edge of the water and unzip the baby buggy's windproof cover. And then she'd glance over at John – he never saw her face – just to show that she'd known he was there all along, and then she'd reach into the buggy and lift out

something

not

very

nice

and John would put his hand into his jacket and bring out the Swiss automatic, and with the weight of the gun in his hand he'd wake. This was the worst part.

He was only awake in the dream, but he didn't know. The reassurance of the dream state, the secret knowledge that none of these dangers were real, was no longer with him. He sat upright in his hotel room, the only light the blue neon spill from the hoarding across the Gate.

The momentary obscenity from the park was now in the corridor outside. He could hear it, soft-footed on the carpet, pausing to try the door to each room as it came his way. His hand was empty – the gun broken down as before, the stripped pieces wrapped and stowed in his pack.

John slid out of bed. After one step he stumbled over the bag, and it crashed to the floor. The pacing outside stopped; it had heard him. He turned his pack over and tried to get it open, but the zips wouldn't work.

There was a light clicking sound, like long nails brushing the door by the handle. Then the handle began to turn, the brass glinting dull in the neon glow, and the door began to open.

The room suddenly went dark as the hoarding hit the beginning of its programmed cycle; first the outlines of the letters, then the fill, and then building up the background to the brilliance of day. Each stage put more light into the room, and the last reached the figure that stood in the doorway.

It was Per Lindegren. The neon reflected on his glasses. One lens was smashed, and there was dried blood on the cheek below it. His anorak was open, and it had been torn. His hands were hanging limp by his sides, the knuckles blackened and bruised, and he carried his head at a strange angle.

He spoke. There was more blood around his mouth, and his teeth were black with it. His voice was hoarse, almost a whisper.

'Whatever's following you, boy,' he said. *'Get rid of it.'*

Jerome Brindsley Fraser, Teamverk payroll number 403535/3, was descending a mountain twelve hundred kilometers away whilst Johnathan James Visco, unemployed but hopeful, was going down to breakfast. The stairway down to the third floor was huge and had been elegant once, with angled mirrors at each turn to multiply the effect; the kind of stairway that Cinderella might have descended to applause. Once, but not any more; the mirrors had no lustre, and rugs had been placed to cover the wear in the carpet.

He saw nobody on his way down, and there were only four people in the dining room; a couple in their thirties who ate without speaking, and two large bald men in dark suits whose conversation across the room was a wordless rumble. The room itself was dark wood and crisp linen, with an immense untended smorgasbord on the central table; there was juice, cereal, lukewarm milk in large silver jugs, four kinds of pickled fish, bread, preserves, cheese, and fruit. An elderly waitress came out a couple of times, once with a basket of boiled eggs and once to top up the coffee in the hostess warmer. John waited until she was out of the way before wrapping extra bread and cheese in a serviette for his lunch. Good times might be around the corner, but his boarding-house habits would take a long time to fade.

He tried to think through what he was going to say when he presented himself at the Teamverk offices. Keep it on qualifications, he told himself, and away from experience. Too much of that had been in small-town libraries in amongst the old men who traded newspapers all day long, trying to retain a grip on his selected discipline but feeling it slip away as new controversies became fashionable. When the coffee grew cold on the table by his elbow, he realised that he was stalling. It was time to get himself down to the Norsemann and make his pitch.

The Hotel Norsemann was in a sidestreet off the Storgata, one of Oslo's main shopping rows. It had seven floors and a dark foyer with lots of glass and cane, and all the south-facing rooms from the third floor up had a view of the cathedral. It was an 'international' hotel with ads in most of the gazetteers and trade directories, and it had an appetite for expense-account viveurs and their American Express cards. Teamverk's Oslo bureau had set up camp in a three-room suite on the fifth floor. It had the cathedral view, which also meant that it had the cathedral bells on a Sunday morning; and as the room adjoining the suite was the bureau chief's bedroom, it meant that Teamverk's affairs generally got off to a slow start on Mondays.

John took the lift alongside the ground-floor coffee shop. The elevator car was lined with burlap, probably a sign of construction work on one of the upper floors. He was starting to feel awkward as he'd known he would, mainly because he didn't have any more suitable outfit to appear in than his travelling gear. He'd combed his hair and put a shine on his cheap boots, but neither seemed to help much.

He came out on the fifth and almost stumbled into an abandoned maid's trolley. There were heaps of towels and bedlinen outside some of the doors in the corridor, and across the landing the door to one room had been propped open with a wastepaper bin. Sounds of vacuuming came from inside, along with the hotel's in-house music feed turned up loud.

He counted his way down to the suite, knocked, waited for a couple of seconds and then opened the door.

This was the end room of the three, and it was being used for some kind of data storage; rented shelving had been stacked with mimeograph boxes, and the furniture had all been crowded over against one wall to make way for more stacks of boxes on the floor. Although some of the boxes had identifying labels, most hadn't. The connecting door through to the rest of the suite was open, and John followed the sounds of voices and the yakking of two typewriters.

He hesitated in the doorway, looking into the main room of the suite. There was a big map of Norway on the opposite wall, with progress charts and two year-planners flanking it. The hotel furniture had been moved out to make way for four desks, all of them littered and two of them occupied. The typing sounds came from the next room along through another open doorway.

There was no obvious reception area, no sign of how to proceed. Two men were drinking coffee from styrene cups over by the datalink, and one of them started to move over towards him.

The man was middle-aged and rumpled, almost shabby. *Glenn Dossman*, John thought, the information supplied by the anxious sub-routine that had been playing through his mind for the last eleven months. And the other one, who was watching as Dossman put on a friendly smile with no real meaning in it? (*The little Dutchman who ran the computer side of things . . .*)

'You're looking lost,' Dossman said.

Fighting the sudden impulse to agree, John said, 'Team-verk office?'

'Nerve centre of the whole operation,' Dossman said with an airy wave. 'Who do you want?'

'Is there somebody called Kendall Riggs?'

'He's tied up on the job,' Dossman said, and the Dutchman (*Paul Steen!*) turned to the datalink so quickly that it was obvious to Visco that he'd walked in on a running gag.

John said, 'Can I wait?' and Dossman shrugged as if it didn't much matter to him either way.

'No problem,' he said, 'just find yourself a seat.'

He was about to turn away, but John stopped him. 'Do you think you could give me a quick rundown on what goes on here?'

Dossman turned back, and studied John with an appraising shrewdness that hadn't been obvious before. 'Are you Press?'

'No, nothing like that. I've got a letter of introduction from Lewis Alexander, he's your London man. I'm here after a job.'

'You left it kind of late. What do you do?'

'I'm a geologist. What do you mean, I left it late?'

'Well,' Dossman said with disquieting gravity, setting

his styrene cup down on the nearest desk, 'to begin with, we don't do any actual survey work here, we just co-ordinate all the teams out in the field. And second, most of the field surveys are nearly over. A couple more days, and we'll have all the data in for the computers to play around with. Have you done any time on mines?' John shook his head. 'Well, it's mines men we'll be hiring next. We'll be out of surveying and into direct development. What did the London man tell you?'

'It was a while ago,' John admitted. 'It took me some time to get the money together for this.'

'Well, I'm not speaking for the boss, but that's how it is. You still want to see him?'

'I'll give it a try.'

Dossman wasn't going to give John a final *no* – that would be Riggs' problem – but as he stepped back and gestured towards a couple of moulded-plastic office chairs that had stacks of files on them it was plain that he felt he'd given all the necessary discouragement. 'Okay,' he said, 'anywhere you like.'

When John had moved some of the files across and sat down, Dossman had already wandered through to the next room and had picked up a telephone. Steen was still watching the new figures as they came in on the datalink, and he glanced up at John for a brief moment.

He tried to settle in the cheap seat, and he wondered what he was going to do next. There was a fear deep inside; all along he'd been calling it creative tension, but now he was starting to recognise it for what it really was.

He was going to blow it again. Whatever reassurance he tried to give himself, that was always behind it.

FIVE

Marcos Navarez stood knee-deep in snow and looked
blankly at the slope before him. The fucking stuff went
on for miles and miles, just ironed out the country and
the road and everything into a flat plain of white. It had
taken him an hour to get this far, and he wasn't even a
mile out of Tromstad. Wherever he'd managed to bring
himself to, he could see that he was no longer on the
road; he'd left it some way back without even knowing,
following some flattened shadow that brought him up into
the woods whilst imagining that the two lanes of tarmac
were no more than a few inches down. Instead the tyres
had been rolling on the frozen ground, but now the ground
was going soft on him. In order to save himself some
airfare he'd bought a car, loaded his gear into it, driven it
straight at the trees and got it stuck. The boys were going
to piss themselves at this one.

Staring wasn't going to get him anywhere, and he was
cold. I bet it's cold enough to freeze spit before it lands,
he thought as he trudged back towards the car, remembering the Jack London story where the guy ended up
trying to stuff his hands into his dog. Marcos spat, but it
only hit the snow like spit would most anywhere else. It
didn't make him feel any warmer.

Marcos Navarez was a Hopi Indian, flat-cheeked and
broad-nosed with straight black hair down to the middle
of his back, two hundred and thirty pounds of beer belly
and muscle. Not many people laughed at him while he
was around, but the man who'd sold him the car was sure

to be laughing at him now. A Citroën 2CV, for Christ's sake – what you needed for scenery like this was something crossed between a half-track and a bulldozer. The Deux-Chevaux was more like a biscuit tin with a lawnmower engine, with narrow tyres that bit down into the snow like saucers on edge.

He went around to the back and lifted the trunk lid, looking with half a hope to see a folding shovel or something that he could use to dig the wheels free and turn around. But it was just as he remembered from when he'd loaded his bags, no tools and not even a spare.

It had seemed such a good idea the night before when three of them had agreed to go equal shares, but then the other two had insisted they'd done no such thing as soon as they were awake again, which was too late because Marcos already had Lidman's old car fuelled up and standing in the square outside the hotel. Bastards. Now if he couldn't dig the car out and turn it around, he was either going to have to roll most of the way backwards to the village or else walk down with all his luggage. *It hasn't been all that bad*, he'd kept telling himself during the low-gear crawl up what he'd believed to be the unploughed mountain road, but from the depth of the snow around here it obviously had.

He let the trunk lid drop, and went around to get in behind the wheel. He didn't want to abandon the Citroën if he could help it, because when the summer thaw came Lidman would probably climb up here and get his car back and resell it to some other dumb bastard at the end of the season.

But then, when he turned in the seat and looked back through the 2CV's narrow rear window, he began to wonder if even that was possible. Because of the height and the angle, he could see nothing of his own wheel tracks.

Marcos groaned, and he closed his eyes. If this was a bad dream, now was the time to be waking up. Home had never seemed so far away – he wanted to be doing what he'd done every winter for the past five years. He wanted to take a garden room in the Kon-Tiki motel down on Van Buren, spending his afternoons in the sun by the heated pool cracking twelve-packs of Coors and his evenings in the water stroking around and occasionally coming to the edge and cracking twelve-packs of Coors. With his eyes still tight-shut he could see the night patterns in the green-blue water, a rippling mesh of refraction shadows from the lights at the bottom of the pool.

He snapped alert. That would be all he needed, to be found stiff and dreaming and dead behind the wheel. Even if the spit didn't freeze before it hit the ground it froze fast enough when it got there, and he could do the same. He reached under the column for the ignition key; he'd run the engine for a while, and then move when the heater had taken some of the chill out of him. What a hope, he was thinking – he'd felt more heat coming out of a peppermint. He took his gloves off and held his hands down by the vent, flexing his fingers and cracking his knuckles. He blipped the accelerator to build up the revs, six hundred ccs of raw power. It sounded like some old man clearing his throat in a reading room.

But soon, he was going to have to admit it. Something was making him uneasy, and he was wary of returning on foot through the woodland.

The heater wasn't doing much good. The little car didn't hold onto any of the warmth, and the canvas roll-over roof didn't fit too well. There must have been some slight effect, though, even if he didn't feel it, because when he looked around he saw that the windows were all misted over on the inside. This scared him a little, although again he couldn't say why. He cut the engine. The silence was sudden and complete, but still he was sure that there was something outside.

It was a certainty that he'd never known before. Christ, he thought, maybe that totem shit's got something going for it. He tried to logic up some reassurance, but there wasn't any to be had. His skin began to crawl, just like it said in the magazine stories, as he realised how isolated he really was. He hated this country, where all the kids spoke English better than the English and even the drunks were fairly well-heeled.

But there *couldn't* be anything outside, not unless it was one of the boys come to set him jumping and give the others a laugh that would follow Marcos from contract to contract around every project for the next few years. Hey, Cochise. (They always called him Cochise, or Tonto, or Geronimo. Tonto was the only one he objected to. There were limits.) Tell us about that time in Norway you got conned into buying some dipshit wagon and got yourself spooked in the woods. Warren Christiansen said it was one of the funniest things he ever saw . . .

Well, if there was somebody out there waiting, Marcos was going to see how slinky he could stay with two hundred and thirty pounds of Hopi crashing down on him. And if it *is* Warren Christiansen, he thought, let's see if we can't pop the fat bastard and have him fizzing around like an over-inflated prophylactic, to which his beachball body with its pimple head had often been compared. Marcos heaved around and reached for the door catch, and found himself face-to-face with the dark shape of a head only a few inches away on the other side of the window.

He converted the motion without even thinking about it, and instead of opening the door he locked it. The head had dropped down to below window level, the details all blurred by the thin layer of mist between them. Marcos reached across to slip the catch on the passenger side, glancing back as he recognised the sounds of the handle being tested.

The dark shape reappeared. It's got to be a joke, he told himself, it'll be one of the boys in a mask or something. He hesitated for a moment longer, and then he reached out and wiped a clean slash across the glass. The face dropped away again and he got no more than a brief glimpse, but it was enough to know that he wasn't looking at any mask.

55

The eyes branded themselves onto his memory, so hard and so fierce that they burned everything else away. They were as shiny and expressionless as knucklebones.

He turned around to check the doors in the back, the seat frame creaking as his weight shifted. It was a flimsy car, a frail shell with no real protection about it. Whatever had looked in on him was now gone from the door and he started to clear some of the other windows to look for it. The condensation was so heavy that it was almost sluicing off. He could see nothing, but then sounds started to come from the passenger door.

They stopped after a moment, and then the head reared up to his level again. Its eyes burned straight through the misted glass and into him. Marcos could hear a low, anguished moan, and for a moment he actually wondered where it was coming from; but then he knew, the voice was his own.

But why was he sitting here filling his pants? He was in a *car*. He tried to restart the engine, but it didn't seem to catch so easily when it was hot – he couldn't believe it, but already the turnover was getting weaker and weaker as the battery ran down. But then he remembered Lidman's dumb-show demonstration, and he started to pump the accelerator pedal; the engine sputtered almost immediately, but then it stalled. With the second try everything came alive, and he reached for the shift. It was a bent stick emerging from the centre of the dashboard, and when he stirred it around he made a lot of crashing and whining. *Manual*, he reminded himself, and he rammed the clutch pedal to the floor and tried again.

The whole car shook, and he felt it drop a couple of inches as its springing took up some extra load. From the corner of his eye Marcos could see something moving in the mirror, something that looked like a scarf being pulled up onto the roof. It was gone before he could fix it, but when he looked up to the roll-over it was bulging down between the cross-members under some hard pressure, and the pressure shifted and resettled as he watched.

He was still trying to find his gear. The stick didn't seem to be connected to anything anymore. Inches over his head and less than a foot away, a scratching began. It wasn't just aimless scrabbling but a strong, measured sweep that would be stripping the vinyl waterproofing off in even layers. Every layer brought it a fraction lower, a little closer. Marcos was sitting like the dogmeat in a can, and he couldn't even get the damn car into gear.

There was a dull pop from the roof. It sounded to Marcos like a gunshot through a drumskin; he looked up and saw a single claw, blue-black and sharp as a steel hook. He'd seen snakes being venom-milked in a tent at the county fair once, and their fangs had punched through the plastic wrap over the mouth of a tumbler about as easily.

The claw started to draw down with the power of a winch, opening up the flimsy roof like a zipper.

Okay, Marcos, he thought with surprising calm, you've got maybe five seconds to live if you don't get your shit together. The engine's running, just take it in stages and find your gear, then get rolling and throw that sucker off the roof. *One*, in with the clutch, *two*, get a hold on the stick, *three*, a bony fist like a rock slammed down into the back of his head and instantly closed up the eighteen inches or so between his face and the windscreen.

He bounced back, sunbursts of shock exploding behind his eyes, only to be violently cuffed again and thrown hard against the door. Whatever was knocking him around seemed to have the weight and strength of a panda behind its paw. He felt the claws brush by his cheek as it swung for him again, *heard* the clean, whickering sound they made as they cut through the air. The car bounced and groaned as weight was shifted around up above as it groped to reach him. Marcos was the prize in the bran tub, and there seemed to be no limit to the number of tries before he could be hauled up in triumph.

Half-blinded and tasting his own blood, Marcos tried to get himself down and out of reach. He almost made it, too, but then the claws hooked into the collar of his checked woodsman's jacket. He found himself being lifted from his seat, the material dragging up tight under his arms and making it even more difficult as he tried to get the buttons undone so he could slide free. He managed the first as he was drawn up – clear of the seat now, only his feet dragging and his knees pressed hard against the wheel. He tried to jam them against it and for a moment it seemed that he was succeeding, that the half-bent iron rod that was laid across his shoulders had now reached the limit of its power.

But then the roof split from end to end, and the beast came falling through.

The cross-braces hadn't been enough to hold it back. Marcos dropped, and he felt as if he was suddenly being buried in an earth fall. The welds that supported the seat-back gave way under the doubled weight, and he found himself being squeezed flat with his feet under the dash and his face being mashed into the patterning of the rear seat. He grunted and squirmed around. The beast was moving too, trying to turn itself about in the narrow space to get to him. A foot like a ramrod punched into his stomach – the car was heaving on its springs like a fair-ground ride, but he wasn't so much aware of that as of the light that he could see overhead. The ramrod hit him again under the arm, sending a jolt of pain down his side and sliding him a foot or more so that he folded up against the seat and felt as if his neck would break at the angle; but now the light was all that he could see, and the light was all that he wanted. It was the deepwater light at the end of the motel pool, a shining green blur through the water that got clearer as he swam towards it. His breath was almost gone but he was putting in some good, hard strokes, tasting the chlorine and thinking of the beer in the ice bucket over by his table.

The light came closer, almost close enough to see the lines of the tiles around its housing, but his breath was bubbling away even faster and the water seemed to be getting thick and heavy. Somehow he knew that everything depended on his being able to reach the glass with the day behind it, that if he gave in now and let himself float upward then he'd rise and rise but he'd never break surface. He started to thrash, to rip his way through the thin curtain that was slipping down over his eyes like a caul. The light spread and grew until it had pushed all of the darkness away around its edges.

His forehead bumped against the toughened glass of the rear window. The beast had come around now, and he could feel its two broad hands on his shoulders. Its breath was on his cheek, like a wind through dead leaves. It started to lick him hungrily around his neck and his ear, and Marcos began to scream. He felt as if he'd been cheated out of some important promise, as if he was a child getting his first glimpse of what the world was *really* going to be like.

In spite of the crushing weight on his back, he managed to lift himself and started to bang his head against the window. The first couple of times it bounced, the third time it spiderwebbed and bulged outward. His skull had pushed the glass out into a blister, and when he drew back and butted in the same place with strength he didn't even know he had, the glass sprayed outwards and his head was through.

He barely had time to taste the air of freedom, before his collar was gripped and he was dragged back inside.

He could barely see. There was blood in his eyes from the cuts all around his face, and the breath was bubbling up out of him in a red froth. One of the kicks had broken a rib and pushed it through into his lung, but he was hardly aware of it. He could feel his fingernails splintering as he did his best to hang onto the seat back.

Wait till I tell the boys about this one, he thought weakly, and then he launched himself. He was hollow. He could fly.

He came down heavily on the edge of the glass, an inch deep or more across his throat. His life was running out in heartbeat spurts as the beast gathered him in. He could feel the power of its love as he slid back onto the vinyl.

He looked up into those eyes, hard as wind-driven sleet, and he tried to smile.

In the yard behind his house, Leif Lokkeberg was clearing the snow from the door to the gate with a broad shovel. He was too old to be doing the work himself, but too mean to be paying someone else for it. He stopped and looked up as a faint sound came down the wind from the *fjellside*; it was a bitter howl, and the harmonies of rage and frustration carried well in the chilled air.

It reached Henrik Lidman a moment later, but in the lower part of the village by the public quay it wasn't so clear. He set down the soft drinks crate that he'd been about to lift and carry into the store, and he listened. He remembered the wolf hunt of twelve years before, and of how he and his brother hadn't been invited along. He thought of the thickset man with the hair of a girl who had bought his car, and he smiled a sharp, ratty smile.

It carried along the slopes to the Teamverk camp, even into the site office where the team leader sat trying to make some sense of the way that Jerry Fraser had marked up his samples. He looked up briefly, thinking that if a man should go into hospital for a tooth pulled and then wake up to find his nuts in a Mason Jar alongside his pillow, that was the kind of sound he'd probably want to make.

And it carried down to the far end of the site, where Skipper Ashton was standing with his hands in his pockets and watching without interest as Earl Bonneau took a leak against the side of one of the Portakabins.

He listened for a moment. The sound was starting to tail away.

'Fraser's wolf,' he said.

'Yeah,' Bonneau agreed. 'Mean-sounding fucker, ain't he?'

*   *   *

Jerry Fraser and Olav Nystrom were better-placed to hear the howling than anybody else. It would be another fifteen or twenty minutes before they reached the base camp, and as the sound began they stopped to listen. They glanced at each other, but neither spoke. When the sound tailed away and didn't restart, they continued their descent.

SIX

It was late in the morning when the two of them finally reached Teamverk's number nine camp. It was set on a plateau of dark shale which fell off suddenly to the railway line below, for this site had originally been a marshalling yard to serve the mines. Tromstad had no rail link with the main Norwegian network, but a transport system had carried the crushed ore down to the docks for loading; now the line was gone, the docks were gone, and most of the service buildings were gone as well. There were only exposed concrete bases to show where they'd been, some plumbing and a few raised thresholds. One building was still standing, two storeys with an open-sided workshop beneath, its folding doors long gone for firewood and oil thick on the floor where the snow hadn't blown. The office above was reached by a side-stairs; this was Ray Kreiger's section. The rest of the camp was terrain-adjustable cabins linked by boardwalks, all in the shelter of this main building.

Dark shale, white snow. The surface cover had been trampled down to ice, and where the sun touched it had become loose and mushy. Nystrom headed off for the cabins, and Jerry Fraser went to find out what had happened to his sample case.

It was on Ray Kreiger's desk. Kreiger had the tagged rocks out and was copying their numbers onto a sheet for transmission to the Oslo bureau. He looked up as Fraser stepped through the door and said, 'Where the fuck were you?'

'Where was I when?' Fraser said, and closed the door behind him.

'Don't play about, Fraser. You know damn well.'

'And you know my lines were down.'

'Which is more than you could manage. I had to send Skipper Ashton and Boney after you.'

That was Earl Bonneau, known as Boney, which he wasn't. Fraser said, 'The whole world loves a volunteer.'

'Talk to them about it and see if they like you being smart. Where's the Rover?'

'Busted. Ask Olav Nystrom.'

'I'm asking you. Busted how?'

'I didn't get stoned and run it off the track, if that's what you mean. Something in the clutch locked up.'

Kreiger stood up. He was taller than Fraser but only just, and he was considerably broader, and he had a couple of badass tattoos on his forearms that he liked to show off when he rolled his sleeves back. He said, 'That's our one transport. Why didn't you coast it down?'

'Down a railway track on ice? Are you serious?'

'There's nothing funny about screwing up, even if you seemed to be aiming to make a career of it.'

'Tell me you didn't want to hire me,' Fraser suggested. 'I didn't . . .'

'And tell me I got dropped on you without warning . . .'

'I'm through telling you anything, Fraser, you're not worth the spit.' Kreiger had been baited before, and he knew he was an easy target. He'd become a team leader because he'd been a competent field man, and he'd moved from being a confident professional to a new state of uncertainty; he was a manager, whatever the hell that involved. And he was also slow to pick up on ironies. He said, 'What was that about volunteers?'

Oh shit, thought Fraser. Kreiger was proud of the fact that he'd jumped in before the draft in the early days. Fraser said, 'Don't ask me, I don't keep notes.'

'Because if it was one of your cheap shots . . .'

'I leave the cheap shots to you, Ray. You're an artist.'

Kreiger moved around the desk. He was eight or nine years older than Fraser, and it was enough to cut away the ground between them. And he was a *manager* – he was in line for all the frustrations, and his responsibilities prevented him from coming up with the most direct answers. Which is why he could strain and boil at Fraser but he couldn't do the one thing in the world that he most wanted to, and that was bust his nose. He said, 'Get this, Fraser. I dislike you, okay? It's only that I've got a responsible position here prevented me from telling you before.'

'Didn't prevent you from showing it.'

'Maybe this will help. There are three types of people in this world, the volunteers and the conscripts and the shits like you who run, and they're in that order.'

'Are we talking evolution or natural history?'

'They shot cowards in better days, Fraser, just remember it. There were no safe roads to Sweden then.'

'And whisky was a dollar a bottle and the niggers knew their place.'

Kreiger glowered across the office. There was nothing else he could do, he was a *manager*. They'd taken away his real authority and given him powers that he didn't know how to use. In a way, Fraser was sorry for Ray Kreiger; a little part of him wished that the ox could just lumber over and take the swing that he wanted to. But most of him was relieved that he couldn't.

Kreiger turned away abruptly. 'You don't know how glad I'll be when you're gone,' he said.

'So why keep finding me things to do?'

'I'm soft, that's why. I think that if you do something over enough, maybe you'll start getting it right.' Kreiger put the heel of his hand to his forehead, as if a little pressure might shake down an over-complicated world. It didn't seem to work. He didn't look at Fraser again, and Fraser backed towards the door.

He believed that he'd got off lightly. Kreiger hadn't even insisted that he stay and take over the logging of the samples, which was technically his responsibility; no doubt

Kreiger had simply wanted him out of the office. Another few days, and it would be a wrap on the number nine survey – goodbye Tromstad, and goodbye to Ray Kreiger.

He'd started early, and now he was going to slip out of the camp before anyone could object to him finishing early. As he stepped down onto the boardwalk, he could see that Nystrom was coming his way and so he waited.

Olav had come from the drill shed. 'I looked for a bolt I could use perhaps for a fast repair, but everything is stowed.'

They left the boardwalk and crossed the flat area that had been left clear as a helicopter landing site. Yellow chalk had been put down to mark it into zones, and there was a group of oil drums to the side that were to be used for signal fires in bad visibility. Fraser said, 'Stowed is how it will stay until some decisions get made. If they fold the project, will you be leaving town?'

'I don't know.'

'Have you discussed it with anybody?'

'At home? No.'

'Wouldn't it help?'

'I don't think so. There's nothing to discuss except I feel I have to leave and that's it. I can't say why and I can't tell them what I want to do. If you were my father and I came to you with that story, how would you feel?'

'I'd probably take it personally.'

Nystrom shrugged, point proven. Now they were on the broader track that would take them down to the village, a road that was the borderline between mining land on one side and the hayfields on the other. He said, 'I'm good with engines, and I know boats. I could join the merchant fleet.'

'You really want to get around, don't you?'

'I want to spend my life knowing there's more than this. Where are you from, Jerry?'

Fraser was looking back up the road but there was nobody following. 'Virginia, first. Then Florida.'

'Florida I know,' Nystrom said, meaning that he'd read

about the place. 'Miami Beach and Disneyworld. Jerry, we have nothing like Disneyworld in all of Norway!'

It took Fraser a moment to absorb the idea. Over in the adjacent hayfield and unseen by either of them, the *fylgja* came angling down. It was panting from a long, hard run, and as it came closer it hugged the ground and crept along in the snow. It followed their scent and the sound of their voices, and these would have to be enough to satisfy it.

For the moment.

SEVEN

'Still okay?' Dossman said, and John looked up, startled. He'd been trying to get a look at his watch without making it obvious; some time soon the office would be taking its lunch break, and he seemed to be no closer to getting to see Kendall Riggs.

He nodded as Dossman set down a coffee from the Cona maker in the next room. 'I don't know how much longer he's likely to be,' the Teamverk man went on. 'You sure you want to hang around?'

'I'm sure.'

He'd been waiting now for more than an hour. Riggs hadn't once emerged from his room, which John had deduced was at the far end of the three-sectioned chamber that was the suite, although Rachel Hellstrom – he assumed it to be her – shuttled in and out a few times. She didn't look much like the sporty seductress that Lewis Alexander had made her out to be, just a competent-looking career woman who'd missed out on beauty and who tried to make up the distance with too much make-up. Dossman spoke to her once and she gave John the briefest flicker of a glance, and that so far had been the total of his progress.

As John sneaked another look at his Timex, Glenn Dossman hitched himself onto the corner of a vacant desk and tried to give some serious thought to the problem of Bjorn Gyllensten.

Keeping the sleeping partner sweet was his area of responsibility. He was, after all, the local liaison officer, although he'd always felt that his own description of the job – bagman for the bribes – was closer to the truth. He'd been talking on the telephone to Gyllensten for most of the time that John had been waiting, and the general line of the conversation was beginning to worry him. The unofficial terms of their agreement were that Gyllensten should take his money and leave Teamverk alone, but now he was talking in terms of active participation. It was up to Dossman to decide whether this was a real danger, or whether it was just a strategy to raise the price of co-operation now that commitments were inescapable.

Everything pointed to the squeeze, so it was really just a case of deciding how much of an offer to recommend. He could stroll down to the Vinmonopolet for a take-out liquid lunch to help him think it over. He slid off the desk and headed for his overcoat, but then the girl was blocking his way.

'Do you handle the money?' she said. Her English was good, her accent local.

Dossman was caught off-guard. 'Not personally,' he said, but before he could go on she'd taken an envelope out of one of the pockets of her duffel coat.

She was attractive in a serious kind of way, clear-eyed and fair with her hair bound up in Swedish braids. The duffel coat she wore was a man's, the sleeves turned back and sewn; the toggles were undone to show a double-thickness of pullovers. Dangling by ties from the sleeves was a pair of knitted gloves, and mittens to go over the gloves. Her jeans were faded, her boots child-sized.

'I'm Sara Hansun,' she said. 'This is Jerry Fraser's salary cheque.'

Dossman looked around for rescue, but there was none to be had – the entire office was suddenly on the move as the lunch hour began, and so he looked down at the piece of paper that was being thrust out before him and saw that it was, as she'd said, a cheque drawn on Teamverk's bankers in Amsterdam.

'Jerry who?' he said blankly.

68

'Jerry Fraser. He's on contract to Teamverk on the Tromstad mine survey.'

'I know Tromstad. But what's the problem?'

'The problem is that he's given me his money so that I can find us a place in Oslo, and I can't get a bank to honour the cheque.'

'There's no reason why it shouldn't. Even if it takes a couple of days to clear . . .'

'They won't go as far as that. The cheque's made out to Jerry. They'll credit it to his account, but they won't give me the cash.'

This should have been bounced straight to Rachel, but as usual she wasn't around. Dossman took the cheque – she was obviously going to hold it there until he did – and turned it over. The back was blank. He said, 'He'll have to endorse it. Or draw another cheque on his own account and make it out for cash.'

'But if the cheque's good, why won't they pay me?'

'This isn't negotiable. That's the way American banks work, but it's different here.'

She took it back and looked at it. She seemed sad and confused, as if it was a favourite pet that had bitten her. Dossman said, as gently as he could, 'Anybody can pay into his account, but only he can draw on it. They should have told you that at the bank.'

'They did,' she said, carefully folding the cheque back into its envelope. 'But it wasn't any help. Jerry's still in Tromstad and I'm stranded here.'

'But he should be back any time. There's nothing more to come from Tromstad after today.'

She shook her head. 'Ray Kreiger – you know Ray Kreiger? He holds Jerry to the letter of his contract. He won't let him leave unless he has to, until the final okay comes through from this office.'

The envelope went back into her pocket. Dossman hesitated a moment, and then said abruptly, 'Look, how much do you need?'

She stared for less than a second, but it was long enough

to make him regret the offer. She backed off with a thin, defensive smile.

'Thanks,' she said, 'but forget it.' And before Dossman could say anything else, she turned and walked out through the open door into the hotel corridor.

Why can't I keep my mouth shut? Dossman thought, and he turned to suggest that Visco should lose himself for a while and try for Riggs again later.

But Visco must have left by one of the other doors. His seat was empty, and his untouched coffee was cold on the desk.

John had only gone a couple of yards down the corridor when he felt an unexpected touch on his arm. 'You're the Englishman that's come looking for a job, yes?' Steen said.

The Dutchman had emerged from the empty store-room; Teamverk's offices had more entrances and exits than a bedroom farce. John was torn between waiting to find out what Steen had to say and running after Sara Hansun; she'd only just disappeared into the stairwell by the elevators.

He said, 'I suppose you're going to tell me what a bad time I picked.'

'If you listen to me, I'll give you some of the best advice you're going to hear.'

John felt the moment slipping away; he made a decision and followed Steen back into the storeroom. 'As long as you're not just telling me to go home,' he said, but Steen made a slight gesture for silence and closed the door behind them. Then he went and looked through into the main room of the suite; Dossman had already gone, and within a couple of seconds John heard him pass by in the corridor outside.

He was about to speak again, but again Steen silenced him. It came to John with sudden absurdity; we're *hiding*, he thought, looking at the way Steen was holding himself back so that he could see the door to Riggs' room without being seen, but then the far door opened and closed and, after a moment, Steen beckoned him through.

There was a murmur of voices fading away as they came into the main room; Riggs and Rachel, on their way to lunch. Steen reached under one of the desks and brought out a fair-sized attaché case. John said, 'Look, I can come back later . . .'

'I won't be here later. That's a part of it. We can talk while I'm working.'

'I thought this was your lunch hour.'

'That's the best time.'

The two of them were now the only people left in the suite. John was beginning to regret his decision, but it was probably too late; the girl would have disappeared into the crowds on the Storgata by now, and his chances of catching up with her would be zero.

Steen took his attaché case through and set it down by Riggs' door. Then he set a three-letter combination to open it and took out a professional-looking set of picks.

'What are you doing?' John said as the Dutchman set to work on the door.

Steen paused, considering the question as if it had some extra philosophical significance. 'Basically,' he said, 'I suppose you could say that I'm robbing them.'

Ten seconds later, they were inside.

The room was an odd hybrid of office and bedroom, with the sleeping arrangements almost hidden around an alcove. There was an expensive-looking leather sofa – which, looked at closely, turned out to be buttoned plastic – backed by a sectioned mirror and flanked by two fake onyx tables. On them were big copper vases which served as bases for low-wattage lampshades. Facing this arrangement across the room was an aircraft-carrier-sized desk covered in black vinyl; Steen was setting his briefcase down on the blotter.

There was a photograph in a frame on one corner of the desk. It seemed to have been knocked so that it faced the wall, and Steen turned it back around. It showed a photograph of a woman with two children, boys in their teens.

'Kind of sad,' he said. 'The two of them together, you know? We shouldn't try to judge.'

'I don't.'

'You a married man, Mister . . . ?'

'John Visco. No, I'm not.'

Steen looked up briefly, and then he started riffling through the stack of memos by Riggs' blotter. Most he discarded, some he transferred to the attaché case.

'This is quite a survey, John Visco,' he said. 'Quite an operation. You know what it's doing?'

'I've read about it.'

'Teams all over Norway and Sweden, all of them checking out mines that are no longer worth the work. The results come here, to me, all the figures. I'm the computer man.'

'Right.'

Now Steen put the memo stack back in order and lifted the waste bin onto the desk. He started taking out the pieces of crumpled paper and smoothing them out, looking for anything of interest. 'You don't understand, I know,' he said. 'What I'm telling you is, all the hard information, the stuff that's paying for all this,' (a quick gesture around the office) 'it has to come to me in the end.'

'Are you saying you can fix it so they give me a job?'

'No, I'm not saying that, just wait. I'm saying that all the information comes to me and I have to, you know, press it down.'

'Crunch it.'

'Press it, crunch it, what the hell. I make it all neat for the big computers in New Jersey. They run it all in with this big programme they've got, tells them if any of the mines is a good gamble to pump money in. You know, watch the trends, predict the market. Lot of crap.'

He returned the bin to the floor and started opening drawers. John watched with growing fascination. Steen found the Dictaphone that he was looking for. He removed the tape and tossed it in after the memos.

'What I'm saying is,' he went on, 'take the information away, and the whole thing has to start again. Maybe they find there's a job for you after all.'

He closed the case and carried it through to the outer offices. John followed like a hungry cat after a sardine. He said, 'And you're taking the information away?'

'Got a buyer lined up in Rotterdam.' A last check to see that everything in Riggs' room appeared to be in place, and then Steen closed and relocked the door. 'No names, you understand – professional discretion.'

Now they went to the datalink. Steen opened the case again and started to shovel the day's printout into it. John said, 'How much is there to carry?'

'Already gone. Code it up, send it through the telephone system.' Steen patted the datalink affectionately. 'To New Jersey I send junk. I make up all of the figures and the computer makes them look good. So now I take the last of it, and goodbye.'

'Why are you telling me?'

Steen looked at him levelly. 'Because you need a break, John Visco, anyone can see. And it costs me nothing. Okay?'

'Thanks.' John was making some rapid calculations; Steen must have some immediate plans to disappear or else he wouldn't be taking the risk of giving himself away. Any useful moves that could be made with this gift of information would have to be made fast. Steen's dirty work might not be discovered until the next day or even later, but John couldn't take the risk.

Steen was finished, and heading for the door. John decided that, with the jackal out of the way, it might look bad if he were to be found sitting amongst the bones; he followed.

73

EIGHT

John made his way back to his hotel along Karl Johansgate. No cars here, only the earth-shaking trolleybuses that nosed their way gently through the people like beasts too tame ever to be thought dangerous. The sky was iron-grey and there was snow in the air, and the bookshop owners in the walking streets had covered their outdoor racks with polythene sheets and dragged them inside. Otherwise, the city moved on without missing a beat.

He knew that Sara Hansun was looking for somewhere to live, and reckoned that she'd probably make the most obvious start and check on the agencies listed in the commercial services directory. The desk clerk at the hotel helped him to identify the category and even provided him with a giveaway map to mark the locations of the offices.

He skipped the first three. He wanted to intercept her, not follow her around. The fourth agency on the list was a short T-Banen ride out of the centre, close to the sculpture park.

The four-colour map was wrong in one important detail; winter made Oslo into a monochrome city, a good sharp print of an old movie. Two white sightseeing buses stood in the half-round before the park's cast-iron gates, empty and with their engines revving. Exhaust fumes had sprayed two sooty airbrushed cones across the snow, a casual fouling of boredom. This would be the three-hour tour, a fast run through all the major sights that would spin you dizzy and drop you back at your hotel, a whole city condensed into a flicker-show and about as memorable.

He found the agency, a big wooden-frame house on the west side of the park. He'd missed Sara Hansun by a matter of minutes, and she'd headed back towards the T-Banen station at Majorstua. John wondered why he hadn't met her on the boulevard; it was this more than anything that took him back to the park gates.

He could see from the gateway that the tourists were sticking together, all thirteen of them picking their way along a gritted path at the far end of the park's central avenue. There were black specks moving across the snow towards them, a horde of ducks from the park's frozen lake snapping and chortling like ankle-high muggers. Beyond the avenue was a bridge, and then the wide dish of a fountain big enough to take a couple of cars; the water had been shut off, and the dish was filled to overflowing with down. From the fountain onwards there were rising terraces, leading the eye to the great stone column that was the park's centrepiece.

There was a single figure on the steps below the column.

The people had all moved on by the time that John reached the bridge, leaving a mess of tracks and some disappointed wildlife. The ramparts of the bridge were the first stage of the open-air gallery display, two inward-looking lines of groups and figures; they were all ages, all naked, and with a dusting of white on their heads, shoulders and breasts. The figures were stylised almost to the point of blandness, their personalities as grey as the stone, caught forever in attitudes of tenderness, agony, jealousy – all the downbeat moments of the human spirit.

He recognised her long before he reached her. She was kicking along aimlessly, working through the kind of problem that would never have a neat solution. He said, 'Can I talk to you for a moment?'

She looked at him sharply, uncomprehending. 'What about?'

'I saw you back at the Teamverk offices. Are you some-thing to do with the Tromstad survey?'

'No,' she said, and walked on. John hurried to catch up, pulling out the notebook in which he kept the jottings for his job strategy.

'I heard talk about somebody called Ray Kreiger. Is he the team leader?'

'There are better names for people like him.'

'And can you tell me,' John went on, 'whereabouts Tromstad actually is?'

She stopped, and studied John for a moment. He'd taken out a Fineliner and was waiting to write her answer down. She said, 'Are you serious?'

'I'm serious. I really need to know.'

'You really need a map. It's about a thousand kilometers –' she pointed vaguely across the park towards the mountains and the distant ski runs – '*that* way.'

John tried to write it down. The fibretip pen was solid. 'I think I'm freezing,' he admitted. 'Can I buy you coffee?'

Sara Hansun stayed wary for a moment. Then she said, 'Coffee and a doughnut?'

'Whatever you like.'

'Deal.'

They squeezed into a corner table in a Baker-Hansen's. John asked questions and filled a couple of pages in his notebook with details, and Sara watched him with an expression that said that she couldn't entirely make him out, and that she wasn't too sure that she wanted to.

'So,' he said. 'Some of the men working on the project had already left before you did?' Sara nodded, brushing sugar from her fingers. 'You wouldn't know how many?'

'No, but I'm sure that more will have left by now. But you're wasting your time – they left because the job was over.'

'Not according to what I just heard.'

'What do you mean?'

For a moment he was going to tell her about Paul Steen,

but then he decided to preserve the confidence he'd been given. 'There's some problem with the results,' he said. 'Some of the work will have to be done again.'

She looked up in surprise. 'But they can't!' she said, loudly enough to make one or two people look around.

'I heard it kind of unofficially. But I'm sure it's true.'

She thought about it for a moment. 'Yes,' she said at last. 'The way this Mickey-Mouse outfit works, I can believe it.'

John glanced at his watch as he closed the notebook. 'Listen,' he said, 'I have to go set something up. Do you want anything else?'

From the careful study that she'd given to the cakes counter only ten minutes before the answer was an obvious *yes*, but she waved him away. 'Go on,' she said. 'You're as broke as I am.'

It was a point that he couldn't really argue. He left her at the table to consider whatever new and unwelcome problem this change in circumstances had brought, and set out to make his last visit before taking action.

To Teamverk again, and this time he was going to be sure that he talked to Kendall Riggs.

'Mister Riggs? Kendall Riggs the bureau chief?'

Riggs looked around, caught in the act of pressing the elevator call button. 'Who are you?' he said.

John stepped forward from the shadowed area of the Norsemann's lobby. 'My name's John Visco,' he said. 'This will explain everything.' And he held out a letter.

Riggs looked him over nervously. Close to thirty, dark and hungry-looking, John seemed to have been dressed from a surplus stores on a budget. He didn't look like a process-server, so Riggs took the letter. The folded paper had been carried around for so long that he had trouble getting it open.

John had waited less than fifteen minutes in the lobby; it was still early in the afternoon, and a check with the desk had confirmed that Riggs and Rachel were still out at a lunch that was getting to equal the running time of *Ben-Hur*. He'd watched as the two of them had made a whispered arrangement to arrive back at the office separately – as if they thought they were fooling anyone – and then made his move as the elevator doors had closed to carry Rachel away.

Riggs said, 'Who's Lewis Alexander?'

'Your London man.'

The elevator arrived and the doors opened. Riggs continued reading as he stepped inside, and John followed.

'I didn't know we had a London man,' Riggs mused.

'This was nearly a year ago.'

Riggs completed his skim, and held out the letter for John to take back. There was a discouraging finality in the gesture. 'Well,' he said, 'a year ago I might have been able to help you. Right now we're winding up all our surveys.'

'I know. But suppose you found that you had to redo some of the work, and most of your men had already left the sites . . .'

'I don't think you've got much of a grasp of the way this business works.'

The workmen's burlap had been removed from the walls, uncovering three sides of coral-tinted mirrors. The lift was like a tiny magic box, a sideshow wonder, a cheap glance into infinity. As the indicator panel counted through the floors John waited. Riggs began to get uncomfortable.

They reached the fifth floor and stepped out onto the landing. Riggs said, 'Look, if it was just down to me then okay, there'd be no problem. Assuming you're qualified.'

'I'm qualified. Degree in geology and postgraduate credits in micropaleontology.'

'After the season we've just had I couldn't tell a micropaleontologist from a microcephalic, assuming there's a difference. You're in the wrong place at the wrong time, and you've picked the wrong mark. There's no Lewis Alexander with Teamverk any more, the projects are all folding, and when they were in operation it was the team leaders who did any extra hiring, not the bureau.'

'Team leaders like Ray Kreiger?' John said as they reached the door to the Teamverk suite, but Riggs was already opening the door onto the scene inside.

All of the staff had been herded together in the main room, and they were chattering nervously. Dossman was by the connecting door to Riggs' own room; it was open, and a hotel security man was crouching to examine the lock. Rachel was inside, looking through the memos on Riggs' desk; she looked up at him, pale and shocked.

Dossman came over. 'Kendall,' he said, 'we've got trouble.'

John cashed in the last of his travellers' cheques and bought the map that Sara had advised. He found Narvik pretty quickly, high on the north-west shoulder of the coastline. It was on a deep-reaching fjord and further protected by the broken offshore chain of the Lofoten islands. Tromstad he couldn't see at all, but Narvik was a good enough start. She'd been right, it was quite a distance to cover.

Exactly how he was going to cover it was the problem; the money that he'd managed to save during the summer was only enough for a one-shot exercise, and the one shot was Oslo. When he'd brought his pack down from his room and paid his hotel bill, it began to look like he'd barely have enough to feed himself over the next two or three days.

He began checking out the possibilities for transport, starting with the shipping offices. In order to connect with the regular coastal service he'd have to make his way back to Bergen, and then four days of steaming on the North Cape route would get him to Svolvaer. He'd have another day to kill in the small island fishing town before connecting with the overnight boat to Narvik – practically one week on the move, and still he wouldn't be in Tromstad. During that time Teamverk could either win through or go under; whichever it was he'd be ignorant until he arrived, and when he arrived he'd find himself beached and helpless.

But it wasn't worth arguing through, because he couldn't even come near to affording the passage. The railways were next; five trains a day from Oslo to the medieval town of Trondheim, two of them connecting with a northbound service to the end of the line at Bodø. From Bodø it was eight hours by coach or another overnighter by sea. The fare wasn't quite so ambitious, but he still couldn't afford it.

A late lunch was some bread, sausage and a beer from an Oluf Lorentzen supermarket near the East station. Most of the hotel's breakfast buffet was wrapped in napkins and stowed in his pack, but he'd need to save that for later. He sat on a bench upwind of the hotdog kiosk in the station's main hall and watched the city's half-dozen drunks in conference over the serious business of the day, which involved sending out scouts to ask tourists for money.

He could get himself out to the main E6 highway and look for a ride, but although that would be the cheapest option of all it would be no faster than the boats. He needed to get to Ray Kreiger before the survey folded completely, maybe offer himself in place of one of the field men who had already walked off the job. Kreiger was sure to be sympathetic. He'd have to be impressed by Visco's determination. Guessing from what John had overheard at the bureau there wouldn't be much more than one or two weeks' work, but it would pay for his keep and the journey home and it would give him what he needed most; field experience, a foot in the door. In his mind, he was already there. Now that the scenario was agreed, all he had to do was to work his way through it.

Take it one stage at a time, he told himself; first get to Bodø, and hit the cash reserve as little as you dare. It would mean getting a cheaper ticket for some intermediate destination and then travelling through – he briefly considered riding a freight, but only long enough to dismiss the idea altogether. It wouldn't only be uncomfortable, it would probably be suicidal at Arctic night temperatures.

So if he was found out, he'd be thrown off; worse things had happened, and he could take it from there. Three hours to the next train gave him plenty of time to think of alternative strategies – or to convince himself that he wouldn't have any problem. He lifted his pack onto his shoulder, and headed across to the small booking hall off the side of the concourse.

Before he got to the line at the ticket window, one of the akvavit scouts appeared in front of him. He was sandy-haired and bleary-eyed, and there was an old scab in the stubble on his upper lip. He swayed before John for a moment, probably assessing the mark before he made his pitch; but then his attention seemed to wander, and he moved on without speaking.

Now, what was that about? John watched from the line as the man approached others, mostly being avoided or rebuffed. He couldn't have been more than about thirty-five, and he'd reached the end of his road already. It was a mean kind of achievement.

The booking system for the State Railways was computerised, and it took only a couple of minutes to run off his ticket and two separate reservation slips. He checked the slips as he came away from the window; each showed carriage and seat numbers. The first would cover him to Trondheim, but the second was only to the next station on the northbound service – after that he'd either have to sit tight and sweat or be sure he could dodge the guard. Reading off the destination on the second piece of paper made him smile.

There it was, in neat teleprinter type. He'd booked himself a ticket through to Hell.

NINE

Steen was jerked awake by the low thunder of an articulated lorry as it swung around behind the Opel Rekord, and the Dutchman immediately had to cover his face as white light flooded through the car. The light moved on and left him trying to blink away a burnt-in after image; he rubbed his eyes, and the sharpness began to fade.

Seven hundred miles in one twenty-four hour period was a punishing schedule. Averaged-out it didn't look so bad, but translated into physical stiffness and the long, hypnotic drone of the autobahns it became a torture. He'd picked up some amyl poppers in Christiania, but instead of clearing his head and sharpening his senses they'd made his heart race dangerously and set him panting. Now he had a sick headache, squatting like a dead spot behind his left eye.

The lorry came to a stop a hundred yards across the parking area, and its lights were doused. Steen tried to stretch, but the confining shape of the Opel stopped him; he opened the door and eased out into the cool night air.

He'd stayed around Oslo until dark. The idea was to make himself impossible to trace, which ruled out the airlines and the car hire companies – Riggs might not react quickly enough, but Dossman was sharp. There was his own car, of course, but that was traceable and it extended the circle of danger considerably. Besides, he'd bought it cheap to make the journey up and he'd had doubts about its reliability even then; it was getting to the kind of age and mileage where a VW tends to heave a dying sigh and punch a hole out of its engine block with a piston. That would be all he needed, rolling to a halt on an autobahn and dribbling oil like a loose-bowelled dog.

No, the Opel was a much safer proposition, and it had been easy enough to get hold of. It had simply been a matter of looking for a car showroom which gave space to the franchise desk of a rental firm, and then waiting after hours until somebody returned a vehicle. Steen had gone along a few minutes later, raised the letterbox flap in the showroom's door, and spiked the envelope containing the Rekord's keys and contract on the end of a length of coathanger wire.

Now, several hours later, he was in a quiet picnic zone on the edge of a service area, an asphalt car park screened from the motorway by trees and overlooked by a land-scaped slope with tables and benches. He'd been there for about half an hour; he hadn't wanted to stop at all, but the blare of angry horns as he'd begun to drift across the carriageway asleep at the wheel had been a warning that he couldn't ignore.

He took an uneven walk over to the weak lights of the washrooms, his joints squeaking as they came back into use. He reckoned that another half-hour or so would bring him through Dortmund and then on to Essen, with a border crossing into Holland somewhere around Goch. One of the northern routes staying nearer to the coast might have cut a few miles from the overall journey, but this way the roads were faster and he'd be coming into the home country at an unexpected angle. Teamverk couldn't know his employer but they might have been able to make an approximate guess at his destination, and he didn't want to risk being stopped at the frontier. So far he'd been lucky – no checks on the ferry crossing from Norway to Denmark, but coming through into Germany a short time later he'd seen the car before him being pulled aside for a random customs inspection. The border posts might have his description, and there was even a thin chance that Dossman might have been able to follow through the strategy so that they'd know the car he was driving.

He stood over the washroom basin with the water running and wished that he'd gone for amphetamines as he'd wanted rather than allowed himself to be talked into the amyls. He'd inhaled from three of the capsules and now they were tearing him apart from the inside. Bright lights became spears and smells became nauseating – the liquid soap dripping from the dispenser over the basin, the pink-disinfectant background of the washroom, the ugly metallic edge of fresh petrol on the breeze as he walked back to the Rekord.

The car had been another problem; it hadn't performed as well as he'd hoped because it was badly in need of a tuneup and a service. It had even cut out on him a couple of times as he'd slowed on the minor roads. Something wrong with the carburettor, he guessed, but his practical abilities with cars were zero outside of being able to steal them.

Well, what did it matter? The car wasn't his, and it could end as a useless and expensive shell as long as it got him to Rotterdam. For a few minutes he sat, seat belt on and waiting until he felt settled enough to drive. When he finally started the engine he blipped the accelerator pedal to keep the car from stalling and then nosed the Opel out towards the service road and the petrol islands.

As the tank was filling, Steen asked the forecourt mechanic to take a look under the hood. The man grimaced and waved the air before his face as the vapours came up to meet him; you're driving a bomb, he told Steen, and the Dutchman could only nod and give him a sick half-smile before walking unsteadily around to the other side of the island. He was almost ready to throw up, but somehow he was holding it down; he pulled out a handkerchief to wipe his face.

It was the one that he'd broken the poppers into. Small bombs went off in his head and deep inside, and he started to dry-heave.

The mechanic found him squatting down with his head

84

hanging, the worst of it over. Steen insisted that he was okay, paid cash, and got back into the car. His sides hurt and he was shivering, but his head had cleared a little.

He rejoined the autobahn and headed for the Dutch border. The mechanic had tweaked the carburettor as far as he'd been able without making it into a workshop job, but there wasn't much difference in the handling. He drove with the window partly open, relying on the steady feed of cold air to keep him alert.

Most of the radio stations that he'd tried to get on the way down had faded on him after less than half an hour, but now he ran through the wavelengths to see if he could tune in to the Voice of America. Different stations came through in bursts between the static, but where the forces service should have been there seemed to be a dead spot on the dial.

He hunted around to either side of it, steering one-handed and weaving slightly. Nothing else was strong enough to be worth holding onto.

With no runup and no warning, the voice of a young girl came through the dead air.

Steen reached again to tune it out – he was looking for big-band jazz, not fairy stories – but then he waited. The girl wasn't professional, but sounded like a teenager reading to somebody's children.

And as the woodcutter came down from the forest, he began to think that there was perhaps somebody running to catch up with him, and because he knew of no reason to be afraid, he stopped on the path and looked back. And there the Follower stood, with his feet planted right in the woodcutter's own footprints.

Steen did his best to hold on, feeling glassy and unreal. The traffic on the far carriageway of the autobahn flowed by in a hypnotic stream of light. Other cars were twinned red jewels in the darkness ahead.

And the woodcutter said, 'Follower, are you hurrying to speak to me?' And the Follower looked into the woodcutter, all the way down to the deepest secrets in the woodcutter's heart. Now, the woodcutter had a wife and a fine home and two fine children, and it was known everywhere that he was the happiest of men. And the Follower said, 'No, woodcutter, I wasn't looking for you at all.' And then he raised his great claws and he struck the woodcutter down. And as the woodcutter lay, the Follower took his shape and lifted his great axe onto its shoulder, and then it set off for the cottage where lived the woodcutter's wife and his two fine children. Sometimes he walked like a wolf, but now he walked like a man. He was a stealer of shapes, and they called him the Follower. Unhappiness and spite, these were what he lived for and these were his wine. As he walked, he sang, and these were his words;

There was a pause, as if the girl might be checking to be sure that Steen was listening. His hands were trembling on the wheel, his knuckles almost white. He glanced in the mirror and saw that he was no longer alone in the car.

> *'I am the beast that follows in your way*
> *To find the one whose sorrow meets my own;*
> *There's none so strong I cannot bring him down*
> *And none so far I cannot draw him home.'*

Steen heard none of it. He'd twisted the wheel hard over and stamped on the brakes; the car was suddenly filled with light and noise as the cars on his tail reacted and swung away, and then he was slewing onto the grass beyond the shoulder and the Opel was trying to fishtail around.

When he scrambled to look into the back seat, it was empty. There was only the nylon rain jacket that he'd worn out of the car during his stopover in Copenhagen, lying more or less as he'd thrown it. He'd felt ready to piss his pants with fear, and there was nothing there. The radio was playing low in the background, Ella Fitzgerald singing Cole Porter.

He collapsed back into the driver's seat. His shirt was so wet that he might have put it on straight from the wringer. *I'm not going to make it,* he was thinking, *I'm poisoned and I'm dying*, and he wondered if he'd be able to get along to the next emergency telephone and call for a doctor.

The mirror had been knocked as he'd turned, so he reached out to straighten it. And then, of course, it all became obvious.

With the amber lighting of the autobahn coming in at an angle, the rear window was picking up a dim reflection of the jacket on the back seat. His own credulous imagination had filled in all the details. He still felt shitty, but suddenly not quite so mortal.

He restarted the stalled engine. As he drove back onto the shoulder he watched in the mirror as the angles changed and Pepper's ghost faded away. His turnoff would be about half an hour ahead, if he kept it at a steady seventy kph.

The crossing-point that he was aiming for was about ten minutes' drive from an RAF camp close to the border. There was a small customs post on the road, hardly more than a hut and a drop-across barrier, but it was locked every night from ten o'clock; what attracted him more was the route across the nearby fields that had been marked out by border-hoppers from the camp returning from evening sprees in Holland.

He'd only seen the way once before, and that had been three years ago and in daylight. Although he took it slowly when he got into the area, the first time through he missed the point where he was to leave the road and strike out across country. *Concentrate*, he told himself as he turned the Opel around in the narrow lane, and he came back slowly looking for some telltale signs of car tracks.

The cattle were a hazard he hadn't expected. Some of them ran when the headlights swept across them, others froze in place. One lay square across his path and wouldn't move, and he was almost forced into a drainage ditch as he pulled over to avoid it. The Opel bounced over the rough ground, and the stench of petrol filled the car.

He was lost, but he didn't know it. The actual route was more than a kilometre away. The tracks that he'd followed were of farm vehicles that had ripped up the grass bringing in pipeline for an extended drainage system. There was a deep trench across the end of the field, but the Opel's low-angled lights didn't show it, nor did they show the electrified cattle wire that had been staked across to keep the herd back from the workings.

The wire carried a low voltage in metal filaments that had been twisted in with a nylon line. A man touching it might get a slight burn, nothing more. If Steen hadn't been forced so near to the edge of the field he might have ripped out the wire and never known it; the Opel's lights would have shown the fresh earth of the diggings and he'd have been able to pull up in time to realise the mistake. But what he hit was the transformer at the end of the line, the buried junction box which took mains supply and ran it down to a safe level.

The beast in the back of the car leaned forward to whisper softly in his ear.

The box came tearing up out of the ground in a shower of sparks. The potent vapour trapped under the hood exploded, and it blew through the car's thin box-section bulkhead into the passenger compartment. The fireball took out all of the glass, lifting out the rear windscreen in an unbroken sheet and flinging it over the hedgerows and into the next field. All of the cattle were together and running when the fuel tank went up, bending the boot lid out of shape and sending it spinning and bouncing with Steen's two suitcases close behind. Their weight brought them down close by, drenched with petrol and burning; the soft plastic outer skins were quickly eaten down to the frames, and then the fire began on the contents.

Suitcase number two was carrying all of the last week's printout. The outside of the stack was charring as the fire-breeze lifted the upper folds, and then it began to burn as fast as it could unravel. Used carbon ribbons from Rachel Hellstrom's IBM Selectric flared and melted, unofficial records of outgoing correspondence that Steen had retrieved and saved. The oil in the Opel's sump had now become hot enough to burn, and the engine block broke with a dull crack.

The car had been quickly reduced to its basics, a black shell of metal at the centre of a self-generating furnace. The yellow heat boiled off into the night, a rising cloud of brilliance that could now be seen for several kilometres.

With it went any last chance that Teamverk's Oslo bureau might be able to salvage its operation without going back to the field surveys. By morning they would be taking out what was left of Paul Steen, and it wouldn't be much. He'd be beyond identification, beyond even a last-ditch effort at dental matching. With the car they'd have more luck – the plates would probably be gone, but the engine number should have survived and would be traceable. It would be slow and procedurally tortuous, but they'd do it; they'd get as far as the records of the hire company, and then a couple of Oslo policemen would be knocking on a door and explaining to somebody how he'd been taken dead from a car that he'd already returned several days before.

It would still be possible to hit on the truth, even though it was unlikely. It would take a lot of ploughing through records, a few inspired connections, but somebody could still match the dates and the circumstances and work up a credible link with the Dutchman.

And there it would stop. Because Paul Steen hadn't existed before Teamverk; he was an invented persona, a

89

fake identity put together for a specific job. The twisted shape from the burned-out Opel would lie unmourned and unrecognised, until someone took the decision to dispose of it.

Steen had served his purpose. Visco was on his way.

TEN

They were fifty minutes late coming into Trondheim. The
Bodø train had been held on the next platform, and there
were about a hundred more people waiting to go. They
stood under the ice-hung awning and at the carriage
windows and in the corridors of the sleepers, watching the
Oslo service coast in because there had been damn-all else
of interest happening in the last hour.

John found his new reservation, and he stood by the
window looking out. The Oslo train was now empty and
dead-looking, and further down the line its belly had been
opened and the mailbags of the Post-Giro were being
pulled out. There was also baggage being transferred
across, a jumble of suitcases and hundreds of skis, two
trolleys' worth of winter hardware being wheeled around
on the snow-beaten platform. He was thinking how, in an
hour or less, he was going to become some kind of crimi-
nal. The idea didn't give him the thrill that he'd supposed
it might.

The service moved out ninety minutes late and in near-
silence. The lights cut to half-power after the first ticket
check, and most people covered themselves with their
coats and tried to sleep. John had probably picked up
more practice than any of them, and within a few minutes
of closing his eyes he was fading away like an old
photograph.

He was still in the train, but it had been cleared of people
and he was alone. When he turned to look out of the

window there was nothing, just a void. The carriage was moving, bucketing and swaying on the long ride down into nowhere – he could feel as much when he got out of his seat and reached up for the pack that was no longer there.

This wasn't right. He'd been through it all in various forms before, and he'd come to expect a certain routine. His faceless hunter would be in the next carriage or in the one beyond that, and he was supposed to be getting ready for it; somebody was playing by the wrong rules. No pack meant no gun, and no gun meant an end to John's last backstop of reassurance.

He got down between the seats and waited; almost immediately he heard the door at the end of the carriage sliding back, and the racket of wheels on rails came through louder from the unsoundproofed boarding platform on the other side. The door closed again, the sound dropped back, and the follower was now in John's part of the coach.

The fearful part of his mind was screaming to him to make himself small, to wrap himself down tight and hope that he might not be noticed. On a more conscious level he was thinking *face it and get it over with*, but without the sustaining power of his two-pound metal totem he was helpless.

Something bounced on the floor of the carriage, a hard crack like wood wrapped in leather. Another bounce much nearer, and it rolled past bringing with it the sharp odour of burned meat. John glimpsed it for a second and then it was gone; red-black and flaking, it was a human head roasted beyond recognition. It left a trail of soot and grease on the vinyl, and a moment later he heard it bump a couple of times against the door at the back of the carriage.

Face it. That was all he had to do; look it in the eye. He tried to raise himself to look over the seats, but he could feel that his brave intentions were all staying down on the floor.

John could see the outline of it against the glass of the end door. It hadn't come any further into the coach, and it was standing and swaying with the movement of the train. It was in the shape of a man, barrel-chested with a wrestler's build and long, straight hair that hung lifeless and smooth. One hand was raised in the air before it, and it was holding something.

And then it stepped forward, and it came under the low-power corridor light. Now John could see what it was holding – his gun, pinched delicately between thumb and forefinger as if it had been dipped in something putrid. *Want to come and get it?* the shape seemed to be inviting, and then it swayed forward a little more and its face came into the light.

It was as grey as stone, and with the light directly overhead its eyes were deep pits without mercy. The stone moved and the follower smiled a golem smile for John Visco, showing teeth as small and as perfect as a baby's – but there were a hundred or more of them, and each had been filed to a razor point.

Still smiling, it started forward.

He might have been making noise, he couldn't tell, but none of the others around him seemed to be awake as he made his way stiffly down to the end of the carriage. That had been one of the worst, no competition, and he was glad to be out of it. As he waited for the toilet to come free, he rubbed a clear patch on the opal-frosted window so that he could watch the day shaping up. Like the first fjord dawn that he'd seen from the deck of the Hardanger car ferry it was coming slowly, with features emerging from the grain rather than being revealed.

They were following an edge of grey water to their left, its surface raised in an even swell by the wind. There were occasional buildings by the waterside, none of them much of a size and none of them obviously occupied. Behind them were hills with an even cover that was slowly washing through from indigo to white. The details began to halo out as his breath recondensed and crystallised on the glass.

Until Hell freezes over, he thought, and the sudden absurdity of it made him smile.

The window in the door through to the corridor linkage was only iced around its edges. John could see the second window only a few feet away and weaving unsteadily, and beyond that a darkened coach that was a duplicate of the one behind him. One of the *konduktørene* was making his way down the aisle, his jacket buttoned up high and fresh snow still clinging to his boots and trousers from the last stop. He was checking the sleeping forms against a folded seating plan in his hand.

John turned around and started to walk.

It was happening much earlier than he'd expected. He wasn't sure what he was going to do. He could keep going and stay ahead of the guard, but only until the end of the train and that wouldn't be long enough; and he didn't feel that he had the nerve to sit tight and let the inspection pass him by. Even though people had been changing seats and moving around, the carriage numbers would have to balance in the end.

When he got level with his seat, he went on past without even hesitating. He was starting to get an idea.

The restaurant car would be two or three stages back down the train. They'd be gearing up for breakfast around now and he could be getting a coffee or something – no, *two* coffees, and he could smile and squeeze past the guard as he was taking them forward. A cup of the hot stuff in each hand might make the *konduktøren* hesitate before asking to see his documentation; more important he'd have an extra credibility, one of a group instead of a single evasive freeloader.

This will work, he assured himself, *just watch*.

But the restaurant car was deserted, lit only by the grey light of the morning. Well, not completely deserted – there was a girl sitting at one of the tables halfway down, an empty wax cup and a half-full bottle of Coke in front of

94

her. She must have saved them from the buffet trolley that had moved down the centre of the train the night before. She was playing with the frayed edge of a Narvesen Catering paper napkin, and she looked up as John came towards her. She didn't seem surprised.

She said, 'So you wouldn't take advice.'

'I never could. Does this mean you're heading back to Tromstad?'

'I don't have any choice. If Teamverk's extending the project, Jerry will have to stay on. And if that happens, I get stranded in Oslo with no money. I suppose you're going to sit down.'

'If it's okay.'

'I suppose it is. I'm annoyed with you, John Visco.'

He slid into the seat across from her. 'Why?'

'Because I told you about Teamverk and you didn't want to listen. Don't think I'm going to start feeling responsible for you.'

'You shouldn't. I'd already decided.'

'But for what? From the sound of it there's two, maybe three weeks' work on offer.'

'I'll take it,' John said. Her English was perfect, almost accentless. Seen close-up in daylight her hair was various shades running from a medium brown through to the colour of honey, too subtle in its shifts to be tinted. Despite her claim of annoyance she didn't really seem to be angry; she glanced over his shoulder and said, 'Going over the records again, that's something a monkey could do.'

But if that's what it would take, John was fully prepared to swallow what remained of his pride and be a monkey for a couple of weeks. He said, 'You're now looking at the best-connected nobody in the rock trade. I've had so much free advice, I could open a bureau. I've been interviewed so many times that for six months I just lived on the expenses. I mean, I'm starting to get desperate. By the time I finally get work, we'll be into a new geological era and all the continents will have switched around. Don't

95

you see how much of a disadvantage that could be in my line?'

She was trying to take him as seriously as he was pretending to take himself, but she couldn't keep it up. She cracked, with an unladylike snort. Her eyes shone in the dawn light, and her skin looked as soft as a doe's.

She said, 'Exactly how long have you been looking?'

'Six years,' he admitted.

'Six years,' she said. 'Time enough for whole new mountain ranges to form.' She said it lightly, but John could see from her expression that his frustration had got through to her. Six years of hard effort and constant rebuff were nothing to smile at; anybody who came through and emerged still ready to fight on had to be either worth respect or ready for a nice long holiday in a rubber room.

'Look,' he said, 'it's no big thing. I mean, I never expected it to be easy . . . but it's turned out to be tougher than selling Smiley buttons at a crematorium.'

'And there's nothing else you can try?'

'There's nothing else I want to do. I suppose you'd say I was born unreasonable.'

Sara Hansun looked out of the window. They were getting close to the end of the lake, striking out on raised track across shallows that had frozen; but Sara was briefly lost in another landscape, one that no-one else would ever see.

She said, 'My father was a forester for fifteen years. He was in an accident, and afterwards the company moved him to an office job at the mill. He wanted to carry on as before, but they wouldn't let him.' She smiled, but there was bitterness in it. 'They took him away from what he loved and sat him behind a desk, and they expected him to be grateful. I used to go with my brother to meet him at the gates, and he looked like . . .' She stared out at the line where the sea and the sky met, searching for a way to describe the image in her mind. 'Like I felt every year when they were choosing the Flower Princess for the Constitution Day parade, and I was never even on the list.

The closest I ever got was carrying a ribbon behind the carriage, and I had to smile and pretend I was happy about it. You could say *that* was being unreasonable, too.' She glanced down at the napkin in her hands, which now was almost confetti. Screwing it all up together, she said, 'I'm sorry if I haven't been encouraging to you. I really hope you succeed. I just think that you're wasting your time with Teamverk.'

'At least I've got this,' he said, and he searched around inside his jacket until he came out with the Lewis Alexander letter. He passed it across the table to her, and she took it and opened it out. Light showed at the thin spots where the corners had been rubbed almost through.

Seeing the date, she said, 'But this is nearly a year old.'

'I know. That's how long it took me to get the money together for this.' He watched her, but he could see she wasn't reading it; something behind him and down the carriage had caught her attention.

The guard, he thought with a sudden flutter of panic.

Sara Hansun said, 'John, I've something to ask. Will you help me?'

'What's the matter?'

She lowered her voice slightly and leaned towards him, dropping the ruined napkin to one side. 'There's a *konduktøren* making his way towards us, he'll be checking on everyone. Will you tell him we're travelling together?'

John dropped his voice likewise. 'I'm not sure it will do any good.'

'But I haven't got a ticket.'

'Neither have I.'

ELEVEN

They were put off about an hour later at what looked like an unscheduled stop, a single building with a bulldozed forecourt and no sign of any town or village to back it up. They got their bags carried for them; Sara had a small brown suitcase with straps and a broken handle. It seemed a strange kind of treatment for a couple of stowaways, first-class disapproval – but then John saw why.

He said, 'They locked up the bags.'

'That's to keep us here,' Sara said, and she sounded like she'd been through it all before. The ground floor of the wooden building on the track side was divided into two, waiting room and office with a sliding window to link them; they were in the waiting room, their bags were in the office. John could see them through the glass, stacked against the opposite wall by a paraffin heater. The office also had a desk with postal scales and document stamps, painted bookshelves with two or three bound timetables, a switchbox for points and signals, and a telephone. Apart from a cheaply-printed calendar on the wall over the desk, it was undecorated.

The waiting room had even less – just two hard benches and another paraffin stove, which wasn't lit. When the Bodø train was moving out the *stasjonsmester* brought them matches, and he stopped to explain something to Sara. He wore so many layers against the cold that he could barely crouch before the heater, and then John almost had to help him up. Sara listened and nodded a few times, but it seemed that she had nothing to add.

When he'd gone she said, 'He's telephoning for the police.'

To him it was obviously nothing personal; he'd been almost sympathetic, but it was equally obvious that he wouldn't be argued out of his duty. John said, 'What will they do?'

'I don't know. Maybe check with the railway company and see if they want to prosecute us.'

'Do you think that's likely?'

'Depends how far we got for nothing. They might just take a look at how much money we've got and make us pay up.'

Then they'd be shaking the dust out of his wallet. He said, 'I'm not sure I've got enough.'

'I know for sure that I haven't,' Sara said, and she started to lay her gloves and mittens along the top of the heater for a long-overdue drying.

It appeared that they'd have some time to wait. The *stasjonsmester* had disappeared, taking a broad shovel that had been rammed into a drift by the door of the outhouse and tramping off down the line. Sara seemed indifferent to conversation, so John buttoned his jacket up as far as it would go and went to take a walk around.

Oslo had been cold, but this was worse. The slopes on the far side of the tracks were almost in whiteout, nothing to see but the slim ghosts of telegraph poles and a couple of lathed wooden snowbreaks some way up. Walking through the fresh snow around the building was like kicking through salt; on the windward side it had piled high enough to reach the ground-floor windowsills and almost bury the oildrums and ladders that were fixed there, but John didn't stay exposed for any longer than it took to plough a way through to the shelter of the building's other face. This was the real frontage, with a three-step framed door at its centre. Over the door was a plain black and white sign with a single light globe above it; he couldn't even attempt to pronounce the name.

They were higher than the rest of the village, which was

why they'd been unable to see any of it. Not that there was much to be seen – the station had been built on a terrace, and standing on its edge John could count no more than half a dozen roofs amongst the trees below. There was one good road, and it even had some traffic; the sight of it set him wondering. It was about half a mile away beyond the houses, running in at an angle that would probably bring it to a close parallel with the railway line a mile or so ahead. If their bags hadn't been locked away they could have slipped off down the track and started looking for a ride before the police could arrive – if.

Five minutes outside was enough. Back in the waiting room he pulled off his glove and touched his face; his skin was like ice and his hand was like fire, and for the first minute or so the thawing was acutely painful. Sara had huddled down into her oversize duffel coat and was either watching the flames of the heater or asleep, it was difficult to tell which.

The area's police deputy arrived shortly before noon, the snowchains on his Volvo Estate ringing like sleighbells as he pulled in by the station's forecourt. The *stasjonsmester* had returned less than an hour earlier, and the two of them talked outside for a moment; then the deputy came into the waiting room, and Sara showed that she was awake after all and stood up. She had some kind of identity card ready, and John got out his passport.

At first the deputy spoke only to Sara and in Norwegian. He wore a belted car coat of imitation leather over his uniform, and he didn't look as if he smiled often. John heard a couple of place names that he could recognise and twice the name *Teamverk*, but most of his attention was on his passport as it was turned over in the deputy's hands. Brown eyes, five-eleven, no scars, a photograph from a coin-in-the-slot booth that made him look like Billy Clanton's corpse; he'd been expecting a reprimand or at worst a night in some rural lockup, but it only occurred to him now that he might be turned around and deported.

'Show him your letter,' Sara said, surprising him with the switch. John did his now-familiar piece of production, and said, 'You'll have to translate it for him.'

'I don't think he needs it.' Sara was handing over Jerry Fraser's cheque, and there was a pause as the deputy studied both of the testimonials. He handled John's letter carefully, in deference to its age and condition.

He looked at John first, and said in English that was almost as good as Sara's, 'This is no proof, this is not even a promise. And it is almost a year old.'

'I know,' John said, accepting the letter back. The deputy looked at them both.

'None of this tells me why you should try to cheat the railway company.'

'Neither of us has any money,' Sara said, and the deputy gestured them over to one of the benches and had them turn out their pockets. The total amount wouldn't have settled the difference on one ticket; John and Sara found themselves giving each other the same sideways glance of disbelief.

They weren't alone; the deputy also seemed genuinely dismayed. 'You try to go a long way on a worthless letter and a useless cheque. What did you intend to do at Bodø, stow away on some boat?'

'I was going to work that out when I arrived,' John said, scraping his change off the bench.

'And afterwards, you no doubt intended to return and pay for all the tickets you used but never bought, for the food you maybe had to beg?' They both nodded, a little too eagerly. He went on, 'Unfortunately, the law has little concern with what you may have intended – it can only respond to what you have done. And you, Mister Visco, seem to have stranded yourself a long way from home without much consideration of how you might survive or return. The word for this is vagrancy.'

'He was going for a job,' Sara offered unexpectedly.

'Without alien's papers and without insurance. How seriously am I supposed to take this story?' He fixed on

John again; 'If I ring the Teamverk mining survey, will they tell me all about you?'

The answer to that one was easy. Even if Kendall Riggs could remember him (and only Kendall Riggs had known his name), he wouldn't want to know. John said, 'What are you going to do with us?'

The deputy was silent for a moment, and it was impossible to guess what he might be thinking – rogues, innocents, or enemies of the state. He said, 'I will have to talk to my chief. Put your bags in my car.' And then he turned and walked out of the waiting room, leaving them to go around to the office with the *stasjonsmester*.

Because of its broken handle, Sara had to carry her brown case held awkwardly across her chest; John thought it made her look like an evacuee. They loaded the bags into the open tail of the Volvo whilst the deputy sat behind the wheel and wrote up some notes, and then they climbed into the back and waited. They didn't dare to speak and he didn't pay them any attention, but perhaps that was supposed to be part of the treatment. After a few minutes, he started the Volvo and they set off.

John wasn't sure what to expect, a district courthouse or a one-man post. They drove down through the village and onto the highway that he'd seen from the terrace, turning in the direction that he'd assumed would run together with the railway line. After little more than one ploughed and gritted mile it did, but they'd hardly run parallel with the embankment for more than a couple of hundred yards when the deputy steered them off the road and into a parking area before a group of buildings. It reminded John of a daylight version of the place where he and Per Lindegren had waited with the Fiat, a grocery store with a telephone kiosk and then a couple of buildings set further behind it. There was a light-up sign on the wall of the store above the kiosk with an arrow that pointed in the general direction of back and the words, *Park Pensjonat 150m*. The deputy left the Volvo across three car spaces with its engine running and went into the store.

When he came out a minute later he was followed by a woman in her mid-thirties zipping a jacket that she'd obviously just slipped into. She headed around the side of the store as the deputy came back towards them and beckoned for them to get out of the car.

He said a few words to Sara, and Sara nodded. Then he raised the Volvo's tail so that they could get their bags, slammed it when they were out and then got back in and drove away.

John watched him go, wondering what next. Sara had obviously been told, because she set off to follow the woman in the direction of the *Park Pensjonat*.

It was a small guest house, apparently owned by the storekeepers and empty of guests – the busy season would be in the summer months with the tourist traffic on the North Cape route. She led them to a twin room on the upper floor with a view of some open land to the side; it was pleasant enough, even though none of the furniture matched and the heat had been turned off. Before she returned to the store she brought them towels and plugged in the convector strip. She didn't give them a key.

Neither had commented on the assumption that they'd be sharing; it could fall into line with a set of more urgent preoccupations. Sara said, 'He knows we can't afford to pay for this.'

What would the room cost? Two, three hundred kroner? Perhaps they could just afford it if they pooled their cash, but it would clean them out. John suspected that it was his nationality that lay behind the non-standard treatment; they were being handled as neutrally as possible whilst advice was sought from somewhere higher up the legal chain. He said, 'The idea's probably that we spend the night worrying about what's going to happen to us. Maybe if we promise to pay what we owe, he'll let us off.'

'Or maybe I'll get a fine and a police record, and you'll get deported.' She sat on the edge of the bed and shivered. Outside was supposed to be cold, but indoors you noticed

103

it more. The convector strip was making a few game clanking noises and no obvious difference to the temperature. John stood by the window and looked out.

Whatever the reasons or the explanations, time was being wasted. The addition of a possible vagrancy charge to his other difficulties made it even more urgent that he should get to Tromstad and persuade Ray Kreiger to take him on. To be turned around and sent home now would be a year's work gone for nothing; for worse than nothing, because it would be a slapdown from which he might never be able to climb back. This was his high shot, a lifetime effort, and it would never come again. If he could get on the payroll he could square his debts – both their debts.

'John?' Sara said, after he'd been staring out in silence for a while. 'You okay?'

'Sure.' He could see across the fields behind the store and houses to a stand of dark trees. Beyond the trees was the place where he most needed to be, out of sight and down the road looking for a ride. And he couldn't be there because – well, because he was *here*. Some intangible moral pressure held him where no locks or guards were necessary.

He stared out of the window in silence for ten minutes or more. Sara watched him for some of the time. At the end of it, he turned abruptly and crossed to the bed where he'd laid his pack. It was underbelly-up, frame and straps all showing, and he swung it around and onto his back. He said, 'I'm going to see if I can hitch a ride.'

'You're asking for trouble,' Sara warned as she turned around to watch him.

'I'm looking for a way to get myself out of it, and it isn't going to happen if I sit here and wait.' The weight of the pack was settled on his shoulders, and he started to buckle the padded body-belt.

Sara said, 'What about me?'

'You sit tight and blame me for everything.'

'So when I have to leave, I stand out there by the road on my own and hope that the first truck to pull in isn't driven by a man with a double sleeping bag and some big ideas?' She got to her feet, and reached for her case. 'Hold back, John Visco, I'm coming with you.'

It took them more than an hour to get to the road, crossing the fields because they didn't want to be seen from the houses. Before they left the *pensjonat* they'd straightened the covers, refolded the towels and unplugged the convector strip; it was like they'd never been there. Part of the way they followed in some fresh-looking ski tracks, and for the rest they stayed where buried scrub held the snow together. John took Sara's case for a couple of the difficult stretches, but mostly she insisted on clutching it and staggering on.

The piece of road where they emerged was ideal, a broad curve with enough of a runup for them to be seen and sufficient space for a vehicle to pull over after a moment's consideration time.

Presupposing the arrival of a vehicle, that was.

They saw three cars in as many hours, all of them going the wrong way. It was getting dark enough for the last of them to be using headlights, and John said, 'Maybe it wasn't such a good idea.'

Sara looked up at him; for the last half-hour she'd been sitting on her case, arms folded around herself to present as small a target to the wind as possible. Every few minutes she'd stand up and try to stamp her circulation back, and then she'd wrap down again. She said, 'You want to go back and hope nobody notices we ever left?'

John started to shake his head. His hair and shoulders had become glazed with a thin crust of ice, and it made him feel brittle. 'We could give it a while longer,' he said. Going back would mean asking for a key at the store, knocking at the jailhouse gates to be let back in. 'Think you'll manage?'

'Give me a shake if I stop moving.'

Their first authentic possibility came along less than ten minutes later, an articulated juggernaut that was a moving

105

lightshow with a roar that preceded it around the bend like a majorette. They both stood expectantly and Sara held up the sign that they'd made as the cab swung into view; seconds later it was thundering past and battering them with the gritty slipstream of its twenty-yard load. A noisy gear-change, a contemptuous flash of the dozen or so tail-lights, and the circus had left them behind.

Probably some rule against him picking up, John thought as he watched the spindrifts settle in its wake, but one shallow layer down was his true feeling, which was, *what a prick*.

Sara wasn't complaining; it was John's show and she'd volunteered to come along, but it was getting obvious that she wouldn't be able to stick it for much longer. One more try, he promised himself, just one more car and that would decide it. Sara sat on her case again, John stood so that he blocked some of the wind from her, his pack balanced against his leg, and they waited for the car that would take them away from trouble.

But before the car came the freight train, an apparently endless line of wagons and flatcars headed by a diesel; it was the powerful searchlight cutting a tunnel through the snowflakes over the embankment behind them that first caught John's attention, and he brushed Sara's shoulder.

'Look,' he said. 'No guards.'

'No carriages, either,' Sara said. 'If this car doesn't stop, then I'm going back to the room.'

She was standing and raising the *Narvik* sign, and John looked down the road to see the throw of headlights that was the first signal of a vehicle coming their way. Okay, he thought, this is the one; already they could hear the snow chains as the Volvo came into view.

Snow chains like sleighbells.

'Oh, shit,' John said. 'Look who it is.'

Sara lowered the sign. 'What do you want to do?'

'I think I want to run.'

The surprise went both ways. The deputy didn't see them until he was almost level and then he hit his brakes, sliding on past as his wheels locked and he half-turned into a broad skid. If John had never seen bad news on the move, he was seeing it now. Sara had thrown the sign away and was getting a hold on her case – so a fast retreat was agreed, but to where? The Volvo's headlights were yellowing the translucent snow that had been plough-heaped at the sides of the road, tyres biting at the hard-pack as the deputy got control and started back towards them; it was going to have to be the freight or nothing.

They ran for the embankment and started to climb; it wasn't far, but every step seemed to pull them deeper and slow them more. The train wasn't moving at much above a brisk walking pace, but that was no use if it was gone before they could reach it.

Two-thirds had passed by the time they reached track level, but it left plenty more. Although there wasn't really time to be picky there was a promising-looking flatcar that would be coming level in fifteen seconds or so, and although John didn't have the breath to shout he pointed and Sara got the message; but would she be able to make it without help?

He needn't have worried – she tossed her case onto the boards and hopped up after it. It was John who had the difficulty – his pack seemed to double in weight as soon as he tried to lift it high enough to throw, and the effort made him drop back almost to the end of the car. He somehow got it on before his legs started to give out, and then he grabbed a chain which kept him running until he could put on the extra burst to swing himself up.

They were leaving the deputy behind. John could see that he'd stopped the Volvo and got out; he was walking through the headlights, putting out rays and shadows to sweep across the snow to the embankment. Already they were losing the road, which meant that John's first idea – to ride far enough to get them out of the deputy's territory and then jump down and look for a lift again – was no longer in the draw.

They were sharing the flatcar with three tractors, red

107

Massey-Fergusons that were chained down and chocked into place. Tarpaulins had been roped around their paint-work so that they'd arrive in presentable condition, and when Visco reached the forward end of the car he found that Sara was pulling on a loose flap and trying to make enough of a breach for them to crawl into shelter. The ropes were tight, and she wasn't getting anywhere.

Suicide. That had been John's first assessment of the idea of Arctic freight-jumping, forgotten in the panic of flight and now coming back with force. So what, if they'd been picked up again? They'd already been on the point of returning to the *pensjonat* anyway, an admission in itself. And the deputy knew enough about them and their destination simply to telephone ahead – as an escape, it scored low in a lot of sections. John wondered if the deputy might simply decide to forget about it. Some hope, but it was better than nothing; they'd still have to be sure they were off the train before it reached Bodø.

If they ever made it so far. Sara wasn't getting anywhere with the tarpaulin, and she looked to John for help; they were picking up speed as they left the village behind them, and it put an edge on the wind that could have flayed the hide from a bull. Even if they could get into the space between the tractor's rear wheels they wouldn't be much better off – the tarpaulin wasn't a tent, and the chill wind would find them somehow.

John had a better idea. Sara looked uncomprehending as he helped her up, but then she quickly realised what he was trying to do as he began uncovering the door to the tractor's cab. She did her best to give him a hand – neither of them was working too efficiently, and it was getting worse.

The cab was never intended for two, so they had to squeeze in together and put an arm around each other in order to get the door closed. They sat hugging each other like monkeys under a tree, too cold and too relieved either to be embarrassed or to enjoy it much. But John hadn't finished; the tractor's paper-tagged ignition key was in the slot, and the battery was fresh enough to turn the engine over and fire it up on the third attempt. He ran it for a minute or more before he switched on the heater. The airblast was luke-warm, but getting warmer.

The cab windows misted up, they started to relax. There wouldn't be much gasoline in the tank, but they had two more tractors to get through after this one. So much of Sara was pressing against him that he had to remind himself, they were strangers. There was also Jerry Fraser to be considered, before he started imagining otherwise.

Sara managed to fall asleep, and John pretended to. The fuel lasted just over an hour before the engine died, and then the temperature in the cab began a rapid fall and they had to move along. This time Sara brought her case with her, and it made John think of the stateroom scene in *A Night at the Opera*. Her hands were too chilled from the transfer to manage the straps, so John helped her to open it. He said, 'What are we looking for?'

'Late breakfast,' she told him. 'About eight hours late, the way I work it out. There's an emergency Toblerone I keep somewhere in here.'

'A Toblerone? What kind of emergency were you expecting?'

'You want to get smart, John Visco, you can do without.'

'If we were on the ground I'd have to dig a hole to get humble enough. Hold it a moment, you reminded me.'

He climbed out of the cab and down to where he'd stowed his pack, and he was back within two minutes. 'Here we go,' he said, 'one emergency beer.'

'And what kind of emergency were *you* expecting?'

'Nothing too big, or I'd have stashed a few more. At least it's cold.'

'At least.' She reclosed the case and pushed it towards John, a distance that was about the thickness of a sheet of paper. 'Here, throw this outside and then keep that can out of my reach.'

'You don't want any?'

'I'll take a mouthful, and that's plenty for a train with no corridor and a few hours to go. We can't all pee off the side of the wagon when no-one's looking.'

And when the winds are sub-zero, John thought as he put her luggage with his own, *none of us can.* He climbed back into the cab and closed the door, and then with his arm again around Sara's shoulders he opened the beer one-handed. She'd already divided the chocolate; 'Here,' she said, 'I broke it in the middle. Count the pieces if you don't trust me.'

He squinted in the twilight. 'It's white.'

'White's harder to get. Better make damn sure you appreciate it.'

'I can safely say I'll remember the moment forever.'

Jerry Fraser. If John needed a model to work towards, Jerry Fraser would do as well as any in that he was over there on the easy side of the wall that John was trying to climb. Meanwhile here he was, stage one, almost as close to Jerry Fraser's girl as Fraser himself could ever be – except that it was just fluke, a pocket of circumstance that meant nothing. He was tense wherever she touched, and he couldn't easily relax because the change would now be obvious; he kept his eyes open, aware of the texture of her hair against his cheek and the light insistent pressure of her body against his side. If he closed his eyes he might sleep, and if he slept he might dream; and considering the setup of the moment, he didn't have the courage to face it.

TWELVE

Somehow they missed the planned dropoff point at Fauske, and before John knew it they were covering the last hour of track with the sea to their left. This would be the Saltfjorden, a long and fairly shallow inlet with Bodø at the tip of its northern shore; pinpoints of light far off across the water threw reflections that rippled and danced with the swell, bobbing and weaving like stars in oil. They came into Bodø at two in the morning, and he saw that his fears had probably been justified – the freightyard lights were on, and the railway people were waiting.

By keeping their heads down in the cab they missed being seen by the two men who stood either side of the track and scanned the wagons as they came in; the men wore day-glo vinyl worksuits, and one of them had a hand radio. The station and freightyards at Bodø seemed to share the same plateau of quayside land, four open tracks with no formal divisions between them – looking out towards the water they could see a line of standing trucks and then an unfenced container yard, and then beyond that the waterfront. The plateau was bounded by a high-banked road on the townside, and by the station and ware-house buildings at its end.

They were blocked in every direction, but it still seemed that they had a chance to sneak out without being seen; the yard lights only covered the immediate unloading areas, and there were plenty of shadows if only they could get to them. John wanted to run for the empty passenger

111

train that stood between them and the road, climbing through one of the carriages and then scrambling up the embankment on the far side, but Sara shook her head. She wanted to go for the water, to loop around by the quay and emerge on the other side of the station hall, and since John supposed that she knew the layout he couldn't disagree.

No more than two or three men were beginning the search at the front of the train, probing the loads with flashlights. It was a good hour for freight-hoppers, a bad hour for raising the staff to pin them down. John and Sara made a run for the cars on the next track and slipped under the linkages between two wagons, Sara first and then turning to take the bags as John passed them over before following. There were no shouts, no sounds of running; next came a line with no train, and the jetties fifty yards away. Bulldozer tracks crossed the open ground to its edge, and there was snow floating on the black water. There were also a few low Portakabins with lights burning outside, but no signs of people.

They waited in the darkness behind an aluminium Majortrans container, but not for long – the snow on the ground around them was sufficiently unspoiled to show a trail, and when the searchers reached their flatcar they'd be easy to follow. As soon as they were sure that the station's meagre security was still being concentrated around the train itself they moved out, past a row of five Nissans that were waiting under factory wax and towards the engine sheds and freight administration building. If they could get past these without being seen, Sara whispered, there would only be the station forecourt left to cross.

The station hall itself was a dull redbrick building with a clock tower and an upstairs restaurant, which was closed. The forecourt consisted of a wide turning circle and a ramp which climbed to road level. There were taxis in the circle before the glass doors, and a *politi* transit van parked at the bottom of the ramp. There were at least two police officers sitting inside it, and they had all the view they'd need.

'Something's wrong,' Sara said. They were behind a corner of the freight offices, with the building concealing them from the police van. 'There are too many people around.'

'You're telling me,' John agreed, but that wasn't how Sara had meant it.

'The waiting room's supposed to close, midnight until five. But look.'

And she was right; John could see a blurred mixing of colours through the glass, and as he was watching a middle-aged couple came out of the doors and got into one of the taxis. They seemed so dog-weary that John felt sorry for them.

'They were in my carriage,' Sara said. 'That was our train.'

But fourteen hours late? They backed off from the corner, afraid that one of the officers might glance up and catch them peeking. Sara said that she'd had an idea, and she explained it to John; he looked at her with the kind of apprehension that he usually reserved for genial dentists, but he had to admit that it would probably work.

Another taxi was setting off and two more were coming back as they swapped bags. Sara's case felt absurdly light to John, and she swayed uncertainly under the weight of his pack – fortunately it wouldn't be for long, as the idea was to scramble any descriptions that might have been sent ahead. He waited in the shadows for a couple of minutes after she'd gone, and then he set out to follow.

He went through the gap between the offices and the engine sheds, and it brought him out at the station end of the passenger platforms. He didn't even glance to see how the search was going on, but he made straight for the doors to the booking hall.

The numbers inside were reducing fast, already down on the crowds that he'd seen across the forecourt. Even as he was walking in there was a group of people leaving through the glass doors directly opposite; most of those remaining were in a single line at the ticket window, sag-eyed and spiky-haired, whilst partners and parents and children camped with their luggage on the waiting-room benches. Sara was near the end of the line; she looked over and gave him a grin, the only bright face in the chain gang. He smiled back, and she indicated that he should sit down and wait.

He planted himself on a bench with a Chinese woman and her two children, both of them asleep. The hall seemed indecently bright for the hour, and after the night air outside it was also stuffy. He wondered what Sara was doing; the plan had been simply to mix with the people inside and to leave with a group of them, but it seemed she'd had another idea. He must have become drowsy, because the next thing that he knew was that he was being shaken lightly by the shoulder.

It was Sara. The Chinese family had moved on, along with most of the other people from around him – the line was down to three, and the others who were left were mostly looking out of the glass doors as if they were wait-ing to be met. Sara was holding a slip of paper. She said, 'Come on, John, I got us a passport.'

She made a point of studying it as they walked out past the *politi* van, and then she handed it to him as they climbed the long gritted ramp out of danger. It was some kind of booking form for a hotel, hastily scribbled out. 'You know where we're going?' he said, and she nodded.

'Only the most expensive crash in town,' she said, 'cour-tesy of the railways.'

She'd managed to pick up the story by standing next to the telephone in the hall and listening to a small fat man making a breathless explanation to his wife; the train – *their* train, the one from which they'd been dumped – had hit a deep snowbank somewhere north of Mo-i-Rana and had tried to push its way through without waiting for a snowplough, with the result that the engine had been ruined and they'd had to shunt all the carriages back to the last station on the line. There they'd waited for almost ten hours without food and with deteriorating sanitation as another engine was brought all the way from Trondheim. Buses were arranged to bring in a number of connecting passengers whose own service had been cancelled at Mo because of the line blockage. The little man seemed more annoyed because he'd run out of things to read.

Now the NSB was offering rooms at the SAS-Royal hotel in Bodø to anyone that needed them, and Sara had thought it worth a try; the booking clerk hadn't even asked to see her ticket, he'd just written out the voucher and handed it over before starting on the next. It was an unlooked-for bonus, something that would keep them from walking the streets until the sunrise; all this, and breakfast too. John was hoping they'd have large napkins.

Nearly three a.m., and Bodø was bright and deserted. He'd been expecting some windswept frontier shanty, but he couldn't have been more off-beam; it was pleasant and urban, with wide streets and shopfronts that blazed like the day. The going underfoot was thick ice but firm, and as they walked the length of the Sjøgata to the SAS-Royal they were passed by the same taxis twice over as the last of the better-heeled made their way to the free shakedowns.

The hotel was a modern high-rise in a square which overlooked the breakwater. Most of the ground floor was given over to a mall, displays of menswear and perfume and a basement delicatessen reached by escalators. At this hour everything was shuttered, and the escalators were still. Sara got in line again, this time for a key, and then they took the lift to the seventh and their room.

John sat on one of the twin beds and looked around as Sara used the bathroom. The walls were plasterboard covered with kapok and the furniture was hotel-forgettable 1960. There was a colour TV, a room service menu in two languages (mainly English), and four channels of junk music at the touch of a switch. The whole assembly could have been anywhere in the world; the

115

SAS-Royal was the kind of hotel where tourists booked in to sit looking at each other.

He kicked off his boots and lay back on the bed. It was bliss, but he knew from long experimentation that sleep could come anywhere – it would be more important not to miss breakfast.

He was dreaming when Sara emerged. She stood by his bed and watched for a while. Then she touched his shoulder, and when he rolled over onto his side she thought he was going to wake; but he didn't, and for the rest of the night he was quiet.

THIRTEEN

'If we can make it to Narvik,' Sara explained over break-fast, 'we'll be okay. There's a helicopter service that's under contract to Teamverk. We can get a ride in.'

'Are they likely to take us?'

'Not as a special trip, but if somebody wants to come out we can tag along with the pilot for the first half of the ride. I hate to say this, but we can . . .'

'I know, show him my letter.'

'And Jerry's cheque. I'm going to wring that useless piece of paper for all it's worth.'

John Visco looked again at the map. They'd cleared one half of the table in order to spread it out, and Sara had made a small mark on the coastline to show him where Tromstad lay. It looked pretty remote, and she'd explained how there wasn't enough traffic to justify ploughing the mountain roads.

He said, 'Hold on, though, Kendall Riggs put a freeze on the project. There won't *be* anyone coming out.'

'You don't know Ray Kreiger, he won't be able to stop them if they want to go. He likes to beat his chest and play the caveman, but they're all better at it than him. Except Jerry, that is. Jerry isn't weak, but he just doesn't want to play.'

'But if we don't get a ride, is there a boat service?'

'Only the village's own boats, when they come to get supplies or deliver their fish. So we can forget it.'

'Has there been some kind of argument?'

She hesitated, and looked towards the windows. The

restaurant was around the side of the hotel, with a view of the small boats and dinghies in the town's innermost harbour. Beyond them stretched the breakwater, and beyond that was the sea and the islands. She said, 'No argument, only that they don't want the project and they show it.'

'Most places would be angling for a decent cut.'

'Not Tromstad. As far as the mines are concerned, nobody's interested. The last time they were worked at a profit was during the occupation. The army took over the village and most of the men were used as forced labour, and then when the Germans pulled out they dynamited all the workings and the machinery.'

'Scorched earth.'

'What?'

He realised that he'd been taking her English for granted, and that this was an idiom she probably didn't know. 'A scorched earth operation, it's when you pull out fast and destroy everything you leave so the enemy can't get the use of it.'

'Well, they didn't leave anything, there's hardly one of the original buildings standing.'

'But it's starting to look now as if there's some value in the mine?'

She shrugged. 'Who knows?'

It was ten-thirty, the end of the breakfast time. Over by the dancefloor, two hotel waitresses began stripping the buffet table and salvaging what they could from the wolverines of the night train. John said, 'Paul Steen probably knows. I suppose we should be grateful to him, he at least tried to give us a warning.'

'Which makes him a poor sort of spy. Considering the way things are going, I'm finding it hard to think gratitude towards anybody. How do I look?'

The question took John by surprise. 'Fine,' he said uncertainly, and after the automatic response he immediately started to wish he'd grabbed the opportunity to say something more positive.

'I mean it,' she said, and it seemed that she was looking for objectivity rather than flattery, 'am I a mess or do you think I look a little bit cute?'

So now he was obliged to study her, to meet her eyes; they were the blue of faded denim. He wondered why she was asking and what he should say. She'd brushed out her hair and retied her braids – that and a cold-water wash had been the most that either of them had been able to manage that morning, because there was some problem with the hot water supply to the room and neither had felt sufficiently hard-faced to complain about it. She'd also, he realised for the first time, added a faint trace of makeup.

'A cute mess,' he said, and inside a voice was yelling *blew it, didn't you*? This is Jerry Fraser's girl, he told it, and the voice was suddenly quiet.

She pushed her chair back from the table. She said, 'Remember that when you're being impressed by how I got us to Narvik.'

'What are you going to do?'

'I'll tell you when it's done. Let me have your letter.' He handed it over, and she went on, 'Wait around and look after the bags. Watch the boats if you want something to do, I might be an hour or so.'

They moved him out of the restaurant ten minutes later so he went through to sit on the Balustraden, a windowless inner balcony from which the hotel guests could peep down through a forest of plants to watch the native wildlife in the mall below. He sat at a table behind someone else's empty coffee cup, feeling slightly alarmed to be alone in a strange country and without his letter – its absence seemed to make a cold space in his jacket, and he felt the urge to unfold and check it even though he knew it wasn't there. It was like an itch.

And there was something else; Sara's absence was making him unsettled, although it was no more than the slightest feeling from a habit only two days old. He wondered if she might be feeling the same – but from the way

119

she'd breezed out of the restaurant without even looking back, the answer to that one was easy.

He kept a watch on the mall below and so he saw her coming, squeezing her way through a crowd of badge-wearing convention people and then past two soldiers in fatigues and red berets. She looked as if she'd had some success in whatever she'd set out to do, and she confirmed it when she arrived on the upper level less than a minute later. Sara was almost glowing as she sat down opposite him.

'We're on our way,' she said. 'How are you in a kitchen?'

'Deadly. Why?'

'You're cooking breakfast for ten sailors in the morning.'

'If I'm cooking breakfast in the morning, what are you doing for them tonight?'

She gave him a sideways knowing look and a wink. Then she said, 'Getting dinner.'

Nothing was going to be happening until the late afternoon, so they took a walk along the town's main quayside. One of the Polar Express ships was loading, swinging a powered hoist around to drop a net to the quay. Two fork-lifts were stacking the pallets, and there were others in line over by the warehouse doors – John saw pre-cut wood, veneers, tagged engine parts, old gas cylinders with new labels, numbered milk churns; small trade but fast turnover, so fast that most of the stuff hadn't even been taken into the warehouse, just set down to be fork-lifted away again within a few hours.

He must have seemed preoccupied, because Sara said, 'Don't you think you can manage?'

It was a moment before he realised what she meant, and then he said, 'I know all the basics. But I've never done it times ten before. What about you?'

'Same. I suppose you just make the portions bigger and hope they don't run out.'

120

'There's nowhere to run on a boat.'

'I meant the food.'

'I was thinking about me.'

The net went up and away, leaving the quayside clear for them to walk through. Sara was about to say something else, but then she seemed to hesitate.

John said, 'How did you manage to fix it?'

'First I went to a freight agent and asked about boats leaving for Narvik. We timed it well, because some of the stuff from our train is being carried up the coast. Then I went looking around the dock offices until I found one that looked promising. I went in and explained the situation and asked for help. I showed the captain your letter.'

'And that gave it away.'

'He doesn't read much English. I only needed the letterhead to impress him.'

'I'm glad it finally impressed somebody.'

They stopped to look in the window of a chandlers' in the next block after the warehouses, at the outboard motors and the survival suits and the fifty different kinds and colours of rope. Sara was hesitating again; John could sense that something was coming, and he wasn't sure that he'd like it.

Finally she said, 'I didn't tell him all the truth about us.'

'What did you say?'

'I told him we were lovers.' She gave him a smile, wan and apologetic. 'I said we were running away because my parents don't like you. You're chasing this job to make some money so that we can afford to get married.'

John nodded slowly. He was dazed by the idea, and flattered by the casting. He said, 'Anything else?'

Sara was staring at a display of Shelby-Teknikk cabin heaters for no particular reason. She said, 'You'll have to remember that I'm pregnant, as well.'

(*For real?* flashed through his mind with horrifying speed, but she went on,)

'It was the first thing I thought of. I told him that I got

121

sick and passed out at a party, and the child isn't yours. But you still love me anyway.' She gave him a cautious, sideways look. 'Did I do wrong?'

'No,' he said after a moment. 'No, you did fine.'

'It got him on our side. And he said that if you'd give a hand with the unloading when we reach Narvik, that would cover our passage.'

She was still uncertain of his approval, so he did his best to reassure her. 'Sure,' he said. 'Why not? I thought I was going to have to sleep with the bo'sun.'

She smiled, and her relief showed. 'Nothing *quite* so extreme,' she said.

Bodø wasn't so big that the afternoon could slide on by without them noticing; passing the time – especially without money – had to be worked at. Best of the bargains was the town's small museum behind the cathedral, because the admission charge had been waived for the off-season. They were the only visitors. Most of the exhibits were about fishing, the boats, the nets, the hooks, the systems; there were dioramas showing how fish could be dried or pickled, and models in large cases like fish-tanks where a sheet of rippled glass stood in for the surface of the sea. Sara translated the captions and added some background of her own. It filled an hour.

An hour was about what it took to cover a circuit of the town's centre, twice. The day wasn't so cold that they couldn't walk to the end of the breakwater, an immense stack of rocks on the seaward side protecting an inner concrete wall and walkway, although it seemed a lot colder when they finally made it back. Sara reckoned that she knew where the cheapest hot drinks in town were to be found.

'The railway station?' John said. 'Are you kidding?'

But she was right. They went, not to the *Cafena*, but to the stone-floored waiting room below it, and there they dug into what was left of their funds to feed the drinks machine. When they'd got two cups of chocolate they fed themselves on what John had managed to make disappear from the breakfast buffet.

'Four boiled eggs?' Sara said with disbelief. 'How did you manage to carry four boiled eggs?'

'Sleeves,' John said. 'And the little bastards were hot.'

His first worry, that by going back to the station they were asking to be recognised and picked up, was groundless. Nobody knew them, and probably nobody cared. It was here that they passed the last hour before it was time to go and look at their ship.

She was called the *Inger Sorensen*, and she was the largest of three boats tied off at a private jetty down from the Sjøgata. The jetty was small, and so the boats were moored in series out to seaward; they'd have to cross the deck of the first to get to their own, and the outermost – it looked like a small tug – would have to be unhitched before they could move out. Together they presented a dense tangle of masts, cables, derricks and cross-riggings, and from somewhere in the maze came the eye-popping flash and crackle of an arc-welder.

She was named for Captain Sorensen's wife, which perhaps made it unfortunate that she rode fat and low in the water. Long dripping hunks of ice had formed under her bilge outlets, and her plates – particularly around the prow – showed patches of rust which had been red-leaded and then frosted over. But for all her age and her scars she was a neat ship, showing the results of a care that could only be found in a family business.

Sorensen himself was on the deck, supervising a nephew with the welding gear ten feet up. He was bigger than John and bearded, somewhere in his fifties. He was wearing a green all-weather suit and a cap with scrambled braid on its peak. The cap was oily and begrimed, and it had the name of the ship hand-embroidered around the front. He seemed to light up when he was talking to Sara – she'd described him as being like a kindly uncle, and the description seemed to fit. It was also literal, because another nephew was called to show them to their cabin.

The boy spoke some halting English. He was called David, and he worked with the engines. There seemed to be a glassy gleam in his eyes that John, if he'd thought about it more carefully, might have identified as a kind of hero-worship. He led them down the companionway to one of the lower decks, opened a cabin door and switched on the lights, and from there they were on their own.

John had been expecting some unused corner, a room crammed with old tackle and perhaps just enough room to stretch out with their luggage for pillows. But it seemed that they'd been given one of the best cabins.

There were two bunks, one porthole, a shallow wardrobe with a sliding door; there was an area on the far side of the wardrobe that John couldn't see into, but which probably had room for a basin and a mirror. The lower bunk was freshly made-up, and someone had tied a red scarf around the light to soften it. Sara crossed to the porthole; on the wall-mounted table below it was a bucket with a bottle standing in fresh ice and a couple of chipped tin cups alongside.

She lifted out the bottle and turned it, dripping, to look at the label. 'Akvavit,' she said wonderingly. They'd been given a honeymoon suite, hastily thrown together with the props to hand.

'I don't believe this,' John said.

She pushed the bottle back into the ice and left it leaning. 'They're good people, John,' she said.

They were both silent for a few seconds, looking around. At the moment they were a couple of frauds standing in for people who didn't really exist; and John, at least, couldn't help envying them.

Sara was the first to move. She heaved her case onto the top bunk, which had no blankets but a stack of life-jackets back in the shadows. John unclipped the body belt and eased out of his pack. There was a painful knot between his shoulders. He said, 'I'll see if I can find any more bedding. What's the schedule?'

'Dinner in a couple of hours, once we're under way and clear of the inlet. Can you see this?'

Her voice had become an echo as she'd moved around the angle of the L-shaped cabin, and John went to join her. He said, 'What is it, a cupboard?'

'Shower and toilet. We pulled first class.'

Over her shoulder he could see that she was right. The cubicle was narrow but it was high, its ceiling a mass of exposed plumbing that had been painted over as had a run of electric cable and an aluminium hood belonging to the ship's ventilation system. There was a single shower head with a couple of lever-cocks around waist-level; it was all dusty, and obviously long unused. John said, 'It probably doesn't work.'

Sara reached forward and twisted one of the levers. An immediate high-pressure blast like an explosion put spray over them both, and within a few seconds it was running hot. 'There, sceptic,' Sara said. 'This is a big boat with a small crew, they probably bought it old and cheap and don't need half the cabin space.'

'Bet it runs out,' he said as she shut off the water.

'We're on a boat, not a bus. As long as the engines are turning, there's hot water and steam. Who's going first?'

'You found it. Want me to take a walk?'

'No need, but you can watch the wall for a minute if you like.'

This was a new experience for him, listening to someone undress whilst he kept his eyes on the back of the cabin door by sheer effort of will. She gave him a call when it was okay for him to turn around. He relaxed slowly, like a violin without strings.

As she was showering, he rummaged and finally found some blankets; they were in a locker under the lower bunk, and when he pulled them out he found that they were warm – presumably the water pipes ran somewhere under there. He was closing the locker doors when Sara called to him again.

'John,' she said, 'I forgot my towel. Can you get it for me?'

'Where do you keep it?'

'Bottom of the bag, stuffed in a corner somewhere.'

Her jeans and the rest of her clothes were in a bundle next to her case. They were warm, too. He had to move most of the stuff in her case to get the towel out; she travelled even lighter than he did, but then because of sizing differences her clothes didn't take up so much room. Her lingerie certainly didn't – the underthings were so insubstantial that they were probably very expensive, in contrast with the rest of her bargain-basement outfit. Presents? Maybe, but it was none of his business. He replaced a taped package and a paperback copy of *Kristin Lavransdatter*, and closed the case.

The shower became a spattering, and then a drip. When John held out the towel and looked the other way, Sara's groping hand touched his own and rested for a second. There were some satisfying scrubbing noises for a couple of minutes before she said, 'That's all of it, I'm coming out.'

She didn't even wait for him to tell her that he was looking away. He heard her giggle, and said, 'What's so funny?'

'You're looking so *serious*,' she said.

She was dressed in a minute, everything clean from her case. She towelled her hair as much as she could and then brushed it out straight to dry; being wet made it darker, and it hung almost to her shoulders.

'I'll see you in the galley,' she said, and left him to it.

All of the must had been washed out of the shower, to be replaced by a soapy sweetness. John felt that the boat was starting to move as he watched the water run grey around his feet, and when he came out he looked through the cabin's porthole. They were out of the harbour and moving into the Vestfjorden, the open channel that would be their route through the Lofoten islands. The first of those islands was on the horizon, bleak, craggy and snow-dusted. As the *Inger Sorensen* steamed north, the land-masses would appear to merge until they became a solid chain of cliffs – the Lofoten Wall, an eighty-mile break-water of ice and rock. He dressed quickly in his last clean shirt and his spare jeans, and then he went to look for the galley and Sara.

She'd been right about the ship, it had seen better days. There was waist-high wood panelling along the companionways with oak grab-rails for rough seas, and even though the nephews obviously kept the fittings more or less polished and the floors more or less waxed this didn't measure up to the easy glow that would come with constant use. Since this level seemed to be for cabins and storage only, he climbed a central stairway to the upper deck.

The galley had been painted a light green colour, and then re-painted so often that all its corners and angles and pipe-joints had become softened and blurred. Its main feature was an open gas range with a safety rail around it, and there was also a large oven that could be locked with a wheel. He couldn't see Sara; she wasn't in the adjacent dining area and she wasn't in the side-room that had the double sink and a meat slicer, but she had to be some-where around because there was a fair-sized ham on the boil.

She was actually in the food stores, one along the deck and down some tight steps. She came in with two large cabbages and a bag of all the vegetables she'd been able to find; when she saw John, she said, 'You manage okay?'

'I managed,' he said. She'd tied her hair back with a loop of elastic. She set the cabbages on a board by the meat slicer, and John added, 'How are you doing?'

'I think I'm doing fine, now I know where they keep everything.'

'Didn't the regular cook show you?'

'They haven't got a regular cook, he left.'

John stepped aside as she crossed to check the ham. He

said, 'Wise man, maybe they were chasing him. Do you want any help, or do you want to take all of the blame?'

'There isn't space for a double disaster, no I'll have to do it alone. I'll let you keep an eye on the expresso.'

The expresso was a two-gallon urn by the serving counter with a number of rinsed mugs on a tray beside it. Coffee grounds went in at the top, and steam came out wherever it could. John stayed at a respectable distance and said, 'What do I have to do?'

'Instructions are on the side.'

'I know, but they're in Norwegian.'

She apologised as she came over; she switched between languages so often that she wasn't always aware of it. When she'd given him a translation from the anodised plate on the side of the boiler he played with the taps for a while; they spat hot water like sten guns. The first time he tried to fill a mug under one of them, it was blown out of his hand to bounce on the floor.

Two deckhands came into the dining area as he was into the next lesson, which was getting something out of all the high-pressure plumbing that actually resembled coffee. This scrambled everything he'd learned, although it was Sara they were watching – they were both about seventeen, and they looked like orphans at a toyshop window. She'd diced the ham and then returned it to the stock, adding everything she'd found. The stew was so dense that it was taking her two hands to get the wooden spoon around, the cabbage strips wrapping it like seaweed.

The deckhands were patient enough as John wasted four coffees to get two, and each took his mug with a polite nod. Then they hitched themselves on the edge of one of the two big dining tables and chatted for a while. Something was amusing them. John said to Sara, low enough so they wouldn't hear, 'What are they talking about?'

'Nothing about us,' she said, 'so don't worry.'

She whipped up some powdered arrowroot to thicken the broth. When the two deckhands had half-emptied their mugs they came to John for refills before they wandered off; this time he got it right. Whilst Sara was lining up plates on the counter he took a look in the pan and said, 'What are they getting?'

'Some of everything, and I'm calling it *lapskaus* to play safe. That's hash, to you, and it's nearly ready. Can you get everybody along here?'

'What do I do, bang on a plate?'

'I think they'll get the message if you just go along and tell them.'

But it wasn't so easy, because he'd already forgotten what he'd observed of the *Inger Sorensen*'s layout. He finally tracked down the bunkrooms by the sound of voices and music from a cheap radio; the door to the below-decks corridor was open, and as he approached he heard scufflings of suppressed panic.

There were four of them in the two-man cabin, and as John appeared in the doorway they were all looking towards him with apprehension and embarrassment. When they realised who he was, they started to relax.

It was a moment before John caught the odour, and it was unmistakable; grass. The smell always made him want to gag, which probably staked him at the bottom of some-body's social ladder. They'd probably been afraid that he was the captain. He said, 'I came to tell you the food's ready. Anyone understand me?'

'Thank you, yes,' the crewman nearest the porthole said. One of the others checked his watch – meals on time, this was something unusual. The first crewman added, 'Have you told Villi and David?'

'Not yet. Where do I find them?'

'Engines,' said the one nearest the door. He was John's age, almost a group patriarch. 'Don't worry, we take care of it. You tell bridge.'

Telling bridge wasn't such a problem, although emerging onto the upper deck made him wish for the jacket that was hanging behind the door of the cabin; he stepped into a hail that came down like beads. Most of the *Inger*

129

Sorensen's superstructure had been raised on the back one-third of the hull to leave extra space for deck cargo, so that the bridge, funnels and lifeboats all seemed to be crowded together so much that they were climbing over one another for air.

There were two others on the bridge with Sorensen, one of them a girl of about twenty-three. This surprised John for a moment, but then he thought, *why not?* She was watching a radar screen. Sorensen had the wheel, and John waited at the back in the green night-sight glow, wary of speaking in case the distraction put them on a reef. After a short time the second man, who was closer to Sorensen's age and probably a brother or a cousin if he was a relative at all, glanced over towards John and asked him a question; at least, John assumed as much from the inflection, which was all that he understood.

He tried to remember Sara's word for hash, and couldn't. 'Smorgasbord,' he said, and that made all three of them look at him in puzzlement.

'Sorry,' he said, 'it's the only word for food I can think of.'

The girl translated it for the others, and it brought a big laugh. John did his best to smile along. Sorensen spoke to the girl and the first officer, and they both moved out; John hesitated before he followed, but realised that the captain had to stay. Sorensen glanced at him, and he chuckled. 'Smorgasbord,' he repeated softly, and chuckled again.

The silent messroom that he'd left was full of noise when he returned. The whole crew was squeezed in around one of the tables except for David, the boy who'd taken them to the cabin. He was through in the galley with Sara, showing her a couple of deep aluminium mess tins with clamp-down lids and carrying handles – one for the bridge, one for the engine room, neither of which could go unmanned. Now that John had some idea of where he was going, he offered to take them along.

Sorensen was too busy to pay him any attention this

130

time. He was tied up in a radio exchange and watching the radar screen. John could see the green shaded blur of the coastline and the blips of two other vessels; there were more, fainter blips to the north-west. John knew that he'd been seen even if Sorensen couldn't acknowledge him, so he left one of the canisters on the chart table and withdrew.

The engine room was two decks down with its door chained open for air. It wasn't actually a room, it was a below-decks area that took up most of the rear end of the ship and cut through the various levels. John went down over his head into a sea of sound, mainly a loud hammering with many other layers of noise beneath; when he reached the bottom of the metal stairway he looked around for Villi.

He was on the other side of four immense cylinders that were capped with interweaving masses of cable and piping, and he was working on a stripped-down pump. Villi was also wearing ear protection, for which John was starting to feel a need. He stepped over an opened five-litre can of red lead and hefted the lunchbox through the gap between the cylinders and a set of massive silver-painted ducts that ran up the outer skin of the ship and overhead to the funnel, and when the engineer saw him he lifted his wrench and used it to indicate some horizontal piping. Villi was obviously David's father, the resemblance was so close.

John looked at the piping, wondering what he was supposed to do. The pipes shimmered with radiant heat, and they were kinked slightly for some reason. And then he saw it; he lifted the mess tin, and it fitted perfectly into the gap.

Villi grinned, and winked. John left with the feeling that, noise apart, there was more fun to be had working with the engines than with the captain.

When he got back to the galley and the messroom, the crew had gone again. Sara had cleared most of the debris to the end of the table to make a space for herself, and she was just finishing a plate of the *lapskaus*. She was almost beaming; she said, 'I got away with it.'

'Nobody died?'

'They actually said they liked it. I don't think they've been used to much.'

The running around had kept John from being hungry, but now he said, 'Is there any left?'

'I saved you some. Help yourself off the range.' He went through, expecting to find some boiled-out cabbagewater with a thin film of fat on its surface and not much underneath, but what she'd actually done had been to skim off a couple of pints of the stew and keep them in a separate pan. As he was ladling out, she went on, 'The regular cook left them six weeks back for a job with the Frederick Olsen line. They've been taking turns ever since and I think it's been grim.'

'They've got a big disappointment coming in the morning,' John said as he pushed some more plates aside and sat down.

'If you can read the labels, there's no problem.'

'That's the problem.'

'Look at the pictures, then.' But when Sara looked around the kitchen she saw no pictures, just the aftermath of the buffalo stampede. She said, 'Am I being lousy if I leave you with all this?'

'There isn't much. It's like clearing up after dogs, one bowl each. Where does it all go?'

'Wherever it fits,' she said, pushing back from the table. 'As long as you can find everything again tomorrow, that's all that counts. You mind if I head back to base?'

'Carry on. You earned it.'

'Sure?'

He nodded. 'I did this for a living, once. Eight weeks in a Norfolk restaurant.'

'Never argue with a professional,' she said, already on her way to the door. 'See you later.'

He started with the French carbon-steel knives, because they'd rust if they weren't cleaned and dried straight away

– in fact they were already slightly pitted and discoloured, a sure sign of the lack of a full-time chef. It was a shame, because they were quality blades even if they were a mismatched set – he'd seen enough hotel gear to know.

He filled the pans with hot water and suds, and put them to one side. Then he ran fresh water into the sink and started on the cleanest of the plates and utensils; the rest would go into the water to soak as the first batch were dried, and the pans would come last. These weren't so impressive as the knives, battered-looking tinware that looked as if it had been bounced around the deck often enough.

As he worked, he found himself yawning. The short-term pickup of the shower was wearing off. The previous night in the SAS-Royal had been no more than a few exhausted hours squeezed between late arrival and breakfast, whilst the two nights preceding that had simply been darker stretches in transit. It took him half an hour to finish which, he reckoned as he walked back towards the cabin, had worked out pretty well; it gave Sara time to get herself straight, pick out a bunk and get herself into it without them having to mess around with coy arrangements. She'd probably be asleep by now.

He tapped very lightly on the door when he got to it, just in case. He listened, but all he could hear was the deep pulse of the engines and so he gently turned the handle and stepped inside.

The main lights were out, but there was still a dim glow from the emergency bulb over the door. All of the life jackets had been moved to make way for the bags, and his own jacket had been laid across them. The lower bunk was empty. He glanced towards the shower, but that angle of the cabin was dark. He started to wonder where Sara had gone, and then her arms came around him from behind.

He froze, not knowing what to do; she took his hand and guided it around behind him, and as his fingertips brushed her skin John knew that she was naked.

133

Still holding his hand, Sara came around before him and gently pulled him towards the bunk. 'Don't say anything,' she whispered. 'Don't say a word.'

It had been a long time, but remembering now didn't worry him – nor, suddenly, did falling asleep. What made him apprehensive as she helped him undress and ran her tongue along his shoulder was the very real prospect of him wasting his strength in one short-lived and uncontrollable explosion.

As it turned out, he didn't need to worry. Because they had several runs at getting it right.

FOURTEEN

At first he hadn't thought that he'd be able to sleep in the narrow bunk with Sara against him, but he was wrong; they curled together like kittens in an intimacy that slowly unwound itself through the night hours. When John came awake – not with the usual snap that dumped him, uncomprehending, into the day, but a more gradual falling-away of layers – they were somehow back-to-back and barely touching. When he raised the blanket and rolled off the edge of the bunk, Sara hardly stirred.

They'd stopped somewhere; it was probably the change in the beat of the engines that had got through to him. Now they were idling, with an occasional plate-rattling surge as a reminder of their true power. He moved over to the porthole, feeling the deck's vibration through his bare feet; it was still dark out there, and he was too low down in the ship to see much more than the old truck tyres which were used as fenders and the overhanging mat of snow on the quay's edge, a few feet above.

This would be Korsnes, the *Inger Sorensen*'s planned stopover. Some stevedore work had been included in the agreement, so he thought he'd better make himself available. He showered quickly, and with the thin partition door closed – the idea was not to wake Sara, partly out of straight consideration and partly because, when they next faced each other, he didn't know what he was going to say to her. The intense activity of a few hours before had taken place without a word, as if they were beasts out of their cages while the keepers were away. Now there were

135

issues that would have to be faced, and this had never been one of John's biggest strengths.

He was getting into his jeans as a low grinding sounded from the hull, metal squeezing against timber for a couple of seconds before the *Inger Sorensen* began to move out. So much for his willingness to help, to establish some kind of equality with the kindergarten crew; but if there had been any heavy unloading he was sure that he'd have heard it, so perhaps this had been no more than a brief contract stop for the Post-Giro or something similar. Sara had turned over, but she was still asleep. Her tawny-blonde hair lay across her face and on the folded blanket they'd used as a pillow. She slept on as he let himself out of the cabin and closed the door as quietly as he could.

Korsnes was about two-thirds of the distance from Bodø to Narvik, according to his map; that should give them another four hours before they berthed, at least. If Sara was right, they'd be in Tromstad by the afternoon. Perhaps he should try to see Kreiger right away, or perhaps he should give himself a chance to assess the situation; he'd have to play it as he found it. Right now, he was playing chef.

Unemployment had helped put a polish on his domestic skills, so he wasn't really worried about his basic competence – the worry was that he didn't know what to give them. He somehow couldn't imagine a ship's crew picking over the lightweight buffets that he'd seen in his two hotels to date; he knew of *rømmegrøt*, a kind of sour-cream porridge, but he didn't know how to make it.

The layout of the cold store was no guide. There seemed to be too much of everything, so that the oldest of anything that wasn't frozen or canned was starting to go bad. Obviously with the regular cook moving out the supply orders had continued, but there had been no systematic rota of menus to run the stocks down evenly.

Fuck 'em, they could find out what an English breakfast was like. He got together a vacuum pack of bacon, a box of eggs, two salami (no sausages), three frozen loaves,

136

and a can of tomatoes that was almost the size of a bucket. He loaded them all into a dumb waiter that Sara had missed the previous evening, and then he ran it up to the galley.

The spinning-wheel oven was racked like a breadvan inside, with shallow trays for shelves that could be removed and placed on top of the range. He could get everything going in relays, eggs last to keep them from hardening, and then he could return the trays to the oven on a low setting until the clientele arrived. The loaves wouldn't thaw in time, but he could break down the slices and fry them.

The door opened. It was Sara. She'd retied her braids and pinned them into place with a couple of gold slides. The sky behind her head was a fishbelly grey, lightening into mother-of-pearl. It felt like someone had taken a hold of his heart and squeezed.

She said, 'Hi, chef. Getting your fingers burned?'

'So far, so good,' he said, and he pulled out the last of the trays and carried it across to the range as she closed the metal door behind her. She managed one-handed, because under the other arm she had the mess tins from the previous night; then she came around by the range and watched as John dropped the tray into place. It was an exact fit, and the top of the cooker was covered from rail to rail. The other trays were already filled and frying, and this was for the eggs; almost a litre of corn oil, on with the heat, and then he started cracking shells.

She watched them lining up, all perfect yolks that started to skin over and go blind as the heat reached them. She said, 'You know, this is pretty fair going. You ever been a cook in another life?'

'I've known plenty in this one.'

She gave it a moment longer as a compliment to his efficiency, and then she took the mess tins over to the sink and started to run water into them. She said, 'I think you've been around more than you make out.'

Now that she was turned away, he let himself glance at

137

her. 'First time it's ever done me any good,' he said. He was looking for a lead, some kind of clue as to how things were going to be with them; was she regretful, embarrassed, delighted? John was prepared for the letdown, gentle or otherwise – but as far as Sara appeared to be concerned, they might have slept in separate cabins.

He turned back to the range as she cut the flow of hot water, so that she wouldn't catch his eye or see his doubt. She came back into the main part of the galley and said, 'How did you sleep?'

'Fine,' John said guardedly. 'You?'

'Okay, apart from the bad dream.'

'Bad dream?'

'Not mine, yours, although there seemed to be enough of it for both of us.'

'Sorry.'

'Don't be sorry. I was worried about you, that's all. It wasn't anything to do with . . .' she hesitated, trying to think of a delicate way to put it, '. . . with the rest of last night, was it?'

'Oh, no,' he said. 'It's an old problem. Nothing to do with you.' And he opened the door to the oven for the return of the trays; he'd preheated it on a low setting and now he started to transfer the food, all of it slightly underdone. It should keep for half an hour and come out fresh.

Sara came and leaned on the rail, out of his way but able to watch him. 'And you don't want to tell me about it?' she said.

'Only because it's dull.' He closed the oven door and spun the locking wheel. 'I'd rather talk about you.'

'Me?' Sara stuck her hands in her pockets, and sighed heavily as she looked around the galley. Then she studied her shoes. 'There isn't much to me,' she said. 'I don't know for sure what I want out of life, and I keep starting things that I can't finish.'

'Like what?'

'Like last night.' She met his eyes now; her own were

138

apologetic, regretful. 'I'm sorry, John. But there's still me and Jerry Fraser.'

'Oh, shit,' John said stonily, as all of the implications of the situation finally caught up with him. In spite of his early reservations, he'd somehow managed to edit Fraser out of the scenario altogether. 'Yes,' he said. 'I suppose there is.'

Sara pushed herself away from the rail, and moved towards him. She caught his hand in both of her own, and held it. 'Don't take it wrong,' she said, 'but we've got an agreement. He's kept me through the summer, so now I've got to work and keep him through the winter.' She smiled wanly. 'What we had, I thought it was going to last longer than it did. But it's a deal, and I've got to stick to it. Best to leave it, John. I like you, but I seem to be bad news.'

He shrugged. 'Whatever you say,' he said.

The crew arrived without having to be called. There was some bemusement when they were faced with a bunch of hot dishes at the centre of the table instead of the cold platter they'd been expecting, but the initial surprise turned into enthusiasm. Recent weeks of crew participation in the galley had made every meal an adventure, since there were some of the boys who couldn't open a pickle jar without getting a thumb in it; breakfast had commonly been delivered with all the finesse of a brick passing through a jeweller's window. Nearly all of them shook hands with John and Sara afterwards. The only one who didn't seem happy was Lars, the crewman who had spoken to John in the bunkroom. Sara asked him what was wrong, and got a rueful reply.

'Something he didn't like?' John asked.

'He thought it was all fine,' Sara told him. 'But he says it's his turn to handle the cooking on the way back, and he's not looking forward to the reception he'll get.'

'Better tell him we're sorry,' John said, and Lars grinned and offered to take the mess tins to the bridge and engine room. Both the captain and the chief engineer had worked through the night without relief. Villi would sleep through the berthing in Narvik, but the captain would have to stay awake to deal with the harbour people – but then, Lars added, that was what you got for being captain.

When the crew had all gone John and Sara split for a while, Sara stacking the plates by the sink ready for washing whilst John went down to the stores to clear out the worst of the perishables. He felt guilty as he emptied the rubbish bags over the *Inger Sorensen*'s downwind rail, but the gulls that hung in their wake seemed to think that it was a fine idea. He went down to the cabin and found that Sara had finished in the galley and was cramming all her gear back into her case; she'd stripped the bunk and stowed the blankets, the last traces covered. They should be getting into Narvik in about half an hour, she told him, and she suggested that they could go up and watch the approach from the deck.

John said, 'Will they let us?'

'No reason why they should stop us. If I stay down here with the engines thumping for much longer, I'll get a headache.'

It was turning out to be the first halfway decent morning that John had seen since his arrival. The sun was a weak yellow blur that had already climbed almost as high as it was going to get, and where the water caught the light it changed from black to silver. They came into Narvik along the headland where the ore railway ended in stockyards and a transport system to the loading quays, passing almost in the shadow of a Tokyo-based carrying ship that ran three city blocks from end to end. Mountains surrounded the deep natural harbour, pine-forested lower slopes with bare rock above, and on the narrow ground between the rock and the railway the town fitted in wherever it could.

The *Inger Sorensen* berthed at a modern wharf a little

way south of the town, and two of the crew wheeled out a gangplank and dropped it to the quay. The others were freeing the lifting gear and untying the ropes that had been used to lash spare pallets over the canvas of the deck cargo and prevent it from lifting in the wind. As Sara was picking up her case, John said, 'You'd better go ahead, but can you tell me how I get to the helicopter service?'

'Why?' she said. 'It's as easy if we go together.'

'I'm helping to unload, remember?'

So she put down her case and said that she'd wait for him, and John looked around and wondered exactly how he might be able to help. On the far side of the metal gallery that ran before the bridge, the captain was descending the outside stairway; he looked rumpled and red-eyed after a night's navigation. John went over to intercept him, and Sara came along to translate.

'Tell him if he'll say what he wants me to do,' John said to her, 'I'm ready.'

Sara translated, and Sorensen listened with a patient, almost indulgent smile. Then he looked at John, and John tried to guess what he might be thinking. He couldn't.

Sorensen put out a hand, as if to shake. There didn't seem to be any other interpretation, so John took it; the captain's palm was hard and scaly, and when he turned John's hand over in his own it showed pale and soft in the comparison. He laughed, and shook at last, clapping John on the shoulder.

'On your way, Smorgasbord,' he said, and then he released him. The captain went down the deck to meet the harbour official who was strolling across the quay towards the ship, and John and Sara went to pick up their bags.

They crossed the yard and the single freight railway track that cut between the goods terminal and the road, Sara walking along with her case held crosswise like an ant with a crust of bread. Some way ahead the traffic ran heavy, snow tyres rippling like rain.

141

As they moved, she gave him a couple of anxious looks. Finally she said, 'John? Are you upset?'

'Christ, no.' He glanced back towards the quayside, where the *Inger Sorensen*'s deck winches were being swung into play and a small truck was being backed around to the berth. 'It's what I was hoping for. Honest work like that would probably kill me.'

They climbed the gentle slope that took the road away from the sea and into the town. This was the main north-south highway, passing through Narvik between ferries on its way to the Cape; if the roads behind Tromstad had still been open, this would have been the place to try looking for a lift. As it was, Sara reckoned that it would take them about an hour to reach the airfield, walking through the town and down the other side of the headland. The air was sharp, because the sunlight that fell on the mountains was coming in at too low an angle to reach them. When they were in the centre they crossed a bridge which took them over the railway, and John asked if they could stop for a minute to watch the ore trains going through. She was more than ready to agree, and she sat on her case and massaged her stiff fingers through her mittens as he looked out over the wall. The bridge was the main link between the split halves of the town, and it was getting busier by the minute; it was the sheer pressure of pedestrians, some of them pushing shopping sleds, that eventually forced them to move on.

John took Sara's busted suitcase from her and carried it for a while, knotting the free leather of the straps together into a makeshift handle. She complained loud and long, but she let him; every few minutes she complained again, mainly to get over the message that she wasn't taking him for granted. As they were tramping down quiet Kirkegata to the sound of their own snow-deadened footsteps, a *politi* van pulled in ahead of them.

For a moment John looked around, even though he knew there was nowhere to run. This was the quiet end of Narvik, a residential suburb – the life had been drained out of it for the day. It was also, it seemed, the end of the line. The policeman had circled around the front of his van and was climbing over the shovelled ice that lay like a bank of flint along the edge of the road. He was alone, and he didn't look much more than twenty. He seemed friendly enough as he spoke to them both, and Sara answered for them; John was thinking this is nothing, wait until they see what's hidden in the towel.

But it certainly didn't look like an arrest; Sara was explaining something and the policeman was looking around as if there might be someone spying on him from a distance. When he saw only the houses and the church and the evenly white common ground between them, he turned and spoke again and waved a gloved hand towards his van; Sara nodded, and he moved to open the side door.

'What's going on here?' John whispered, and Sara checked that she couldn't be heard before she replied; the young policeman was half into the Transit and moving some accident gear to make room.

'He's giving us a lift to the airfield,' she told him, and when John looked disbelieving she added, 'It's his first day out alone with the van.'

So the *politikonstabel*'s expansiveness, his eagerness to do someone a favour and seem casual about it, suddenly became comprehensible. It was pride, solid and simple. John sat in the back of the van whilst Sara climbed into the front alongside the driver. He felt like a fox with a ticket to the hunt ball.

After some medium-rise apartment blocks the road took a steep hairpin, and suddenly they were looking down on the airfield. There wasn't much to it, just a narrow strip between the mountain and the fjord; two light aircraft were tied down in the turning area, by a yellow building which had *Narvik Lufthavn* lettered on its side. There was a telephone kiosk standing next to the building, and there were five cars parked in a row outside the perimeter fence. Modest wasn't the word for it.

143

They'd been in the van for less than five minutes, and could probably have walked it in fifteen. The policeman threw them a salute as he left them by some broken-down baggage trolleys and brought the van around to make the return climb up the valley side. His retreat cut the number of people on the airfield by one-third.

They entered the building through a door marked *Ekspedisjon*, but there was obviously no-one around. Presumably the control tower would be manned, but that was some distance away from the main field to take advantage of the extra height of the slopes. They pooled their change for the krone pieces, and John stayed with the bags while Sara went out to make a telephone call. As he was waiting he looked out of the windows onto the strip; the snow had been scrubbed right down to the tarmac. Presumably there was some regular paying service that was enough to keep the strip open through the winter, probably something like the twin-engined Navajo that he could see weighted down at the wings and tail by loaded tyres. There wasn't the runway length or the backup for anything bigger, so the Teamverk men who were heading out would probably have to use Narvik as a transit stop to Bodø, and then take an SAS internal flight to Oslo as the springboard for New York or Seattle.

Sara came back from the kiosk. 'There's a pickup flight booked to Tromstad,' she said, 'but the helicopter's tied up running medical supplies to one of the islands.' The pilot would have to come back to refuel, so they'd have to catch him then. Apparently he'd be going out empty, so it wouldn't be worth an argument to him.

The *Lufthavn* building was ticket office, baggage check and travel bureau all in one. As a waiting room, it scored low. They pushed some chairs around, and tried to get comfortable.

John said, 'You want to give me any advice? This could be your last chance.'

'Like what?' Sara said, sitting on one of the low vinyl chairs and rearranging her duffel coat to cover the gaps.

If there was any heat around, someone was saving money on it. 'I honestly don't know what I could tell you.'

'How did you come to be linked with Teamverk?'

'I'm not. Jerry's linked, and I'm just along for the ride. We met up when I was at the university in Oslo.' She looked at the ceiling, and sighed for a time when life had been simpler. 'Jerry advertised on the bulletin board.'

'For a girlfriend?'

'For a translator. He wanted someone in modern languages to translate mining journals and geology papers for him. I had to read them aloud, and he'd make notes. He'd bluffed his way into a job with a land survey team, and he needed to catch up.'

The approach sounded encouragingly familiar. John said, 'And everything developed from there?'

'We couldn't use the library and I was sharing a place, so we used his flat. After a while I began to stop over.' She gave him a narrow look that was only halfway serious. 'We seem to be getting away from the subject here.'

John held up his hands in innocent protest. 'Don't blame me,' he said. 'I only asked for advice.'

'I'm probably the last person in the world to give advice. You'd better make do with good wishes.'

'Right,' he said. 'This is real progress.'

Sara raised an eyebrow. 'Progress?'

'The first time I asked you, you told me to forget it.'

It was too cold to sit for long. Sara went to look through the travel brochures, and John wandered over to the window. Beyond the airstrip, the fjord ran flat and calm to the cliffs of the next headland a couple of miles away.

Something was beginning to make him uneasy, and pinning it down was proving to be difficult. It wasn't the job-hunt, or his chances, or even the way in which he was going to handle the no-ticket problem when it finally caught up with him; it was the kind of disquiet that wouldn't step out and show itself.

And it couldn't be anything to do with the previous

night, because that was ground that he'd already trodden. Although it was true that he'd never had an affair that was quite so short-lived before, none of the others had left him with the kind of mark that wouldn't heal . . . not unless you included the first, and that was the special little nick in the heart that everybody gets on the first time that they fall. Her name had been Caroline Thompson, and she'd been fifteen years old – a whole year above him in school, totally unreachable. On several Sunday afternoons he'd walked the streets around her home, hoping that she'd spot him and recognise him as he ambled by; it was only afterwards that he'd learned that his geography had been out by about a mile and a half.

He'd met her again, seven years later at a friend's party. She hadn't known him. She'd been Caroline Vickers then, and she'd spent most of her short evening casting nervous glances towards the telephone, half-convinced that the babysitter was going to call up with news of some disaster. But the strange part about it was that Caroline Thompson still had a warm little corner of his memory all to herself, still fifteen years old, never changing. Sometimes he suspected that when he was old and whacked-out and on his deathbed, his last thought would be of Caroline Thompson, and the arch of her slender schoolgirl's body as she leaned across to close his eyes and bless him away.

He wasn't sure how he'd been led onto that track, but a faint sound brought him out of it again; it was the distant beat of rotors, somewhere out over the water. Sara heard it, too, and was moving across the room as he looked for a speck in the sky. He saw it after a few moments, the glint of a perspex bubble as the helicopter dipped around to make its approach.

'Here he comes,' John said, but Sara was already behind him. She put a hand on his arm, and gave it a squeeze.

'Let's go see if we can get a ride,' she said, and started towards the door.

It was then that he knew; it was the end of a slow

process of realisation that had begun with the vision of Sara in the galley doorway with the morning sky behind her.

A special little nick in the heart.

Oh, Jesus. This was all he needed.

FIFTEEN

Her name was Kristin, and she was fifteen years old. She was marking off the distance she'd covered by the beat of her snowshoes, counting off the shuffling paces that would bring her down from the mountains and into Tromstad – and because she had no real idea of the distance, she had to keep moving her target.

It all seemed so different in the winter. The snowcover had turned their cattle run from a distinct path into a piece of guesswork, and even the landmarks didn't look the same. For as many summers as she could remember she'd made the journey two or three times in a week, usually with one of her parents or her cousin Olav, but on the trips when she'd covered it alone she'd never once had to stop and consider her bearings. She'd been thinking that she'd be able to get up to the *seter* and back again by noon, so that no-one would ever know that she'd gone against her father's orders; now here she was, mid-day long behind her and no backup explanations arranged with any of her friends.

Even the *seter* had been transformed, half-buried on the hillside with its verandah jutting out over the valley. Somehow she hadn't expected its rooms to be so cold and empty when she walked through them, or the three-sided view from the large sitting-room to be so bleak. For the first time that she could remember, she'd actually been glad to leave. The schoolbooks that she'd needed had been in the bedside cupboard where she'd placed them almost four months ago, fully intending to get around to reading the set passages sometime during the summer; but good intentions regarding school work seemed to fall apart in the grazing season, when there was always something more interesting to pull her away.

Of course, she knew the real reason behind her father's edict. It wasn't the presence of the wolf at all, although the animal gave a useful cover for the truth – which was that every man in the village feared for his wife or his daughters, not because of some rangy old mutt that was desperate enough to want to make off with one of the animals from the fold, but because of the Teamverk men. It was true that nobody had much wanted to see the mines reopened, but when news got around of the incident at the house of her uncle, the light-keeper – and rumours made it worse by suggesting that Roskva wasn't entirely innocent – then feelings of resentment and non-cooperation had hit the bell for the carnival prize.

In some ways it was Olav who got the worst of it, stranded between the two camps. He was at the age when a sense of alienation was easy to encourage, and although Kristin didn't exactly understand it in those terms, she was aware of his tendency to interpret the family's dislike of his friends as a resentment of himself. They'd been close, she and Olav – until about a year ago, that was, when the changes in her that were to drive them apart had become too obvious to ignore.

Those same changes might have put her in danger with the project men. Whilst the slow boys of the village were barely awake to the fact that a young woman was emerging from a child's body, the hard-core half dozen from the survey had whistled and shrieked at her every time they'd gone bouncing and skidding past in the Land-Rover with the beady-eyed man behind the wheel. Until the beady-eyed man ran it into a snowbank, that was. But now the project had been run down almost to nothing, so what kind of danger did that leave?

It left the wolf, and she was starting to believe it.

Getting late. Soon they'd be putting the lights on in the main square and the quay. With that, her last chances of getting by unnoticed would be gone. Three generations of Nystroms lived in the courtyard-related complex of the old wharf house, the sons marrying and bringing their wives into the family; with such closeness it was common for the children to be swapped around to make the most of shared bedroom space, and nobody could keep track of all of them all of the time. It might be that everyone was assuming her to be somewhere around, but if she missed the start of the late meal they'd know for sure she was missing. And at this moment, her father's anger was something that she feared more than any wolf.

She tried to put on some speed; but there was only one ideal, energy-conserving pace for snowshoes, different for everyone. She soon fell back into her own, habit and training pulling her down. They'd been fine going up, but for most of the way down she'd been wishing for her skis. The books didn't help, because they put her off-balance and made it difficult to keep up a rhythm.

Some way ahead, beyond this next stand of trees and over the dip, she could look for her first view of the village. By now she was no longer counting her steps, and it would give her something more concrete to aim for. The snow was taking on a bluish cast, a sure sign of failing light, and the dark masses of the trees were starting to merge. Her fear was beginning to settle, to become a localised ache whose root lay somewhere between her hips – it shocked her slightly that it should take this form, a sensation that she'd barely begun to recognise and identify even though her mother had patiently explained it all to her a couple of years before. It had sounded like a horror story to her then, and even now she had a tendency to reject it on an intellectual level; but sometimes her body would cry out on its own behalf with an edge so keen that it made her want to groan, and for some reason that she couldn't explain it was crying now.

Fifteen years old, untested in so many ways. She came over the rise and eagerly looked for her first view of the roofs and lights of Tromstad. She'd been wrong. All that she saw was another fold in the land, another treelined stretch of the snow-changed landscape.

Could she have mistaken her route on the return? Surely not, because on the way down she at least had her own tracks to follow. Even so, the way ahead was unaccountably strange, as if somebody had given the world a quick twist like a puzzle-cube when her back was turned. It was easy enough to check – all she had to do was glance down and there were the marks of her snow-shoes, still crisp from the morning. And there, equally fresh and running parallel, was a set of tracks she hadn't seen before.

She immediately looked behind her, and there was nothing; all around her, nothing. She looked at the tracks again, deep and well-spread with a powdery kickback of snow from each stride. It's a dog, she told herself, Leif Lokkeberg's mongrel, maybe – it would follow anybody that didn't kick it. But Leif Lokkeberg's mongrel was old and lame now, and hardly ever left his yard; this, she knew, was the mark of the wolf.

She'd see the village lights from the next rise, she was sure. It wouldn't follow any further – she'd heard Olav's story of how he and Jerry Fraser had seen it one day at the old mine workings, how it had run from them. Besides, these prints were as old as the morning. It couldn't have trailed her for much further than this, or she'd have seen the marks before. It probably wasn't even trailing her; their paths had simply coincided several hours apart, both of them taking the same line of level ground through the mountain pass. This was how she was thinking when she came across the dead animal.

It was a rabbit, long-legged and in its white winter coat, and it was stretched out to its full length across her old tracks. There was no way she could have missed it earlier. It didn't seem to be marked in any way, although the ravens had already had its eyes; the sockets had both filled with fat beads of blood. It lay there like a signal, or a gift. The killing seemed casual, automatic.

Kristin tried to circle around it, but she lost the sliding beat of the shoes and foundered in the snow. She was clutching the schoolbooks tightly to her chest, making them take on a greater value than they had in order to justify the fear that she was now feeling for real. The truth was that they weren't really so important after all; texts could have been borrowed, notes could have been copied, exercises could have been redone. What had seemed like a tremendous bore the previous evening now appeared to be quite sane and sensible. She forced herself to be calm, and regained her footing; then, without looking back at the blinded shape that lay behind her, she pressed on down the trail.

Now she was counting again, making the words sound out in her mind. She'd have counted aloud, but she was afraid of attracting attention. There wasn't much comfort, but at least it was making her concentrate.

And by the time she was up into the hundreds, she was also calmer; nothing had happened to her yet, and nothing was going to. Five hundred and fifty brought her around a bend in the trail and to her first view of the village lights and the fjord beyond.

This would be the final run, through the hayfields and the pastures to the streets of upper Tromstad, and then down through the cobbled alleys to the footbridge and the village centre on the headland. No wolf would dare follow her *there*. Already her imagination had consigned it to her past – the idea of it trailing her with patience, watching her back as she slogged on uphill in the early morning light, gave her a small fix of terror that thrilled rather than sickened. Her real fears now were back where they'd started, with her father.

She was eager, and she was also more tired than she realised. From here the descent was steeper, and with the first couple of steps her legs gave way. She came ploughing down into the snow as if they'd been roped from under her.

She was more surprised than hurt; in fact she wasn't hurt at all, but she'd obviously been pushing herself harder than she'd known. Getting up this time wasn't as easy as before, because she'd managed to lose one of her shoes; that's what came of keeping the webbing ready-tied so she could be lazy and simply slip her boots in and out without any extra work. She could see the orange plastic mesh a couple of yards away, bright even in the twilight. She hoped she hadn't snapped a buckle.

The snow was too deep and too soft for her simply to walk across, so she'd have either to slide her way along or else get up and manage some kind of hop. Either way it was going to be a struggle, because there was nothing solid for her to get a hold on.

It was while she was trying to decide which course would be best that the wolf came into view around the turning of the trail.

It seemed as surprised as she was. It stopped, watching her.

The animal was much bigger than she'd expected, full-coated and powerful, and it continued to hold back at a safe distance. By Kristin's reading of the situation, it hadn't really intended catching up with her, just to pace along and keep some kind of regular gap between them; she couldn't imagine why, but she did her best to get some reassurance out of the idea. All her confidence went, however, when she perceived the beast's eyes.

They were blue, and they glowed. No reflection of the snow-twilight could explain it, they glowed like they were lit from behind. The effect was cold and impersonal, lightning on ice. Then, before she could move, came something that scared her even more; it tried to stand.

It wasn't simply a wolf trying to get onto its hind legs, it was something else; something halfway between, because it started to lose its wolf-shape as its paws came clear of the ground. But then, when it tried to take a

153

faltering step, it was with an animal's posture and unsteadiness.

Kristin tried to rise and run, but she'd forgotten about her missing shoe and she fell again. She went deeper into the snow, and it slowed her and pulled her back. Without looking around, she could hear the soft, even crunch of footsteps coming nearer. Her other snowshoe was still a yard beyond her reach, although if sheer desperate will could have affected the distance it would have contracted with a snap.

She looked over her shoulder, ignored the powdered snow that clung to her face. The effort of standing seemed to be exhausting the animal, and when it dropped back to all-fours it hadn't covered a third of the distance between them. It glared at her; those brilliant eyes were the only detail that she could make out in its otherwise shadowy outline. She didn't want to see any more, but she kept a fix on it as she started to inch back through the snow towards her fallen shoe.

The wolf was watching and panting, aware of what Kristin was trying to do but momentarily unable to reach her. She started to feel around behind, and when her fingers didn't hit the plastic she had a sudden fear that the snowshoe had been quietly taken away while she wasn't looking; but she was still a couple of inches short, that was all, and when she pushed back a little further she caught hold of the webbing. The buckle was still in place.

She brought it around and put it on, nervous enough to fumble it on the first attempt but cool enough to get it on the second. The wolf followed every move, like a starving man at a bakehouse window. It started to pant more heavily as it saw her stand, getting her feet under her in the loose snow that she'd kicked up and then stepping forward onto the pure surface. The shoes wouldn't let her reverse; she could only shuffle forward, which meant that she'd have to make a tight circle putting her back to the animal in order to head for the safety of the village.

But she didn't have her books; and whilst she knew that

they'd become a concern too trivial to be bothered with, there was a small and irrational part of her mind that was reminding her about them loudly enough to break her concentration. She couldn't see them. Behind her, the sounds of effort as the animal again tried to stand. She should have been moving; instead, she looked back.

She was just in time to see it dropping to the ground, defeated. However much it wanted to be like a man, it stayed as a wolf and was crushed by the attempt. This brought Kristin's nerve back; enough of it, at least, to look for the books that had baited her into this situation. The wolf glared on, a prisoner of distance and incapability.

She'd have to approach it to get her books. Only a little, but the fact was enough to make her hesitate. I'll be safe, she thought; even standing, it's too slow to catch me now. She moved around to face it again, and started in towards where her carrying-strap lay on the snow.

And as she pulled the books out of the hole they'd dug for themselves, the wolf got upright again. It swayed triumphantly, and its breathing steadied; Kristin's new confidence seemed a little less sound. She hastily shuffled about and started on the trail, and the man-animal followed.

She'd been mistaken. It was learning, and now it was faster. Its breath was sounding less like the grinning gasp of a wolf and more like a man's. There was the village, not so far ahead, every pinprick of light a window to a room with a door and a lock; surely nothing could happen to her so close to the safety she'd known all her life. She couldn't glance back without breaking her stride and falling, but she knew that the beast was getting nearer. She started to count, to keep herself going and to bring up her speed. She couldn't remember what came after six.

But more than a kilometre went by, and still it hadn't reached her. They were almost at the livestock fences of the summer pastures, the fields where the hay was strung out on wires to dry in Tromstad's brief sunshine; the trail would lead alongside the fence for a short distance and then end in a stile. If it could barely stand, it would never be able to manage the climb. She'd be home in minutes, and during the night the men of the town would be out to hunt the animal down just as they had ten years or so before. She made the turn at the fence and went alongside it, almost running; the snowshoes flapped against her heels and the loose surface powder came up around her like spray, but it felt like she was going too fast to be stopped.

The day hadn't yet faded completely, but it didn't have far to go. The snow reduced everything by its contrast to the barest silhouette, a shadowplay version of reality against a washed-out blue background. Here was the fence, a finely-cut effect of sticks and rails, and there ahead was the stile. This was more substantial, a four-foot ladder in a double A-frame of logs. Kristin slung her books over into the field, and climbed to follow them.

It was as she was swinging herself over the top that she saw the animal hurdling the fence with doglike ease, landing on all fours and then standing again within a couple of steps. As it started to round back towards her, Kristin's snowshoes tangled in the bars of the stile. She was pitched headlong into the snow.

All of the air had been whacked out of her. She couldn't move, she couldn't scream; and she was so close, close enough maybe to be heard. She couldn't even lift her head to see it coming.

She could hear it, though, and even sense its presence as it stopped beside her. It had a clean-sawdust smell, like a puppy. It breathed deeply a couple of times, and then stooped; Kristin tried to shrink down into the snow, but a hand was thrust under her head. At least, it was the approximate shape of a hand, but as it took hold of her chin and lifted she could feel the dry roughness of pads against her skin.

It raised her head, and she looked into its face. Almost all of the wolf had been driven from its shape – only the

156

eyes burned on, bright as stars and only inches away. For the rest – there was nothing.

Kristin screamed then. But there was a helicopter coming down the mountain, and the clatter of its blades lifted her agony and whirled it away.

SIXTEEN

Sara had volunteered for John to sit in the front whilst she kept company with the bags. He'd thought it was good of her until he saw how there was nothing but a rail and the thickness of a sheet of plexiglass between him and the ground below. He shared the forward section of the Bell Ranger with Andy Quinlan; Quinlan had put in his hours piloting bubble-fronted Loaches in Vietnam, and his flying style was one-handed and expressionless. In conversation he had the kind of slow smile that ought to be friendly but isn't, the kind that has you checking your flies the first opportunity you get.

An overland short-cut brought them in for the approach, a low skim over a pass that was unnerving when John considered how bad the light was getting. Quinlan put the 'copter into an immediate banking turn to bring them out over the woods, and as he levelled out John got his first view of Tromstad. He saw one central group of buildings on a peninsula of the strandflat, sufficiently developed to have a formal layout of streets and street lighting even though everything was fairly squeezed together, and then other buildings and groups of buildings that had spread across the adjacent bays and inlets. There was no harbour, no need for a breakwater; the village's boats were moored out in the shelter of the fjord itself, which beyond them ran a mile or more to the high crags of the glacier-cut valley sides.

When he'd set the machine down in the yellow-chalk ring alongside the mine ruins and the fibreglass huts,

Quinlan swung himself out and left them to manage. Two men were on their way over, one carrying a navy-style kitbag and the other a suitcase that was so overstuffed it was creaking. The second man had the build of the Goodyear blimp, and Sara told John that this was Warren Christiansen. The other, a middle-aged babyface with eyes as black and expressionless as sewn-on buttons, was Herschel Kerr. It seemed that they both had ideas about leaving.

As soon as he was near enough to be heard, Kerr said, 'We waited for you, see?'

'Like you had a choice,' Quinlan said, saving empty apologies for nobody. Perhaps flying brought that easy self-sufficiency as an automatic bonus; if Andy Quinlan had a soul, it would be wearing aviator sunglasses. John climbed down to the ground and reached inside for their bags. He already envied the pilot a little and thought that, given time, he could dislike him a lot.

The bags came down onto the snow and Sara came after, taking the hand that John offered. He could almost feel Herschel Kerr's button-eyes drilling him from behind, and as the two men came forward to board the Bell Ranger he noticed that Sara sidestepped far enough to put herself beyond Kerr's reach. Kerr saw it, too, and grinned briefly. There was nothing friendly behind it.

John and Sara backed off as the rotor sweep increased, evening out into a blur before Quinlan laid on the power and lifted from the ground. He turned the machine neatly about its own centre, dipped the nose, and slid off into a low-altitude power run across the *fjell*. By the time that he got back to Narvik, Quinlan would be navigating almost entirely by compass and shipping beacon.

Sara led the way into the main part of the camp. John said, 'Two of them gone. You think that's promising?'

'Don't ask me. I've stopped giving advice.'

'I wasn't asking for advice.'

'That's okay, then. You already know I think your plans are mistimed and way off-centre.'

'I wasn't asking for encouragement, either.'

159

There was a look-at-me hammering from the windows above as they passed by the two-storey administration block. Sara didn't even glance up; Skipper Ashton and Earl Bonneau, she told John, so far up Ray Kreiger's ass that they have to take a peek out to see if it's daylight. John looked back when they were past the block and saw the Lenny-and-George outline of a hulking giant and a smaller man, both crowded up against the window and shouting something that couldn't be heard.

On the boardwalk alongside the cabins, Sara said that Jerry probably wouldn't be around; he had his own piece of survey ground some distance away, and he came into the camp as rarely as he could. After only a few minutes, it wasn't hard for John to understand why; there was an unpleasantly cliquish feel about the place, an atmosphere that might come from a rodeo crossed with a Monday Club meeting. Anybody halfway normal would stand out as a misfit.

'We'll look for Olav,' Sara told him. 'He can bring us up to date.'

Nystrom wasn't hard to find, because most of the cabins weren't showing any lights. He was in the third storeroom along, and he had some of the seismic gear disassembled on the floor for cleaning – with both Rovers out for the rest of the winter, he'd been given responsibility for more or less everything that ticked or unscrewed.

He was surprised to see Sara. He started to say so, but she quickly switched him to English for John's benefit. Nystrom got to his feet and dusted off his jeans.

'You a friend of Jerry's?' he asked John, but Sara slipped in first.

'Olav here is probably Jerry's biggest fan,' she explained, and Nystrom shrugged and smiled shyly. She went on, 'John's here to look for a job with Teamverk, and he's going to see Jerry before he goes any further.'

'Jerry's giving out jobs?'

'Advice only.'

John was looking over the equipment on the floor. Almost without exception, it was unfamiliar to him. He said, 'What do you do on the project?'

'I fix things,' Nystrom said. 'Engines, mostly. Jerry calls me a token viking.' He turned again to Sara. 'Why did you come back, anyway?'

'Because of the extension. How's it all going?'

Nystrom looked out of the window. The afternoon was well over, and the evening was starting to get a hold. He said, 'Jerry's okay, his records are good, but the rest of it . . . Ray Kreiger's in big trouble. In deep shit without a snorkel.' And he seemed almost pleased.

'It couldn't happen to a nicer person,' Sara agreed. 'Is Jerry at the mine now?'

'Out on the *fjells*, looking for his wolf. You know . . .' Nystrom mimed the use of a camera, and again Sara had to turn to John and explain.

'Jerry thought there was a wolf hanging around his part of the site,' she said, but Nystrom broke in almost before she'd finished.

'It's real,' he insisted. 'We saw it. Not ten metres away.'

Sara was impressed – or at least, John thought, as impressed as Nystrom obviously wanted her to be. Their eyes met for a moment, and he caught the half-concealed message to play along. It was a brief smouldering of the previous night's fire.

John didn't have to try too hard. To be less than ten yards from a free-running wolf – he *was* impressed.

There was no point in waiting around, so they left Nystrom and the makeshift camp and made for the track which would lead them down to the village. They came close by the hayfields where the wires sang in the sub-zero winds, but they were sheltered by the high banks of snow on either side. Tromstad was ahead and below them.

Sara said, 'Olav's okay. One of the few people on the project who is. Taking the job gave him a lot of trouble with his family.'

'What kind of trouble?'

'Just a big dislike for Teamverk and the whole idea.'
She stopped unexpectedly, shifted the weight of her case
so that she could hold it under one arm, and pointed. 'You
see that house over the other side of the water?'

John followed the line to where the land came around
on the far side of the inlet. It was getting too dark to make
out much detail over the distance, but his eye was drawn
by the pulsing of the shore beacon. The two-storey frame
house was just a little way down from the light.

Sara said, 'The girl who lives there, she married into
Olav's family. Her husband's an old man. She got friendly
with one of the project men and invited him around one
afternoon. The one called Andy Meador heard about it
and turned up first. He tried to rape her. He had to get
out of the village within the hour, because they were going
to lynch him. She's a mad woman now.'

She stared at the house for a moment longer before she
moved on. A mad woman lived there. Something in the
way that Sara said this seemed almost to suggest that she
approved.

Ten minutes later they came to the first of the buildings,
a haybarn with a crust of icicles along its roof's edge long
enough to reach most of the way to the ground. Each of
the glistening spikes was the thickness of a man's arm.
Some way ahead the track became a street, lit by the spill
from the wooden houses on either side. Sara was making
the turn into a side-alley between two of the houses when
she realised that John hadn't kept up with her. 'Here's
where we call home,' she started to say, but then she
looked around to see that he was hanging back, indecisive.
'What's the matter?'

'I think I ought to fix up somewhere to stay.'

He didn't have a sou, and they both knew it. Sara said,
'You may not be around long enough. Come on.'

These were some of the oldest buildings in Tromstad. The
peninsula below the hill had been settled first, but it had
twice been almost cleared by fire and rebuilt so that the

162

wharf houses were all that remained of the original layout. The alley led them to a small courtyard where the upper storeys overhung and split logs were stored beneath, and Sara set her case down in the snow by a door in a plain wall. She'd no key – after all, she hadn't expected to be coming back – but it seemed that she knew a trick with the door, because by unpinning the slide from one of her braids and fishing around with it by the lock she was able to get them in.

They came through into a small sitting room, sparsely furnished and with a bottled-gas fire as its centrepiece. As Sara was lighting this, John took a look through into the kitchen; even smaller, with another door and some steps that led down to a private yard filled with snow like a sugarbowl. Sara took her case upstairs, and John waited in the main room until she reappeared.

She'd unpinned her hair and brushed it out. She said, 'Have you got a sleeping bag?'

'No,' John said. 'For once I didn't think I'd need one.'

She glanced at the couch, but it was too small to be worth considering. 'I'll see Lokkeberg about getting a spare bed.'

'I feel like I've put on you enough already.'

'Come on, John, we both know you've no option. Tomorrow you either get yourself employed and move to the hotel, or you don't and you leave town.'

'What about Jerry?'

'What about him?'

'Won't he mind?'

'There's no reason why he should, unless somebody gives him one.' She looked at him. 'You wouldn't be thinking of it, would you?'

'Not me,' he said quickly.

'Good,' Sara said, but she watched him for a moment longer as if she wanted to be sure and also wanted him to know it.

In order to see Lokkeberg they had to go back along the alley and around into the street. Sara explained what

163

they needed, and Lokkeberg led them down to the cellar where old appliances and rolls of carpet were stored. He was somewhere in his sixties, bent but still strong; age had focused its attack on his hands, which were knuckled with arthritis. He watched as John struggled to pull a folding bed from under some boxes of old curtains, and finally came forward and tried to help. There wasn't really much he could do, and John had to unfold the mattress and be happy with that. Lokkeberg's dog was waiting at the top of the cellar stairs, lame as his master, and John was starting to feel like the elephant in the circus parade as all four of them shuffled around to the annex – one carrying, two giving advice, one simply doing his best to keep up.

When Lokkeberg had gone, Sara went into the kitchen and started to look into cupboards. She said, 'I don't know what he thought he was going to eat tonight.'

'He could have intended going out,' John said, and he left the mattress propped against the wall behind the couch and went over to see.

'There's nowhere to go.' She had all the cupboard doors open, and she gestured towards them. 'Look at this, he's run everything down.'

John looked, as instructed. He saw a tin of cocoa and a bag of sugar, and a lot of unmatching plates. In the refrigerator was half a tub of soft margarine, sharing the back of the door with two litre bottles of lager. He said, 'Maybe that was the idea.'

'He forgot about it, more like. Jerry never stayed in one place long enough to get domestic. How much have you got left?'

'Money? Just a few kroner.'

Pockets and purses got emptied onto the chopping board, a half-dozen coins and a couple of notes. Sara did some fast miracle-working calculations and said, 'We can get some eggs and some cheese, that's about all. Jerry's probably got money, but we never leave it around.'

Reasonable policy, if all a would-be thief needed was a hairslide; so they got back into their outer layers and went

164

down to the general store in the village centre. They crossed the bridge that linked the mainland to the outer spit and came in through some quiet back streets where the school and the library had been built side by side. They were walking over ski and sled tracks, and the obvious herringbone imprint of the plough that kept the streets clear; no cars, or at least none that John could see any sign of.

Lidman's store was a sell-anything venture that rambled through three connecting buildings between the main square and the public quay. One end of the labyrinth was a chandler's smelling of wax and tar, the rest was an unsystematic mix of groceries, books, patent medicines, hardware, and second-hand batteries. Lidman himself was outside as they approached, sweeping down the path with a stiff brush; he was wearing a greasy tan mackintosh, wellingtons and a beret. He followed them into the shop, wiping his hands on the overcoat. John looked through a box of Disney comic books in Scandinavian versions as Sara was being served; it didn't take long, and they were soon back on the bridge to the mainland. Sara told him that the business was owned by two brothers, and the story went that they'd set it up after getting engaged to twin sisters from Harstad. The twins then rounded off the picture with a double-jilting and the Lidman brothers, like it or not, found themselves cast as tragic figures with all of their lives as rehearsal time. This had been thirty years ago. The village still talked about it.

Sara didn't really mind Tromstad, but on the other hand she wouldn't miss it. 'Last summer was better,' she said as they reached the alley. 'We were in Ulefoss.'

'Rare earth survey, right?' John said. 'Fenco and Union Oil.'

'Near Telemark. You know about it?'

'I read about it. As close as I ever get.'

'Well, here's your chance to get a little closer. Jerry's back.'

Lights on the upper floor of the annex were the

giveaway. John carried the food through into the kitchen as Sara called up the stairs.

'Jerry,' she said. 'Are you there?'

John's heart was hammering. He nearly fumbled the eggs. A voice from the floor above said, 'I just got in. When did you appear?'

'We've got a guest. Try not to scare him away.'

'Who is it?'

'Come on down, and I might have enough voice left to tell you.'

Of course, he'd only have to see Sara's case to know that she'd returned for some reason. What he might make of John's pack was something else – suspicions might already be forming to such an extent that any rearguard defence on John's part would be as transparent as jellyfish shit. Besides, he was such a lousy liar. He couldn't manage a grin without it looking sick, so he went through to meet Jerry Fraser with his face a blank.

Fraser was halfway down the stairs. He looked, thank God, like an ordinary human being. He was older than John, and thin almost to the point of delicacy; this, along with his dark eyes and washed-out skin, gave him an air of carefully-controlled neglect that would probably be a major part of his appeal to Sara. He was limping slightly, and Sara said, 'Have you been trying to run?'

'I fell a couple of times where the snow got deep,' he admitted. 'It'll be okay now.'

'This is John Visco,' Sara said, halfway formal. 'He's from England.'

Fraser turned around to take a look, and John put out a hand. Both squeezed, and both released at the same time; neither was trying to make a competition out of it. He said, 'I'm guessing Sara's invited you to stay over,' and he nodded towards the couch and the mattress.

'Only if it's okay with you,' John said, and to Fraser it was obviously something that wasn't worth argument.

'I didn't know anybody was coming to Tromstad out of choice these days,' he said. 'What brings you in?'

166

'It's kind of difficult to explain,' he began, but Sara helped him over the hardest part.

'John's a geologist,' she said. 'He's looking for a job.'

Fraser's eyes widened. 'On a project that just died on its feet? You should have warned him, Sara.'

'I did, but he's got some unusual ideas. Tell him, John.'

So John tried. 'I said that it was difficult. It's not the job itself that matters, it's the way I can use the credit afterwards.'

'Speaking of credit,' Sara cut in. 'Your cheque bounced to me. That's why I had to come back.'

'It was no good?'

'For you maybe, but for me it bounced. Wrong name on the top line.'

'You should have taken it to the Teamverk bureau.'

'Teamverk bureau couldn't organise snow at Christmas. It was John helped me get up here with no money.'

Fraser raised his hands as if to defend himself from information that was insisting on coming all out of order. He said, 'So what's this about a job that doesn't matter?'

They sat around the gas heater as John went over the approach that he'd first explained to Sara in the NSB dining car. Sara said, 'I already told him, he's running at a wall.'

But Fraser wasn't quite so ready to dismiss. 'I don't know,' he said. 'It might work. It's no worse than the confidence job I had to pull to get in.' He looked at John. 'Let me get it straight. You want to work for Teamverk, but you're not bothered whether it's actual work or just the appearance of it.'

'That's right,' John agreed. 'Either way, I get one step further on.'

'What's your background?'

So John told him about Scotland, and about micropaleontology, and Fraser said, 'You should be trying for oil exploration.'

'I did. Nobody was hiring. Second or third time around, you get the feeling they'd rather you didn't bother.'

'You ever do any seismic work?'

'Not seriously, but we went into the principles. Is that what you've been doing?'

'Personally, no, but a good sixty or seventy per cent of the project depends on it.' Fraser was massaging the side of his knee with his fist, as if it was an old ache that he didn't expect to go away. 'If you can offer that kind of background,' he said, 'you're ahead.'

'Is there any chance of picking some up?' John was remembering the strange gear that he'd seen in the storage cabin. He might be able to bluff his way in, but he'd be blown when they saw how he didn't even know how to open the boxes.

'If you'd arrived a couple of weeks back, yes. But all that's been folded now.'

'But you could at least give him some idea,' Sara suggested, and Fraser glanced across at her.

'That's no problem,' he said. 'But give me a chance to think.'

She got to her feet. 'Can you think and eat at the same time, or is that too risky?'

'Only if I stick a fork in my ear. What have we got?'

'Omelette eggs with cheese. You want anything more, you can dig out your bankroll.'

'That'll be fine,' Fraser said, and he stopped punching his knee and straightened his leg to get the best of the heat; or rather, he didn't, because John noticed that he seemed to be missing a few degrees of play in the joint. Fraser went on, 'And I've got some beers I was saving for an emergency.'

'We had that kind of emergency before,' Sara said from the kitchen doorway. She was rolling up her sleeves for battle with the paupers' shopping list, her slim forearms in contrast with the bulk of her pullover. John looked from her to Fraser and said, 'Would anybody mind if I took over your bathroom for ten minutes?'

There was a perceptible change in the atmosphere. Sara hesitated with a sleeve halfway turned back; 'Sure,' she said, but she didn't seem certain that she meant it. 'Jerry?'

'It's okay,' he said, and Sara seemed to relax. John said, 'Thanks,' and he took his pack up the stairs as Fraser got to his feet and wandered through to join Sara in the kitchen.

Upstairs was smaller than downstairs, not by any freak of relativity but because the kitchen had been tacked on as a one-storey extension, an annex to the annex. John could see the shingled slope of the kitchen's roof under the bedroom window as he made his way through to the bathroom. Its snowcover was starting to shear and break away, lost heat from the kitchen working to loosen the underlayers. It was a sign of bad insulation; the sharpness of the air in the bedroom was another.

He was going to wash and shave, not because he needed to but because he wanted to give Sara and Jerry Fraser the chance to argue about him. If they were going to, that was, but if they weren't, how else could he know for sure? He could hear their voices below, hardly muffled by the thin boarding of the floor. As he set his pack by the clawfoot tub and tugged at the zips to get to his kit, the playback downstairs was conversational and without any hint of tension – not even, he noticed, the brightness that might be expected when old lovers first get back together. He tried not to listen, but the slim chance that he might hear himself mentioned made that impossible. It was only when the taps were running that the voices became sufficiently scrambled to be ignored, and he couldn't quite bring himself to keep them that way.

'Did you get a picture?'

'Couldn't even find its tracks. The whole day was a disaster.'

'Whereabouts did you fall?'

'Those fields where they string the hay out in summer.'

'You got as far as that?'

'I got all over, but that's when I decided I'd better head back. I fouled up when I was climbing over to reach the *trail. I maybe got snow in the camera, I don't know.'*

Sara said something then, but she dropped her voice and John couldn't hear what it was. He realised that he'd been standing with his razor poised for more than half a minute, and the lather from his hotel soap was almost dried to a crust.

Fraser could be heard moving through into the sitting room, and Sara was beginning to clatter around in the kitchen. John ran some more hot water – it was cooling fast in the bathroom's chill – and reworked the lather before he started to scrape his way through it. His disposable razor should have been disposed of a long time ago.

At least there was one thing to be said for the cold, because it took some of the soreness away. He'd be okay in half an hour, he was thinking as he emerged back into the bedroom, but until then he'd be feeling as raw as a beetroot. The furnishings up here were as spare as those below; a double bed that was hardly raised off the floor (unmade, three pillows in the middle), two hard chairs that doubled as bedside tables, and an oak wardrobe so big that the walls must have been nailed up around it. The door was open, and some of the stuff inside was obviously Sara's. Fraser probably intended to pack it along with his own, as long as he could charge the baggage costs to the bureau. Sara's case was open at the end of the bed.

John left his pack on the tiny landing at the top of the stairs. When he got down he found that Fraser was still in the sitting room, staring into the blue flames of the heater and seeing something else altogether. John joined him, a little selfconsciously; so far they were strangers with only Sara as the common ground between them, and in a lot of ways that was worse than nothing.

Fraser looked up at him. 'I think I know what you need to do,' he said, and he seemed fairly confident; so confident that John forgot his awkwardness.

'Really?' he said, and Sara looked through from the kitchen and said, 'If you're going to talk, do it in here. This is nearly ready, and it won't keep.'

There wasn't the space for a table, but Sara had cleared the top of one of the cupboards and there were stools that they could pull in close. She'd beaten all the eggs together in a skillet and sliced the cheese onto them as they'd cooked; now she had the pan under the grill, and she was crouching to watch the mixture rise.

Fraser brought one of the beers out of the refrigerator and set it down next to some glasses, the thin plastic kind that came polythene-wrapped in hotel bathrooms. *Best Western*, the coloured logo on the side read, but it had almost been worn away. 'Here's the plan,' he said as he produced a horn-handled pocket knife to lever the cap off the bottle. 'Does Kreiger know what you want?'

'We went by the office, but I don't think he noticed me.'

Sara muttered something about Ray Kreiger that didn't need to be heard to be understood, and Fraser said, 'Right. Go to him, and tell him that Teamverk sent you to help out.'

'What if he checks?'

'If you put it like that, he won't question it – he'll just sling you the lousy stuff like humping records around or cleaning down the gear ready to be shipped. It isn't survey work, but that's all finished anyway. Kreiger's having kittens because he couldn't stop everyone walking out, so if he thinks you were sent by the bureau he's not going to rock a boat that's already full of holes.'

'Won't the same thing apply if I just ask for a job straight out?'

'No, the point is not to get him to think.' Fraser folded the knife and pocketed it. 'Point two, keep a record of everything you do. Keep it on Teamverk letterheading if you can get some. What you're after is some kind of evidence you can use after the event.'

'But I could fake evidence like that anytime.'

'The idea is,' Fraser explained patiently, 'that it isn't fake. After this is all over and the project's died the ugly death that's in line for it, you go to the moguls and start howling about how you got ripped off.'

171

Sara came between them with the hot skillet, with a fish slice ready to cut the omelette into three. She said, 'That won't get him very far if Teamverk's collapsed.'

'I don't mean Teamverk,' Fraser told her. 'I mean the holding company. Teamverk's only the shell they use to show local participation, it's nothing for them to junk it and cut their losses.' He looked at John again. 'You go to them and say Ray Kreiger hired you on the site and then failed to process it as a formal employment. Team leaders have got that kind of power.'

John thought about it for a moment. 'But what if he tells them different?'

'He won't be around, that's one of the few things I can say with confidence.' And without much sympathy, if Fraser's tone was anything to go by. 'He not only screwed up, he made it more spectacular than fireworks night. He'll be lucky if he ever gets to lead a scout troop.'

The food was divided and everybody had a plate in front of them; as Sara climbed onto her stool, John said, 'So I'm howling at the moguls. What comes next?'

'That depends on how they're feeling and how you play it. The main thing is to keep making a noise, not to let them give you the brushoff.' He filled one of the glasses and pushed it across to John, and started to do the same for Sara. 'The least you should get out of it is a couple of weeks' token salary and the start of an employment record. But that's your lever, and you can maybe do better. The holding company still needs to get money into the Norwegian economy somehow, and that means other projects next season – which isn't so far off now that we've over-run the last. What you should be working for is a place in one of them.'

'Any clues on how I do that?'

'You're on your own. When it reaches that stage, it's every man for himself. Me included.' He lifted his glass and drained off most of his lager in one pull, as if he'd talked himself dry. John hadn't touched his own, and he hadn't even picked up his fork.

'I like the idea,' he said. 'I like it a lot, but it leaves me with a problem.'

'It leaves you with several,' Fraser told him, 'but you have to handle them as they come.'

'This one's here already. My last krone went on eggs.' John's plans, limited and unrealistic as they were, had all revolved around the fairly straightforward notion of getting himself taken on so that he could then ask for an advance on his money, or at least start running up bills against its security. Next to the subtle politics of Fraser's proposal, they sounded like the expectations of a backwoods hick as he climbs onto the big city bus.

Fraser said, 'Your last one? You mean you're completely broke?'

'Stripped and skinned. And the police took my passport.'

That got Sara's attention. 'When?' she said, as if she'd missed something underhand in a conjuror's shuffle.

'After they threw us off the train. The deputy kept it.'

'And you still ran away?' She seemed bewildered. 'How did you think you were going to get it back?'

John shrugged. He picked up his fork and stabbed at his slice of the omelette, just for something to be doing. He said, 'I'd kind of put it out of my mind. I suppose I thought I'd . . . well, get a job and maybe pay the railway what we owed them . . .'

'That was very . . .' Fraser began, but there wasn't a word to describe it. There was a silence around the makeshift table, and John's embarrassment got worse.

Sara broke it. She said, 'Lend it to him, Jerry. Please.'

Fraser looked at her for a long moment and then – so briefly that he might have been trying to disguise it – he glanced towards John. Then back to Sara again, and she said, 'The money belongs to both of us.'

Outside the window, there was a spattering as snow rained down from the shingles into the yard below. John tried not to look at anybody. Fraser said, 'Sure,' and he said it quietly.

*   *   *

While John was helping to clear away, Jerry took himself and his lager through into the sitting room. The lights were out, and he didn't put them on. He stood by the window and looked out into the alley, where there was really nothing to see.

He would never understand Sara Hansun, he was sure of it. They probably suited each other as well as any couple ever could, but she was of a cut more complex than any diamond. He couldn't understand her taste in music, or in the friends that she left behind in Oslo. To Fraser they all seemed half-fulfilled, doomed. He felt excluded whenever they were around, which was often – towards the end of the year they'd started to regard his flat as an extension of their territory, a permanent free floor whenever they were passing through without money. He'd let it go simply because he'd known it was going to end; but now here they were in one of the most remote corners of the Nordland province, and she'd managed to turn up another one.

John Visco was across the room. He'd been standing there quietly, waiting to be noticed. He said, 'I wasn't trying to put you on the spot. I wouldn't like you to think I was.'

Fraser didn't feel up to discussing it. Instead he said, 'What do you know about hard-rock mining?'

'Just the basics, the stuff you get from books.'

'Ever been down one?'

'No.'

'Tonight's your chance.'

John was looking blank. 'You mean, right away?'

'This may be the only opportunity you get. First thing in the morning, you're presenting yourself to Ray Kreiger.'

'I should think it would help me,' John said, and Fraser said, 'You bet.' Then he turned again and looked out of the window.

You start by giving someone a bed, and you end by protecting an investment.

SEVENTEEN

The wharf houses were at the seaward end of the Tromstad peninsula, extending it out over the fjord by the timber platform and jetty that were a part of their foundation. They'd been built in 1850 by Thor Gulbrandsen, master of a whaling ship and then the richest man in the village; in the 1920s two of his grand-daughters had married boys from the Nystrom family and by the 1950s the Gulbrandsen name, almost like the whale, had been quietly wiped out. It had taken some time to make the change, but the wharf house complex was now generally known as the Nystroms' place; Olav's grandfather had survived to see the changes through, although the brother had died in his bed ten years before.

The buildings were all run together as a U-shaped block around a central courtyard, three wooden floors with a common shingled roof and with attic space that had once been used for equipment storage. When the attics had been needed for bedrooms, a warehouse and a small shed had been added to the jetty by the sea-steps. They gave the wharf some extra privacy, and raised the Nystrom prestige by a couple of notches. The bedroom that Olav shared with his cousin Svein was a part of the attics on the side that looked out across the fjord, and through its tiny storm windows it was possible to get the first glimpse of the boats as they rounded the distant headland on their return from the fishing. When he'd moved across from his parents' place at the age of twelve, he'd thought that he'd been given the best room in any of the houses. These days he wasn't so enthusiastic, because the angle of the roof stole so much of the wall space that there wasn't enough room for his books.

He kept most of his paperbacks on improvised bedside shelves, with the overspill in cardboard boxes under the bed itself. They were mostly American popular novels, linked by the strong associations that each had with a specific part of the USA; Raymond Chandler for Los Angeles, John D. MacDonald for Florida, and some occults that made the far north-eastern states look like a pretty uncomfortable place to be. What he knew of New York came from a run of two dozen of Lester Dent's *Doc Savage* pulp reprints under the Kenneth Robeson house name – a knowledge that was either way off-target or closer than most, depending on how you looked at it.

He lay on the bed with his boots off, turning the pages of *The Spook Legion*. He read almost as easily in English as in his native Norwegian. The door was partway open, and two floors below he could hear Ingrid and Anja in the kitchen. They were singing their alphabet, stumbling, giggling, starting it again. Otherwise the house was quiet – the men were all across the yard, talking about the fishing season ahead.

His father didn't much approve of his library. It was strange that the same disapproval didn't also extend to Svein, who didn't even *own* a book apart from a dog-eared collection of Gestapo tortures that he kept well-hidden, but it was one of the inequalities that Olav had grown used to. No privacy at home, no company out of it; that was the basic nature of his problem. The village was a tight fortress of relationships against the bleak, hard country and the sea. It stifled him to be a part of it, but the idea of moving away held a subtle terror.

He closed the book. Down below, the alphabet was starting over. On the locker at the end of his bed was the Sony portable stereo-cassette that he'd bought with his first wages from Teamverk. His father hadn't approved of that, either. Next to it was a framed photograph of an

176

old girlfriend, now working in Bergen and who no longer wrote. He pulled on his felt slippers and went downstairs.

Ingrid and Anja were at the kitchen table, with storybooks open in front of them. Too small to reach without support, they were kneeling on the chairs and making crayon copies of the pictures onto scrap paper. The table was covered with their drawings. 'What are you reading?' he said as they looked up.

'Wolf stories,' they chorused together. Mop-haired and sparkling, they were sometimes difficult to tell apart although Ingrid was a year older, almost. Nystrom went over and sorted through some of the pictures.

'Wolf stories?' he said as he looked. 'What kind of wolf stories?'

'Scary ones,' Anja said, and Ingrid added, 'Fru Mathiesen gave them to us,' and Anja tacked on, 'All about the bad wolf in the forest.'

The pictures were a riot of colours. Purple forests, red forests, a bright blue animal with five legs that was presumably the wolf in question. He said, 'Any old wolf, or has he got a name?'

'The *fenriswulf*!' they shouted, so enthusiastically that they made his ears ring. As he moved around behind them to get to the stove and check the coffeepot, he took a look at the large-format book from which they were copying. The illustration covered the double-page spread and showed forests and snows, and a man with an axe striding purposefully along. Two paces ahead he'd be stumbling over a small block of text in the lower right-hand corner. Somewhere over the page, the next part of the story was waiting for him to catch up. Ingrid was close to finishing her version of the woodcutter, the pink tip of her tongue showing at the corner of her mouth as she bent in concentration. She was colouring his head a solid block of green.

No coffee, so he started some fresh. He said, 'Is your papa home yet?'

Anja was holding up her own woodcutter for him to see. There hadn't been the room to fit his legs on, so she'd

177

continued them on the other side of the paper. She said, 'He came home and he went out.'

'He went out looking for Kristin,' Ingrid added, her head still down and her voice muffled.

'Why?' Nystrom said, making an admiring face at Anja's picture. 'Where did she go?'

Ingrid said, 'She didn't come home *all day*. He thinks she's got a boyfriend.'

Anja slapped her picture down and stared at Ingrid, her mouth a little shocked *O*. Ingrid was grinning with the pleasure of true mischief. Nystrom said, 'He does, does he? Is he right?'

Ingrid started to say yes, and Anja started to say no, so Ingrid came out loud and triumphant with, 'Yes, she's going to marry Sverre the cripple!'

Sverre was the hotel-keeper's son, sixteen years old. When he'd been Anja's age he'd broken his arm so badly that it had withered and hardly grown since. Nystrom looked pained in a gentle attempt to show that he didn't really appreciate the joke, but Anja had already thought of something better. 'I know where she went,' she began, 'she went out to meet the . . .'

'. . . the bad wolf in the forest!' Ingrid joined in, and they both squealed with delight at the aptness of it all. Nystrom took a mug down from the shelf over the kitchen door, and when he'd filled it he went to join the two girls at the table.

'What's this about wolves, all of a sudden?' he said, clearing himself a space. He was guessing that most of the village children would have been warned off with mild horror stories about what might happen if they should hike off to remote spots while the wolf was about, but if these two were any example the effect had been miscalculated; instead of causing apprehension, it seemed that the dark figure of the wolf had temporarily supplanted Ole Brumm the honeybear in their imaginative landscapes.

Anja said, 'Fru Mathiesen was telling us all about it.' Fru Mathiesen was their teacher at the *barnskole*.

178

'She said we'd to stay away from the forests,' Ingrid said, reaching across to get fresh sheets of paper for herself and her sister, 'because the *fenriswulf* would be after us.' The woodcutter with the emerald head and the pan-dimensional legs joined the rest of the heap, and she turned the page for the next illustration. Now the wood-cutter was standing his ground with the axe raised over his head as the wolf advanced on him. The animal was standing upright, wearing britches and a waistcoat; it was grinning as it held out a large paw of friendship, a grin that looked as real as a cardboard crown.

Nystrom said, 'Is this the *fenriswulf*?' Animals that dressed and behaved as men were standard storybook stuff, but there was something vaguely unsettling about that two-legged stance.

'No,' Anja said. 'That was another story she told us.'

'About how the *fenriswulf* was Loki's son and he was very bad,' Ingrid said, 'so all the gods got together and decided they were going to tie him up.'

'But they had to pretend.'

'Yes, they were all scared of him so they had to pretend it was a game, and they got this ring of hair . . .'

'It wasn't just hair, it was all sorts of things.'

'And they said, let's see if you can break this. And the wolf thought they were trying to trick him so he said all right, I'll break it, but only if one of you puts his hand in my mouth while I'm doing it.'

'And none of them wanted to.'

'No, none of them wanted to because they knew they'd get their hand bitten off.'

'And then,' Anja came in, taking over the story, 'one of them said, I'll do it, because if nobody put their hand in his mouth the wolf would know it was a trick.'

'His name was Tyr,' Ingrid supplied.

'So Tyr put his hand in the *fenriswulf*'s mouth and they tied him up with the ring, and he couldn't break it and they all laughed.'

179

'Except Tyr, he got his hand bitten off.'

'But it made him a hero, so he didn't mind it much.'

Nystrom said, 'I suppose that kind of takes the edge off it.'

But Ingrid hadn't finished. 'So then they took the *fenris-wulf* down a deep cave and put a sword in his jaws and a big stone on top of him, and he stays there till the *Ragnarok*.' And she rocked back on the chair triumphantly, and nearly tipped it over.

Nystrom was impressed. The power of the old stories went on forever, whilst the calculated social relevance of the more recent books in the children's library could be forgotten in a day. He said, 'That's quite a tale.'

'She told us others, too,' Ingrid said. 'She told us about the Follower.'

Anja was frowning. 'But she never told us what the *Ragnarok* was, did she?'

'It's when the wolf gets out,' Ingrid said, as if it ought to be obvious, and Nystrom saw that it was up to him.

'Well,' he said. 'That's part of it. The wolf breaks loose and the big world serpent comes up out of the sea, and there's a last battle between good and evil. All the fighting men who were ever killed in wars come up out of their graves and take sides with Odin or Loki, depending on what kind of men they'd been.' At least, that's how he *thought* it went; it was so long since he'd read anything outside of his US collection that he couldn't be sure. On Jack London's Alaska he was an expert, but his Norse mythology was getting shaky. It suddenly struck him that this was pretty strong stuff for children so small, but they seemed to be lapping it up.

'Who wins it?' Anja said, but Ingrid already had the answer.

'I know that,' she said. 'Jesus wins.' And she looked to Nystrom for confirmation.

He hesitated; the fact was that the gods, Odin, Thor,

Freya and the rest, were wiped out at the *Ragnarok* when their own weaknesses were turned against them.

'That's right,' he said. 'Jesus always wins.'

There would be plenty of time for them to find out otherwise as they grew older.

EIGHTEEN

Nystrom hadn't been entirely correct about the rest of the family's menfolk. They weren't all discussing the season ahead; at that moment, two of them were meeting in the narrow street that ran parallel to the public quay.

'None of her friends have seen her,' the first man said, the larger of the two. His name was Mattis, and he was Kristin's father. 'You still think I shouldn't worry?'

'I think now it might be wise to begin,' the other man said. He was older by a couple of years, but he carried his age better. 'I checked with Nils at the hotel.'

'And?'

'His son Sverre gave me a list of the ones who have left. Three Americans remain, including the leader. All three were in the bar since the mid-afternoon. The leader got very drunk, and the others carried him upstairs.'

'What about the limping one,' Mattis said. 'The one who lives out?'

The other man, whose name was Jan-Erik, said, 'Nobody knows. Nobody saw him. Was there nothing at all from her friends?'

They started to walk down the street towards the wharf houses. There was no-one else around. Mattis said, 'Only from Ann-Marie Sandø, something I'd rather I didn't hear. She said that Kristin had been worried about some schoolwork that she'd done in the summer. She'd left it up at the *seter*. I'd forbidden her ever to go up there alone . . .'

'Did you tell her why?'

182

Mattis shook his head. 'She's so young.'

'Old enough,' Jan-Erik said quietly. 'To be of interest.'

Mattis sighed, and kicked at the ground in front of him. 'You never had daughters,' he said, and his tone implied a whole world of complex diplomacy and apprehension.

'I know. I think it's time we got the family out.' Mattis nodded miserably, and Jan-Erik went on, 'We'll probably check the trail and come back frozen and footsore, and she'll be in bed pretending to be asleep. You can give her the telling-off of her life.'

'I don't want that,' Mattis said. 'I just want her home.'

Nystrom had been reading aloud from the story of the bad wolf in the forest when his uncle Mattis appeared in the doorway to the kitchen. 'Papa!' the two girls chorused, but Nystrom could see right away that there was some kind of strain behind his uncle's fatherly smile. When Mattis indicated with a slight movement of his head that Nystrom should follow him into the hall, he got up from the table immediately.

'We have a problem of the family,' Mattis said. The door was still open, so he kept his voice low.

'What kind of problem?'

'Kristin. All day long she has been missing.'

'She's not with her boyfriend?'

'Kristin has no boyfriend,' Mattis said stiffly, and Nystrom nodded towards the kitchen.

'Those two seem to think different,' he said.

'I have been to all her friends, she's with none of them. Now we're to search the *fjells*, and if you think you should not come then that is your decision.'

A search of the *fjells* – there had to be some reason why Mattis was taking it so seriously, and so soon. But what surprised Nystrom was that there should be any question about his wanting to be involved; he said, 'Of course I'll come. What about them?'

He was referring to Ingrid and Anja, who would be left alone. Mattis said, 'Someone will sit with them. Flashlight and snowshoes, before the hotel as soon as you can.' And he turned and went down the hall towards the courtyard access door, leaving a wet trail on the boards behind him.

Take the narrow coast road out of Tromstad centre and head East, and in twenty minutes you could drive around to the headland where the *klipfisk* racks had stood for more than a hundred years. Take a small motor boat across the bay, and you'd be there in ten.

There were only four buildings on the headland. The best-kept and most modern of them belonged to the man who tended the harbour light, a concrete-based electric beacon on the furthest outcrop of rock. The house faced out across the water, which made it badly exposed when the weather got rough; but the walls were painted every year and the storm shutters were of galvanised metal, because the exposure had been deliberately planned. Every sweep of the light put a thinned-down glow into the bedroom at the forward corner of the house. The man who tended the light had come to live by its regular beat, and if ever it failed he would be awake within a few seconds.

A woman moved to the window of the bedroom. She was the wife of the man who tended the light, and she was alone. Her straw-blonde hair reached down to her waist, and her eyes were a pale blue like washed-out ice. From the window it was possible to see across the bay to the town square and the hotel that faced the public quay. The first flashlights were assembling, tiny pinpricks in the shadows as they bobbed around and were switched on and off to test. There was another light down on the water, the navigation light of the small boat that was taking her husband across to join them.

She was used to being alone. When there was a trip that could be managed to return before the hours of darkness, her husband would always be out with the boats. At night he would sleep easily, breathing slow and even to the heartbeat of his beacon. She would bury herself under the covers and pull the pillows over her head, but still the light would manage to find her.

Her name was Roskva Brøndsted.

'Where's the mine from here?' John said as they climbed the cut along by the hayfields.

'Another half mile,' Fraser said. 'And you'll be in the middle of it. Open-cast ores.'

'Of what?'

'Copper, mostly, and there's supposed to be some pyrites around but we've never seen it. Without the snow you can see how all the lower slopes have been terraced by digging, but in winter it's not so obvious.'

'In summer it's ugly,' Sara said from a few yards back, where she was trailing along with her hands pushed deep into her pockets. It was turning out to be a clear, cold night, but the effort of walking was keeping them warm.

Fraser said, 'There isn't much for vegetation to get hold of. The mines were worked from about 1910 to 1944, and they stripped off most of the surface stuff that was worth having.'

'What's left, then?'

'It depends how far the bands continue under the surface, how deep they go. There's no point digging after the ores if the layers squeeze down to nothing after a couple of hundred yards.'

John thought about this for a while. Then he said, 'What do you think the site's chances are?'

'I never worked on the main part, but I'd say they were pretty good.'

'So how come nobody moved in before?'

'Because the mapping techniques we're using only became available in the last few years.'

'This is the seismic profiling.'

'Right.'

John was running through what he knew of the ore business, and he was wondering how up-to-date his knowledge really was. Any mine would be a gamble, and it seemed to make sense to get as much information as you could to stack the odds in your favour; he said, 'Seismic profiling isn't new, is it?'

'The profiling itself isn't, but the analysis behind it takes some hefty computer power. We're not just banging the ground and listening for an echo, we're actually making an underground map as detailed as a photograph. For that you need to section the site off into blocks and do a number of intersecting profiles giving you complete coverage of each of them.'

'What's the technique?'

'Thirty-metre boreholes with ten pounds of dynamite at the bottom. Core samples from the holes give you extra information that you can use when you're interpreting the picture later. There's an instrument called a wire line log that you can drop to give you conductivity readings as it goes down. When the charges are placed we run a line of geophones from one of the Rovers . . .' Fraser hesitated. 'Or we did, until Skipper Ashton totalled it.'

John said, 'They pick up the reflections, right?'

'And record the signals on magnetic tape with a paper copy for protection. The tape gets processed here to convert the information into digital form, but that's all we can do with it. The next stage of interpretation is in Oslo, in a computer run to compare the inputs of the geophones and screen out all the unwanted noise and stray reflections. That gives you a fairly clean picture of each seismic section, a straight cut through the earth along a single line. Every time the shock wave meets a change in the density of the layers, it shows.'

'And is that the picture you base your viability estimates on?'

'No, there's bigger and better to come. The New Jersey programme takes all the intersecting lines and fills in the gaps to give a three-dimensional underground view of the whole site. Then it not only gives you a picture of the mine's immediate viability, it relates it to the trends in

186

world markets and outlines the best development strategy.'

'Or it doesn't,' Sara put in from the back.

'No,' Fraser agreed. 'It doesn't when the man in Oslo runs off with the cookies half of the way through.'

Sara came up alongside them. 'I hope John's getting something out of this, because it's making my head spin.'

They'd covered the necessary half mile and more, and they were coming to the old marshalling yards and the clear pad for the helicopter. The cabins and the administration block were only a couple of hundred metres ahead. Nothing was lit, but so far that hadn't presented any problem – their eyes had adapted quickly, and it wasn't hard to follow the crisp edge of the cut against the snow. John had been surprised at first by Fraser's proposal that they should go look at the mine in darkness, but in fact it made no practical difference, day or night.

He said, 'So you didn't work on this part of the site at all.'

'That's right.' Fraser was getting out a bunch of keys as they approached the cabins; Visco could tell from the sound. 'We stop here for batteries and lamps, and then I'll show you my little piece of Tromstad.'

It wasn't so mild that John and Sara wanted to hang around outside while Jerry went into the equipment hut, so they blinked in the sudden harshness of the electric lights. Right now these were running off accumulators; during the working day, two Honda generators supplied the power. The night supply was for charging the portable units that were racked at the back of the equipment store.

Fraser got them three lightweight hard-hats, and he showed John how to adjust the suspended headband for size. Sara, it seemed, had done all of this before. She'd already slung the heavy orange battery pack around to the small of her back and buckled the webbing belt to hold it there by the time that John had got his hat to fit. The lamps went onto metal clips on the front of each helmet, and the rubber cable went over the shoulder. Fraser double-checked each of the lamps before they moved out. On Sara, everything looked about four sizes too big.

They wouldn't actually need any of this until they got underground, but there was no easier way of carrying it all. John could feel the difference immediately as they returned, light-blinded, to the trail; seven or eight pounds of nickel-cadmium riding low was making him feel unbalanced, but he expected he'd get used to it.

As the ground started to rise again before them and the details of the landscape drifted into focus, John said, 'So, what's Ray Kreiger's problem now?'

Fraser flicked his lamp on for a moment to check that they were following the telephone guidewire staked alongside the cut. 'He concentrated on transmitting the data for each of the survey blocks, and as he moved on he dumped all the records in one of the huts and didn't bother back-referencing or indexing them. Now he's being asked to pull out specific samples, and he doesn't know where to start. Most of the people who could have baled him out have walked off.'

He waited for a moment, seeming to expect some kind of comment from Sara. There was nothing. When he and John looked around together, they saw that she'd stopped a little way back and was looking down across the *fjell*. Fraser said, 'What's the matter?'

'The lights,' Sara said, and she pointed. In the fields down by the village was a ragged line of stars, almost too faint to make out. Flashlights by the look of them, maybe a dozen or more.

John said, 'What are they doing?'

Fraser watched them for a while. The line was moving outwards, spreading slightly. 'I don't know,' he said. 'Lost an animal, maybe.'

It wasn't long before they reached the gnawed-through section of the guidewire that marked the beginning of Fraser's encounter with the wolf. As they left it behind them, he was explaining to John how the cut ran through the snow directly over the mine's gravity railway. John by now was starting to get overheated by the climb, but Fraser pointed out some dense shapes on the mountainside at a shallow angle above. The pithead works and the cable house, about ten minutes further on.

The disabled Rover was almost buried in a steep drift that had built up over the last few days. Fraser snapped on his helmet lamp and focused it to take them through the shadows of the loading bay platform. Sara was on the edge of the levelled area, and for a moment she'd turned to look back. The lights were no longer tight enough together to be called a line, but there was still a method in the way that they were moving out.

She said, 'Maybe they're looking for your wolf.'

Fraser didn't even bother to go over. 'At night?' he said. 'I wouldn't much rate their chances.' And with John Visco following close, he led the way through into the roofless shed.

NINETEEN

Olav's part of the search took him fairly high into the woods, and when he looked downslope he could see the flashlights of the others as they moved out beyond the trees. The more open part of the *fjell* was being quartered by Svein and some of the others who'd brought their skis along; these lights moved faster and were quickly lost, and Olav turned and began to climb away. He didn't believe that Kristin could have strayed as far as this, but he kept his beam low and watched the ground for any odd-looking patterns that might be tracks. No-one would be able to say that he'd argued, or that he hadn't kept up his part of the search until he was called in; yet he felt sure that he wasn't going to find any trace of her, and he was hoping to the point of certainty that no-one else would.

Every dip and every reed put forward a long shadow, and every shadow moved around and stayed hidden as the light went by. She's already home, he was telling himself. Or she's with friends. Or she's . . .

He stopped, and he raised the flashlight high. Angling across the ground before him was a set of tracks that couldn't be there. He moved in closer to look, but even at a distance there couldn't be any mistake.

They were tyre tracks, and they looked at least two or three days old. But *here*, where the snow lay thick over ground that was rough enough to stop a four-wheel drive? Whoever had brought a vehicle this far along must have managed it on good luck and ignorance, because there was nothing else that would serve. He speared the beam ahead until it faded with the distance, but the twin ruts went on and on like the first slow climb on a rollercoaster. This is unreal, he was thinking as he started to follow.

Two hundred metres further on, he got his first sight of the Citroën.

At first he could hardly make it out, because it had sunk in the snow to its axles and then a curving snowbank had been built up on its windward side; but it was such a distinctive shape that before he reached it he recognised it as Henrik Lidman's car, fifteen years old and rusted half away in most of the places that mattered. Every summer season the storekeeper put out a sign, *Car for Hire*, in the hope of catching some of the trade from Tromstad's few tourists, but either his bait wasn't good enough or his sign wasn't big enough, because they never bit.

Not only was it halfway buried, but the flimsy sunroof had been torn from end to end and the rear window had been smashed. It was more than odd, it was almost calculatedly absurd. People were getting grants from the government to set up situations like this. The nearest road was more than a kilometre away, with nothing other than *fjell* and woodland in between. Whoever had managed to bring it this far must have been following the long straight firebreak through the trees, for what reason he couldn't even guess.

He came alongside and shone his light through a side-window, but the car was empty. The inside looked as messed-up as the outside, but when he tried the door it was locked. Which didn't seem to make much sense, as the whole of the roof was open to the night sky, but that was only in line with the rest of the scene – weird and somehow arbitrary, an echo from a land where the rivers ran uphill.

So he went around the back to try from the other side. Kristin was hidden in some safe corner in the back of his mind, remembered and stored where no harm could come to her, but she burst through screaming when he fell over a buried shape in the drift against the car.

At first he couldn't handle all the input, the sudden darkness as his flashlight was rammed into the snow, the halfway resistant bulk underneath him, the complete disorientation of being sprawled on the ground without even having known that he was on his way down; but then when he pulled himself back and his light came out of the drift like a sword from the stone, he could see that he'd been tripped by somebody's luggage.

There were two soft holdalls and an airline bag, and they'd been stacked in a neat row as if they'd been waiting for collection. Olav's heart slowly let him down from its hammering, and the adrenalin high began to subside. For an instant the three bags had been something else altogether, the uneasy part of his mind seizing on the pieces and briefly forcing them to fit.

Way down below, someone was calling. It came through thin and distant on the edge of the wind. Nystrom turned his head to listen, but already he knew that it could have only one meaning; the search was now over, for whatever reason.

Word came up from the village, she's safe, she's home. That's the way it always is, here in the land where the rivers run downhill. But he couldn't leave yet because something was incomplete, a tonic scale with the last note missing. Before he could leave, he was going to have to raise the trunk lid. When someone's gone to the trouble to take the bags out, they don't give you any choice.

It wasn't locked, and it wasn't even closed properly. He crouched down and shone the light inside, almost into the face of the beast that was sleeping there.

Overload.

On the way down to join the others his memory would shed the details, one by one; of the body rolled up tight in its metal womb, of the chrysalis lustre of its skin, of the gentle movement of its sides as it slept and dreamed, all of it shelled and discarded as he stumbled back along the trail. If a heresy couldn't be contained it would have to be driven out, and here was a cabala set to blast through

192

the cellars of reality and open its house to the void.

So Nystrom's mind worked beyond his conscious control to edit and to censor and to sanctify. It wiped him clean and left him sane, dropped the trap on the demons and nailed it down. Everything was back in order as he left the woods and ploughed his way across to where the track ran level with the hayfield fence.

There are no such things as stealers of shapes. That's the way things are, here in the land where the rivers run downhill.

He was the last to arrive. All the dark figures of the party were in a circle as he climbed the stile, and none of their flashlights was pointing towards the centre of the ring. Then Jan-Erik called out, and two or three of the beams swung around reluctantly. Where they crossed, Mattis was revealed; he was kneeling in the snow, and Jan-Erik crouched at his shoulder. Before them was a flattened shape, three-shadowed and unmoving. Nystrom knew that it had to be Kristin. He let himself down from the lower rung of the stile, and went no further.

Mattis dug his hands into the snow, and gently tried to turn his daughter over. She'd begun to stiffen, and Jan-Erik had to help him. They raised her like a wooden doll, her wet hair sticking to the snow. Now Nystrom could see her face. He felt as if he'd been gutted with a hot knife, and over to his left one of the cousins began to whimper. Mattis tried to smooth the hair back from the blue-chilled skin of Kristin's forehead. Her body was slowly relaxing, subsiding into the fatherly crook of his arm.

She sleeps; she's growing, but she's growing wrong.

Now Jan-Erik was speaking to Mattis and had put a hand on his shoulder. Mattis shook it off angrily but immediately seemed to regret his reaction, and he gripped Jan-Erik's forearm for a few moments as he did his best to listen. Then without a reply he delicately lifted Kristin and started to carry her, and the circle fell open before him. Her legs stuck out awkwardly, one showshoe hanging

193

by a snapped buckle. As they'd moved out of the light it had seemed to Nystrom that she was unmarked; it didn't look like any wolf attack, unless the wolf had scared her so much that her young heart had stopped. The bad wolf in the forest, the *fenriswulf*; probably Ingrid and Anja were still colouring them.

Jan-Erik spoke to Agnar, the town librarian who had married one of Nystrom's younger aunts. From where he was standing, it looked like he'd been one of the few with enough presence of mind to hold his flashlight steady when Jan-Erik had called for it. Nystrom's own flashlight hung useless by his side, throwing long shadows from some churned-up tracks alongside the stile. Agnar was taking a deep breath and nodding – because he was one of the few older men who'd come out on skis, it appeared that he was getting the job of taking the news back to the wharf houses ahead of Mattis. Mattis himself was a couple of hundred metres away and still going, refusing all help and seemingly intent on carrying his daughter every step of the way back to her home. Agnar glanced after him once, and then he struck out for the far corner of the field; he'd be following the fences down, staying away from the danger of the haywires. He passed close in front of Nystrom, the snow-dust raised by his passage glittering in the flashlight beam.

Nystrom looked again at the marks by the stile. If they were prints, they didn't belong to anybody here and they didn't look as if they'd belonged to Kristin; he'd seen for himself the tracks of the wolf, and these were nothing like them. When he looked up, he realised he'd been missing something; Jan-Erik had gathered everybody together, and as Nystrom went over some of the cousins were already starting out.

He came in like a guest at the end of a wedding, too late to wipe out the hurt. Jan-Erik was talking to an oversized, homely man who seemed to be put together out of rocks and straw; Nystrom was surprised, because he hadn't even known that Per Brøndsted had joined the search party.

194

Their conversation stopped abruptly as Nystrom got close enough to hear. Per Brøndsted's face was twisted like an old glove with something near to despair. Jan-Erik looked at Nystrom – it was the first time that he'd acknowledged him all evening.

Nystrom said, 'What are we looking for?'

Jan-Erik hesitated for a moment, as if he wasn't sure that he wanted Nystrom's help at all. Then he said, 'Whatever we can find. Go back up the trail and look for tracks, see if there's anything that might have followed her.'

He was starting to turn away again, but Nystrom said, 'It wasn't a wolf.'

Per Brøndsted was looking intently at the night sky as if he'd lost something in it. Jan-Erik said, 'No. It wasn't a wolf.' And then it was pretty clear that Nystrom was expected to walk away, so he did.

He glanced back once, after he'd climbed down the other side of the stile. Per Brøndsted was staring at the spot from which Kristin had been taken, and he was shaking his head slowly at something that Jan-Erik was saying to him. Everything considered, he seemed to be taking it worse than even Mattis. Olav was wondering as he followed the trail, wiping the ground before him with the flashlight's beam; Per Brøndsted must have crossed the bay and caught up with the group after it had left the village, and it meant that the harbour light was unwatched. Nothing much was likely to happen to it – the lamps got changed before they could fail, and the mechanism housing was protected by a foot of concrete – but Per Brøndsted was known to take his duties with dogged seriousness. He'd first been married to another of Nystrom's aunts, but she'd died; technically he wasn't even family anymore, but it seemed someone had still asked him along.

This was a waste of time. If there were any clues or traces around, they'd been stamped into the snow by a rush of teenaged boys all eager to show how concerned they could be. He checked himself; that was unfair. He no more knew how to handle tragedy than they did – he was emotionally blank, blown by the overload and with nothing to show. To anyone else, it would look like he didn't care. That was even how it looked from the inside.

But the trail wasn't going to tell him anything, because all he could see were fresh ski and snowshoe tracks. His beam was getting weak after more than an hour of on-off operation, and as he ran it along the ground it was beginning to flicker. He switched it off. A couple of minutes, and it would be bright enough to use again – but not for long.

There was something going on, and he'd almost missed it. On the slopes below him, the others were coming together; from the way they were gathering it looked as if a discovery had been made. Using the flashlight for a moment to check the steepness of the ground ahead, he started down towards them.

There was excitement, he could sense it as he got closer; everyone was bunched around some object held at their centre and everyone seemed to be talking while nobody listened. But the buzz stopped as soon as he was seen, and people were moving back to let him through.

Svein stepped forward. His flashlight was in his hand and he turned it on something small and dark that he held in the other. Nystrom tried to make it out, but the close-range brilliance was almost too much for him. The family males were all watching for his reaction as he took the leather cylinder and turned it over.

It was lighter than it looked, because it was empty. There were two slots cut into one side for a narrow strap to be threaded through; the leather between the slots had been torn, and that was probably how the lens case had come to be lost. There was a plastic dymoprinted label stuck around one end of the cylinder, and on the label was the name *J. B. Fraser*.

'What does this prove?' Nystrom said. 'This proves nothing.' But they were all moving out, ignoring him, turning their faces back towards Tromstad with the difficult issues now made simple in their minds. Only Jan-Erik waited, and as he put out a hand to take the case there was something in his eyes that, for the first time in a long while, might have been sympathy.

TWENTY

Fraser's mine twisted down through the rock like the trail of a burrowing snake. The first fifty yards or so had been by wooden steps that came down alongside a railed transport system, but after that it was bare rock in a continual downward slope. Most of the shaft had been cut with plenty of headroom, but in places it came low enough to scrape along the top of Visco's helmet. Other diggings branched off along the way, where a piece of a mineral vein had been discovered and dug, but the main work had been in the galleries where richer seams had been found and then chased out in every direction. The first of these was like a wide cave with a honeycomb of passages around it, and a heap of flintlike tailings that had been shovelled against one wall. There had been enough space here to make it worth putting timber supports under the ceiling.

'Well,' Fraser said, 'what do you think?'

John wasn't sure what he was supposed to be looking at. Whatever had been in the mine had also been taken out, leaving plain rock walls with mineral traces that had geological interest but no obvious value. He said, 'All I've seen is a lot of stones. Is there supposed to be something down here?'

'Jesus,' Fraser said incredulously, 'and you a geologist?'

Sara said, 'See, Jerry, not everybody shares your enthusiasm for this hole.' She was sitting on a boulder that had drill-holes through the sheared face of its side, and she'd taken off her helmet for a couple of minutes. The plastic headbands made them uncomfortable after a while.

John said, 'I can't really say anything about a mine that's been worked out. Not at first glance.'

'Well, take another look at it. Hard rock, and that means hard work.'

'Which means,' John said, picking up on the logic, 'that whatever gets pulled out of here must have enough value to justify the effort. Which lets out the iron and copper ores.'

'So?'

'Try gold.'

'Pick up one of those tailings and try again.'

John did as he was told. He got a piece of rock the size of a half-brick, and he turned it over in the beam of his helmet lamp. The surface appeared to be speckled with soot, but as he turned it the soot glittered.

'Silver,' he said.

'Right. Four galleries snaking down into the side of the *fjell* to nail down the veins. There's no way of dating when the first cut was made, but the top level is about three hundred years old.'

'The timbers aren't.'

'They were put in when the other levels were opened in the eighteen-hundreds. Nothing touches them down here, and they're still fresh.'

John went over to check the nearest, a foot-thick sleeper that had been placed under a low point of the roof and then raised to fit with wedges. The wood still showed the pencillings of the mining engineer, and they looked as if they might have been done only hours before. Only a dry mine could preserve wood so thoroughly. John straightened from his inspection and said, 'What are the prospects?'

'On the surface, it's a washout. All the good veins had been worked by the twenties and the place was closed. The Germans tried to reopen it in forty-one, but they gave it up. Now come and look at this.'

Sara replaced her helmet and dusted off her jeans, and Fraser led them on into the mine. Their combined lights

199

took all of the threat out of the darkness; the helmet mountings made it so that anywhere you looked, the light was already there. The floor got steeper, and in one place it had been cut into steps. They went through two more galleries that had been even more heavily-worked than the first, and which were linked by a passage so narrowed by a rockfall that they had to squeeze through sideways; but Fraser's target was the fourth gallery, the deepest part of the mine with more than a half-mile to walk back to the surface. This level had collapsed into another below it, and they made the descent over loose rock with the help of ropes and pitons that Fraser had placed as a part of his survey.

'I hold my breath every time I come down here,' he said. 'They dynamited the shafts while the buildings up top were burning. Take a look over there.'

John followed the angle of his lamp and saw a dark band that ran across the ceiling, ten feet wide or more in places. Fraser went on, 'Pity they didn't try it earlier. They uncovered a new vein and they never knew it.'

Some of it appeared to be almost solid black. John said, 'Is it a good one?'

'It's fair. Maybe it wouldn't be worth Teamverk's time on its own, but as a second string to the main operation it could be worked at a profit.'

John chose a level-looking heap of rubble and took his turn sitting with his helmet on his knees. He looked up at the vein again – slightly disconcerted when his light didn't automatically follow – and said, 'I don't suppose you'd have any idea how deep it runs.'

'None at all. It was risky enough just chipping samples off the face without knowing what kind of state the roof was in.'

Sara said, 'There was already one fall, early on.' She sat down by John, which left Fraser standing like a tour guide.

'That's right,' he said. 'Luckily I wasn't here when it happened, or nobody would have been able to persuade me to come down again. They were doing a profile about half a mile downslope and the bang brought one of the gallery floors through. Or one of the roofs, depending which level you're looking from.'

'What were they using,' John said. 'An atom bomb?'

'No, just the usual charge, but everything must have been stacked like kiddiebricks waiting for somebody to blow hard enough. It screwed all my maps.'

John nodded, as if he'd had maps of his own screwed by similar disasters. He said, 'Can you tell me what kind of brief they gave you when you started?'

Fraser was faintly amused. 'What kind of brief, eh?' he said, but then he let it go.

Basically, nobody else had wanted the shaft. It looked like a certified waste of time, to be checked over only as a formality – it had originally been charted by the company that had done most of the digging, and there was still a copy of the Nazi survey report kicking around somewhere. Fraser had begun with the maps, which had to be redrawn – they were way out and their scale was a joke, and then the collapse had changed half the details anyway. He'd charted all the worked-out veins and made guesses at the yields, and then he'd made guesses based on guesses to estimate the possible yield of the new vein.

No big rock dumps outside, which probably meant that the miners had taken out only the silver-bearing ores and used the rock waste to fill in behind them. Estimate the total volume of your shafts, and then work out some way to put a figure on the amount of loose stuff underfoot . . .

John said, 'That sounds reasonable.'

'Reasonable as shit. When they were back-filling they started at the floor and worked up. How are you going to know whether you're standing on two feet or twenty feet?'

'Drill a hole?' John hazarded, and Fraser corrected him.

'*Dig* a hole. A drill would get stopped by every hunk of rock and you'd never know when you hit ground zero. And if Teamverk wanted to get that serious, they could send somebody else with a spade. Your uncle Jerome finds intense physical activity in bad taste.'

But on paper it had all looked impressively scientific, and Fraser had followed it up with an unasked-for feasibility study – the kind of work that would have to be done to install a modern transport system, the potential value of the silver that had been left behind in the tailings, the nearness of a piece of flat ground where the metal could be washed out of the rock with cyanide . . . it looked as if he'd done everything that he could short of paint the walls and sweep the floors. Even though he tried not to be, John couldn't help being a little impressed.

'I got bored,' Fraser explained. 'They put me up here to forget about me, but I had to think about my portfolio for next year's contracts. Then everybody started getting jealous when it was snowing outside . . .'

He stopped, because Sara was making signals to him. After a moment they could hear what she'd heard, a rattling sound that came far-off and echoing. It wasn't much, but in the sudden silence of the mine it was an attention-grabber.

'If the walls are closing in on us,' John said, 'I don't want to know about it.'

Jerry was tensed and craning slightly, as if his experience of the mine might help him sniff out what was happening in the slight currents of air that moved between the shafts. He said, 'There's some loose fill on the next level, maybe we shifted it on the way down. Stay here.'

He got a hold on the guiderope to brace himself, and then he started to climb the rubble that either dynamite or the recent collapse had brought down. Going up was slightly faster than the descent, but it didn't look any easier. As the arc of Fraser's helmet lamp rippled off across the roof of the shaft above, Sara said, 'Loose fill? Is that something geological?'

'It's just stones in a heap,' John told her, and he glanced up to check the shaft again. Black as jet, now – the lip of rock cut the shadow of his own beam in a distinct edge. He said, 'Sara, I think he suspects something.'

'He's got no reason to,' Sara said.

'It was when you asked him about the loan.'

'In case you didn't notice, you just had a perfect demonstration of how well sound can carry down here. Now, leave it.'

They waited for a while, side by side and in silence. Then, without exactly knowing why he should be saying it, John said, 'Think you could find your way to the surface if he doesn't come back?'

She threw him an angry look, but she didn't reply. John was the one who started to worry as the minutes passed and Fraser didn't reappear; he strained to listen, but he could hear nothing.

When Fraser finally did return, Sara put on a warm smile and said, 'See?' John was still blinking at the suddenness of the switch as Fraser called down, 'It all looks stable enough. I think we're okay.' He didn't have to raise his voice much.

Sara was first up the rope, leaning back as she walked to take most of the weight on her arms. Fraser held it clear at the top, ready to haul her in if she should slip, and John was thinking that it would be easy enough for Fraser to pull the rope on after and leave him alone. He felt an urge to take hold of the end of the line, but he fought it down. He put his hands in his pockets and clenched his fists.

Fraser called out that he was ready, and John started to climb. Fraser wasn't trying to hold his weight; instead, he'd hooked the line over one of the larger rocks to bring it away from the surface of the slope. It was about the distance of a department-store escalator, but steeper. When John was less than halfway up, the line slipped free.

Fraser couldn't have been watching it, because his lamp was turned away and he was talking to Sara. John suddenly found himself leaning back with the rope loose in his hands, too far over to stop himself falling. He tried to take a fast step back, but his foot only clipped the edge of a rock and stabbed on into nothing; the rest of him was following through when the line snapped taut as he reached the end of the metre or so of free play.

He managed to hang there – Fraser was calling to him to do exactly that – but he was still pivoting around and trying to get a foothold, and his helmet light wouldn't come about far enough to let him see what he was doing. For a moment he almost had it, but he only managed to kick some rocks free and send them clattering down into the lower gallery; then with an effort and some unexpected help from the rope he managed to swing himself back and land in a stance that was square-on to the ascent.

John looked up, as soon as he was able. Fraser had pulled in the free line to get him back at a manageable angle, and now he was holding it as he'd held it for Sara. He was bending with the effort – he obviously wasn't strong. Ignoring the fire in his hands, John began climbing again. When he got within reach of the edge, Sara grabbed his sleeve and helped him over.

It would be difficult to say who was in the worst shape. John seemed to recover fastest, and the chilled air of the mine had taken a lot of the soreness out of his rope burns by the time that Fraser was over looking sick. There wasn't much that Sara could do for either of them, so she sat on the tunnel floor with her arms folded around her knees and waited to see if there was going to be any kind of accusation or argument between them. Fraser was looking bloodless and grey, and a couple of times he wiped his nose on the sleeve of his parka. If John had any resentment, watching Jerry's slow and miserable recovery killed it.

When he was fit to speak again, Fraser's first observation was that John's rockslide had sounded like the noise he'd been chasing without success in the upper levels. He hadn't gone up as far as gallery one, but now he was becoming convinced that what they'd heard was a shift in the gallery's tailings pile. There was no reason for it to have happened, unless somebody that didn't know the route was stumbling around up there.

Sara said, 'Could someone have followed us down?' and Fraser was pretty firm about the way his thoughts had been going.

'I know what might,' he said. 'That fucking wolf.'

Sara glanced nervously up the tunnel. Her light made it safe as far as the next curve, and no further. 'I don't know, Jerry,' she said, but most of it wasn't so much doubt as an attempt to reassure herself.

Fraser began to get to his feet. 'It's found its way in before.'

'But you said you never saw it.'

'I didn't have to see it, I could tell. If you were right and those lights meant a hunting party, it may well be looking for somewhere to hide.'

John couldn't remember ever seeing a wolf, not in real fur and flesh. If ever he'd come across one in a zoo, presumably the safety of bars and glass had been enough to keep the experience from taking a hold. He said, 'What do we do if we meet it?'

'Try not to look too appetising,' Fraser suggested, and he checked the focus on his lamp before leading the way up the gentle slope of the tunnel.

They didn't simply retrace their steps, because the lowest part of the mine had been cut into a loop as part of an attempt to head off a vein that never reappeared. If anything *had* followed them down, it could either be ahead of them waiting or lapping up their scent from behind. John was at the rear, and his hard hat got a battering because he insisted on doing most of his walking backwards. The rugged oval of the shaft danced in his beam, the rocks themselves changing shape as the shadows flowed across them, and always the place that he most wanted to be able to see was the area just beyond the soft edge of the light.

They came out into gallery Number Two at an unexpected angle. Three lights ran over the walls and into the shadows and came up with nothing. So far, so good –

because if there *was* some animal down there in the mine with them, they'd nothing that would really serve as a weapon. They could throw stones, or at best Fraser might still be carrying his horn-handled knife; but by the time he could get in close enough to use it, probably it would be too late to bother.

Fraser didn't seem as apprehensive as he might. In fact he didn't seem apprehensive at all – as he started for the dug-out steps that would lead them on to the next level, he was showing the eagerness of the fireman on the hell-bound train. John put another sweep through gallery two before he followed Sara onto the steps.

They continued to climb. A couple of times John didn't realise that the others had slowed for some reason, and he backed on into Sara; the first time he caught her to stop her falling, and the brief touch reminded him of her litheness under all the cold-weather layers. The second time was when they got to the upper gallery, but now he was expecting it.

The gallery was clear. Fraser threw stones into the shadows to be sure, but nothing leapt out. As they crossed the floor it seemed almost certain that the shifting of rocks they'd heard had been nothing more than that, gravity shaking down material that they'd disturbed on the way through. All the same, it would be a relief to get out into the night air – by now they'd built the spectre in their minds, and it needed only silence and darkness to feed and grow stronger.

It raised itself in the shaft before them when they were less than a hundred metres from the entrance. Fraser got a look at it first, just before he forgot himself and smashed his lamp against the roof.

He staggered back into Sara, and John piled in from behind. They were stopped as if by a wall. Fraser wasn't hurt – his helmet had taken the bang from the dip in the rock above – but his head was ringing and his light was out. In the darkness of the shaft ahead, whatever he'd seen was now standing up straight.

'Who the hell's that?' he said, and the two surviving lights were everywhere other than where they were needed.

'Me, Jerry, it's me,' Nystrom said quickly, and he snapped on his failing torch to show himself.

'Olav?' Fraser said, as the firework show behind his eyes faded and let him see the young Norwegian coming down the tunnel towards them.

'I've been waiting for you,' he explained, and he showed his hand in the beam of his flashlight. It had been wrapped in a handkerchief, and a dark stain had spotted its way through the cloth and dried. 'I would have followed you down, but I fell.'

'We heard you. Are you hurt?'

'Not much, but it scared me.'

Fraser took off his helmet and shook what was left of the broken glass out of the lamp's reflector. Behind him, John and Sara were apologising to each other. He said, 'Like you scared us. What are you doing here?'

'I had to see you, Jerry. It's about this afternoon. About my cousin.'

Nystrom sounded serious, but Fraser couldn't guess why because the boy's flashlight was turned full on his face. He said, 'Turn the light away, Olav, I'll be blind for an hour. What about your cousin?'

The light didn't move, although the batteries behind it were starting to give out. Then abruptly, Nystrom swung it away. 'It's Kristin, Jerry,' he said. 'She died.'

Kristin, Kristin . . . Fraser thought quickly, because the name was obviously supposed to mean something to him. As far as he could remember, Kristin was a girl of about fourteen or fifteen, very good-looking but so self-absorbed that she hardly ever smiled. He'd seen her around the village, and Nystrom must have pointed her out at least once for him to be able to link up a face and a name; but as to why Nystrom should be here and waiting in the dark with his information, Fraser couldn't guess.

'That's . . . that's bad news,' he said, aware of how

207

uncertain it sounded, but now Sara moved around by his side. She'd picked up on something else, because there was suspicion in her voice as she said, 'Why come here to tell us, Olav?'

'I'm not part of it, Jerry,' Nystrom insisted. 'Please believe that.'

To John, it looked like a play rehearsal where the wrong scripts had been passed around by candlelight. Fraser said, 'Not part of what? Have I missed something?'

'They think you killed her.'

Silence. Fraser tried to take it in. He couldn't.

It was Sara who spoke first. 'Who thinks that?'

'All of Tromstad, by now.' He looked at Fraser again, desperate to keep some part of his good opinion. 'You dropped something with your name in the field.'

'It's a mistake,' Fraser said blankly.

'I know it's a mistake, that's why I'm here. I checked the lamps and saw there were three missing, that's how I knew where to find you.'

Fifty metres above, the stiffened canvas over the shaft head must have been lifted by a breeze. The chill mine air dropped a couple more degrees. Fraser was recovering fast, and the defences that he'd worked hard and long to perfect were going up; the world was his enemy. He said, 'You knew where to find me. So you could take me back, maybe get yourself in favour with the clan again?'

'I'm on your side, Jerry.'

Fraser was remembering the over-long fix with the flashlight. 'But you were waiting to see which way I jumped, weren't you?'

'It was Kristin. She was my cousin.'

Nystrom was so plainly miserable at the way everything had fallen, Fraser couldn't keep it up. After a moment he said, 'I know. I'm sorry.' And then he pinched the bridge of his nose in an attempt to get his head clear; he was going to need it, because here was one situation that he wouldn't be able to coast through with his aggressive instincts and his ego in neutral.

Sara said, 'What happened, Olav? Perhaps there's some way it can be explained.'

So he went through it all – how Kristin came to be out on the *fjells* for most of the day, how the family search had found her body, how Svein had discovered the 'clue' which was no more than the random spark that everyone had needed. Fraser said, 'Shit. Another week or so, and I'd have been out of it.'

'It was a coincidence,' Sara said. 'That's all.'

'That's all it needs to be.' Fraser was still holding his hard hat, gripping the rim as if he wanted to break it. 'They already had a dress rehearsal with the Brøndsted girl. I'll be lynched.'

John stayed well back, feeling helpless and for once glad that he was being ignored. Nystrom glanced around the mine and said, 'Sooner or later they'll think of coming here.'

But Fraser wasn't in a mood to accept suggestions with grace. 'Where am I supposed to go?' he demanded. 'They all know where I live.'

'You've got to go to Ray Kreiger.'

'Kreiger wouldn't use me to wipe shit off his shoes.'

'There isn't a boat would touch you, and the helicopter won't come until Kreiger calls it.'

'And when it lands, it's in the middle of a big circle of fishermen and they've all got wrenches and chains. I can't run that fast and I can't jump that high.'

Sara said, 'What if Kreiger called Narvik and got the police involved?' But Fraser was shaking his head even before she'd finished.

'He wouldn't do it,' he said, but Nystrom was with Sara.

'It's the only way, Jerry,' he insisted. 'Unless you think you could persuade my uncle.'

'How much persuading can you do in the time it takes to knot a rope?' From the way he was looking from one to the other, John could see what was happening in Fraser's mind; his close friends were slowly changing their shapes before him, crossing the line to join his enemies. But the truth was that Nystrom was showing a concern that was both innocent and impotent, and Sara was obviously doing her best to find a diplomatic formula for handling someone she knew to be potentially explosive to the point of self-destruction. She said, as if she was discussing some problem over the dates of an airline ticket, 'Then one of us will have to make the call.'

'They're watching for all of you,' Nystrom warned, and he even glanced at John, which shot down Sara's next suggestion.

Fraser was looking closely at Nystrom. He said, 'Then it's got to be Olav, right?'

Nystrom hesitated. Only for a moment, but it was long enough. Nineteen years old, and Fraser his only real friend in the village; his mentor, his confessor, an example to be followed. He only needed a moment to raise his nerve, but Fraser got in first.

'No,' he said, and his expression had hardened, 'we don't want to come too far into the open over this, do we?'

Nystrom did a lot of growing up in an instant. He met Fraser's accusing stare and said quietly, 'I'll make the call. If they'll let me get through.'

Fraser couldn't hold it. Instead, he turned away to look for devils in the dark. 'Then where the hell do we hide?' he said.

They couldn't stay in the silver mine. Even if Fraser's association with the diggings wasn't already common knowledge amongst the people of Tromstad, Skipper Ashton would be sure to set them right. He'd probably even work out some kind of underhand approach that would get him and Earl Bonneau taken along to watch the fun. As they climbed the wooden stairway to the pit entrance, Fraser was trying to get Nystrom to admit to the possibility of borrowing or hiring a boat, and Nystrom was shaking his head; if it had been difficult before, it would be impossible now. John and Sara tagged along behind, in silence for their different reasons.

No breeze had lifted the canvas at the shaft head; it had been a hand. Someone was sitting at the top of the steps, and as the lights reached him he stood. There had been a shotgun across his knees, and he now brought it around so that he could cover them all without being too dramatic about it. Descending a couple of yards brought his face into view. It was Jan-Erik.

'I came alone, Jerry,' Olav said with the defeated voice of someone who knew he wasn't going to be believed, 'I promise I did.'

Jan-Erik nodded slowly, as he looked at each of them in turn. 'He tells the truth,' he said in heavily-accented English. 'I followed.'

Fraser looked down from his gaze, wiped out. 'Doesn't make a lot of difference to me,' he said. There was nowhere for him to run – for all the underground space in the mine, it was a plugged hole.

Jan-Erik started to speak, but then he impatiently switched to Norwegian. Nystrom seemed surprised; after a moment he asked a question. John glanced at Sara, but she appeared to be having some difficulty. 'Landsmal,' she murmured. When Nystrom had finished he turned to them, uncertain of how to make his announcement.

'You're being offered a place to hide until the *politi* get here,' he said. 'Our *seter*, the summer farm in the mountains.'

'Sorry,' Fraser said, 'I don't believe it.'

'You can trust him, Jerry.'

'How do I know I can?'

'He's my father.'

John looked from one to the other. It wasn't that there was no physical resemblance – there may have been, but it was slight – it was more a strangeness that stood between them, a distance that made it difficult to believe. Fraser said, 'What's the catch?'

'No catch,' Nystrom said. 'He knows you didn't do it.'

211

'Does that mean he knows who did?'

'I'm not going to ask. The offer's good, Jerry.'

Nystrom's expression was such that it was obvious no pressure would have him trying to get anything more out of the older man – the word *father* somehow wouldn't sit right, and it had even given Olav difficulty saying it – so Fraser said, 'I don't have a lot of choice. Okay.'

They doused their lights as they emerged from under the canvas, and they dumped the belts and the lamps by the entrance. They'd only be dead weight to carry, a giveaway on the *fjell* in the dark. Nystrom and Jan-Erik were in conversation again and John, dizzy at the speed with which the world had flipped around him, was wondering how he might fit in with this new pattern.

Fraser, meanwhile, was keeping a close watch on the two Norwegians. He couldn't understand any of what they were saying, but he followed every flux of tone and emphasis. Jan-Erik was being firm about something. First chance he could get, Fraser said, 'What's the matter?'

'I was going to lead you to the *seter*,' Nystrom explained, 'but my father says no. It'll be assumed that I'm with you, and someone might make a guess.'

Sara said, 'So how do we find the place?'

'You'll have Kristin's tracks to follow.' Nystrom might have sensed the irony, but this wasn't the time to be showing it. 'He says there's a box of emergency supplies, food for two or three days – you're to stay until somebody comes for you.'

An hour later, they'd reached the spot where Kristin died. They'd tracked across the *fjell* in silence, moving with care over the crusted surface of deep snow. Fraser stayed ahead and never even looked back – he could have lost the others without knowing it, and from appearances without caring. From his place at the end of the line Visco could see Fraser's limp returning, slowly at first but getting worse. Sara was in the middle, and she ploughed on patiently.

The place was obvious, because the snow in a wide circle around it had been trampled flat. Fraser stood in the middle and looked around with dismay, almost as if he was imagining himself surrounded with echoes of the hatred that was now being moulded to his name. Then he looked up in the direction of the trail to the mountains; somewhere ahead, all of the mashed snow would thin out to a single wavering track.

'I can't go,' he said, almost too low to be heard, and Sara moved to his side.

'It's only for a couple of days,' she said.

'That doesn't matter. I can't.'

'You've done it before.'

'But not like this.'

She tried to comfort him with a touch, but he pulled away. As John watched, he found that he was learning the precise limits of his sympathy for Jerry Fraser.

She said, 'I'll go down to the village. I can meet you at the *seter*.'

Fraser took his time replying, and then he didn't look at her. 'I'd do it,' he said, 'but . . .' he trailed off uselessly.

Sara said, 'I know,' but they both turned around when John spoke.

'Why can't I go?' he asked. They were looking at him as they might at an old photograph of a distant relative; some recognition and some surprise, but not much of either. Sara said, 'This isn't your problem, John,' but he'd been in the baggage-car for long enough.

'It seems to have adopted me,' he said, and Sara glanced at Fraser for an opinion. He shrugged, and seemed again to be distracted by the churned-up snow around him; but he dug in his pockets and brought out his bunch of keys, and Sara took them and crossed the circle to John.

'Jerry needs something from the cabin,' she explained as she twisted one of the keys around to get it off the ring. 'They'll be watching it.'

'I'll be careful,' John said. He'd intended it to sound sardonic, but somehow it didn't come over that way.

213

Sara handed him the key. 'We'll be taking it slowly. You may catch up with us on the trail.'

He nodded, and slipped it into his pocket. There didn't seem to be anything else to say.

TWENTY-ONE

When he reached the barn that he'd come to think of as the unofficial edge of the village, he slowed. He had a thin kind of story for if he was stopped, but he wasn't even sure they'd give him a chance to tell it; anyway, there was no-one around, so he kept in the shadows and soft-footed along to the alley which ran by the Lokkeberg house.

And there he hesitated. He'd seen nothing to make him suspicious, but it didn't seem reasonable that they'd be leaving Fraser's place unwatched, not if there was a lynching on the rails. There ought to be people in the streets, lights burning in most of the windows – if this was mob fever, it was a shutters and closed-doors version. He eased along to the corner and took his time leaning around. This gave him a narrow view of most of the alley, enough to see the annex door and the downstairs windows. They were dark, and there was nobody standing outside.

John relaxed a little, and he started forward out of the darkness. At the same time, he heard the low buzz of voices. He stopped, and sank back against the clapboard wall behind him; one more step would have put a long shadow down like a marker. The sound was of someone deliberately keeping his voice low, and it wasn't encouraging. At a guess, it came from the wood store under the building across from the annex. Even as John was thinking this, confirmation came with a brief on-off flash of torchlight, somebody messing around because his hands didn't have anything better to do; at least two voices hissed in censure, although John was still seeing the after-image of a single face, a kid with a flashlight under his chin playing monsters. He started to take himself back, slowly in order to make no noise, walking on eggs and flowing around the corner like a stain.

He was here to get a package for Sara, not to put his head on the block in place of Fraser's. The kids under the woodstore were around sixteen or seventeen, if the face in the light was anything to go by; old enough to be vicious in lots of creative ways, and big enough to get together and carry it through. Of course, they might just be scouts, messengers to watch for Fraser and then run to their elders – but personally, John didn't believe it. He circled back before the Lokkeberg house, and went down the next alley.

It all looked different from the outside, although he knew that this had to be right. The annex bedroom and the kitchen extension below it both looked out onto their own yard, an irregular enclosure that backed onto one of Lokkeberg's outhouses. The yard was big enough for a couple of trashcans and not much more. There were no direct lights around the backs of the houses, so he had to feel his way along the outside wall and count the gates; when he got to the one that he reckoned he needed, he gave a quick check around and then tried it.

Nothing. He could get the latch to lift, but the gate wouldn't move – it had to be bolted on the other side. Rats, as Snoopy might say. Sara had explained how the annex key would fit both locks, alley and kitchen, but she hadn't mentioned this. John was frustrated enough to forget himself and give the door a kick.

It went in a couple of inches.

There was no bolt, it was simply being held shut by the weight of drifted snow in the yard behind it. He put his hands against it and really pushed, and he got it open almost enough to squeeze through; but the more he pushed the harder it got, because the snow behind the door was getting more compressed and solid. Swinging it back and forth a few times widened the gap by fractions, and after a minute or more of thumping at the snow, listening out and then thumping again, he was able to get in.

He'd climbed the steps to the kitchen door before he realised that he'd left the gate open, so he waded back across the yard to close it. The kitchen door itself obviously hadn't been opened at least since the cold season started, and it had swelled in its frame; it broke free with a jerk that rattled all the glass in its upper half, and then it somehow seemed too big to close again. He didn't try to force it shut – he'd be needing it in a couple of minutes.

Lights were out of the question. The danger area was the foot of the stairs, where somebody with his face pressed against the sitting-room window on the alley side would be able to see John as he came through and around; but there was no-one watching, and he made it to the upper landing safely.

He thought that it would be worth risking a look from the bathroom window to get some idea of what was happening in the alley. If it was just three boys playing stake-out, he needn't worry; if they had a crowbar, that would be something else. He cracked his shin on the toilet bowl, and felt a damp towel slide and drop over his feet like a cat; otherwise he had no problem, and he raised himself on tiptoe to get a look over the frosted plastic that had been stuck across the lower half of the glass.

At least he'd been right about the number. They'd come out of hiding and they were standing in the middle of the alley, and they seemed to be arguing about something – well, maybe not so much arguing as talking to convince themselves about something they'd already agreed. The one he'd seen with the flashlight was the youngest. The other two were both about seventeen. They all moved towards the front door, out of John's eyeline.

A few seconds later, they started scratching around the lock.

John banged into the toilet bowl again, but this time he didn't even stop. He was careful enough to move quietly on the thin floorboards, but when he got to Sara's case at the end of the bed he fumbled with the catches so impatiently that it was several seconds before he realised that they were already open. He raised the lid, and worked his way through by touch; his fingers remembered the coarse wool of her pullovers, the silk and lace of her lingerie, and then – the stiff paper made a noise when his knuckles brushed it – the sealed packet that Sara had asked him to bring. She'd wanted it for Fraser, but that was a technicality. He was doing it for her. It was just the right size to fit into one of his outer jacket pockets.

The scratching downstairs had become even and regular, as if the boys were rats trying to scrape their way in. There was an uneasy familiarity about it all, a ghost-overlay on the situation that told him all of this had happened to him before; and when it hit him, the sense of immediate danger fell away like breaking glass.

He was dreaming, he had to be. This was the phase that had always fooled him before, the part where he believed he'd woken up when he'd actually only moved to another level of the nightmare. It was the same situation – alone in the dark, a locked door, and someone . . . *something* . . . patiently working to get through from the other side. A dream. Realising it had to be some kind of breakthrough.

But when he levered himself up to his feet, the double-bruise on his shin reacted with a pain that was definitely less than dreamlike. The chill of the unheated room was enough to make a fog of his breath and to stiffen his hands, and as he was pulling on his gloves he heard something that told him no, this was no midnight allegory being played out inside his head, this was more.

What he heard was a voice – two voices – added to those in the alley below. The newcomers weren't so worried about being heard, but then Ashton and Bonneau had never made much of a reputation out of their discretion.

John couldn't make out what was being said, but the

tone was enough. The two project men were signing up on the side of the hounds, whether they were welcome or not. They might do better with the lock – he'd have to leave, and fast. He went across the bedroom and through to the upper landing.

That was as far as he'd reached when the sitting-room door burst in.

They hadn't messed about with the lock, they'd simply kicked it open. By some freak of air pressures, the door from the kitchen slammed shut a moment later. There was a stunned silence from the other side of the house, and then a whoop; they were thinking they'd caught somebody on the hoof, and if John couldn't think of a way out fast, that was exactly what they'd be doing. They all charged through, thundering past the bottom of the stairs. If anybody had glanced up sideways they'd have seen him, but they'd also have been trampled flat by the people behind. He backed off, his mind racing; the place was so *small*, and there was nowhere to hide.

His pack was where he'd left it, standing against the wall in a corner of the landing. He crouched by it and unzipped the lower pocket. In the kitchen, they were banging at the swollen door to get it open. Out came the towel, and from the towel came the SIG automatic. Any moment now they'd be finding his one-way tracks in the yard. He was relieved that he hadn't stripped down the gun and scattered the parts through his baggage, which was his usual way of transporting it. He checked the magazine, five rounds out of a possible eight, 9mm Parabellum ammunition. He stuffed his towel behind the pack frame and went back into the bedroom. He got to the window as Jerry Fraser's would-be pursuers emerged into the yard.

The tracks that he'd left weren't so obviously one-way; he'd been forgetting that he'd gone back to close the gate. This opened up another possibility, that Ashton and the others might stampede on through in the belief that Fraser didn't have much of a start on them; but a lot of the heat had gone out of their charge, and it was apparent from the way Skipper Ashton was kicking through the drift in the yard that he'd guessed the real reason for the kitchen door slamming, and that the trail was anything up to a few hours old. They all started filing back into the house.

John moved to the side of the window, in case one of them should glance up. He heard their voices moving in below. Only one thing terrified him more than the idea of not having the gun, and that was the possibility of having to use it.

He looked around the bedroom again, as if there was a chance that he might have missed something. The bed was too close to the floor to crawl under. The wardrobe was big enough, but they were sure to look. Downstairs, all the lights went on.

Ashton and Bonneau were doing all of the talking. The three boys were probably standing back and watching, unsure of what they'd started as the two survey men strolled around and touched what they liked, demons let out of their bottles. By the sound of it, Bonneau was the one who was climbing the stairs.

John lifted the pistol. It was impossibly heavy. He seemed unable to keep it level, and it shook too much to be a credible threat. The only credibility he was going to get would be when he pulled the trigger, and with every creak of the risers under Bonneau's weight the certainty got nearer.

'Hey, Earl,' he heard Ashton call from the sitting room. 'What do you make of this for a camera?'

Bonneau stopped, turned, began to descend.

It had bought John no more than a minute or so, and he knew it. He put the automatic inside his jacket and turned to the window; from downstairs he could hear the motor drive of Fraser's reflex camera spitting off six frames a second, over and over. He tried to time it so that the sound of the ice breaking out around the window as he opened it would be covered by the noise.

The sloping roof of the kitchen extension was directly below. Ice had re-formed on it, and there was a thin scattering of fresh snow over the ice. The eaves came low, close enough for him to hang onto them. He stepped out onto the roof, took a hold of the guttering overhead, and gently closed the window behind him. The catch was loose, and it dropped into place as the sash met the frame.

That was his first intention wiped out, to stay out of sight until they'd turned the place over and then make his way back inside. Now he'd have to find another way back to ground level, preferably not the fastest or the most direct. He turned his head as far as he could without unbalancing himself; along the eaves, onto another half-roof at ninety degrees, over the ridge . . . whatever came next would be chance, because then he'd be in Lokkeberg's yard. He was bracing himself to move, when the bedroom light came on.

It was Bonneau. He was staring at the bed, almost as fascinated as if there had been somebody in it to watch. But then he saw the three pillows in the middle, an obvious sign that someone had been sleeping solo, and that took all the fun out of it. He flipped back the lid of Sara's case. A couple of seconds later, he dived in with both hands as if he'd seen a fish in there. He came out with three pairs of Sara's lace pants. John wanted to look away. If he'd stayed, it might not have been so difficult to use the gun after all. Bonneau was out the door and on his way down to show his prize to the others.

John began to shuffle sideways, before Bonneau could get back. His cheap industrial boots gave him a decent grip on the shingle, even if they weren't really warm enough for the latitude. Shadows moved across the yard below him, a puppet-play version of something that couldn't be dignified by the name of a search. He went carefully, so they wouldn't hear him.

He made the transfer, but on the other side of the ridge he slipped. He went down the iced-over shingles like a chute, and he landed heavily in a snowdrift in the yard below. It happened so fast, he never had the chance to be scared.

He was lucky; when he staggered out and shook himself down, he saw that the snow was piled highest in his corner of the yard. A couple of metres' difference would have dropped him on a cover too thin to have been any protection. As it was he felt a tenderness where the gun had been pressed hard against his ribs, but that was all. Sara's package hadn't even been creased. Another bonus was that the drift had given him a silent landing, so there was no alarm from the annex; he was now separated from that part of the building by an outhouse and the dividing wall, so there wasn't much danger of him being seen.

Back into the alley, and away. So now he knew what a hero felt like.

TWENTY-TWO

For most of the way, Fraser had been pushing on a couple of steps ahead of Sara. It wasn't so much that he was avoiding talking to her, it was more that he seemed to have forgotten that she was there; he'd drawn back into himself and slammed down all the shutters, which left Sara tagging along like a stray dog behind a butcher's wagon.

But he was pushing too hard. Already his gait was becoming irregular, and he was slowing. She'd seen all of the signs before – if there was something that he couldn't simply ride out then he'd run until he dropped, and then he'd watch with bitterness as reality overtook him. She'd used to think there was something noble in it, but lately she'd been coming around to the truth; Fraser was a born loser, not because the world hated him but because deep inside he was set for eventual self-destruction.

Sara couldn't blame him for this, not when she felt the same yearnings for damnation working somewhere inside her. Every mistake, every bad move she'd ever made had been in the pursuit of something that she'd really wanted – and she believed that, even with hindsight, if she could be given some of those choices over again then her actions would be exactly the same. Maybe a life could be managed better, but she'd never been able to work out how.

Nor had her father, all those years ago. He'd been a sawmill wages clerk in Rakkestad, himself the youngest of seven children who realised as he got older that the happiness he'd known in his parents' house was never to be re-created in his own. It had been a Michaelmas eve when he'd written out a note for Sara and her brother to take along to their grandparents' place a train-ride away in Mysen, packing them a bag each with all the care that their mother had never shown (Sara's mother was on one of her 'trips away', the ones that were always preceded by raised voices and slamming doors late at night). Ninety minutes later her grandfather had opened the sealed envelope and was reading the note, and then he ran – *ran* – to rouse a neighbour for his help and the use of his car.

There was chaos until morning, and talk of an accident. The *politi* came and asked them questions, and later on one of their cars brought Sara's mother. Her grandfather didn't come back until late the next day, and he sat in the kitchen with his head in his hands and didn't seem to hear half of what was said to him.

She'd had to put the pieces together herself, because nobody would tell her straight out; they only said that her father had loved her, and that she must never forget it. After he'd sent them out to the train, he'd locked all of the doors and lowered all of the blinds. Then he'd crammed his mouth with newspaper and pulled a polythene bag over his head. No reasons – at least, none that could readily be understood by a fifteen-year-old.

It kind of knocked your view of a universe where things would come together to make some final sense.

Fraser was beginning to weave a little, and his breathing was like a rusty saw. Somewhere ahead they were going to have to stop, she knew it. Visco would be at least an hour behind them – poor John Visco, she'd never intended to set him wanting a girl he couldn't have any more than she'd meant to hitch up her own life to that of a man she didn't love. And Jerry, if the truth ever came out, would never have love left over for anyone besides himself; the three of them together had an almost geometrical perfection, interlocking pieces set to delight any connoisseur of human frailty.

In fact, she wasn't so far out in her guess about John. At that moment he was passing the spot where he'd left

224

them, a small grain of happiness somewhere in him that he carried like a light.

Where the trail met the edge of the woodland, John started to climb. He was supposing that he'd made it from the trail to the village and back without being seen, but that wasn't so. His parting from Fraser and Sara had been watched with some apprehension from the treeline a little way above the start of the newly-beaten path, and now after a safe interval the watcher broke cover and came down to the clearing.

It drank the air, one final dip from the aura of misery that would hang over the trampled ground for days. And then it turned its face to where John had walked, and it began to follow.

TWENTY-THREE

John was finding that climbing was easier than descending, because the traction was better. The long-haul effort was making him desperately thirsty. He tried eating snow, but it didn't do him much good; a handful of snow seemed to render down to no more than a few drops of water, and somehow this was worse than nothing. He started to keep a lookout for a dip or a hollow on either side of the track that might indicate a spring or a frozen-over stream bed, and he promised himself that when he found one he'd stop and rest.

More than once, he had a feeling that there was something behind him. A couple of times it was strong enough to make him stop and look back, but he could see for quite a distance and there was nothing. Anybody coming after him from the village would be exposed and out in the open, visible against the blue-white of the snow even if they didn't carry lights. He watched for a while, but there was no movement; and when shapes that were static began to dance, he knew that he'd been staring for too long.

He found his stream almost by accident. He'd thought that he could save himself a few hundred metres of walking by making out across the *fjell* to avoid a long curve, but he hadn't gone far when he realised that this was a mistake – a few hundred metres on a gentle snow-covered incline was a fair deal against the iced-over rock that he found himself trying to climb, so he gave in and started to make his way back down. He stayed low and used his hands, and that was how he came to see the bubbles.

The rock was old and weathered, patterned with cracks. The ice had formed over it like a skin but the stream was still running underneath; he picked what looked like a weak point and stepped on it, and the glaze broke and lifted whilst the air-bubbles scooted and re-formed. There wasn't the depth to use his hands, so he bent to the stone and drank.

After this, he had to take a rest with his collar pulled across his face – the water had numbed it, and the wind chill would make it worse. He tried to snuggle down inside his jacket and waste nothing, not even the heat of his breath, but he was on a loser. The night air was too cold, and his clothing wasn't good enough to keep it out. A minute or so, and he'd have to be moving again.

At least it gave him time to do something that hadn't even occurred to him before, and that was to take a look at the package he'd taken so much trouble to collect. Not that he could see much of it in the dark – turning it over in his hands was the best he could do, and this told him nothing useful. It wasn't heavy for its bulk, a waxed-paper bag with the top rolled over several times and an invoice of some kind stapled to it. After the Big Fall a light shake couldn't do it any harm, and he thought he could maybe hear glass – which might be bad news, but that was for Sara to say. He returned it to his pocket, and then set about returning himself to the trail.

Back on the path, he stopped to listen. There was only the distant wind over the peaks on the other side of the fjord, and the hammering of his own heartbeat in his ears. This notion of being followed was just a reaction to solitude, a way of covering up his nervousness at being further away from streets and houses and people than he'd ever been in his life before. That's what he told himself.

But when the woodland started to close in on either side, it wasn't so easy to believe.

Half an hour later, he was past the point where he'd be able to see back the way he'd come for more than a hundred yards or so. The land was banked to either side, a short scramble up to the edge of the forest. The going was steeper, and the track had begun to wind. This time, it wasn't his imagination; he heard a soft, powdery sound in the still air.

He turned to face whatever was coming. Out in the open had been bad enough, but here he could see almost nothing; his eyes had adapted as far as they'd go, but the trees were keeping the faint bounce light of the snow down to near-zero.

The sound came again. A dark shape broke from the shadows and came towards him, arms thrown wide and barely balancing.

'John,' Sara called to him, 'John, we're here.'

She stumbled out of the deep drift onto the slightly more compact snow of the trail, breathing raggedly from the effort as she waited for John to come back.

'You didn't need to wait,' he said. The silence of the woods made him want to whisper. She wasn't much more than a silhouette before him.

'Jerry had to stop,' she explained. 'This way.'

She led him over the shoulder of the cut, to where the rise concealed a fallen tree. It was as sheltered a place as anybody could hope for, considering the circumstances. Fraser was seated on the trunk, his leg stretched out before him. He'd pulled up the hood of his NATO parka and his hands were gripping the fur edge tightly, knuckles almost resting on his cheeks. He was staring straight ahead, and when John came alongside it was a few moments before he was noticed.

Fraser's apparent indifference was beginning to annoy him as he produced the sealed paper bag from his pocket. He thought that somebody in trouble and with others working to keep his neck out of the noose ought to be paying more attention to his PR. He held it out and said, 'I got it. You want to know if I had any problem?'

Fraser stared at him for a moment, a trick of the darkness putting a glint on the wet of his eyes. Then he lowered his eyes to the package and stared at that, without making any effort to take it. Sara was the one who reached out.

'Thanks, John,' she said. 'You did well.'

Fraser looked up again, taking in the two of them standing together. Then he made an abrupt move to get up, his bad leg stiff. He stepped towards the path. Sara moved out to help him and he swayed neatly to dodge her, limping on past and downwards.

She watched him descending. John's paper prize was still in her hand. He said, 'I didn't open it.'

Sara put the bag inside her duffel coat, and then she found John's hand in the dark with her own. She gave it a squeeze. Even through the double layer of their gloves, the affection leapt like electricity.

And then she was following Fraser, and John was left behind. Back to the hike without a recess – apparently that was a privilege reserved for the victim. John scrambled down after.

'Now we know, don't we?' Svein said, and behind him Kristofer was nodding like a good lieutenant. Nystrom didn't know what they were talking about, but he could make a guess.

'Know what?' he said, and Svein glanced across the alley to where the door of Lokkeberg's annex stood open.

'About your friend,' he said. 'The one that ran. Word is that he makes a habit of it.'

There were lights in all the windows, and people were moving around inside. Lokkeberg had been called down with his keys only to find that they weren't needed; the lock on the alley door had been splintered off the wood with a kick, although nobody was admitting that they'd been there first. It wasn't really necessary – Svein and his friends were looking smug, but Nystrom hadn't fully understood why until now. They might stop at forced entry, but Skipper Ashton wouldn't – and it was Skipper Ashton's words that Nystrom was hearing played back at him, probably Ashton and Earl Bonneau together. He said as much, but he couldn't dent Svein's outer shell.

'At least,' Svein said, 'somebody knows which is the right side to be on.'

'Those two always did,' Nystrom said. They were all around him now, attentive as a jury. Espen, the youngest, didn't even come up to his shoulder.

Svein said, 'And what about you, Olav?'

'What about me?'

'Nobody saw you for an hour, and we're all wondering who told your friend it wasn't safe to come home. Where are you hiding him, Olav?'

'He can't stay buried forever,' Kristofer added, but he nearly choked on the words as Jan-Erik's hand fell on his shoulder.

'Olav took me to check the mining camp,' Jan-Erik said heavily, looking at each of the boys in turn and seeming to see all the way through them. 'And what about the job you were given, Svein?'

'I'm of more use here,' Svein mumbled, but the fantasy had been shattered.

'You lost your sister today, and now you stand here doing nothing while Ingrid and Anja are alone.'

Svein was starting to redden. He'd always blushed easily, and he hated it. 'They're kids,' he said. 'It's women's work to sit with them.'

'The women are with your mother. Go home, Svein.'

Jan-Erik stayed by his son as the boys trailed off reluctantly. Nystrom was expecting him to say something else, but he didn't. Over at the annex, Agnar appeared in the doorway and shook his head. He looked unhappy, as if he'd been doing something that made him feel ashamed. Not so the others who came out after him, their loud voices echoing in the wooden alley. Without looking at Nystrom, Jan-Erik moved over to exchange a few words with them. The search had turned up nothing, not even the camera gear from which the lens case had been torn. That had to be incriminating in itself, because it meant that Fraser was hiding the evidence and he wouldn't hide

230

it if he wasn't guilty – this came from Solberg, who ran
the village's tanked fuel supplies and doubled as the local
stringer for the *Lofotposten*. Something was happening
that Nystrom found hard to understand – as soon as there
was an enemy on offer, those around him began to find
exhilaration in tragedy. They went down the alley yapping
like hounds, off on an endless hunt that would last as long
as human unhappiness.

Jan-Erik watched them go. He didn't seem to share
their feelings, it was more that he was acknowledging the
inevitability of them. They were on their way up to the
Teamverk camp as the next logical place to look for Jerry
Fraser. Silence returned gradually to the alley and to the
violated annex with its lights blazing and its doors thrown
open to the night. Only Lokkeberg was still inside, moving
around on the upper storey. Jan-Erik seemed to have forgotten that his son was behind him. For a moment he
covered his eyes with his hand, and all the iron seemed to
drop from his soul. He recovered himself quickly, but
when he walked over and into the annex he seemed vul-
nerable in a way that Nystrom had never understood
before.

Nystrom followed. He hesitated at the doorway, but
he went in. He kept his hands in his pockets, determined
to touch nothing and to keep himself clean of the shame
of it all. It wasn't as bad as he expected, because Fraser
and Sara had brought so little that was personal to the
place that there wasn't much to be turned over. The
Englishman's backpack had been brought down and
emptied onto the sitting-room floor. Jan-Erik was
upstairs with Lokkeberg, and it was easy enough to
follow what was being said.

'Don't hate me for saying this, but they seem happy.'
This was Lokkeberg, from over by the front of the building. He must have been watching the others as they left.

'I know what you mean. Let them run around and burn
some energy. None of them know the truth.'

'We can pray they never need to. How is Per?'

'No better than you'd expect. He feels as if he's to blame.'

Nystrom hadn't intended to make any secret of his presence on the lower floor, but now he stood completely still. There was something about the tone of the voices from upstairs that told him, *listen hard. Here comes the truth.* He looked up at the boarded ceiling, as if that might help him to hear better. Somebody was crossing the floor slowly, over towards the window with its view of the yards.

'If we're going to blame anybody,' Lokkeberg said with unexpected force, 'blame the island bitch.'

'Make it the Americans,' Jan-Erik suggested. 'They brought us this disease. Now one of them can take it back.'

'If everything works as it should.'

'It will. Tomorrow we call out the fleet.'

'Even Mattis?' There was a creak, someone sitting on the bed, or more likely one of the hard chairs beside it. That was probably Lokkeberg.

Jan-Erik said, 'Especially Mattis.'

'The catch will be bad.'

'That's the price. Everything has to be paid for.'

'They broke in the doors.'

'That too.' The weariness that Jan-Erik had been concealing in the alley was now coming through into his voice.

'That's not what I meant,' Lokkeberg said, anxious to show that he wasn't trying to drag the whole issue down to bills of repair. 'There's a cruelty coming out in all of us. Is that part of the price, as well?'

'Better ask the island bitch,' Jan-Erik said. 'She's the expert.'

Someone was starting to come down, and Nystrom looked around quickly. He didn't want to be discovered but the place was too small to hide. He stepped back through the doorway, hoping that the floor wouldn't creak for him or that it would be covered by the old wood of the stairs. He crossed the alley and ducked under the eaves of the log store opposite, getting himself concealed just as Jan-Erik emerged from the annex. His father didn't stop or look around, but headed down towards the bridge and the main part of Tromstad. Upstairs, a light went out and a door slammed; Nystrom eased out of the shadows and started for home.

Everyone seemed to be at his grandparents' place over in the far wing of the wharf houses. Kristin would have been laid in the main bedroom – that was tradition – and one or other of her parents would be up there with her. The rest of the family would be in the rooms below, providing the massed emotional strength of the clan. Nystrom couldn't face it. Even Svein was preferable.

But Svein wasn't around; the girls weren't in the kitchen, and there was an empty sound to the house that he recognised even before he'd hung up his jacket and propped his boots to dry on the mat inside the door. Their drawings were still all over the table and their crayons hadn't been put away, but when he padded up the stairs to check the small bedroom they shared he found it empty.

This bothered him. Svein should have been sitting with them, and Svein wasn't home. Their pint-sized anoraks were still in the hall, but he couldn't believe that they'd been taken over to be a part of the mourning, not so young. He came back down the stairs, calling their names aloud to identify himself and to reassure them.

The broom-cupboard door opened a crack, and a small piece of a nervous Ingrid peered out.

'Hey, what's this?' Nystrom said as he opened the door wide. The two girls were in their pyjamas, and they'd cleared themselves a small den in the middle of the newspapers and the buckets and the bleach.

'We were hiding from the wolf,' Ingrid explained as he lifted her out.

'What wolf?'

'The wolf that got Kristin. We thought you were it.'

'There isn't a wolf and it didn't get Kristin. She had a bad accident.' He reached in for Anja. 'Didn't Svein come back to sit with you?'

233

'He went out,' Anja said. Like Ingrid she felt so delicate, all bamboo and paper.

Ingrid said, 'He said would we be all right, and we said yes and he went out.'

With his conscience clear, Nystrom could assume. He said, 'Was it him that told you this story about the wolf?'

But Anja was looking at him wide-eyed. She said, 'Is Kristin coming back?'

He hesitated, just long enough to be sure that a lie would be a mistake. He set her down and said, 'No, she isn't.'

There was a silence, as the two of them absorbed this. For the moment, the full implications seemed to be sailing right by them. This would be a good time to lay some groundwork for all the understanding that would have to come later; leave all of the misunderstandings and half-formed impressions to develop on their own, and they'd become fears that might never be fully outgrown.

He said, 'Look, wolves don't have to be dangerous if you respect them and leave them alone. There's nothing evil about them and they don't come into houses looking for you. It's best to stay away from them when you see them, but you don't have to be afraid.'

'But this isn't a real wolf,' Ingrid insisted, as if he'd managed to get the wrong idea altogether. 'It's a made-up one.'

'There's even less reason to be afraid of a made-up wolf.'

'But this one got Kristin,' Anja said. 'We heard uncle Jan-Erik telling grandfather.'

'It's a follower,' Ingrid added, as if this explained everything. Alarm bells started ringing in Nystrom's mind, and he didn't know why.

He said, 'What's one of those?'

'You make it up when you're unhappy.'

'But you have to be really unhappy,' Anja added, 'or it won't come. It can be a wolf or anything it wants to be.'

Nystrom frowned. 'Did Fru Matheisen tell you this?'

234

'No,' Ingrid said. 'It was uncle Jan-Erik. He was telling grandfather.'

He gathered them up, one arm each, and he started to carry them up the stairs. Ingrid was yawning, and then Anja caught it. Ingrid said, 'I tried making one, but it wouldn't come. You have to think too hard.'

'And what did grandfather say to all this?'

Ingrid tried to tell him, but she was yawning again. Anja filled in with, 'He said they'd better be sure it can find someone it would like.'

They had a single bed between them, sleeping one at each end with plenty of room in the middle. 'All right,' he said. 'That's enough stories for today.' He set them down on the bed; they promptly crawled across to swap ends.

They had a night-light, a thickly shaded lamp with a fjord scene all the way around it. The windows of the houses on the shore had been cut out so that the light could shine through. He said, 'You want me to leave this on?' and they both said, 'yes, please,' together.

Anja said, 'Are you going out again?'

'No, I'll be right upstairs. I can hear you if you call.'

'Will it be wolf stories again tomorrow?' Ingrid said. She was trying not to sound anxious, but it still showed through.

'No,' Nystrom said, 'I don't think it will.' They both seemed relieved. Somewhere during the evening, wolf stories had stopped being a simple source of macabre thrills. They'd become instead a source of insecurity, the raw stuff of childhood terror. He said goodnight, and switched off the main light. The nightlamp glowed soft and yellow, the windows of the printed houses shining their welcome across the waters.

He left the door slightly open, and went down to the kitchen. The table was covered with their pictures of the *Ragnarok* – a riot of colours, mostly red. He stacked them together and put the crayons back in their boxes. On the way back to his own room, he looked in on them again;

they were already asleep, and probably had been before he'd reached the foot of the stairs. Words they'd overheard had raised their fears, and then a few more words had calmed them.

He lay on his bed and stared at the angle of the ceiling, too preoccupied even to think of his books.

If there were words which could calm the fears that Olav Nystrom was having, he didn't know them.

TWENTY-FOUR

It might have been midnight when they reached the *seter*, but John couldn't see his watch to check. They'd been starting to think that it would be impossible, looking towards the dark massif of the mountain range before them, but then the trail had levelled out into a pass through the ridge and they'd begun to descend into the next valley. The going got worse as they climbed. It also got colder, which put a limit on Fraser's rest stops.

From the little that they could make out, there was more to the farmhouse than any of them had expected. Instead of a two-roomed weatherboard shack with a turfed roof, it had more of the look of a shooting-lodge. Someone had gone to a lot of trouble to cut a deep terrace into the valley side so that the verandahed end of the *seter* could be built out to give a spectacular three-way view. And this was about all that they could see as they tramped down the last couple of hundred yards by a rail fence, although what they really cared about were shelter, food, and the chance to build a fire.

It seemed they'd have to wait just a little longer, because the place was locked and they didn't have a key. John left the others on the verandah by the main door and went around the back. In an enclosed yard which had stone walls to shore up the hillside behind them, he worked mainly by touch and by moonlight (the night sky had been clearing over the last hour) to grope his way over some cardboard boxes that had gone slimy with the wet, a stack of four-foot gas cylinders that had to have been brought up by tractor, some torn lead pipes from old plumbing, and finally, under the pipes and wrapped in a piece of sacking, two adjustable wrenches and a cold chisel. The wrenches had rusted solid, but the chisel was fine; driven by a rock from the top of the wall, it took out the lock on the backyard door with a single blow.

He could see that he was in some kind of scullery, but the kitchen beyond it was no more than dim planes and shadows on the other side of the door. When he put the chisel down on a flat surface to his right, he heard the metal clink against stone.

He had no idea where he was going. It would have been simplest to backtrack and bring Sara and Fraser in through the yard, but now that he was under cover John didn't intend to go outside again if he could help it. Feeling his way around the kitchen table, he knocked into one chair and sent another crashing over before he found the second door that let him through into the central hallway. This was a T-shaped passage, and he was at one corner of the intersecting end; directly across was the main door at the end of the verandah, only now he was looking at it from the inside. He went back and lifted the latch, and the door slammed back into him.

Fraser had been leaning on it. Sara followed him through and closed the door behind her. Fraser then did something that John hadn't even thought to do, which was to feel for a lightswitch. There was one by the door in the kind of place that you might expect, but nothing happened when he flicked it.

'Power must be off,' he said, which didn't seem unreasonable. John was unsticking himself from the wall, where he'd been flattened like Wile E. Coyote.

He said, 'Maybe there isn't any.'

'You don't get switches without it,' Fraser said, and he flicked up and down a few more times to make the point. 'There's got to be a junction box somewhere around.'

'How about the kitchen?' Sara suggested, as if she had some idea of where the kitchen might be.

'It could be anywhere.'

John said, 'But it's most likely to be near one of the main doors. Then you don't have to fall around in the dark.'

So they fell around in the dark looking, and decided that it wasn't in the hall. Then they all shuffled through to the kitchen, holding sleeves like blind beggars with John in the lead. Fraser was cursing at leaving all of the mine lamps behind. Sara dropped off the chain and stayed in the kitchen as the two men went on into the scullery, and they could hear her opening and closing drawers as they got on their hands and knees – or knee, in Fraser's case – and carefully ran their hands along the skirting.

The sink and the work surfaces around the walls were all stone, and they were supported on pillars of brick that had been painted over. John checked this by banging his head against them, twice. Fraser had the easy wall, the one that was a straight run of wood panelling – except for the junction box. It was an old-fashioned type with a switch handle on the side like a stopcock; Fraser couldn't move it, and when he tried it neither could John.

There was a sunburst in the kitchen. Sara had found some matches in one of the drawers, and the glow of the flame was enough to hurt their night-tuned eyes for a moment before they could adjust. Fraser called for her to bring some light through, and she appeared with an inch of candle in a cheap tin holder.

It was enough to show them why none of the switches worked; the junction box had been stripped out a long time ago, and several layers of paint had fixed the handle in place. 'So much for the juice,' Fraser said, and he looked up at the candle. 'Any more of those?'

'It's all gas,' Sara said, and she held the candle up higher to show a square of asbestos and a mantle fitting on the wall above Fraser.

'Great,' he said as he used the wall to get back to his feet. 'A little gaslight haven in the mountains.'

'At least it's somewhere,' Sara protested as if she was

taking the bad feeling personally, but Fraser shook his head.

'It barely qualifies,' he said. 'Let's see what we've got.'

First was the kitchen. Its windows turned black as the candlelight spilled in, cutting off any chance of seeing the night outside and throwing their own reflections back. There in the middle was the big table that Visco had stumbled around, enough space for a dozen people and more, and beyond it was a hearth on a similar kind of scale. The effect of this was reduced by the small light-up heater in the middle. The walls were panelled in honey-coloured wood – dark honey, mellowed with age, close-fitting boards under layers of old wax. John took the candle and used it to flame the gaslights, because Sara couldn't reach and Fraser didn't seem interested; he'd found another piece of candle stuck to a plate, and as soon as he'd lit it from the first one he was off into the hall and looking around. Sara was beginning a methodical check of the kitchen to track down the food supplies they'd been promised – she was assuming that it would be a stock of cans and unperishables to be kept up year by year – so John took the other candle and got out of her way.

He wandered down the hall, with the candle flame putting spook shadows all around him. It was like trying to find his way out of the ghost train when the fuses had blown. Fraser had gone all the way down to the end and into the main room of the lodge, but there was a pair of opposed doors halfway along that he appeared to have skipped. John tried one; beyond it was a bedroom with a stripped-down mattress, and a curtained walk-through to a bathroom that deserved some kind of award for the survival value of its fittings. Across the hall was a mirror-image, with the same dark, solid furniture that bugs seem to prefer hiding under.

He made sure that he closed the doors behind him. There were enough draughts cutting through the place already. When he got into the sitting-room, he found that Fraser was working his way around and closing the curtains. He had some way to go, and John thought that he seemed to become selfconscious as soon as he realised he wasn't alone.

'No point advertising that we're here,' he explained, although he didn't say who he thought might be doing the observing.

John said, 'I don't think they'll make much difference. We'd be better in the kitchen.'

'We'd freeze.'

'There's a heater.'

'It's gas, and we don't know how long it will last.' He pulled some more of the thin material across the limelight of his own reflection. That's the ghost he's hiding from, John thought, and as he watched Fraser limp around the open fireplace he said, 'You think we're in for a long stay?'

'Who knows? I thought you were used to expecting the worst.'

'I'm not used to it, I just had a lot of practice.'

'So stick with an expert,' Fraser said, and he got the last of the windows covered. 'Let's go see what emergency rations look like.'

Sara was in the doorway to the kitchen, already on her way to find them. She said as she backed in again, 'Did you see anything like a box or a basket?'

'Not a thing,' Fraser said, and he looked around. 'What about the food?'

'That's what I meant. This is it.' Sara pointed towards the table. On it were a box of oat cereal gone damp and rotten, and two packets of dried soup which were waterstained but which otherwise seemed to be okay. In the walk-in larder behind the scullery she'd also found some fresh candles and a stack of old newspapers, and that was all of it. The only other item on the table was the package that John had brought from the annex.

He said, blankly, 'There's got to be more,' and there wasn't a better way he could have annoyed Sara after she'd all but torn the boards off the kitchen walls.

She said, 'You find it, then, John.' Fraser had a rueful

little smile on his face, and he was gazing up at the spiderweb pattern of shadows on the ceiling thrown by a rope-and-pulley drying rack that was tied off over the hearth. The slowly warming air was moving it slightly, and the shadows danced. He looked as if he'd just won a long-odds bet for a prize he didn't want. John tried to patch over his own damage by saying, 'Maybe we're in the wrong place,' but that only made it worse.

Sara said, 'We followed the only tracks to show up in the snow.'

'Which means,' Fraser added, with a smile that John had decided didn't look so much rueful as stupid, 'someone else could follow us just as easily.'

'But where's the point in making the place into a trap?' John argued. 'Four hours back you were on the wrong end of a gun.'

Sara was staring again at the meagre haul on the table. She said, 'There must have been some mixup. That's all it is.'

'Right,' Fraser agreed. 'And tomorrow we go around the block and steal from the Seven-Eleven. Face it, Sara, Olav and his uncle set me up.'

'But Olav's supposed to be your friend.'

Fraser was taking care that he didn't look directly at anyone. He said, 'I never had one yet that didn't try to cheat on me.' And then he gave each of them a smile in turn, as if he'd just said something really encouraging about their prospects for tomorrow, and picked up the waxed-paper bag. With that and his candle, he walked out of the kitchen.

Well, thanks a lot, Jerry. John glanced at Sara, but she was already reading what still showed of the instructions on one of the soup packets. John didn't feel hungry, but that was training; if he needed to he could go for a day without even worrying about breakfast, but then the first bite would trigger him off and he could eat like a pig. Since she obviously thought there was nothing to discuss, he reached across for a couple of the newspapers; they

242

must have been on an upper shelf, because they were dry. He took them and a couple of the matches, and he went down the hall to the sitting room to set a fire.

Fraser wasn't there when he arrived. Apparently he'd picked himself a bedroom.

TWENTY-FIVE

There were six of them, riding a truck on a specially widened trail in the late afternoon. The trail was swept regularly and was about as safe as any trail in the area could be, but safety was relative. They weren't far from the base camp and there had been traffic all day, and now it was raining; the discomfort was always mitigated by the fact that rain took the edge off enemy activity as well as their own.

A mine went off under the front of the truck, blowing pieces of the wheel and the engine up through the cab. The driver and the man beside him were immediately shredded, and as the shrapnel carried on through into the back it took a neat piece out of the head of the war correspondent who'd hitched a lift out towards the action. The man next to him had his chest punched through by the gearstick, and the truck dropped and folded as its axle snapped. Fraser fell from his place near the tailgate, through the canvas cover as it ripped under the sudden weight of bodies, and as he hit the scrub at the jungle's fringe someone else fell heavily on top of him, wrapped and struggling in the canopy.

The truck was almost on its side, and there was a fire under the ruined engine as the sump oil burned; there was probably a tyre burning as well. A few yards away somebody scrambled to his feet in a panic, ran a couple of yards and collapsed.

The man in the canvas was struggling to get free, but he wasn't putting up enough of an effort. Fraser tried to push him off, but didn't have enough strength himself. He was afraid that he might suffocate; the canvas was as restricting as one of the army's green rubber body bags. He worked an arm free and reached up to uncover his face. The rain-soaked air seemed cool and welcome.

His view of the truck was tilted and unreal; the burning tyre was putting out black smoke into the rain. Only one man was standing, the short Vietnamese scout who'd been riding near the tailgate, and his arm was hanging oddly. Some way closer, Fraser could see the body of the correspondent; fatigues unmarked, head mostly blown away and helmet with it. Then two Viet Cong came out of the jungle, AK-47s levelled and ready, and one of them shouted across to the scout. There was a short exchange, and then they ignored him and moved around to cover the upturned rear of the truck. The man who had tried to run only seconds before was now trying it again; it wasn't that he'd seen them, it was more like his brain was out and his legs were trying to panic on their own. They didn't make it, and neither did he; as he fell for the second time, one of the VCs cut him open with a burst of fire.

As the runner lay making terminal wet noises and trying to hold onto the slick earth with his fingers, the two Viet Cong started to put bursts into the back of the truck. The bursts were random, but then they were obviously in a hurry because even as they fired they were backing towards the cover of the jungle. The weight on top of Jerry spasmed a couple of times as bullets hit, and then it shivered for a few seconds. One of the VCs was yelling at the scout, and the scout was shaking his head and showing his arm. The other was looking at the sky and backing off faster – the rubber smoke was a beacon, and a gunship could be with them in seconds.

The argument ended abruptly when the Cong put a burst into the scout and slammed him back against the worn-out roof of the cab. Then they both turned and were gone, even before the scout had slid down to the clay. Seconds later there was a big Chinook transport overhead, and the grass and the trees began to whip and shake in the batter of its downdraught. The machine came as low as it could without fouling its rotors, and Fraser could see it tilting delicately to one side as the door gunner scanned the upturned belly of the truck and the broken dolls that had spilled from it. He wanted to struggle out and wave, but the weight on him seemed to have increased and spread. After a moment, the Chinook was moving off and skimming the tops of the trees, too big and too heavy for Search and Destroy but unlucky enough to be handy.

He began to get frantic. He was yelling now, forgetting the nearness of the enemy on the ground, but he was drowned in the rotor beat. The Chinook was out of sight but its guns were raking the jungle, either chasing a glimpse of the VC or putting down random bullet tracks in the hope of pinning them. Fraser squirmed and kicked and managed to get his elbows on the ground, and then he used his leverage to draw the rest of his body out. The canvas resettled heavily behind him.

The Chinook hadn't been able to put down, because there wasn't enough space in a road's width. Ground transport would be on its way, though, probably called in as soon as the smoke started to rise. They'd be moving cautiously, expecting an ambush and waiting for a reassurance of safety from their air cover. Fraser got to his feet and stumbled; he tried it again, but he couldn't stay upright.

When he brought his leg around, he saw why. There was a neat dark slash in the canvas alongside his knee. He knew that he hadn't been shot, so it had to be shrapnel and as he stared at it the leg began to hurt. From nothing the pain started to rise; and although he tried to wait it out, squeezing at his thigh with both hands in an attempt to hold it back, there seemed to be no upper limit to the agony.

He hopped around looking for a medical kit. They'd been carrying one somewhere on the truck, but everything had been scattered as it had bucked and overturned. The search wasn't comprehensive – he made a wide detour around the flayed remains of the driver, who had been black but who was now no human colour at all. He finally spotted the kit hanging from a tree, and he had to jump to get hold of it. The webbing pulled free and the pack fell to the ground with him.

Ripping the cloth back wasn't easy, it was too much like reaching into the wound to open it out. There was some white powder that he poured into the length of the slash, following it with a big dressing to hold it down; and then, because the pain wasn't dropping, as much of the morphine as he thought he dared get away with.

He bound the leg as tightly as he could, and after a couple of minutes the pressure and the morphine started to make it manageable. He hopped across to where the correspondent lay, almost headless. An M-16 rifle was jammed barrel-first into the mud a couple of yards away, and Fraser collected that and a rumpled poncho. The rifle was a lever, and the poncho was some protection from the mud as he turned the reporter over onto it.

Less than half an hour, and the rescue squad arrived moving slowly behind minesweepers. They found only one survivor, a correspondent with some West Coast magazine who had been on his way to see his first action, and it showed – he'd retrieved his duffel bag from the trees and was sitting on it like he was at some Trailways country stop. He was dazed and bloodless-looking, and his fashion-tailored fatigues didn't sit so well as when he'd been measured for them in Saigon. Nobody paid him much attention as he limped across and climbed into the back of the transport, and he didn't speak to anybody apart from the lieutenant who asked for his account of what had happened, not really listening because a reading of the ground was all the story that anyone needed.

Although the jungle belonged more or less to the VC, the US Army had no competition in the air. They made the most of the territory – choppers linked the LZs and the outposts in a fast and frequent taxi service, and Fraser was out of the home base within an hour. He hadn't even been recognised. He got through to the strip at Danan and caught a transport down to Saigon, keeping his fla jacket closed across the name tab. The last of the mor phine went just before the plane took him out, but i Saigon he was able to get more.

A week got him in touch with the Dutch network. The fixed him a passage on a boat, steerage to Australia, an then they lent him the airfare to Stockholm via London It didn't hit him, but it filtered through slowly. He' deserted.

In Stockholm, the aid organisation finally got him doctor for his leg. The shrapnel had worked its way we in by then, and an operation didn't get all of it. That' when Fraser got the punchline to the biggest joke he eve heard. Because if he'd lain still and waited for the rescu squad, they'd have stretchered him back to the aid statio for army attention; the medics wouldn't necessarily hav made a better job of the leg, but they'd have rec ommended his discharge.

He'd have been home within a couple of weeks.

Sara could always tell when Jerry was dreaming. He didn' moan or toss about, he just lay with his knuckles tight o the covers and his lips moving as if he was whispering prayer. She was watching him now, by the faint glow c the bedroom's heater. He'd never say afterwards what th dream had been about, but she could guess.

She sat up halfway, and propped herself on an elbow The blanket slid from her shoulder, but she didn't reac to pull it back; she was almost fully clothed, and the roor was starting to get stuffy. Fraser appeared to hesitate i his wordless monologue, as if the gentle bucking of th mattress as Sara moved might be bringing him out of it but after a moment he was off and rolling through night mare country again.

She wondered why she stayed with him, and it wasn'

for the first time. She wondered if it could be explained as some kind of paternal fixation, an unwilling search for a close substitute, but Fraser was nothing like her father had been. Maybe they shared the same kind of broody self-preoccupation that could turn into self-destructiveness under pressure, but that was all. Perhaps it was enough. Fraser's grip on the covers had tightened, and his breathing had become shallower; his lips were forming the only words that she could ever recognise, *why me?* repeated over and over. It had been written on his helmet, she'd seen it in the only photograph that he'd kept of himself and three friends, all trying to look as if there was something good in front of them as they spent the last morning of a few days' stopover at China Beach. He'd torn it up and thrown it away after one of his worse nights.

She could never describe what she felt as she watched. It wasn't sympathy, and it wasn't concern – whatever it was, she couldn't give it a name. It wasn't pity, either. It saddened her that the biggest part of her life was such an unholy scramble, and that nothing she did ever seemed to help it.

The gas fire seemed to be getting weaker, a steady hiss that was running down in volume. As Sara looked over, it died altogether. She lowered herself back onto the bed and pulled the blanket to her chin. Then she stared into the darkness above, and waited for the dawn.

Across the hall, John hadn't really been sleeping. He'd fallen into a drowsy stupor where thoughts chased themselves around in no particular order, but everything came into sudden focus when his own heater died and the metal started to clink and contract.

This bedroom wasn't such a good deal. It had plenty of cracks and gaps where the warm air could get out and the cold night air could get in; he'd covered as many as he could find, but it didn't seem to have helped. His head ached from the cold, his mouth was as dry as if he'd been eating kitty litter, and he needed to pee. Wearily, he threw

back the thin wool blanket and went to look at the heater
It had cooled to a cherry glow, not much to see by; his
hand traced the hose along to where it met a small-bore
feed pipe on the skirting, and when he found the tap he
twisted it a couple of times. There was a low-pressure
popping, and then nothing.

He pushed the curtain aside and went into the bath
room. On top of everything else, he was hungry – half a
pint of thin soup had been worse than nothing at all. A
good shiver brought him fully awake – he couldn't see why
they couldn't simply have slept in the cracking leather
armchairs before the fire, but then all of this had been
Fraser's idea. Visco could have stayed there on his own
but there was something about the atmosphere of the big
room that had soured that proposal.

Now there was no water. It ran for less than a second
just the pipes emptying out; it was the same for both the
bath and the toilet cistern. He went back into the bedroom
and felt around for his boots and jacket, and when he'd
got them on he went out and along to the kitchen.

The big table showed like a gravestone, a glowing slab
that was the only immediately visible feature of the room
Earlier on he hadn't been able to make out anything at
all, so it had to be getting lighter outside. It was showing
up even better in the scullery, where he tried the tap over
the stone sink; not even a splash, although it had run as
a steady trickle when they'd made the soup only a few
hours before.

The supply might be blocked, or frozen, or anything
He wouldn't know where to start checking, but he could
do something about the gas; he opened the door – there
was no way of securing it after he'd busted out the lock –
and stepped out into the yard.

The lodge was fed by a two-cylinder arrangement with
a linking valve and a meter just beside the door. When
one tank emptied, the drop in pressure ought to switch
the supply across to the other; the empty tank could then
be changed without a break. It was already light enough

for him to see that there was a red flag showing in a window on the switchover mechanism, so he tried the handle in case the pressure hadn't tripped it. He felt something shift, but the red flag stayed up. Then he tilted each cylinder and rocked it; in both cases, he heard only a faint splash of liquid down at the bottom.

Every tank in the stack was the same, empty. He didn't have to lift any of them, just twist the valves at their necks and listen to the short-lived gasp that came out. They'd probably all get changed in the spring, when the farm was coming ready for use again.

There was a distinct hump in the *fjellside* that came angling down towards the yard, hardly more than a ripple in the surface of the snow, and from the way it ran against the slope John guessed that it had to be man-made; it didn't take a genius to go one step further and decide that this could be the line of the water supply. It might lead to a spring, or to a reservoir. He climbed out of the yard, and started to follow it.

There were outbuildings only a few yards upslope from the *seter*, a barn with no roof and what looked like they might once have been kennels. Behind the barn he had to climb a split-rail fence, and beyond the fence on the edge of the woodland he found a stream.

It was partly iced-up, but still running. The pipeline now followed the stones of the stream bed, and even though it had been lagged all the way with old rags bound on with wine John thought that it was a miracle that any water had been able to make its way through. Fifty yards or so upstream he came to the supply tank, a zinc cistern big enough to dip a sheep in. The top was partly covered by a metal framework, but it was mostly open to the sky; the cover was topped with a four-inch layer of snow, and in the snow were the tracks of some animal that had stepped down from the overhanging slope to drink. It was fed by a small dam of stones which diverted water aside. There seemed to be nothing wrong with the supply, so he picked his way across and looked into the tank itself.

There was a solid crust of ice inside, several times collapsed and several times refrozen. John made his gloved hand into a fist, but it was like pounding on iron; he looked around for a sharp rock, and when he found one he used it like a hammer. The ice broke, floes bobbed and the water glittered black. He threw the rock aside and gave the pipes a kick for luck; if that didn't work, he was out of ideas.

For the first time, he looked back. He could see a part of the *seter*'s roof some way below him, and a lot of the valley for some way beyond that; the trees and the fences were etched grey on white, and the *fjells* bottomed out into the opal glass of an iced-over lake. But what interested him was something only a half-mile or so away: another roof and presumably another building, invisible from the *seter* itself.

He looked into the barn on his way down, and found that one half of it gave enough shelter to be used as a log store. They'd already emptied the basket alongside the fireplace, so he got as much wood as he could carry and took it back into the lodge.

The cold morning light lay on the walls and floors in silence. He was still the only one around. With the gas out, it would have to be a fire or nothing; last night's embers were still warm without being enough to build on, so he dropped the wood by the hearth, opened a few of the curtains that Fraser had closed, and went back to the kitchen to get some more newspaper.

When everything was ready to go, he looked around for something to use as a taper. Then, on an impulse, he reached inside his jacket. Lewis Alexander's letter was almost in three pieces. He read it for one last time, and then he folded it lengthwise and put a match to it.

Fraser came in as the fire started to get a hold. He was looking noticeably brighter, John thought, less sullen than the previous evening, but he was going to wait for the evidence before he started making concessions.

Fraser said, 'I was going to say what are you doing, but we can manage without stupid questions.'

'You were right about the gas,' John said. 'It spat a couple of times and ran out.'

'I feel like doing the same.' Fraser came over towards the fire, walking without any difficulty. 'I never spent a night so cold.'

'Doesn't seem to have hurt you much.'

'That's optimism at work. We're going to need it by the bucket to get us through this miserable assault course.'

'This is a change from yesterday,' John said, and Fraser lowered himself into one of the big leather armchairs. Like so many other things about the place, the furniture seemed subtly wrong.

'That was yesterday,' he said. 'The day we found the bastards didn't leave us any food. Today's a whole new programme, the day we find the bastards didn't leave us any gas. You check for pressure?'

'Both cylinders.'

'There you go, then. Be happy today, it's going to get worse.' He almost succeeded in looking as flip as he sounded.

John said, 'Not if we're in the wrong place.'

'Can't disagree, but then we both know the chances of that are zero.'

'There's another building further down the slope.'

'Probably a tin shed with a crapper in it.'

John shook his head. 'Too big,' he said, and he explained what he'd been able to see. He didn't want to oversell the idea, but there was a possibility that they'd made a wrong turn somewhere and that the promised food was only an hour's walk away.

There was no danger of Fraser grabbing it too quickly. He said, 'You sure it isn't just a cowshed or something?'

'No, I'm not sure, but I'd say it was worth a closer look.'

'And I'd say you were definitely earning your passage, John Visco. We'll wait until we've all got the nerve to face some weather, and then we can check it out.'

John didn't know how to take Fraser. He was being almost genial. It was as if the night-shift personality had gone home to sleep and left the day man in charge. John said, 'What happens after that? Do we wait for someone to come and get us?'

'I've been giving it some thought, and the simple answer's *no*, we don't. Narvik's Finest aren't going to make an appointment two weeks ahead when they get a murder call from Olav Nystrom's old man – a day or two days at the most, and it's safe to bet they'll be in town. I want you to go in ahead of me and make contact, explain to them how I had to take some time away for my health.'

'And what if they grab me as the first likely-looking stranger on the scene?'

'You've got an alibi, remember. You were a couple of thousand feet nearer to heaven when it all happened, which gives you the cleanest hands in all of Tromstad. So worry about me, instead, I'll be coming down a couple of hours behind you to turn myself over and get protected.'

'So many people worried about you, Jerry,' Sara said from the doorway. 'Mind it doesn't go to your head.'

She made straight for the fire, and Fraser said, 'Don't spoil a good start to the morning, Sara, John-boy found us another foxhole to run for.'

She knelt by the hearth, as close as she could get without cutting out anyone else. 'Does it have a sauna?' she said.

John said, 'Hot water would be an improvement on what we've got now. You know the gas ran out?'

She nodded, although the way that she was chilled almost blue was enough of an answer. 'You call this a good start,' she said. 'What's a foxhole?'

John explained again about the roof that he'd seen. Now he was trying to play it down, because it was already sounding too much like an accepted certainty. Sara said, 'Score one for observation. It makes me wonder how we managed to search this place last night and miss three of the rooms.'

254

'Is there an upstairs we didn't know about?' Fraser said, and Sara looked towards the door.

'Take a look for yourself, the far side of the hall. Make it a two-purpose trip and bring what's left of the soup.'

She obviously wasn't going to move until she was done through, both sides. John and Fraser went out together, and when they reached the far end of the hall they could see what she'd been talking about; in the panelled wall opposite the main entrance was a door, disguised to blend in with the run of the wood. It was hard enough to make out in daylight, and at night they'd have had no chance. Fraser pushed it open, and they went through.

They came into a very sparse bedroom; two single beds, two bedside cabinets, one chest of drawers with a mirror that needed re-silvering, and two more doors; one of these went through into a dead end, a slightly larger bedroom with three berths and its own basin, whilst the other led to a single room and yet another door.

'I don't get it,' Fraser said. 'Anywhere else, and I'd say these were the servants' quarters.'

'Why not here?'

'Because this isn't cattle-baron country, and fishermen farmers don't have people to button their flies for them.'

The furthest door of the complex obviously wasn't used, because it opened onto the back of some kind of shelf unit. Fraser put his shoulder to it and tried to make it move; John helped, and together they pushed it back far enough to get through.

They came out into the kitchen. Also behind the shelves – apart from a lot of dust and cobwebs that made the two of them as grey as the bogeymen in a late-night horror show – was a service indicator board. It was electrically powered, which would put it around the same period as the defunct switches and light fittings.

They left the shelves away from the wall, partly so Sara could see but mainly to save themselves the effort of pushing them back. John checked the tap in the scullery, found that it was working again, and drew off a couple of pints of water into a pan. Fraser only carried the packet of soup, but at least he had the decency to open the doors for them both.

Sara looked up as they returned to the sitting room. She was beginning to warm through, and it showed. She said, 'I hope the place you saw is worth the trip. I don't think I like this one.'

'Any reason?' John said as he set the pan down on the hearth, but inside he knew the answer; Sara's reasons were the same as those which had sent Jerry around closing curtains to keep out the dark, and John opening them again to bring in some light.

She said, 'A bad atmosphere, maybe. Were you never anywhere that you knew you couldn't feel safe?'

'I'm told you get used to it,' Fraser said.

Less than an hour later, they were on their way down. The morning light was clear and cold, and the snowcover of the *fjellside* damped all sounds other than the ones they made for themselves. They cut their own path, the surface giving at every step, and their descent was a half-mixed sound-track with the background effects left out.

Until they came around by the side, all they could see of the second building was its roof, spikes of turf pushing up through the white in an even stubble. Their first sight of the building itself was a disappointment.

Even before they got in close, they could see that it was derelict. No glass in the windows, the weatherboard split and rotten, the door off its hinges. Sara said, 'I think we can forget it.'

'I *know* we can,' Fraser said.'Look at the place.'

John was determined that he wasn't going to feel guilty, but he couldn't help feeling just a little bit responsible. 'It was an idea,' he said. 'That's all,' but Fraser was shaking his head as if he knew that there were much bigger and less kind forces at work than chance alone.

'The usual junk at the rainbow's end,' he said. 'Any-body for going back?'

'We might as well see what we came for,' Sara said, and she passed between them and started on her way over the last few metres. John and Fraser didn't look at each other, but they both followed.

It was more like the traditional *seter* than the one they'd left behind, a couple of rooms below with a loft above, and some outbuildings to the side which formed an irregular yard. Fraser split himself off to take a look at these, and John went into the main building behind Sara.

He'd expected just a shell, but he'd been wrong; the *seter* was furnished, table, chairs, dresser and shelves; all of them plain, none of them expensive, and everything covered with a light glaze of wind-blown frost from the broken windows. There was even a rag-rug on the floor, although the boards were lifting under it and the rags were probably full of weevils. Sara had already gone through into the back room; her voice came back dead, the walls too damp and soft to hold an echo.

'There's some animal been using this as a hide,' she said, and John followed her through to see.

The back room was obviously the bunkroom, straight hammer-and-nails carpentry looking like something out of an old prison camp movie. There was sleeping for six, and a ladder running up into the dark space of the loft above. Sara was looking at a kind of nest of old blankets in the most sheltered corner – they must have been dragged off the three lower bunks, because the blankets on the top bunks were still in place – and stirring at something with the toe of her child-size boot. When John got closer, he could see what it was; a heap of bones, small ones like sticks, nothing larger than a cat or a rabbit.

'That's the only use it's seen in years,' he said, with a nervous glance at the open trap to the loft. It wasn't likely that anything on four legs could have climbed the ladder, but they were two doors in from the world outside and there didn't seem to be any other exit. He said, 'I picked us another dud.'

'You didn't pick us anything,' Sara said. She bent and

picked something from a fold in one of the blankets; John thought that he heard a noise from the room behind him. Before he could turn and look, Sara was up again, holding out a wisp of grey-white fur. John reached out to take it, but it was so fine that it seemed to turn to smoke in the air and leave him with nothing; when he managed a glance at the doorway a couple of seconds later, Jerry was standing there.

He'd crossed the old boards so quietly that his near-silence must have been deliberate. He took in the scene for a moment, and there was no way of telling how he was reading it; nor was there much expression in his voice when he said, 'How's the ten-cent tour going?'

'Don't waste your money,' Sara said, and she dusted off her gloves.

'I found something interesting out back.'

'Is it edible?'

'You'd need a hell of a strong constitution, but it explains something.'

They followed Fraser out and around to the yard and the three low sheds that formed it, and John gave one glance back to the left window above the main door. It was dark, and its glass didn't seem to have been removed or broken. Somehow the idea of all that secret space overhead had been making him nervous, as if something might have backed up there before them and pressed itself low to listen; but he knew that it couldn't be true, and for the same reasons that Sara hadn't been worried as she'd discovered the predator's traces – nothing was around because the snow would have given it away, and the only tracks leading up to the building were their own.

What Fraser had found was the body of an old generator, a rusted mass that filled half the floor space of one of the sheds. It was bolted onto a concrete base, and there was just enough room to get around between this and three of the walls. Fraser was looking at it as if its presence made everything clear, and John said, 'What does it explain?'

'Number one, why there's no power where we're staying. This thing burned out years ago. I checked, and there's a buried line running from here straight back up the hill.'

Sara said, 'What's number two?'

'You're nearest,' Fraser said, looking at John, 'get a close look at that casting.'

Metal that had once been oiled and gleaming was now under a thick coat of grime, and the raised letters weren't easy to read. He peered at them for a moment in the shed's dim light and said, 'Nineteen thirty-eight.'

'That's just the date of the design. What about the rest?'

'Something about Krupp, and Essen.'

'And what does that tell you?'

'Krupp of Essen made generators,' John hazarded. He didn't much like the way that Fraser was prompting him like the slowest child in the class.

'They also made guns and tanks. It's even money that the lodge up the valley was a weekend retreat for the army of occupation.'

'With servants?' Sara said doubtfully.

'Officers only. The kitchen and the annex were for the enlisted men who waited on them.' He looked towards the door, where a small part of the main building showed across the yard. 'My guess is that this humble shack was for the common grunts, well out of earshot. Maybe they imported whores.'

Sara said, 'And maybe they just helped themselves from the village. No wonder Olav's people never wanted to see the mines opened again.'

'It didn't stop Olav's people taking over a decent building for their summer farm. Shall we head back?'

Sara looked at John, John shrugged. She said, 'We may as well. There's nowhere else to go.'

The untethered scullery door banged shut behind them as they filed through into the kitchen. At the far end of the lodge, the fire was almost out. Down the hall and into the sitting room, all in silence; Fraser went to one of the windows and stood looking out across the covered board-walk as John stacked fresh logs in the grate and Sara watched. This was the last of the dry wood; they'd already had the last of the food.

It was a while before Fraser spoke. Then he said, with-out turning around, 'How does everybody feel about a two-day fast?'

'When there isn't a choice,' Sara said. 'It's called starving.'

'A couple of days won't kill us,' John suggested, but Sara knew the country better.

'Hunger won't,' she said, 'but exposure might if you get weakened.'

The flames were getting a hold now, and when Fraser saw this he started over. As he came around the back of the old lizard-skinned sofa he said, 'Well, the nuts and berries seem to be pretty scarce this winter. I don't see what else we can do.'

John waited for a while, just in case anybody was going to come up with anything; but as far as he could see the others were only staring into the fire and out of ideas, so he said, 'We could try hunting.'

Fraser glanced across at him for a moment, without much respect or conviction. 'With what?' he said.

Sara was looking hopeful, slightly. 'Didn't the army teach you to live off the land?'

'Everything we ever needed was airfreighted from home. It wasn't that kind of army.'

John said, 'We could use this.'

He was holding up the SIG P210 automatic, one of the most expensive and accurate of all military-issue handguns. Fraser was staring as if he couldn't believe it, as if John had somehow made a hole in the air before him and pulled the automatic out of nowhere. But all he'd done had been to take it from inside his jacket, where it now left a cold space pretty much as the Lewis Alexander letter had once done. Fraser reached out a hand, and

John reluctantly turned the gun around and gave it to him butt-first.

'It's a Swiss nine-millimetre,' he said. 'Supposed to be very accurate.'

'Supposed to be?' Fraser said, sensing a hitch. 'You mean it isn't?'

'I mean I never actually fired it to find out.'

Fraser started to go over the weapon, at first just testing its weight in his hand but then giving it a closer look to see how it came apart. Sara said, 'What are you doing with it, John?'

'I just carry it around.'

'Is it licensed?'

'No. I bought it two years back from a Dane – we were both working in the same hotel in St Andrews. He'd managed to keep it somehow when his national service ended, but he needed cash in a hurry.'

'What did you pay him?' Fraser said. He'd first checked that the breech was clear, and now he was holding the gun open so that he could squint down it in an attempt to see firelight.

'I think it was about fifty pounds,' John said, trying to sound casual when he knew the amount down to the last note.

'You got a bargain. This is a seven-hundred-dollar gun back home. What kind of grease is this?'

'Vaseline. It's all I could get.'

'Doesn't seem to have harmed it any.' He returned the slide, and then dropped the magazine. 'How many rounds?'

'As many as you see. I think it's five.' As if he hadn't counted them, over and over whenever he reloaded.

'Is that all?'

'I told you, I never used it.'

'You just carry it about.'

'Right.'

Fraser shook his head, obviously thinking John a little screwy but not wanting to say so. He snapped the magazine back into place and ran the slide once more to bring a round up into the breech; the working design was the basic Browning type, nothing he couldn't handle, although the standard of finish was higher than any other gun that he'd seen so close. John was avoiding looking at Sara, even though he could somehow feel that she was looking at him.

Fraser hefted the gun, getting the muscles of his wiry arm used to the weight. He said, 'Well, we could be in business. That's if the charges haven't deteriorated and left us with a dud or a one-handed booby trap.'

'Do you think you can get anything?' Sara said, and he shrugged.

'It'll have to be something big enough to hit and small enough to die. Five rounds doesn't give us any margin, I could waste them all just learning to shoot straight.' And he tried levelling the two pounds of blued steel, as if he might try to blast out the fire through the back of the grate. He seemed pleased, and it was the pleasure of having an edge at last, of being in control. John watched, and tried to fight down his sense of loss. He didn't look at Sara – whatever she was thinking about him, he didn't want to know it.

TWENTY-SIX

They went out into the woods above the lodge, strung out in a line and watching for tracks. Sara had been explaining to John how they'd seen the spoor of a deer or a stag alongside the trail before he'd caught up with them the previous night, but Fraser had told her to forget it: 'I've got no chance of a killing shot with a pistol, so don't be getting too ambitious. We're talking about a couple of days, not the siege of Paris. Three of us could barely drag the damn thing back, and that's when the *real* problems would start.'

Butchering the kill was an aspect of the hunt that Sara hadn't even considered until now, and it quietened her. Now she and John were taking the outside line with Fraser in the middle, armed and ready to go for any game that they could scare up. They carried sticks, and they banged them on the trees as they walked; if anything should bolt, John was hoping that it would have the decency to run forwards instead of back. He didn't warm to the idea of being in Fraser's line of fire as he swung around to bear on it, because of the two targets John would be the bigger and probably not the faster.

It would be a good excuse for an accident, if Fraser felt like arranging one.

They were all watching the ground, which was how they almost managed to miss seeing the two birds that started out from a tree over John's head; Fraser spun around with the gun and John tensed himself as if for a punch in the chest, but the prey was already out of easy range and flickering through the woodland. They'd have been no big prize, anyway, and one of them alone wouldn't have been worth carrying back.

The line moved on, and John kept his eyes down and tried not to think of his gun, twenty yards away and being carried by *someone else*. Even if he got it back unfired, it would never feel the same.

He decided that if he saw any tracks, he was going to say nothing. He could last without food for two days, and so could Sara if she'd only recognise her own strengths and admit it. As for Fraser, he could clutch his belly and howl. If the whole world should give him a round of applause, he'd still consider himself singled out to be spat upon. What really ate at John was that he'd produced the gun and suggested the hunt at all; any respect that it might have bought him from Sara had quickly faded with the admission that he was no more than a midnight cowboy, carrying a totem that was way out of his league.

The snow under the trees was peppered with worm-holes, yesterday's drips from the sunwarmed branches overhead; but there was no sun today, and even though it was only early afternoon they'd be able to keep this up for no more than an hour. John ducked a branch, and then moved aside to go around a stand of reeds that had gathered a small drift. He could carry on for an hour, no problem. But then Sara called out that she'd found something.

John had the most ground to cover, and when he arrived Fraser was crouching down and doing his best to work out the direction of the tracks. It wasn't so easy, because whatever had made them had been moving fast and it had kicked up a lot of snow. John's disappointment lessened when he saw this – the animal probably had a lot of distance behind it, and Fraser's chances of catching up with it must be slight. Sara was looking uncertain, as if she was sensing that her simple gesture in pointing out the tracks was no less than a death sentence written small.

Fraser made his decision, and left the two of them standing under a tree as he set out alone. They watched him moving through the pines, walking carefully and keeping his eyes on the ground ahead; a couple of times he had to stop and look around, and it was obvious that the trail didn't always show up clear. Bad leg or not, Fraser was moving like a cat. Sara shivered. It was cold enough, but John knew that the cold wasn't all of the reason.

Fraser came into a slightly raised clearing, and they got a good view of what happened next. Something broke from the ground near his feet, something that he would have walked on past if only its nerve hadn't failed it. They saw Fraser recover quickly from his surprise and bring the gun around, by which time the animal was a streaking blur almost at the edge of the clearing and into cover. He fired once, and it was checked – not hit, only jerked still by the wall of sound and moving again in a sideways dodge as Fraser got the next shot away, missing again but causing it to switch direction and lose ground in a feint. Then, as it had almost made up the wasted distance to safety, another shot which flipped it up in the air and then crashing down in a tangle; and there was a high-pitched whistling note that John had never heard before.

Sara had never heard a rabbit scream, either, and the realisation brought her up short of the clearing with John a little way behind. The animal was in its white winter coat, and there was red on the snow where most of one of its back legs had been blown away; the rabbit itself was on its back and flailing around madly. Fraser was approaching from the opposite side, and he was looking pleased with himself.

'Finish it, Jerry,' Sara said, 'please!'

'I wasted two already,' Fraser said, and he threw the gun to John. He caught it awkwardly, and he felt the heat of the barrel even through his gloves. The rabbit had managed to get its usable limbs underneath itself, and it was making an attempt to scoot as it saw Fraser reaching down from above; but it did no more than scrabble in the snow as he took hold of its back and lifted it, squirming, into the air. The smashed leg fell apart, stringing out flesh and sinew to the snow beneath. Fraser gripped it by the scruff, and eased back its head. There was a crack, and the rabbit stiffened.

He held it out by the ears, but it was now quite limp. 'There's some tradition says you hang it from your belt,' he said. 'But I think I'll skip on that one.'

They'd be back at the lodge in twenty minutes or less. Fraser went ahead, the others followed in silence. The rabbit's white coat was bloodied and dirty, the body twisting unnaturally from the broken neck, the mangled leg streaming in the cold air. Sara was trying not to look at it, but when she looked at the ground instead she saw the trail that it dripped. John put the gun into his pocket. Now it was just metal, all of the magic blasted out of it in three sharp bursts.

As the lodge came into sight, Fraser said, 'Maybe it's my imagination, but the company seems damn quiet today.'

'You could have spared another shot,' Sara said, so quickly that it had obviously been in her mind since they'd started to walk.

Fraser said, 'For what? Blast off another leg and make it scream some more? You saw the way it was flapping around.'

'I saw the way you killed it.'

'What I did was neat and fast. Who was it talked about starvation?'

John said nothing, and neither did anybody else until they'd entered the lodge and were coming through into the kitchen. Then Fraser dumped the rabbit on the plain wooden table and turned to them.

'All right,' he said, 'that's it. I assume I'm in the presence of a couple of bleeding hearts who never had the moral inconvenience of having their lunch die in front of them before, right? Well, here's something to make you feel better about it. I've seen it done to people, and they scream louder.' He unbuttoned a side-flap on his parka

266

and dug deep; he came out with his horn-handled knife, and he slammed it onto the table.

'Now it's got to be skinned and cleaned,' he said. 'Enjoy yourselves.'

He walked out of the kitchen and shut the door hard; they could hear him all the way down the hall.

John picked up the knife, and opened it. The blade came stiffer than he expected. It was well-honed, and slick to the touch with a thin film of oil. He looked at the rabbit; long-legged, short-eared, thick pads of fur between its toes to support it on the snow. Its eyes, which were open, were large and dark. It was probably no longer warm at the surface, but deep inside . . .

Sara said, 'Can you do it?'

'I don't think so. You?'

She shook her head. 'I've cleaned fish, but . . .'

He put the knife on the table. 'I know,' he said. 'It's not the same.'

The rabbit just lay there, as dead as any in a brace outside a butcher's shop; it was watching it die that seemed to have made all of the difference, just as Fraser had said.

'He knows, doesn't he?' John said.

Sara closed her eyes slowly, as if he was giving her more than she could handle. She didn't have to ask what John meant; she said, 'Yes. I should think he's picked up the message by now.'

'Doesn't that change things?'

'I still owe him. That doesn't change.'

Fraser burst through the door.

Shit, was John's first reaction, *he sneaked back to listen*, and he was glad that the automatic was safe in his own pocket and nowhere else; but then he realised that Fraser's eyes were alive with a different fire.

'Somebody came to call while we were out,' he said, and he beckoned for them to follow. Sara came around the table, with Visco close behind her.

She said, 'Who?'

'He didn't leave a message, just his tracks.'

Fraser led them to the main door, the one they hadn't used since they arrived, and he lifted the latch and opened it wide. They looked out down the covered boardwalk of the verandah, to the corner of the building where it jutted out over the valley. Windblown snow had piled on it, undisturbed the last time any of them had looked; now, emerging from the trampled mess of their own prints around the gate and the doorway, there was a single line of paw marks. The path of whatever had made them could be easily traced, stopping at the first window and looking in, carrying on to the next and looking again, and then on around the corner and out of sight. They followed the line out to the corner and around to find that it was the same again, not a window missed, and then back down side number three to the other end of the verandah, where the wider spacing of a running leap had ended abruptly as the animal cleared the rail. A little snow had been brushed from the balustrade, but not much.

'That was one powered jump,' Fraser said, and he looked over the rail for where it had landed. John was taking more of an interest in the last of the windows which wasn't actually a window but a flimsy-looking access door which would open directly into the sitting room. Ideal for officers to come strolling out with an after-dinner brandy and get homesick for Bavaria, but for security it wasn't much. It looked as if a good rattling would get it open.

He looked again at the marks. He said, 'Any idea what made them?'

'Wolf,' Fraser said confidently. 'The damn thing isn't going to leave me alone.'

He turned, and started the trek around the building to get back inside. Sara met John's eyes for a moment, and then she followed Fraser.

TWENTY-SEVEN

Around the time that the three refugees in the mountain cabin were discovering that they didn't have the far-off valley entirely to themselves, Olav Nystrom was watching the last of the fishing fleet disappear around the headland. It was still too early for the big winter shoals, but the idea was to run a check on the seaworthiness of the boats that had been more or less laid up for the summer. Jan-Erik's announcement had been a surprise, but not a big one; the general opinion in the village was that nothing would come of adding ruin to grief, although the speed of the turn-around had set a few people rocking.

For a moment he forgot himself, and his breath misted the glass of the attic window. When he rubbed it away, the last of the boats had winked out of sight. He bounded down off the bed and went downstairs.

Even if they had to turn back for some reason, he'd have more than an hour. Jan-Erik had wanted him along, but Nystrom's dissociation from the fleet was now so complete that his father couldn't insist without it looking suspicious. He'd offered instead to catch up on a job he'd been putting off for more than a month, the overhaul of Mattis' ancient grey Volvo. All it really needed was new plugs and a tweak on the chain to get the timing back into line, but to Mattis it had sounded as if the old car was slowly dying. It had given Nystrom the excuse to dig out the snow before the wharf shed doors and bring the battery into the kitchen to be charged; and if anybody should happen to mention later about seeing him drive along the coast road and back, he'd have his explanation ready for that, too.

The kitchen was empty. Ingrid and Anja were at the *barnskole*, their mother was still keeping vigil with the other Nystrom women in the house across the yard. Nystrom got into his boots and his outdoor gear and then disconnected the battery from the mains, carrying it out with charger, cable and everything across by the sea-steps and into the shed.

There wasn't much space to move about inside, and he had to open the double doors to give himself room to work. The lower floor of the warehouse was supposed to be the tackle store, so the shed had become a kind of tackle dump, the place where all the junk and the odds and ends left over after refits and repairs got rolled up and stacked in no particular order. Nystrom had to bring out four bicycles and a paper sack filled with holed waders before he could get the Volvo onto the wharf.

He drove slowly down the quay, not wanting to trust the snow tyres completely with the unguarded edge so close, and when he reached the main square he turned into the long street that would run down by the school and loop into the coast road tunnel. This was always the best-ploughed, with banks pushed up before the shops and houses on either side that could get ten feet high or more by the end of the winter. When you heard the big wagon going past, you came out quick with a shovel and started digging your way through; leave it for more than a few hours and you might find that you were walled-in for good, and it would take a couple of men with pickaxes most of an afternoon to get you out.

The Volvo handled well, even though there had been hardly any other cars along to help compact the snow; its age gave it an advantage in weight – if it hadn't been in use during the Occupation, it couldn't have missed it by much – and the weight gave it traction. He was going to need it, because the coast road didn't get cleared more than twice a week, and then only to keep open a backup access to the light in case the sea-route couldn't be used.

He came in by the old *klipfisk* racks, frameworks of open timber that stood higher than any house in Tromstad. In spring the fish would be hung here to dry in the sea breezes, but now the racks were empty apart from a few dried-up bundles of feathers that had once been birds, strung up by their legs to keep others away. It wasn't the racks that he'd come to see, but he steered the Volvo into the warehouse yard where the plough had turned and left it in the shelter of one of the empty buildings. He'd have to walk the last couple of hundred metres to the Brøndsted house.

From the path over the rocky headland he could see down to the light-keeper's jetty, a private wooden pier in a cove that was reached by a long cut of steps. Per Brøndsted's motor launch was tied up there, bobbing slightly in the flat swell of the fjord waters. It meant that he probably hadn't gone out with the fleet as Nystrom had hoped he might, but at least it removed a possible complication – Roskva had already been at the centre of one low-key storm of bitterness and rumour, and it wouldn't take much to start another.

It was a long time since he'd last been to the house, and as he got close he began to look for the new woodwork around the window that had been involved in Roskva's 'accident'. What he saw instead was that the light-keeper's windows now had bars.

They were new-looking and unpainted, probably Sven Lidman's work. They were held with bolts on the outside. Nystrom came up to the door and raised his hand to knock, but the door was already open.

The house seemed to be empty. A strong draught raised itself and entered the hallway with him, suggesting a window or another door open somewhere around the back. The wind lifted curtains and riffled through papers on a bureau as he moved from room to room.

271

What he saw was a mess, uncared-for and in some places actively damaged. It seemed all wrong – Roskva had always kept the house obsessively neat, but now there were stains on the rugs and the sofa had been slashed. He stopped by a doorway and ran his fingers over some deep scratches in the woodwork of the frame; they were at the right level for fingernails, but they felt as if they'd been cut with a chisel. So where was Brøndsted, and why had the door been open?

Nystrom came back into the hallway and looked around, uncertain of what to do next, and it was then that he heard a scuffling from upstairs.

It was hardly any sound at all, and it didn't come again for almost a minute as he stood at the bottom of the stairs and listened. Nosing around like this hadn't been part of the plan, and it was making him feel uncertain and embarrassed. He called out a couple of times, as much to establish his innocence as an intruder as anything else, but nobody answered; then the noise came again, and he started to climb.

Although most of the doors on the upper landing were halfway open, it was fairly dark; the inside shutters on the bedroom windows must all have been closed. It was an odd feeling, a darkened house in the middle of the afternoon, and it suggested something illicit and faintly entertaining. Perhaps she'd kept it like this when . . . but he couldn't bring himself to finish the thought.

He gave one of the doors a push and then took his hand away quickly, as if it wasn't too late to pretend he hadn't done it. But there was nobody inside, just an empty main bedroom with a few streaks of light to show where the shutters didn't quite meet. When he took a step through he noticed an unpleasantly sour smell like that of a sickroom or an untended nursery; it was also a few degrees colder than the rest of the house, and from the insistent edge on the air he guessed that the window on the other side of the shutters had been opened as far as the bars would allow.

A table-lamp had been upset just by the window,

knocked almost over by the draught but held from top-pling by its flex. It leaned against the shutter with its shade awry, and as the breeze stiffened for a moment it began to rock from side to side. It made the scuffling sound that had drawn him in.

So it seemed that he was alone in the house. There was an unsettling, disjointed feeling about the place, like the world glimpsed on the other side through a funhouse mirror. He turned to go. Roskva came at him out of the darkness.

He came around in slow stages. First came the thunder, all out of tune and out of time, but then the input started to arrange itself into the patterns of the outside world again and became a bone-breaking pain in his chest and shoulder. There was another, duller ache at the back of his head; he'd slammed back into the wall, and it was resting against the bruise. Somebody was going through his pockets.

He opened his eyes. Roskva stopped and stared at him, like an animal disturbed in feeding. Then she carried on, fumbling through his jacket with a lot of haste but not much method.

He could barely recognise her; the change was almost as much of a shock as the hammerblow she'd given him. She'd been – how had Jerry described it? – a china doll, so perfect that memory couldn't hold it all and seeing her was always like being hit for the first time. Now she was like a mad woman, her golden hair in unkempt strands and her clothes a rag-bag arrangement that had become grimy and torn.

Nystrom tried to raise himself, but he picked the wrong angle. The arm on his mistreated side couldn't support him and he fell back against the wall, dazzling himself with a lightshow in white and purple. Something clicked by his side, a small sound of metal on metal, and when his vision came back Roskva had gone. He touched his shoulder; it was a web of soreness with a white-hot centre, but at least

273

he could move it. As he was getting his feet under him, he saw Per Brøndsted.

The light-keeper swayed into view in the doorway of a room across the landing, trailing a bloodstained sheet behind him that he'd pressed to a bad wound on the side of his forehead. With his big hands and his clumsy build he'd always seemed like a beast to Roskva's beauty, but now he was just crumpled and old. *Olav, your boat,'* he was saying as he reached out for the wall to steady himself, and the sheet whispered around the doorway behind him like a snake.

'I'm in a car,' Nystrom said, 'but she took the keys.' Ordinarily he'd have left them in the Volvo, but a summer spent with some of the Teamverk men had taught him different habits.

'Where did you leave it?'

'The warehouse yard, by the racks. Can she drive?'

'She can try.'

The cold air helped to revive them both when they got outside, and Per Brøndsted led the way over the headland path. When they reached the Volvo there was no sign of Roskva, and only Nystrom's own tracks led in a single set from the wide loop where the plough had turned. Brøndsted looked back over the headland, his breath hanging ragged in the cold air.

'She doesn't know,' he said. 'She's gone for the boats anyway.'

All of the steps down to the cove had been shovelled clear, and as Nystrom descended he could see most of the pier. There was nobody on it. Per Brøndsted could see as much, but it didn't slow him. He was weaving dangerously, missing steps and coming close to stumbling. He wore a thick-knit pullover with darns on the elbows but no jacket, and the scab on the side of his forehead couldn't have been more than ten or fifteen minutes old; Nystrom did his best to keep up, but he was still on the last run of steps as Brøndsted made it onto the boards of the jetty.

He went straight to the launch and climbed aboard. The

boat moved with his weight and there was a rasp of metal over wood. Nystrom saw as he got closer that the rope hawser had been replaced with a chain, and the chain had been padlocked through a couple of cleats on the jetty's mooring. Like the bars on the house windows, it looked like new work; there was a raw spot on the edge of the boards where the chain had been rubbing.

Holding his shoulder, which had been starting to get better but which was now worse from the jarring of their descent, Nystrom crossed the planking and looked down into the launch. Roskva was there, collapsed against Per Brøndsted's chest and weeping bitterly. She'd been trying to force the Volvo's keys into the boat's ignition; one of them was jammed half-way in, and the ring with its leather tag hung crookedly from the dash. She was hugging Per Brøndsted for comfort, and he was stroking her hair.

'It's all right,' he was saying. 'Everything's all right.'

'I won't lie to you, Olav.' Per Brøndsted sat on one of the hard kitchen chairs with his hands on his knees, holding himself still as Nystrom worked with a lint pad and some disinfectant to clean up the wound on the side of his head. Brøndsted looked sideways as much as he could, and said, 'You believe me?'

'Sure.'

'That thing out there, the thing in the mountains. It's a part of her. She made it.'

'Made it how?'

But Per Brøndsted's answer was to shrug and sigh heavily. He could accept the impossible, but the mechanisms of the impossible were beyond him. Nystrom could see over the big man's shoulder that the kitchen door, leading only to the yard where Brøndsted kept his gas cylinders and fuel-oil drums, had been bolted and padlocked on the inside. The extra security dated back, Nystrom was sure, to that disastrous afternoon of several weeks before; but its purpose was not, as he'd first assumed, to keep others out, but to keep Roskva in.

She'd been waiting behind the door as Per Brøndsted returned from clearing the jetty steps. They'd found the heavy spanner she'd used on them both when they'd taken her back upstairs; Brøndsted had been using it to switch cylinders the night before, and then he'd locked it in a drawer that she'd somehow been able to open. Now she was back on her bed, curled tight into an unresponsive foetal ball. When nobody was around, Per Brøndsted had told Nystrom, she would creep downstairs and he would find her in the same position on the bare floor of the second bedroom.

'She needs help,' Nystrom said as he wrung out the bloody cloth into a basin. 'She needs a doctor.'

'What she needs is to be whole again. But it's too late, she can't take it back. It would kill her.'

'Like Kristin.'

Per Brøndsted bowed his head miserably. 'Now tell that to your father and the others. I asked for their help and they told me to let it run. They wanted it to harm the mines men and maybe drive them away.'

'Whose idea was it to set up Jerry Fraser?'

'I don't know. That came after Kristin.'

'And whose idea was it to involve me?'

Per Brøndsted sighed again. 'I don't know, Olav,' he said, 'I really don't.'

But Nystrom already knew the answer. It had been the price for trying to walk away.

He didn't look back at the house. He went down to the rocky shore by the *klipfisk* racks and turned his face to the salt sea wind; it plastered his hair flat and started cold tears in his eyes, but it had no power to cleanse him.

The first of the boats was a small blip on his horizon, already around the headland and steaming for home. It still had a lot of the fjord to cover, and he could get the Volvo back into the shed and stripped down before the ropes were being thrown onto the quay. His trip had served its purpose, as had theirs – the informed and the

276

ignorant alike had been kept out of the way whilst the calf had been staked to draw the wolf.

But this wolf wasn't an innocent in search of prey. It was something far more dangerous in a borrowed shape, and it was looking for a home of its own.

Jan-Erik hadn't called the police in Narvik, and he didn't intend to; his answer to the danger had been to set up not a single calf but three, Fraser, Sara and the English stranger – none of them family, none of them his own kind.

There was no point in trying to make the call himself. Fru Sandø at the exchange had to be part of the scheme, or she'd be wanting to know why nothing had yet gone through. Again he was nine years old and hiding under the table, a witness to events that he couldn't control, events that no longer made any rational sense but which moved to a cruel logic of their own.

He put his back to the open water and descended to the yard. He thought that he was doing pretty well, so far. It wasn't often that you had to adjust to a new outlook on the world, to come to terms with a place where – just every now and again – the rivers might be found to run uphill.

TWENTY-EIGHT

They'd brought in more wood to dry on the hearth, but it didn't burn well. It wasn't just the way that the fire flickered and spat, it was the whole day that worked to make the three of them listless and depressed, and when the light started to fade and Fraser went around again to close all of the curtains, nobody suggested that he was wasting his time.

He hadn't forced home his argument over the rabbit – at least, not as hard as he might. After the point had been made, he went alone to the kitchen and gutted and skinned his catch. What remained after the fur and the insides had been thrown away had hardly seemed worth the effort, but they'd stewed it in a pan on the open fire anyway.

Every now and again, the timbers of the lodge would shift, as if the place couldn't get comfortable with the corner of warmth they were making. It was used to sleeping on through the winter cold, and it did its best to let them know that they weren't welcome. Fraser stared into the fire, Sara hugged her knees and stared off into the dark.

John said, 'Maybe we'd have been better taking our chances in the village.' He was only putting into words what each of them was probably thinking, but Fraser dived onto it straight away.

'You, maybe,' he said. 'What do you think *my* chances were?'

'Sometimes people take running like it was a confession.'

'Look, I've been getting this all season from stoneheads like Ashton. You didn't have to come with me.'

'I didn't have much choice.'

'You had all the choice you could want. What scared you was the idea of standing out on your own. Well, I'm sorry if I didn't stop to explain it all to you, but I had other things on my mind.'

'I wasn't trying to complain.'

'Like hell you weren't. You're trailing lines, and then as soon as somebody grabs one you cut it loose. Don't throw out an argument if you're not prepared to stand with it.'

Sara said, 'Come on, Jerry,' but she only made it worse. Fraser looked angrily at her and John together.

'And don't think I've missed what's been going on with you two,' he said. 'If you're wondering why I still dragged myself out to show you the mines, it's because the only thing that keeps me going is the knowledge that there's one straight guy left in the world, even if it's only me. I suppose you told him about me and the army?'

Sara, who seemed to know that nothing she could say was going to divert Fraser onto another set of rails, said, 'It was mentioned.'

'I bet it was,' Fraser said, and he took a breath as if there was a lot of spite built up and ready to break through; but then, at the point of bursting, he seemed to lose his energy. He sank back into the old armchair and rubbed a hand across his face as if he might reshape it and come out as someone else, but all he did was to scratch himself raw on his day-old beard. He was sick of defending himself. It had become such a habit, he was doing it even when no-one attacked him.

Outside on the verandah, something was moving.

John was watching Fraser. Sara had obviously heard it all before, and she wasn't interested. What fascinated John was a single thought; that of the three, Jerry had become the outsider.

'What the hell,' Fraser murmured. 'Even I'm getting sick of the sound of it.'

Sara looked up suddenly, and she frowned. Nobody was paying any attention, but a moment later they all heard it, a faint combination of wood on wood and the squeak of a hinge, the balustrade gate on the verandah being pushed back over a wedge of snow.

'Somebody found us,' she said, but Fraser turned back to stare into the fire.

'Let him bang on the door,' he said.

But they waited, and nothing else happened.

No knock, no bang, not even a rap on the window to get their attention. Sara slowly raised herself from her armchair. The fire was their only light in the room, and it put her shadow across the wall. John reached for one of their candles and lit it as Sara crossed the floor to the end window, and then he followed her over.

Fraser tried to pretend that he wasn't interested, but he couldn't keep it up. A mob would be making more noise, and if it was Olav come to tell him that he was safe – well, why was the kid standing out there on the boardwalk without making another sound? He got up to join the others.

Sara was by the window, and John was standing well back. All she needed to do was to reach out and draw back the flimsy material of the curtain, and the light would fall through the glass and show whoever it was that was standing out there. She halfway raised her hand, but she was hesitating. She couldn't do it.

Come on, Fraser was thinking, angry with her although he knew well enough the apprehension that was holding her back. It was the same kind of feeling that he'd always got outside the freak show, terrified of what he was going to see when the reality always turned out to be common-place and even pathetic.

There was another noise, a kind of shuffling sound. Fraser said, 'Either somebody's in bad shape, or we've got wolf trouble again.'

Sara looked alarmed, and the show of her fear was somehow deepened by the light of the candle. She said, 'Can he get in?'

'Not as long as we don't open up to him.'

'What about the next time we go out?' John said.

'I don't know. Down by the village I'd say we were okay, but here . . . depends how hungry he is.'

The wolf, if it *was* the wolf, had started to move down the boardwalk. The three of them on the inside followed it along to the next window, and when it seemed to stop, they stopped.

'It's winter,' Sara said, 'he'll be hungry, all right. Let's take a look at him.'

'No,' John said, but Fraser was already reaching out to jerk the curtain away. He couldn't have put a name to the things that he'd been shutting out when he'd pulled the drapes earlier, but the wolf was different. He'd seen it, chased it, almost been close enough to touch it; he'd lost count of the number of times that the animal had nosed around his gear at the mine and chomped at his telephone wire, and he'd wasted nearly three days with his camera just trying to get another sight of the beast. When it came to the Tromstad wolf, Jerry was the expert.

He said, 'Maybe the light will scare him off,' but the faint panic noise that escaped from John was enough to make him turn.

John had backed off. He had an expression as if he'd managed to sneak an advance look at the scenario they were playing, and he knew that it was all about to turn very sour.

Sara said, 'Is it because of the dream?' and John nodded.

'A *dream*?' Fraser said, incredulous. 'Jesus.' And he ripped the curtain back.

He was too late, the animal had moved on. There was a faint mist of its breath on the glass that was already turning to frost. Fraser tried to catch up, but he almost fell over the furniture on the unlit fringe of the room, and he called to John to stay with him.

Another window, and too late again. The candlelight showed a faint square of the verandah, a section of the balustrade, part of one of the column supports for the overhang; the shadows moved and lengthened as John came around, but the wolf had already reached the first corner of the building and there would be no way of seeing it from here.

Now Fraser was beginning to get angry. He threw a chair aside so hard that it rocked over and crashed to the floor, but then he almost tripped on a corner of a rug that he'd lifted; it was as if the layout of the room had been carefully planned for this moment, to slow him down and keep him always one window behind as the wolf padded on around them.

The snow outside wasn't so thick on the boards that they couldn't hear the scratch of its claws; the wolf and Fraser were heading for the corner window together, Fraser desperately clearing his way through whilst the wolf was taking its time. 'Come on, come on,' Fraser was muttering, either at the wolf or at himself – it was difficult to tell as he was clipped by a bureau that nobody could even remember seeing before, bouncing off and reaching for the curtain to jerk it down, rod and everything.

And then he stopped.

It might have been some kind of game, everybody freeze, although the sound that had caused Fraser to pull back was nothing to laugh at. It came through the thin wall as easily as if the animal had been in the room with them.

The wolf was struggling painfully into an upright stance.

Fraser's hand slowly dropped, and the drapes stayed closed. They could still track the animal's hoarse breathing as it came from near floor-height almost to a level with themselves, falling back the first time but making it on the second attempt. And then came something that all three of them knew, even though there was no way that they could see it; in the same moment they were aware that the beast was turning its head and looking into the room, its gaze unchecked by anything that could be placed before it. They were held for a moment by an energy so fierce that they couldn't have moved even if they'd wanted to. The only imaginable option was to run but they had nowhere to go, just this tarpaper shack that suddenly didn't seem half as solid as they'd all believed.

There was a fourfold click, and a very faint squeak as of damp chamois. It was leaning on the glass and panting hard as it watched their shapes on the thin cotton, but then it swallowed noisily and pushed itself away as if to prove that it no longer needed help. It started to move again, only now it wasn't with the wolf's easy stride but with an awkward strut as if bones and muscles wouldn't quite fit together, a counterfeit man assembled without plan or pattern.

Fraser didn't try to race it any more. He stayed where he was and listened with the others as the animal took its time to cover all of the verandah, checking on them from every side. It paused at each window and, cold as it was, for a few seconds the room got colder. The last window of all was one that John remembered from the outside. Because it wasn't a window at all, it was a flimsy-looking door with its top half glazed to match the window beside it, and he remembered idly thinking that it would only need a strong hand and a firm shoulder to bust it inwards.

One of the armchairs was blocking the door on the inside – that was why they hadn't seen it earlier – but the chair wasn't close enough to keep anything back, it had just been rolled across the gap because there was nowhere else for it to go. Each of them probably had the same thought at the same time, which was to get across the room and push the chair hard up against the wall, jamming it against the door so that its weight could serve where the thin pine couldn't; but nobody moved except Fraser, and Fraser moved too late.

He took one faltering step, and the handle began to turn. The woodwork groaned as it was pushed inwards. Fraser hesitated, caught in the firelight. The pressure on the door increased, and then there was a single, snapping report; it sounded as if the frame was breaking in, but it was the handle springing back as the animal lost its grip. There was a scrabbling of nails on wood, as if it was trying to manage with broken hands. The panting got harder – it was either with the effort or with the frustration, they couldn't tell – and the handle started to jump up and down, making a sound that echoed down through the empty lodge like a Gestapo team's midnight hammering.

The noise stopped as abruptly as it started, and it left nothing; no breathing, no presence, no claws on the boards, no slow groan of muscle on wood. John appreciated then that Fraser, whatever his other hangups might have been, was no coward, because it was Fraser who got up the nerve to stride forward and pull the drape aside.

Nothing there. If it had stayed with the pattern they'd followed through the snow that afternoon, it was over the balustrade and away across the *fjell*. Even if they'd had a light powerful enough to seek it out at a distance, none of them would have wanted to use it.

'What's the dream, John?' Fraser said quietly, and this time there was no mockery in his voice; it was as if the fabric of his world was starting to give way under pressure, and believing that he was no more than a part of someone else's nightmare would be an easy way out.

There was only one answer that John could honestly give. 'This one,' he said, letting Sara take the candle from him as she passed. If events ran true to the plan this should be the awakening, the worst part before he came out into the silence and the safety of the night; even as he tried to believe it, he knew that it wasn't going to happen, that the nightmares had been no more than the nursery slopes for the reality now getting set to play itself out.

Sara did something that hadn't even occurred to either of the two men. She stood close to the glass with the candle raised high, and she looked down for tracks. The snow was so stamped-over and disturbed from the afternoon, there was no way of telling what had gone past or how it had been formed.

She turned back to face the room. 'What about the scullery door?' she said.

Pretty much the same sequence of thoughts ran through everybody's mind. The scullery door had no lock, not even a catch to fox something that couldn't manage a simple handle; but it let out into the yard, and the gate to the yard was shut; but then the safety of that was illusory, because the yard was a part of the terrace that had been cut into the *fjellside*, and the high ground ran level with the top of its wall.

And if that wasn't enough, there was bait. Without even thinking about it, Fraser had thrown the rabbit's offal out onto the snow.

He was on his way. 'Bring the gun,' he shouted back at John, and then he was running into the darkness of the hallway with Sara close behind. John's jacket was over the back of one of the armchairs by the fire, and as he dived for it a door somewhere slammed with immense force and the fire went nova, more than doubling its brightness as it surged with an updraught. John had been around when something similar had happened before, in the tacked-on cabin annex to Leif Lokkeberg's place when Ashton and Bonneau had forced their way in; it meant that a door to the outside had been opened.

His jacket seemed to be fighting back at him. He got the wrong pocket first, and almost turned the whole thing inside out trying to put himself right; and then, when he found it, he could feel the hard shape of the gun but it had got itself jammed in somehow and he couldn't pull it out, and he only finally ripped it free when he was halfway down the hall and stumbling over the coat as it trailed out behind him.

Jerry and Sara were at the end of the hall. The kitchen door was closed, and Fraser had his hands around the brass doorknob; only his fingertips were touching, waiting for the first sign of movement from the other side. John could read enough of his expression in the dim light to know that he should be silent.

They all listened. They could hear the quiet, unexcited scratching of claws on the stone floor of the kitchen. The sound changed as the animal crossed the rough matting before the hearth, and then was back as before. It was circling, investigating, checking out every corner of the room. Fraser must have tightened his grip without meaning to, because there was the faintest touch of metal against metal; the animal was across the room and behind the door in less than a second, bouncing like a pup to the clatter of the dinnerbowl.

Sara put her hands over Fraser's, and together they held the door firm as it started to shake. If its paws (or whatever they were) could barely manage a straight handle, they'd have even less chance with a round doorknob. Somehow, that wasn't as much consolation as it should have been, and Visco was also finding that the flat coldness of the gun in his hand didn't give him the same kind of reassurance that it did in the security of a hotel room. He'd never fired a shot in his life, there were only two rounds left in the magazine, Fraser and Sara and two inches of solid door were between him and his first-ever target, and his first-ever target was a beast that left tracks like a wolf but tried to walk like a man.

'Don't just stand there,' Fraser told him, looking over his shoulder at John while the shaking of the door gave way to a much harder battering. Its hands might not bend as they should, but it didn't lack strength. John hefted the automatic, and hoped that he looked as if he knew what he was doing.

'You're in the way,' he said, 'move back.'

'And let it in? No chance.'

'Then take the gun!'

'How many fucking arms have I got?'

He couldn't see what Fraser expected him to do – put a shot through the door? The SIG delivered a punch that was harder than most, but it seemed over-optimistic to expect it to break through so much solid wood and still come out deadly. Sara was gripping Fraser's hands so hard that there were flecks of blood where her nails had dug in.

And then, as abruptly as it had started, the hammering stopped.

Fraser looked at John, and John nodded. Sara got out of the way first, slipping well clear and then standing back to watch as Fraser reduced his contact with the door all the way down to fingertips again, at full stretch and with most of his body out of the firing line. John levelled his gun, feeling less than confident behind its wall of stopping power. He didn't even know what stopping power *meant*. Fraser snapped the door open and slammed it inwards, and before it hit the wall he was back with Sara.

Nothing came out, but John almost put a shot into the empty doorway. Beyond it, the kitchen seemed undisturbed. No movement and no sound; he stepped forward into the darkness.

The kitchen was too full of angles and shadows. Through the scullery he could see that the back door was wide open, spilling a greyness through to pick out the surface of the big table and put a dull shine on the glass-panelled front of a dresser. Please, God, he was thinking, let it have run. And for once, it seemed that God had got it right by John Visco.

His sweep took him as far as the door without any unwelcome surprises. He kicked it shut and put his back to it; 'We're clear,' he shouted through to the others two rooms away. 'Get me a chair or something.'

Sara brought lights, Fraser brought one of the chairs from around the kitchen table and they wedged it at an angle behind the door. It wouldn't be foolproof, but they hammered it in as tightly as they could. John watched, mostly, holding the gun in a kind of daze. Nobody even mentioned what had happened, probably because they were still wondering whether or not they believed it. Soon it would be the time to start rationalising, to start questioning memories, to beat them out on the anvil of the familiar until they could be fitted in without too much difficulty. Until then, it was open season on the credible.

Something caught Fraser's eye as he stepped back in the scullery, and he reached out and lifted John's right hand. He turned the gun slightly to catch the light and said, 'You can improve all our chances with the safety catch off.'

He let it drop, and left John staring at the impotent weapon with alarm. As he came through into the kitchen, he said to Sara, 'Any ideas on who came knocking?'

Sara hesitated. There was something in Fraser's tone that told her the first of the shutters was already down. She said, quietly, '*Fenris*.'

'Is he from the village?'

'He isn't from anywhere.'

After a beat, Fraser rolled his eyes heavenward. 'Oh, great,' he said. 'Listen, why don't you both get together and swap stories while I do something useful and check all our windows?'

As Fraser walked out into the hall muttering to himself, John came through. 'Fenris?' he said, but it was as if she'd tried the idea once with Fraser and didn't like the results enough to try it again.

'Leave it, John,' she said, and she left him alone as she went out to help with security.

John pulled out a chair and sat down. Let the others handle the work for a few minutes, John Visco was the jerk who went hunting tigers with no cork in his popgun. He laid the gun on the table and switched the safety off, on, off. It was easy enough, you could unlock the slide one-handed if you needed to. He'd done it lots of times, snapping around to draw a bead on water glasses, vases, framed prints on the wall. Gideon bibles, or mostly on his own reflection in the mirror.

But then, that was John Visco's way. He only ballsed things up when they *really* counted.

TWENTY-NINE

He sighed, and ran a hand over his hair. He'd cut it himself with a pair of nail scissors, that was why it always looked so ragged. Fraser and Sara were moving about at the other end of the building – he could hear their voices, but they were too far-off for him to make out what they were saying. There was enough antagonism in it for him to suppose that he was being discussed, although it was an assumption that he'd made at other times and under other circumstances, and he usually turned out to be wrong. It was a perverse kind of vanity. Still, if they *were* arguing, and they were arguing about him, it meant that somebody had to be taking his side.

Fraser could say what he liked, but let him remember who'd been first through the door. John was wondering when the full meaning of this would get to him, especially the possibility of what might have happened if he'd tried to use the automatic; when all the might-have-beens came crowding in together they'd probably bring him to his knees, but for the moment he seemed to be holding it off without really being sure how he was doing it.

In a minute or so he'd go and help out, he told himself. It wouldn't matter what they were saying or who they were saying it about. A minute to unwind – he'd been first through the door, they owed him that.

The next chair along had been knocked out from the table in the rush. John realised that he'd been staring at it, and that it had set off a harmonic in his memory. For a while he listened to it singing, and then he had it.

290

Ten years ago, the kitchen in the big house that his father had bought for his mother, two years before the site accident that had killed him.

John Visco was only a few weeks away from finishing at school. He'd had reasonable offers from three of his five universities, and he still glowed with the reflected shine of other people's expectations for him. This time was still his sharpest memory, more so than the early years – these were just a blur, three or four towns and schools run together in a mismatched jigsaw, and the times that came later grew less and less pleasant as they went by.

The house had been his father's way of buying off his mother. She'd hated being unsettled, but even now it hadn't turned out the way she'd wanted because John's father simply left them for months at a stretch whilst he worked out contracts in other parts of England or abroad. His mother kept the place as prim as a museum, and the old man didn't disturb it much when he came home – he had neat and economical habits that he'd learned from his para-bachelorhood.

There was a certain discomfort whenever he was with them, like having a stranger around. John would lie awake, hearing him moving about downstairs when everybody else had gone to bed. One night – the night he was remembering now – he'd gone down and found his father in the kitchen, a large and randomly assorted meal on the table by the light of the open refrigerator door. John had pulled out a chair and joined him, thinking of how the scene confirmed his mother's description of the man as a gypsy in name and habits. It was the only time they ever really talked, and it was the only fragment of his father that John carried in his mind.

He didn't remember the conversation at all, but the moment and the atmosphere were with him now. As an escape, it wasn't much, and only hindsight showed that it had been a peak of happiness with only the downhill slopes ahead. At the time he'd thought it negligible, an

291

unworthy base for somebody who was going to fly so high. Looking back, he'd trade an age of his days for that one evening.

Why had it come back to him now, and why so strong? The kitchen was different, but the two chairs and the table had been just so, and the light of the open refrigerator had fallen across as the light of the candle did now; and in the more hazy sketching-in of the background, the dark space of the open doorway to the rest of the house had been in more or less the same place as the shadow cast by the unit that he and Fraser had pushed away from the wall that morning.

John stared. Memories sank back under the surface of the pool, but he was no longer paying attention. Without looking down, he reached for the gun with his right hand. He stood, and the chair behind him scraped a little on the stone. For a moment he waited, and then he slid the tin candle-holder across the table towards him and moved forward.

The safety catch was off. This time, he knew it.

The concealed door to the servants' bedrooms was still open, as was the door beyond that. He and Fraser had left them that way. They looked like an invitation.

He walked into the darkness, his light in one hand and his gun in the other. He found the beast in the furthest corner of the furthest room.

It had never even occurred to John that it might be as afraid as they were. It crouched in the shadows and wouldn't face him, hunching even lower and trying to press itself into the floor as he placed the candle on the flat top of a washstand by his side. John couldn't make out any details, and from the sounds he'd heard on the boardwalk he wasn't sure that he wanted to; but he knew that he couldn't simply spike it when it was cowering, not with the endless scream of Fraser's rabbit so fresh in his mind.

Fraser and Sara had moved through into the hallway. Their voices came over more clearly now.

'I didn't expect to get floored by competition from a soup-kitchen Casanova, that's all.'

'Whatever we had going, Jerry, you already ruined it. Maybe I just had a good teacher.'

'So why did you come back?'

'Because we've got a business deal.'

'You call it a business deal? Come on.'

'Think what you like, Jerry, it doesn't really matter.'

The animal turned its head to look at John. He saw the eyes first, twin fires of blue, their glow meeting his. He was aware only of the dim shape of the animal behind them as it began slowly to rise to man-height.

Is it you? The voice in John's mind said.

At that moment, he understood what it wanted.

Is it?

The animal – the *fylgja*, the follower – was incomplete. It was half a spirit, a single face of a coin of misery. Shut out by the girl who had created it, the beast was looking for a new home.

There was a sensation like a blade of ice forming at the centre of his heart.

Yes, a part of his mind over which he had no conscious control seemed to be saying. *Yes, it's me.*

The animal's eyes glowed brighter, and the ice began to spread.

He could feel it seeping through him, flash-flooding through his veins and arteries and setting hard wherever it reached. He wanted to cry out, but even as he tried it was as if his chest had been bound in steel hoops. He tried to raise his hand, but the ability was quickly and neatly taken from him.

The beast itself, meanwhile, was fading away.

He could actually see the pattern of shadows on the wall behind it. The follower was shedding its animal body, an unsatisfactory patchwork of the shapes that it had tried and found wanting. It was taking Visco over, drawing him on like a glove.

He strained to make it out, willing it to stay visible;

until the takeover was complete, perhaps he still had a chance of turning it around. But even the shadows were going grainy and losing their definition; the beast was taking his eyes.

So that was it; John was to be compressed down into a space where there was no light, no sound, no sensation. He wanted to try to fight it off, but he didn't know how. He felt like a man chained and weighted at the bottom of a pool, with light and sound a thousand miles away and his life bubbling out of him in silver.

The follower had now dismissed him, pushed him over to one side to be ignored as the process completed itself. The beast was too busy getting the measure of its new tenancy, riffling through his memories and picking out the sore spots and the more promising areas of unhappiness. As in a dream, John felt his fingers being flexed, his body being turned.

The gun being raised.

It was tracking along the wall, making a guess at where Fraser and Sara ought to be. They were moving towards the kitchen, two walking scores that had to be settled. He had to try to fight it somehow, to claw his way back. But how?

The pistol bucked, hard. The bullet punched through the wall as if it was made out of paper. Sara's scream was like the turning of a broken wheel at the other end of the world; the thought of her being harmed, he realised suddenly, scared him even more than what was happening to him now.

And that was his lever.

Knowing that the follower was no longer watching him, John concentrated all of his remaining energy into the forming of a single thought, the memory of their one night on the *Inger Sorensen*.

He was gently closing the cabin door behind him. The lights were dim, there was a single bunk made up with rough blankets. Sara Hansun's arms came around him from behind. On the rerun there was no surprise, only the powerful wave of happiness that in reality had come later. He took the memory, and projected it with all the force he could manage.

The follower reacted as if it had been speared from behind; John heard its silent howl, and felt its grip on him loosen all at once. He shook with its rage, but he didn't share it. Instead, he bore home as hard as he could.

It tried to turn on him, but it was too late. Kicking and clawing, he prised it free.

The effect was spectacular, like a glittering wave tearing free from his chest; it lit up the room like lightning, but even before it hit the floor it had begun to change. It regained its form, and landed on four paws; after skidding on the wooden floor for a moment, it was up on two legs and running for the exit.

'Get the chair away!' John shouted hoarsely, hoping that somebody would hear. 'Give it somewhere to run!'

He tried to raise the gun with its one remaining round, but his hand wasn't fast enough. The follower was changing as it moved, like a series of overlapping still frames run together; it was a wolf-dog and a child, a Hopi Indian with streaming black hair, the little Dutchman burning alive and screaming. As it dived out of the door it was changing again, reverting to its first and fastest shape. John started to follow it through, but he was left way behind.

When he got to the kitchen, Sara was backed-up against the wall by the door. The door itself was wide open to the night. The only other immediate detail that John took in was Fraser, on the floor but stirring slightly to get up. He went on past, kicked the door shut, and started to fit the chair back into place.

'Did you see it?' he said, but Sara was too dazed. She tried to answer, but then slowly shook her head.

The door was jammed as firmly as it would ever be, which now could never be firm enough. John said, 'Is Jerry hit?'

'You blew splinters off the ceiling. Jerry took a dive.'

So there it was, the would-be assassin and his victim reduced to a couple of *farceurs*. As John and Sara went back into the kitchen, Jerry was sitting upright. One arm was held crookedly across his chest, and when he saw this John said, 'You okay?'

Fraser looked up, but he didn't seem to be able to speak. John helped him to stand, an uncertain business with Jerry still hunched protectively over his arm. John said to Sara, 'Are you sure he wasn't hit?'

Sara was hanging back nervously. 'I don't see how.'

'There's blood.'

Not much, and not really enough to indicate a gunshot wound, but there were a few spots on the stone floor and more were being added. They guided Fraser around and sat him at the table, and John lifted the arm as carefully as he could manage and laid it flat on the bare wood. Already it was looking wrong. He asked for a knife, and Sara brought him one from the kitchen cupboard. It was too blunt to be useful, so he just sawed through the cuff of Fraser's woollen shirt and then ripped the sleeve back in one.

The arm was broken, and badly; it was twisted out of shape like a rag-doll's just above the wrist, and the bones inside must have been pulled completely out of line.

John said, 'Does it hurt?'

Fraser was staring at it with an expression of stupid vacancy, as if he couldn't understand that the limb was his own. He said, 'Can't feel a damn thing.'

John didn't want to attempt to turn it, but there was more blood in a sticky patch on the tabletop. He moved the light in closer and crouched down to look. There was a definite hump in the forearm that raised it almost half an inch from the flat; on the underside he could make out a ragged edge of skin with a white sawtooth of bone protruding through. Fraser must have wrapped it around the table leg as he'd gone down, hitting so hard that he hadn't even felt it.

Sara had backed off again. John went around the big

table to her. He spoke quietly, so Jerry wouldn't hear; as she listened she became more apprehensive.

'What are you going to do?' she said after a while. 'Operate?' She was barely managing to keep her own voice down. 'You're talking about two people who couldn't even get together to skin a rabbit.'

'This is different.'

She looked back at Fraser. 'I can't do it, John,' she said weakly, and so he did his best to fake up enough confidence for both of them.

'Just help me, okay? I'll do the pulling, all you have to do is tie the splints off.'

'Forget it, Visco,' Fraser said thickly.

'Don't worry, Jerry, you won't feel a thing.'

'Lying bastard.'

He told her that he'd need the package from the cabin, all of it. She studied him warily for a moment, but she went. It's as simple as that, John thought; just put up a good enough front, and the wheels will start to turn around you. Fraser was watching him as he moved over to the old open hearth, fixing him with a stare like the one the big cats save for the keeper who brings their meat.

John unhooked the lines to bring down the drying frame, and when it was low enough to reach he withdrew one of the six-foot slats. Fraser was still watching as he broke it down into splint lengths.

He said, 'She told you.'

'She didn't tell me,' Visco said, 'I guessed. What's the maximum dose you can take?'

'Why?'

'Because you're going to get it.'

Sara brought the package, now a roll of lint padding without the waxed paper. It opened out to show three neat rows of glass ampoules taped into place, of a kind that had been designed to work together with an added needle and plunger to make a disposable hypodermic. Two had been removed already. John asked Fraser where he took it and Fraser said in the leg, near where it hurt.

He looked at Visco with defiance, and added, 'I'm no junkie.'

'What is it, morphine?'

'The only thing that works. I get it prescribed. They tried me with others but I keep going back.'

John considered for a moment. Then he said, 'Okay, you'll have to stand for a couple of seconds and drop your pants.'

'No.'

'Come on, Jerry, you can't jab through your jeans.'

Fraser shook his head. 'I'm starting to feel it,' he said desperately. 'I can't move. Slit my pants leg.'

'The knife's no good,' John objected. It had barely served on Fraser's shirt. But Fraser had other ideas.

'Check my pocket,' he said. 'The knife I used on the rabbit.'

He managed to brace himself with his good hand against the table and lift himself a little so that John could work his hand into the pocket of his jeans for the knife. When it was clear he eased himself down, taking an age to be sure that his mistreated arm didn't get shifted. Swelling had started to set in and make it look even more grotesque, and a bruise had begun to form from the underneath up.

Sara came in as he let out the long breath that he'd been holding. Jerry couldn't make up the dose, but Sara said that she knew how. John could hear paper seals tearing and the ampoules clicking together behind him as he crouched by Fraser's leg and opened the knife. It was plain steel, well-sharpened and oiled, and after the tough work of the double-hem it slit through the denim easily.

There was a support bandage around Fraser's knee, and the pink ends of a crescent-shaped scar showed above and below the kneecap. There was a long track of needle marks down the inside of his thigh, scars over scars. He'd started the shots close to the damage, moving further away as the skin had become too puckered and torn, but then when the skin had healed he'd gone back to the beginning.

Sara had made up the hypos as Fraser had directed, four of them laid out on the linen tablecloth that she'd found to use for bandages. Fraser was shifting around on the chair to get the best angle, working in millimetres and trying to keep his shoulder always at the same angle to the table.

John said, 'Can you do this left-handed?'

'Both hands and eyes closed. I've had plenty of practice.'

Visco moved the hypodermics within his reach, and he picked up the first. He tried to bring it around to the needle zone, but his hand was shaking. 'Steady me, somebody,' he said, and Sara came around to help. The shot went in, raising a little goosebump under the pressure of the needle. Sara took the empty hypo and passed him the next. He gave her a grateful look for a moment, and then bent to concentrate again.

John watched as each went in, half an inch spacing between the jabs. Only a part of his attention was on Fraser; the rest was on Sara. Item one: he'd admitted to himself that he was in love with her. Item two: he couldn't have her – whatever her own feelings were, the moral obligation that she felt towards Jerry Fraser was stronger than anything. John could wish it wasn't so, but he couldn't do anything to change it.

He'd sprung the first item on the beast, and the beast hadn't liked it at all. It had been looking for somebody at an all-time low, somebody cleaned-out of good feelings leaving plenty of space for a wanderer to move in. It had reacted to an exposure of true emotion like a cat dashing out from under a burning house.

But suppose that it had the chance to analyse what it had observed; suppose that it had the intelligence. Item two meant an uncertainty that would almost be as good as outright rejection as a means of undermining his one defence. It could get him on the mat again, and this time it could keep him pinned. He'd be closed down into that little dark box forever, with maybe just the odd piece of bad news being passed along to make his agonies worse.

He already knew what the first piece of news was likely to be. As long as Sara lived, it wouldn't feel secure.

Sara took away the last of the hypodermics. Fraser sat back and tried to breathe deeply.

John said, 'How long, now?'

'I don't know. They tried to cut me down, but I've got resistance. It may not be enough.'

'That's all you get,' John said. 'We don't want an overdose.'

'And you can keep your hands off me until it works. Take a walk, or something.'

Fraser closed his eyes, and started the deep breathing again. John said, 'Give me a hand, Sara. We'll boil some water.'

THIRTY

The morphine wasn't enough. Fraser whimpered at the first sensation as his arm was lifted, but that was the only sound that he made.

His hand was like a dead man's, limp and cold with nothing to grip back. The arm above it was like a badly-packed sandbag. John had to pull harder than he'd expected, because the muscles that were deforming the arm resisted him.

It came out slowly, straightening and regaining something like normal length. The tooth of bone withdrew, and the blood started to run again. Sara brought the splints in and tied them off, and then John steeled himself to feel for the break through the skin. The bones seemed to have settled in more or less the right places, but he knew that this would only be a botched job to carry them over until they could get Fraser some real medical attention. There might be loose bone in the wound, bleeding inside, tissue caught between the broken ends as they'd been brought together. The whole thing would probably have to be broken and re-set, and Fraser would have another ache to nurse through the long winter months.

They strapped the splinted arm to his body for protection. John supported him as he stood to move through to the sitting room and the fire.

Sara led the way down the hall with a candle. Before they reached the sitting room, Fraser almost keeled over with delayed shock. They got him to the sofa and laid him down; two minutes later, he was asleep.

For a while they watched him anxiously, like a new baby. His breathing had become shallow, but at least it was regular. If there were going to be any complications or an infection linked with the rough-set bones, they probably wouldn't start to show for at least a few hours; the immediate dangers would be from the high morphine dose that he'd taken. John knew nothing about it, but four of the ampoules seemed a pretty stiff measure. Taken with the wasting trinity of cold, hunger and fatigue, they might even be a permanent cure for Fraser's discomfort.

John sat on the rag rug before the hearth, and Sara stretched out in the warmth beside him. Pushing back a straying wisp of hair, she looked up into his eyes.

'John,' she said. 'What really happened in there?'

For a few moments, he thought about telling her the truth; bizarre as it was, he knew she'd believe it. But instead, he said, 'You tell me something. That night you waited for me, on the *Inger Sorensen*. Was it to get your own back on Jerry for seeing that village girl in the afternoons?'

She stared at him. He was coming at her from a completely unexpected angle. The first time she tried to speak, nothing came. Then: 'How do you know about that?'

'I guessed. You as good as told me. But what about us, Sara? It's important for me to know.'

She reached for his hand, and took it in both of her own. 'It wasn't revenge, John,' she said. 'Please, don't ever think that.'

'So, where do we go from here?'

She turned away from him, looking into the fire. 'I don't know,' she said. 'I know you want a straight answer, but right now I can't give you one.'

Her eyes shone in the reflected firelight. She was being honest with him and he knew it, but he also knew that honesty wasn't enough. A feeling that was more than disappointment was settling through him; this was fear, open and uncomplicated. Sara's uncertainty offered him no protection at all.

And protection was what he was going to need, because he knew that in the morning he was going to have to take the gun with its single bullet and make his way down to the village. He'd force somebody to get the police – he was sure they hadn't, yet – and he'd bring back a doctor.

The follower would be out there, for sure. He was also sure that it would come after him, looking for its second chance.

He wouldn't look behind him. Not once.

But somehow, he wasn't sure that it would make a lot of difference.

THIRTY-ONE

Fraser was no better when the dawn came. But he was no worse, and they tried to get some comfort out of that; a couple of times he moved without waking and once he muttered something, but John couldn't make out what it was. He thought that Sara had fallen asleep, but she followed him when he went down the room to the mahogany dining table, and she pulled around a chair with him and watched as he stripped down the gun.

He didn't make it the full job, just the slide, magazine and frame, checking on the positioning of the recoil spring and trying a few test pulls on an empty chamber. Perhaps it looked impressive to Sara, but after a while he had to admit that he was stringing himself along; nothing that he was doing was going to have any effect either on the efficiency of the pistol or on his own chances of hitting anything with it.

He slipped in the last round, pushed the magazine home; work the slide once to bring it in ready to fire, safety catch on.

'I suppose I'm ready,' he said.

He left by the main entrance, stepping out and onto the verandah. Sara closed and locked the door quickly behind him as they'd arranged, but he still heard her muffled '*Lev vel da,*' coming through.

There was a flat wedge of snow cleared by the verandah gate as it had been pushed open. He could read off the tracks in two layers, those belonging to the three of them from two nights before partly filled in by drift and then

304

overlain by the animal's from only a few hours ago. Even these were starting to get indistinct.

John started the climb to the rail fence that would be the first marker of his journey. Sara might have been watching from one of the windows of the lodge but, as he'd promised, he didn't look back. The morning light was dull and soft on the snow, and he threw no shadow. He kept the fence within touching distance of his gun hand, sticking as close as he could to the line they'd taken coming in. After ten minutes of this their old tracks had faded away, their follower's with them.

He tramped on, as his breathing got laboured and the going got worse. The weight of the automatic was enough to unbalance him slightly; when all of this was over, he told himself, he was going to take the gun and dump it. He'd take it out over the deepest part of one of the fjords, and he'd drop it in the water. It would be just one new start out of many; he could also dump the weird plan that had sent him chasing after Teamverk and decide instead what his *real* capabilities were, (*the effort was already starting to wear him down. It should get easier after the mountain pass gave way to the descent, but it would still take hours. As he left the fence behind, he started to count off his paces*) by which time Sara would be free of her arrangement with Jerry Fraser. All that he'd need then would be her answer.

The suspicion that something was seriously wrong had been growing for more than half an hour, but he'd been forcing it down and ignoring it as he'd concentrated instead on the life that was only just out of reach. Now he couldn't ignore it any longer; the track should have levelled out and started to drop some way back, but he was still climbing. The woodland above and around him was too dense for him to get much sense of the landscape, but the distance covered alone told him that he'd missed the pass.

He started to turn around to make his way down.

But then he stopped himself, just in time.

If he couldn't backtrack, he'd have to try cutting across somehow, descending on a line that would bring him back to the path he should have taken. He couldn't go by the sun or the fall of the shadows, so he'd have to take his line from the trees, doing his best to stay on a straight course.

He only hoped that he'd know the cattle-run when he crossed it. He'd missed it easily enough the first time.

When he found running water a half-mile or so down, he was ready for it. The going was a lot steeper now, and he was less confident. But self-doubt could wait until he'd taken a drink; he was coming to a stream and waterfall, rocks and mosses frosted over and grass that had been combed flat wherever it had been uncovered. The upper levels of the falls were sheer and bearded with icicles around which snow had formed itself, and he climbed down past these to where a fast-running pool was no more than two-thirds icebound.

He crouched by the edge, and took off his gloves. Seen close-up, the grasses were rotten and black, plastered down over the rock by the constant flow of water. The surface rippled and danced, and he plunged his hands in quickly; if something was trying to look over his shoulder, he didn't want to see it.

Take a look, a small voice seemed to say. *Just a quick one.*

He wiped his hands on his jeans and got back into his gloves as fast as he could, which wasn't too fast because he'd lost so much feeling that he fumbled the job badly. He wrapped his arms around his sides to put some warmth into them so that he could pick up the gun and carry on. It lay on the flat beside him. He'd misjudged the effects of the water's chill – for a minute or so he doubted that he'd be able even to lift it two-handed, much less make any effective defence.

The snow by the edge of the stream had been smoothed and refrozen and sculpted by the flow. It looked like polished white stone. John stared at it, waiting for sensation to return. The urge to look behind him was getting more difficult to resist.

Is it you? Are you there?

He told his fingers to flex, and he could see them doing it. He told them to pick up the gun, and they did. He began to follow the stream-bed downhill, because he knew that it would take him on the most direct line.

He'd fouled up, completely blown his route. He'd paid too much attention to the ground in front of him, and not enough to the land ahead. Since he couldn't go back, he'd have to complete a loop and start again; the stream-bed would lead him down to the lake, and he could make his way along the shore until he got sight of one or other of the two buildings as a reference point. He'd already lost more than two hours of daylight, and he was going to waste at least another.

The stream petered out and went underground fairly quickly, but the gully that it had cut deepened and carried on down. Well, it made everything simpler; the rock walls that came up on either side made a four metres wide corridor that even he couldn't wander out of by mistake.

He had to be careful. The gully floor looked like a rippling stairway, but most of the rocks under the snow were irregular and loose and they shifted when he tried to put weight onto them. Every now and again, he spared a glance ahead; this was how he was nearly on the lake before he realised it.

There was no shoreline, not for some distance. The end of the gully met the edge of the water with a sheer rock wall running out on either side. There was nowhere else to go but the ice.

Still, it seemed to be solid enough, especially in the shallows where it was a translucent white. He took a couple of steps out, testing his way. It was slick and glossy underfoot, but if he didn't rush and just shuffled along he'd probably be okay. Further out he could see broad swathes of lighter frosted areas, and darker bands where the ice appeared to be at its thinnest. As it had frozen, the surface must have broken and re-formed to make layers of varied depths.

He stayed as close to the side as he could, and he took it slowly. The surface was oily, treacherous; and after a few yards it started to darken.

It had to be the black water of the fjord showing through. He knew that he was in trouble when he saw an even darker shadow locked into the ice itself, a crack pattern that had refrozen. It looked like a buried branch, or trapped lightning. Obviously the shallows only spread in a fan-shape around the mouth of the gully, a long-term buildup of material that had been carried downstream and dumped.

John tested his next step. It was almost certainly his imagination, but he thought he could feel the ice flexing.

A dousing in the fjord at these temperatures would kill him in minutes. He was going to have to turn back.

He wasn't even feeling apprehensive about it, because the cold and the utter drudgery of his journey so far had worked together to drive most of the superstition out of him. What could have happened last night, he asked himself, I mean *really* happened? And how come I was so convinced?

Still trying to puzzle it through, he turned around. It was waiting.

She stood on the ice by the gully. She was about sixteen years old. Her hair was long and free, but her skin was greenish and marbled like something that had been stored in a jar for too long. Her eyes had the dull shine of silver coins in river mud. They drilled John with the intensity of their hunger, and he was unable to move.

The chill wind from the lake lifted her hair. She smiled, a hundred baby-teeth filed to razor points. Somewhere behind John, there was a sound like rocks being squeezed together.

The ice was starting to give.

Her smile widened, but the glitter of her eyes was

unchanged. She held out a hand towards him. It was dirty, the fingers bent, the nails all torn.

She called to him.

We need each other, she said. *Please . . . I want to come home.*

The ice began to splinter.

THIRTY-TWO

As she'd watched John walk away, Sara felt a loneliness
that clamped down over the lodge like a dome. Three had
been a crowd, sure enough, but in his present state Fraser
was no company at all. She glanced down the room to
where he lay; she couldn't see much of him beyond the
high back of the sofa, but he didn't seem to have moved
When she turned to the window again, Visco was out of
sight. He hadn't looked back.

Well, it was going to be evening before she saw him
next, and she planned to spend the long hours until then
stoppering every crack and chink in the place. Four of the
windows weren't as secure as she'd have liked, and there
was nothing to stop the main door other than a cylinder
lock identical to that around the back. The fireplaces were
probably safe, even though it wasn't much of a jump from
the *fjellside* to the roof along by the yard; the flue in the
kitchen was bricked-up, and the fire in the sitting room
ought to discourage anyone or anything from playing
Santa Claus.

She made one more check on Fraser, telling herself that
after this she'd leave him alone. He'd moved slightly and
pushed some of the blanket away, and his breathing had
become more rapid as if the pain was now managing to
get to him through the sleep. Also he was starting to whisper, the same thing over and over like a loop, and Sara
didn't have to lean in close to know what he was saying.
She pulled the blanket back over him and then went
through to the kitchen.

310

Respecting the Nystrom family's property somehow didn't seem as important as survival. They'd already scored one door and an airing rack, along with some holed panels and the linen they'd used to bind Jerry's arm back together, and she now set about adding two kitchen chairs to the list. They were cheaply made, and they broke easily when she laid them on their backs on the stone floor and stepped down hard on the legs. She wasn't just doing it for the kick of destruction, although the explosive crack as the wood gave way under her was some kind of satisfaction after the way they'd been duped and trapped. When the chairs were down to just seats and struts and plenty of splinters, she crouched down and began sorting through.

She was after the double-headed nails that had been holding them together. She picked out six that were usable, leaving the others either because they'd rusted or because they were too firmly into the wood for her to get them out. Nothing was going to be wasted, because the long timbers of the chair-backs would make door wedges and the rest could be burned. There was no way that she'd consider going outside for more logs when the hearth stack ran out; and if old man Nystrom wanted to know what had been happening to his furniture, she'd tell him to go look where the emergency supplies were kept.

They weren't all straight, but they'd do. She found a chunk of carborundum sharpening block in the knife drawer and used it to hammer them as flat as they'd go. Then she went through to the scullery, where they'd found the nearest of the suspect windows the night before, and drove the nail through the sash and into the frame. It was a rough-looking job and she'd bent the last half-inch over, but it wasn't looks that were going to count if it turned out to be needed.

She took the two chair-backs through into the hall and wedged one of them under the knob on the main door, kicking it into place as tightly as she could. It looked barely adequate, but the weakest point in the whole lodge was probably that for which the other chair-back was

311

intended, the verandah access door. She could hardly hope to nail *that* shut, so she'd have to do the best with what she had. But first, before she had to risk disturbing Jerry, there were more windows.

The remaining three were all on the same side, in the bedroom and bathroom that John had been using on their first night in the *seter*. One of the windows was a bitch, it didn't look more than three or four years old and it was of harder wood than the others. There wasn't even a catch on it – obviously the people in the village didn't feel threatened by their own kind in the way that the builders of the place might have, but now everyone was playing by a new set of rules. It gave her a kind of sick thrill to see how easy it was to raise the sash a couple of inches and to think that something on the outside could have done it with as little trouble, without even needing hands that were half-way human . . .

She made herself stop thinking about it. Visco would be back by evening, and it would all be over. She closed the window with more force than she'd intended, and then she wasted two of the nails when she drove too hard with the block and broke them. Bastard things – but then it wasn't really the nails, or the wood, because when she'd stopped and taken a couple of breaths and told herself to be calm she found that she had no more trouble than before.

Less than an hour gone. The day stretched ahead like a long and wasting illness.

Sara thought that she remembered closing the sitting-room door to keep the noise from Jerry, but it was open again when she got there. The reason became obvious when she stepped through from the hall, because Fraser was no longer before the fire.

She found him in the kitchen, sitting in the same place that he'd been for the rough surgery of a few hours before. He looked up when she came in, but he didn't speak. His eyes were red-rimmed and gritty, and his skin was grey like old candle-wax. She could see three of the ampoules

312

empty and rolled aside on the table, and he was just finishing off the fourth around the other side and out of sight. He must have swayed through on his own and then broken out the needles and assembled the hypos one-handed; maybe he didn't have the energy or the will to call her, or maybe he'd known that she'd have refused to let him have the dose that he wanted.

He threw the ampoule with the others, scattering them, and then he braced his good hand against the table to prise himself up. He'd never liked to be watched, and he didn't seem to want it now. His injured arm was still cross-strapped to his body, but it had turned slightly. It didn't even seem to belong to him, and it occurred to Sara for the first time that he might lose it.

His slit pants leg flapped like a sail as he took aim at the door and staggered through it. Sara followed him down the hall, keeping her distance but ready to step in and catch him if he should begin to founder, but he made it all the way on his own. He didn't drop until he was back at the sofa, and then he used what was left of his strength for a slow descent. He'd only looked at her the once, and he hadn't acknowledged her at all. When she came around before the sofa to help him get back into the blankets, his eyes were already closed.

Sara knelt to watch him for a while. He'd managed a lot more than just the walk for his shots – although considering his condition, that was enough – because he'd first gone around and re-covered all of the sitting-room windows. Where drapes could be pulled across, he'd pulled them again; and where they were jammed or broken, he'd lifted the material and stuffed it in around the frames. Now his ragged breathing began to settle, and he seemed to be relaxing. This was no surprise – eight of Jerry's shots within twelve hours on a man with no resistance would probably put him on a slab in a plastic bag.

She watched for a little longer. He stirred once. *'Why me?'* he whispered, and then he quietened down.

There was no point creeping around in silence now,

because he probably wouldn't hear anything. Sara brought the second chair-back through and put it against the verandah door, and then because that didn't seem to be enough she rolled one of the big armchairs across and pushed it against the wedge as a second defence. Then, either as a third line or simply because she was exhausted, she sat in it and fell asleep.

When she woke her first thought was that it was dark, that she'd been sleeping for hours, that the evening had arrived and nobody had come for them. The truth started to sift through in layers; the fire had burned down but not out, and the daylight spilling in around the edges of the drapes was as bright as it was going to get around this time of year. She'd been out for only one hour, two at the most.

She had the beginnings of a sick headache, a migraine that was settling as a ring of pressure behind her right eye. It was probably a result of the enforced hunger-strike. There wasn't much that she could do about it, except perhaps try to fool herself by drinking some warm water.

The hearth logs were dry now, but there were only a few of them left. Within the hour she'd be stripping out the lodge for kindling. It would be something to look forward to. Sara used half of the wood to build up the fire, and then she went to the kitchen for some water.

At least, that was her intention, but on the way she decided that she would have to undo some of Jerry's cover-up work. He'd turned the place into a mausoleum and then laid himself out so that he wouldn't have to look at it; just a couple of the windows uncovered would bring some light in without panicking him when he woke.

This time, he'd reversed the damage. He'd pulled the drapes over so hard that she couldn't get them back. Oh well, what the hell, so we sit in the dark until rescue comes. She was going to let the material fall when she saw John Visco, a hundred metres downslope and climbing.

*   *   *

He was coming up with his head down and his arms spread for balance, and he looked tired. Snow had settled all over him, either kicked-up or windblown. The gun was still in his right hand – it caught the light with a dull gleam as he swung it around – and he was carrying something else in his left, something long and loose like a bag of stones. Sara didn't know what to think, or what to feel; seeing John again helped wipe away the unwelcome pressure of their isolation, but he wasn't supposed to *be* here. He was supposed to be getting close to Tromstad, warming the gun inside his jacket in case he should have to use it, counting off the paces that would bring him to the hay-fields and the final run down into the village.

John looked up and saw her. He was almost too tired and too cold to smile and show recognition. She managed half a smile herself, and then she dropped the curtain and went through to the main door.

The brace was still there, as she'd left it. Some part of her didn't want to take it away. She could hear John now, clambering onto the boardwalk and breathing heavily, every breath as cold and deep-reaching as a dose of ether. After a few seconds' wait without the door opening, Sara heard him call her name.

'John?' she said, uncertain. 'You're back so soon?'

'I didn't get through. All the snow's moved, it's changed, I couldn't find the way.'

'Did you . . . were you followed?'

'Jesus, Sara, I'm freezing!'

She made her decision. She knocked the wedge free, and opened the door. The cold air came in like a moving wall. John stood there, bedraggled and chilled, and seeing him so close was enough to wipe out her doubts.

'The wolf?' she said as he came in past her, and he shook his head.

'Not a sign.'

He stamped off the snow on the rough matting of the hallway as Sara closed the door and put back the brace. He said, 'How's Jerry?'

315

'He woke up for a while.' She wasn't going to tell him about the extra shots; Fraser didn't have a lot of dignity left to him now, and Sara didn't want to make herself mean by cutting it any more. 'He's got like a hangover,' she added. 'He's sleeping it off now.'

John went on into the kitchen, and Sara followed. 'Well,' he said, 'I didn't waste the day, I bagged us another bunny.'

He swung the rabbit up and slapped it onto the table, landing it so heavily that it farted out a teaspoonful of air. Sara was looking at it, but her mind was really somewhere else; she said, 'John, what are we going to do?'

He slid the automatic into his jacket pocket, and then he started to peel off his gloves. They didn't come easily. He said, 'Well, I don't think we need to worry. We've got food and we've got fire, we can last a little while longer.'

'And what about Jerry?'

'Jerry will be fine.'

'He needs a doctor, you said so.'

'That kind of depends on whether or not he improves, doesn't it?'

John moved out into the hall towards the sitting room. Sara looked doubtfully at the rabbit. Its dry eye glittered back at her.

'You made the place secure?' John called over his shoulder, and she moved to catch up with him.

'I put nails in the windows and wedges under all the doors. Nothing can get in.'

'Or out. Now, why don't I take a look at this arm?'

Sara stayed well back as he crouched in the firelight before the sofa and gently turned back the edges of Fraser's blanket. He leaned in as close as he could get without actually touching anything, moving around to get the best out of the bad light. Then he nodded.

'I think the worst of it's over,' he said as he put the blanket folds back again. 'It's the bruising makes it look so bad.'

'Suddenly you're an expert?'

John stood up, smoothing his hands against his jeans. 'I set it for him, didn't I?'

'John, it can't be left. If you don't want to try again, I'll go.'

He started around the sofa towards her. 'Sara,' he said, with the kind of insincere gentleness that might be used to explain an unpleasant fact of life to a child, 'you don't know what it's like out there. You didn't see it.'

'I lived in Norway all my life, I don't have to see it. We can't wait here for people that will never come.'

The annoyance in her voice had stopped him, but he was smiling. He said, 'I was thinking about that. We got ourselves into a panic last night, didn't we?'

'Nothing that wasn't justified.' Something was wrong, horribly wrong, and Sara couldn't make out what it was.

'Come on. Some animal got in here and we squawked so much we scared it off. Then we started making plans that don't really hold up in the daytime.'

'They still sound good to me.'

'Believe me, Sara, we're best just riding it out, the three of us here together. We've got what we need.'

He started to back off, and then he turned around. He put the backs of his hands out towards the fire.

Sara said, 'John, how did you get the rabbit?'

'I feel like ice,' he said. 'I can't believe how long I've been outside.'

'The rabbit, John.'

The question seemed to get through to him slowly, as if it was in pieces that he had to reassemble. 'What about the rabbit?'

'How did you manage to get it?'

A moment's pause, check the index, look up the answer. 'I had the gun, remember?'

'There was no blood.' In fact, as far as Sara had been able to see, there wasn't a mark of any kind showing on the white fur.

'Well . . . I don't think you could have looked too closely.'

Something hit the verandah gate hard, banging it back another couple of inches over the snow, and the same something landed heavily on the boardwalk. Without a pause, it started to hammer at the main door.

But it didn't stay there for long, just long enough to find that it wasn't going to get in, not that way; after a couple of seconds it turned, and a second later it was at the first window.

The whole frame shook, so hard that the glass seemed to come loose, and it was still reverberating when the next window started. Another burst of violent effort, and on to the third.

The third window started to open.

The catch must have been faulty, and they couldn't have tried it hard enough to make it show. The drapes began to lift as the cold air poured in through the crack, flapping and billowing as it widened. The check that they'd given the windows had been enough to show up any opportunities for a wolf that was trying to walk like a man, but they hadn't been expecting anything as fast or as forceful as this.

The window jammed. Two inches, three inches, no more. It moved on.

As it came around the boardwalk onto the end wall of the lodge, Sara went to try rousing Jerry. She wasn't sure that she could get through to him, but she was going to try.

He hadn't moved for a while. He'd pulled himself up tight in the blankets, as if he was trying to get as small as he could. His eyes were slightly open, his lips slightly parted. There was a thin trail of blood from his nose that had run and dried.

She touched his face. Towards the fire it was still warm, but the shadowed side was starting to get cold. It was the first time she'd ever touched dead skin, but this was *Jerry*. He must have been gone an hour or more, while she was asleep.

I think the worst of it's over. The sickest joke she ever

heard. She looked at John, but John was watching the wall.

It had reached the access door, the weakest link. Sara braced herself for the hammering, but it didn't come.

There was a silence that lasted several seconds, then the scratching started. It wasn't just an impotent pawing; it was the purposeful, economical sound of something that knew what it was doing.

John's face was a bloodless mask. He took a step back, and then another, as if there really was somewhere to run. Sara was wondering if the cheap wood of the kitchen chair would hold against the door. She was thinking of how easily it had snapped when she'd put her weight on it.

There was a noise which couldn't be anything other than that of a latch flying up. The door gave in a half-inch and then was jammed by the brace under its handle. The handle started to turn back and forth and the brace started to shake loose, hopping in little centimetre jumps towards the door's edge. There was a raw squeal of castors as the armchair moved a half-inch towards the middle of the room.

The brace worked its way a little further, and then stopped. It had been pushed as far as it could go, and now its corner was hard up underneath the handle. It was holding. The rattling of the handle stopped.

There was a hard kick which shook the door and boomed all the way through the lodge. With the next one, the chair-back broke cleanly in two and the door burst inward.

Olav Nystrom came through with it, his father's shotgun already halfway to his shoulder. John Visco read his expression in an instant, and he turned and ran for the hallway.

The armchair slowed Nystrom down, and they could hear the kitchen door slamming by the time he was over it. Sara was bewildered to find herself in the middle of a scene where everyone else knew their parts but her; when

319

Nystrom raced past without pausing to explain, she followed him.

He was moving so fast, he nearly didn't make the stop at the end of the hall. He grabbed the doorknob and pushed; it was solid. There wasn't a lock, so John must have put one of the remaining chairs behind it. Somewhere further in, they could hear the sounds of wood splintering; he was stamping through the brace that held the door to the outside. Nystrom backed off, and took a running kick at the woodwork; he was through first time, skidding to get his balance on the kitchen floor and to make the turn towards the scullery where the door was still swinging back against the wall.

'Block it behind me,' he shouted to Sara, and he was out and running. He was waving the shotgun more like a club than a firearm. Sara hardly understood, and she had to force herself to concentrate and look around.

She was looking around for another chair that she could use, but all she seemed to be able to see was matchwood. She was wondering what she could do next when she felt the hard pressure of the SIG 210-2 rammed up underneath her ear.

John's breath stirred the down on her neck. His left arm came around her all the way, and he drew her tightly to him. His left hand gripped her breast, and squeezed hard enough to hurt.

What he'd done was obvious, now that it was too late. The back door had been a dummy, and as soon as he'd got it open John had slipped behind the shelves and into the old servants' quarters. He'd cut through the bedrooms to emerge into the hallway, safely behind Nystrom's mad charge.

He squeezed again, harder. *'You, bitch,'* he whispered hoarsely. *'The bullet's for you.'* He was pressing the muzzle hard into the soft hollow behind her jawbone, and she could feel the slight shifting as he thumbed the safety catch off.

'No, John,' she said through the blinding pain as he bore in on the nerve. 'Please . . .'

'You're wasting your time, Sara,' Nystrom said from the doorway. He'd been through the yard gate before he'd realised that it had been closed, there were no fresh tracks, and he'd blown it. 'That isn't him. Not any more.'

Even against the pressure of the gun, she tried to turn and see for herself. John might be in there somewhere, but he was buried deep. There was no echo of him in the sounds that it was making now. Nystrom's shotgun was pointing at the floor; there was nothing that he could do, because Sara was between them.

Their eyes met. His were bleak, alien, empty.

'I love you, John,' she said, knowing that she said it too late.

The follower studied her. Then, using the pressure of the muzzle, he turned her head around again so that she faced Nystrom.

There was a hot wire running through the middle of her head, a link between the gun and the ache that had been growing behind her eye; but even though her vision was beginning to break up, she could see an expression of puzzlement coming onto the young Norwegian's face.

Sara tensed, waiting for the last sound she would ever hear; but then, without warning, John's grip loosened. She almost fell away as he let her go, but she caught her balance in time; John had taken a faltering step back, and she had to spin around to see why.

John was looking at her strangely. She tried to read what was in his expression, but she couldn't. His eyes lowered from her to the gun, which he was still holding before him at the same angle.

After a few moments, the hand began to quiver. It was as if somebody was using all of their weight to hold it down against him.

'John?' she said, uncertainly.

He glanced at her once and held it a fraction too long; it almost cost him the contest, but she'd seen enough to know that John had managed to fight his way back. The gun hand started to move; slowly, painfully, he managed to bring it up, away from Sara altogether.

The last few inches were the hardest. He almost lost ground, but he got the muzzle under his chin and held it there.

'I heard you, Sara,' he said, and he pulled the trigger.

AFTERMATH

The first thing that he became aware of was the sunlight, angling down into the room through the half-closed slats of a venetian blind. As he struggled to bring this into focus, a shadow moved across the window.

He knew her immediately. It was Caroline Thompson, fifteen years old, as pure and as poised and as cool as church marble. Her long hair was brushed out and falling around her shoulders, and her white school blouse was unbuttoned at the neck to show the silver chain she always wore.

Oh, perfection. Looking at her, he'd sometimes been so moved that he'd begun to hurt . . . but that had been back in 1967, the year when Procul Harum bowed in and Che Guevara bowed out, when the Beach Boys sang *Barbra Anne* and Jane Fonda played *Barbarella*, when a colour TV in a rental store window was enough to attract a crowd in the street. Now it was just the shadow of a hurt, an echo from a thousand years away.

She was moving towards him from the window. He knew why she was here; she'd come, as he'd always known she would, to close his eyes and to bless him on his way. She reached out to touch him . . .

. . . and was gone.

Sara Hansun stood in her place, close by the side of the hospital bed. He could see an IV stand with two bottles of drip and a switchover valve just behind her, and there was a background *blip-blip-blip* keeping track of his life signs.

He felt as limp as a puppet. He wondered if he was paralysed.

'Welcome back to the world, John,' Sara said. She didn't touch him after all, but let her hand drop to her side. She was only just managing to hold herself together, he could tell.

Was he going to be able to speak? He wanted to ask about the damage, but on the other hand he didn't want to hear. So he said, 'How long have I been out?' Or at least, he tried; his voice came out in a scratchy whisper, his lips making the shapes with almost nothing coming up from behind.

'Five days,' Sara said, lowering herself onto a chair alongside him. 'Olav raced back to the village and sent a Mayday on one of the fishing boat radios. We brought you out by helicopter. You're in the Central Hospital, in Narvik.'

Flat out for five days in a hospital bed. They must have been having a high old time, wiring him back together. What must he look like? Again, he wasn't sure that he wanted to know.

And there was something else that he needed to ask, first.

He said, 'Did I kill it?'

Sara understood immediately. 'I never saw anything like it,' she said. 'The thing just . . . dived out of you. It was like it had been hit with a flamethrower.' She shook her head, unable even to begin to explain or interpret what she'd witnessed. 'It went for the door, but it was screaming and burning away. Before it reached the outside . . . pouf.' She made a small, throwaway gesture to illustrate. 'Nothing but snow on the floor.'

He closed his eyes. He'd beaten it, but at what cost?

'We agreed a story,' Sara went on, 'but don't worry about it. Just say you remember nothing. Nobody would dare to call you a liar.'

Why? he thought. *Because I left some of my brains peppered on the farmhouse ceiling?*

He couldn't avoid the big question any longer. He said, 'Exactly how much of me is there left?'

Her face became suddenly serious, but then an immediate wave of emotion took it over. He couldn't tell if she was giggling or crying; she seemed to be doing both.

'Oh, John,' she said, leaning over and taking his face in both of her hands. 'You bloody fool. You'd left the safety catch on the gun again.'

It was a moment before he understood what she was saying. Then he managed a weak smile.

'How embarrassing,' he said.

STEPHEN GALLAGHER

CHIMERA

No school until further notice.

The village schoolhouse is in use as a morgue. There has been a tragedy at the remote Jenner Clinic. It has always been a place of secrets – and now, something terrible has happened.

Meanwhile, high in the valley by Ravens' Crag Farm, the Gaskell children reach home. The farmyard is quiet. The gate stands open. The Gaskell boy tugs at his sister's sleeve. 'Look,' he says, and Sarah nods.

In the middle of the yard, the Strange Boy is waiting for them.

Waiting to play . . .

HODDER AND STOUGHTON PAPERBACKS

STEPHEN GALLAGHER

OKTOBER

The dogs were used in tests.

Beyond the experimental labs, the three operating theatres were used mainly for *post mortem* dissection.

Security was tight. High in the Swiss mountains, the research station was only a small part of the giant Risinger-Genoud drug company. A small but very important and very secret part. The clinical results were fascinating – and terrifying.

But there had been a security breach. An outsider, skiing on the edge of the glacier, had had an accident, was lying unconscious near the animal pens . . .

When James Harper came to, he knew only that something had happened to him that was destroying his sanity.

The dogs howled in their madness, not understanding that a human being had now joined them as a subject of the Oktober experiments.

HODDER AND STOUGHTON PAPERBACKS

STEPHEN GALLAGHER

THE BOAT HOUSE

Back home, some called it the Yellow House. You didn't even have to be mad to get in. *Because once they had you, madness would surely follow.*

Slipping un-noticed from a country in the turmoil of rebirth, a young Russian woman escapes her shadowy past to find peace in an English lakeside town. Stateless and without papers, she begins to rebuild her life. At last, she believes, the torment of the prison hospital is behind her.

But for others, the torment is about to begin.

Boatyard worker Pete McCarthy watches in dismay as the stranger in his house becomes a menace in his life. She walks at night and the innocent die. The first to see it, he is the last to face it; after all, Alina Petrovna is no-one's idea of a monster.

But her losing battle with darkness goes on. And her Children of the Lake are growing in number . . .

'A master of pace and suspense, Gallagher has the dark, neon-splashed imagination of a true original'
Glasgow Evening Times

HODDER AND STOUGHTON PAPERBACKS